"Eileen Wilks writes what I like to read."
—Linda Howard, *New York Times* bestselling author

BLO[...]

"Action packed . . . [An] exciting, twisting thriller."
—*Genre Go Round Reviews*

"Full of intrigue, danger, and romance . . . The Lupi series is one
of the best Were series I have ever read." —*Fresh Fiction*

"An intense and suspenseful tale. For anyone who enjoys werewolves and romance, *Blood Magic* is a must-read . . . Eileen
Wilks is a truly gifted writer. Her newest novel is truly a work
of art as her words paint a picture of a modern-day Romeo and
Juliet." —*Romance Junkies*

"Wilks's storytelling style is so densely layered with plot com-
plexities and well-defined characters that it quickly immerses
readers in this fascinating world. There is no better way to escape
reality than with a Wilks adventure!" —*RT Book Reviews*

"Another great addition to the Lupi series, Eileen Wilks's *Blood
Magic* is an engaging paranormal tale full of action and adventure
that should not be missed!" —*Romance Reviews Today*

MORTAL SINS

"Filled with drama and action [...] number five in the
World of the Lupi series and [...]

"Ms. Wilks has a skill with [...]
brings a world and its chara[...]

"Fabulous . . . The plot just sucked me in and didn't let me go until the end . . . Another great addition to the World of Lupi series."
—*Literary Escapism*

NIGHT SEASON

"A captivating world." —*The Romance Reader*

"Filled with action and plenty of twists." —*Midwest Book Review*

BLOOD LINES

"Another winner from Eileen Wilks." —*Romance Reviews Today*

"The magic seems plausible, the demons real, and the return of enigmatic Cynna, along with the sorcerer, hook fans journeying the fantasy realm of Eileen Wilks." —*The Best Reviews*

"Intriguing . . . Surprises abound in *Blood Lines* . . . A masterful pen and sharp wit hone this third book in the Moon Children series into a work of art. Enjoy!" —*A Romance Review*

"Quite enjoyable, and sure to entertain . . . A fast-paced story with plenty of danger and intrigue." —*The Green Man Review*

MORTAL DANGER

"Grabs you on the first page and never lets go. Strong characters, believable world-building, and terrific storytelling . . . I really, really loved this book."
—Patricia Briggs, #1 *New York Times* bestselling author

"As intense as it is sophisticated, a wonderful novel of strange magic, fantastic realms, and murderous vengeance that blend together to test the limits of fate-bound lovers."
—Lynn Viehl, *New York Times* bestselling author of the Darkyn series

"[A] complex, intriguing, paranormal world . . . Fans of the paranormal genre will love this one!" —*Love Romances*

Books by Eileen Wilks

TEMPTING DANGER
MORTAL DANGER
BLOOD LINES
NIGHT SEASON
MORTAL SINS
BLOOD MAGIC
BLOOD CHALLENGE
DEATH MAGIC

Anthologies

CHARMED
*(with Jayne Ann Krentz writing as Jayne Castle,
Julie Beard, and Lori Foster)*

LOVER BEWARE
(with Christine Feehan, Katherine Sutcliffe, and Fiona Brand)

CRAVINGS
*(with Laurell K. Hamilton, MaryJanice Davidson,
and Rebecca York)*

ON THE PROWL
(with Patricia Briggs, Karen Chance, and Sunny)

INKED
(with Karen Chance, Marjorie M. Liu, and Yasmine Galenorn)

DEATH MAGIC

EILEEN WILKS

BERKLEY SENSATION, NEW YORK

THE BERKLEY PUBLISHING GROUP
Published by the Penguin Group
Penguin Group (USA) Inc.
375 Hudson Street, New York, New York 10014, USA
Penguin Group (Canada), 90 Eglinton Avenue East, Suite 700, Toronto, Ontario M4P 2Y3, Canada
(a division of Pearson Penguin Canada Inc.)
Penguin Books Ltd., 80 Strand, London WC2R 0RL, England
Penguin Group Ireland, 25 St. Stephen's Green, Dublin 2, Ireland (a division of Penguin Books Ltd.)
Penguin Group (Australia), 250 Camberwell Road, Camberwell, Victoria 3124, Australia
(a division of Pearson Australia Group Pty. Ltd.)
Penguin Books India Pvt. Ltd., 11 Community Centre, Panchsheel Park, New Delhi—110 017, India
Penguin Group (NZ), 67 Apollo Drive, Rosedale, Auckland 0632, New Zealand
(a division of Pearson New Zealand Ltd.)
Penguin Books (South Africa) (Pty.) Ltd., 24 Sturdee Avenue, Rosebank, Johannesburg 2196,
South Africa

Penguin Books Ltd., Registered Offices: 80 Strand, London WC2R 0RL, England

This is a work of fiction. Names, characters, places, and incidents either are the product of the author's imagination or are used fictitiously, and any resemblance to actual persons, living or dead, business establishments, events, or locales is entirely coincidental. The publisher does not have any control over and does not assume any responsibility for author or third-party websites or their content.

DEATH MAGIC

A Berkley Sensation Book / published by arrangement with the author

PRINTING HISTORY
Berkley Sensation mass-market edition / November 2011

Copyright © 2011 by Eileen Wilks.
Excerpt from *Mortal Ties* by Eileen Wilks copyright © by Eileen Wilks.
Cover art by Tony Mauro.
Cover design by George Long.
Interior text design by Kristin del Rosario.

ISBN: 978-0-425-24512-5

BERKLEY SENSATION®
Berkley Sensation Books are published by The Berkley Publishing Group,
a division of Penguin Group (USA) Inc.,
375 Hudson Street, New York, New York 10014.
BERKLEY SENSATION® is a registered trademark of Penguin Group (USA) Inc.
The "B" design is a trademark of Penguin Group (USA) Inc.

PRINTED IN THE UNITED STATES OF AMERICA

10   9   8   7   6   5   4   3   2   1

*This book is joyfully dedicated to
my daughter Katie
and her wonderful fiancé, Matt.
I couldn't be more delighted.*

ACKNOWLEDGMENTS

Typically writers use this space to acknowledge the help others provided. I'm using it to offer an apology. There are inconsistencies between what we call the real world and some of the details in my fictional world that may disconcert some readers. A female president, for one. The building and security systems at the FBI Headquarters in Washington, D.C., for another. There are more, but if I describe them, I'll give away too much about the story.

What can I say? The realm Lily and Rule live in isn't ours. For some reason, they elected a female president a couple years ago. We didn't. The architect of the FBI building there had a slightly different plan than ours did. And they have lupi. And dragons . . .

ONE

~

LILY Yu was at the shooting range at FBI Headquarters when she saw the ghost.

Her ears were warm beneath the headgear. Her bare arms were chilly, with her left arm out and steady; the right one ached and trembled. She'd fired a few clips right-handed before switching, which was dumb. Should have started with the left so her bad arm wouldn't be bitching so much. To bring her new Glock in line with her dominant eye while keeping her stance and grip neutral, she had to twist her right arm in a way that her damaged bicep objected to.

It objected to a lot of things. The humerus might be healed, the skin grown back nice and smooth over the entry wound, but the exit wound was bigger, bumpier, and dented. Lost muscle didn't regrow.

Except that Lily's was. Slowly, but it was returning.

A whiff of sulfur hung in the air. Sound slapped at her ears through the protective muffs as her neighbor to the right fired steadily on the other side of the divider. The fur-and-pine tickle in her gut—the reason her shattered bone had knit so quickly, the cause of her muscle's gradual, impossible regeneration—made her feel as if she should burp.

Fifty feet away, a drift of otherness obscured the paper target she'd been putting holes in.

It was white. Maybe that's why she immediately thought *ghost*. It drifted on a diagonal like three-dimensional rice paper—translucent, not transparent, its edges too clearly defined for smoke, shaped right for a human, but faceless. Even as it floated closer on a steady, nonexistent air current, it remained out of focus—four limbs and a trunk in human proportions, the details blurred like a smeared chalk-drawing.

It was coming straight at her. The quick clamp of fear stiffened Lily's spine and widened her eyes.

As the faceless thing floated closer it stretched out one hand—and yes, that was clearly a hand. For all the vagueness of the rest of the form, that milky hand was painstakingly vivid, as if an artist had etched in every minute detail from the mound at the base of the thumb to the lines crossing the palm to the wrinkles at the joints. There was a ring on the third finger of that hand.

A gold ring. Glowing. On the left hand, palm up. Beseeching.

Lily's heart raced and ached under the weight of a terrible pity.

The filmy shape drifted to a stop. As if it were, after all, only smoke, it began to tatter in an ethereal breeze, wisping away into nothing.

TWO

~

AMERICA was not a classless society.

No place was, of course. Not if that place counted humans among its residents. Humans were every bit as hierarchical as werewolves, from what Lily could tell. Just less honest about it. The official line was that the United States was a meritocracy: the talented, the dedicated, the extraordinary would rise to the top.

Maybe so, if you were willing to stipulate that money equals competence. Lily wasn't. That tidy metric also didn't account for another American preoccupation that fed into class: beauty. A woman who had both, she reflected as she zipped her jeans, might come across as cold because she felt isolated and wary of other women. Or she might be a stuck-up bitch.

Maybe today she'd figure out which was true of her boss's wife. Their one encounter last spring inclined Lily toward the "bitch" summary, but it had been a very brief meeting. Maybe she was wrong. After all, Ruben had picked Deborah and stayed with her, and the woman did teach seventh grade, so . . .

"You're sure it was a ghost?"

"Of course not." Lily saw red for a moment—the red of the stretchy sweater she tugged over her head. Then it was down and she saw the gray walls and pale wood of the bedroom, and the man she shared that bedroom with. "How can I be sure? I'm no medium."

"But it looked like a ghost." Rule sat on the bed to pull on his shoes. With his head bent, his mink brown hair fell forward, hiding his face. Rule had been overdue for a haircut even by his standards when he got the subcommittee's request for "clarification of your expert testimony from last March." He'd promptly cancelled his hair appointment.

That was stubbornness, not lack of time. The request had come from an überconservative senator pursuing sound bites for his base. He'd wanted to ask Rule annoying questions to get them on the record, and Rule refused to look as if he'd raced out to trim himself to fit conservative notions of grooming.

"White and filmy. Floating. Yeah, it looked like a ghost." The remembered ache of pity closed Lily's throat. It had wanted something from her. Needed something.

Ghosts, she told herself firmly, were not people. She'd been told that by an expert. Whatever that fragment of ectoplasm wanted, it had come to the wrong place. She didn't have any answers.

Lily turned to check herself in the full-length mirror. She could see Rule behind her. The aging athletic shoes—no socks—he was tying suited the worn-to-white jeans with a hole in one knee. Oddly enough, they also went great with the whisper-light black cashmere sweater that had probably cost as much as one of the car payments Lily had finally finished making on her Toyota. "I know Ruben said casual, but—"

"You think the jeans are too casual?"

"No, not you. You're fine." Rule could pair ragged jeans with cashmere and look like a film star. Lily couldn't. First, she didn't own cashmere. Second, a sane woman who wanted to stay that way didn't compare herself to Rule Turner. He could make Bubble Wrap look good.

He stood up. His grin flashed white in a way that still sliced right through her. "You are not wearing one of your work jackets to a backyard barbecue, Lily."

"That would be stuffy."

"Which means you can't wear your shoulder harness."

"I know that."

"You're wearing your ankle holster, aren't you?"

"Of course." It held a little snub-nosed Beretta that had started out as a loaner from Rule's father. When Isen wanted to gift her with it, she hadn't argued. Range and accuracy were no more than you'd expect from a snub-nose, but it had good stopping power. It made an excellent clutch piece.

The Glock she'd been practicing with earlier was now her main weapon. It had a comfortable grip, which was always a factor when you had small hands. It had range, too, and accuracy, and kick-ass stopping power with the right ammo. But it was not her SIG. That was back in California, buried beneath a few tons of earth and rock. She missed it.

But she would not have carried it to her boss's barbecue anyway, she reminded herself, so that didn't matter now. She gave her reflection a frowning study. This was the first time she'd been invited to the Brookses' place socially, and she wanted to get it right.

The jeans looked okay. The sweater . . . something wasn't right. Red was a good color for her, so that wasn't it. The material was stretchy, but not too snug for her boss's party. Nor was the scoop neckline too low. It showed just enough skin to say "social" instead of "on duty." But that skin looked awfully bare.

She wasn't wearing the *toltoi*. That was the problem.

The *toltoi* was a charm the clan had given her when she became Rule's Chosen—meaning that their Lady had picked her for him as mate. At first Lily had thought the lupi's Lady was their deity, more myth than real. But there was a difference between worship and service, and the Lady was as real as a sunrise. Or a sock in the jaw.

Last week, a dumb accident had broken the chain and started her worrying about losing the charm. So it was back in San Diego being remade into a ring by a special sort of jeweler, one who worked with Earth magic as well as metal. The *toltoi* wasn't exactly magical, but it wasn't exactly null, either. It had . . . something. Something Lily couldn't define, which was deeply annoying, but whatever that might be, it needed to be handled with respect.

And this sweater needed a necklace. She headed to her closet.

Lily appreciated order. Her bracelets were in the silvery box on the dresser. Earrings were in the acrylic box next to it. Necklaces were in the hanging thingee in the closet. She dug into one of the hanging thingee's pockets.

"A shooting range is a funny place to see a ghost, isn't it?" She took out a double strand of small black beads. "And I've never seen one before, so I'm relying on hearsay about what ghosts look like."

Rule came up behind her. "They're usually bound to the place they died, aren't they? I suppose people don't die often at a shooting range."

"Better not," she said dryly. "Though they can also be tied to an object instead of a place, and some ghosts break the rules. Or so I'm told." She considered the necklace, put it back, and took out a choker with polished wooden beads. "Fasten this for me?"

"No, not that one." He plucked the choker from her fingers. "Maybe your ghost is tied to one of the guns at the range."

"It's not *my* ghost." Lily had had a ghost, or something like a ghost—a part of her soul, anyway, from a Lily who'd died. A part she hadn't really had access to for several months, but that was over. She was all together again. She frowned at Rule over her shoulder. "And I like that choker."

"The wood is lovely against your skin, but you might want to try this on before you decide." He slipped cool, slinky metal around her throat, his fingers brushing her nape.

Three tiers of delicate chain fringe in silver and brass cascaded in dainty splendor from her collar bones to the midpoint between her breasts. Three white stones studded the tiers. It was stunning and stylish and nothing she would have bought for herself—and not only because of the undoubtedly high price tag. Oversize necklaces were not for her. They made her look like a kid playing dress-up.

Not this one, though. This one was just right. She fingered one of the white stones and turned, tilting her face to look up into eyes the color of bittersweet chocolate. "Have I forgotten an occasion?"

"Don't tell me you forgot our eleven-months-and-five-days anniversary."

That made her grin. She went up on tiptoe—he was too tall, but she'd adjusted—and gave him a quick kiss.

At least she meant it to be quick. But there was the skin of his cheek, freshly shaved. The clean scent of his hair . . . Rule used baby shampoo because he disliked carrying artificial scents around on him all day. And that approving rumble in his chest, felt as much as heard, when she tasted him with her tongue.

"I'm looking forward to seeing you wear this without the sweater, bra, jeans—"

"But not, I think, at Ruben's barbecue."

He smiled, his eyes slumberous beneath the dark slashes of his brows. "Perhaps not."

"Though it would make cleanup easy." That made her think of Toby. Last month, Rule's son had proposed a strategy to keep from getting food on his clothes: eat in his tighty whiteys. A little pang pinched at her. "Sometimes my job sucks."

"I could have sworn you liked barbecue, I know you like Ruben, and since there's nothing you could be except a cop, I'm not sure what about your job sucks for you right now."

"I was wishing Toby could be here, or that we were back home."

"Ah. Me, too." This kiss was soft, consolation or appreciation, she wasn't sure which. They lingered in the circle of each others' arms, enjoying the moment. "I miss him, but your job isn't the only thing dragging us to D.C. I received my own invitation."

"Until we found out I had to testify, you were going to tell Senator Bixton to suck it."

"I assure you, I never tell powerful senators to suck it." He smoothed her hair, but his gaze snagged on his wrist, where he wore a watch worth more than Lily's first car. "Scott hasn't dinged me. I'd better see if . . ." He patted his pocket and frowned.

"Your phone's downstairs on the dining table."

"Thank you." He started for the door.

"You aren't going to turn into one of those men who can't find his socks without help, are you?"

There came that grin again. "Wait and see."

Lily shook her head and reached into the shoe bag for the flats she'd bought on sale last week back in San Diego. Back home.

D.C. wasn't completely strange territory. She'd been here a few times since switching from a local cop to the federal version last year, including a stay of several months while she completed accelerated training at Quantico. The house was familiar, too. It was a two-story brick colonial in Georgetown owned jointly by Rule's clan and two others. Rule had been coming here off and on for years. He was the public face for his people, and sometimes that meant lobbying Congress.

Sometimes it meant being asked asinine questions by politicians posturing for the cameras. He'd handled that the day before yesterday with his usual panache. Being absurdly photogenic helped, but he was just plain good at PR. That's how he saw this particular appearance before the subcommittee doomed to endlessly masticate the Species Citizenship Bill— which did not, he thought, stand much chance of being brought before the full Senate this year.

Lily's testimony was more of a command appearance and would be for a different committee, though Senator Bixton was on it, too. At least it would take place away from C-SPAN; the stuff they'd be asking her about was all classified. Her appearance wasn't until Monday. She could still hope Ruben would pull off a miracle and get her out of it.

Lily stepped into her flats and headed for the stairs. The new necklace felt cool against her skin.

It was a lovely gift, thoughtful and elegant and snazzy, and she was not going to obsess over the fact that he could afford to spend more on her than she could on him . . . though that sort of led into why the thoughtful gift was also a problem.

Rule's birthday was two weeks and three days away.

Oh, she had a present for him—a custom-made black silk shirt. Lily's cousin Lyn was a dressmaker, tailor, designer. Last month Lily had snuck out one of Rule's favorite shirts and taken it to Lyn to use for fit. The new shirt would have black embroidery on the collar, very subtle: a stylized depiction of the *toltoi*.

Lupi could be so damn male sometimes. They always spoke of her having been chosen for Rule. It never occurred to them that Rule had been chosen for her, too. The embroidered *toltoi* was Lily's way of pointing that out.

But one gift was not enough. She needed something fun or funny or sweet. Two more somethings would be best. Then there was the wedding, which wasn't until March, sure, but she had no idea what—

A stabbing pain at the base of her skull brought her to a stop halfway down the stairs. Ow. That was really . . . gone. She blinked, gave her head a cautious shake, and continued downstairs. Weird, but she felt fine now. No way was she going to mention a here-and-gone headache. Who knew what kind of crap-all tests some conscientious doctor might want to run?

Lily had been on sick leave for four weeks. She was on limited duty now, and it chafed. Aside from the lingering weakness in her right arm, she was perfectly fit. Unfortunately, no one would believe her without running some of those stupid tests, and that was likely to raise questions she couldn't answer. Mantles were a deep, dark lupi secret.

Rule was talking on the phone in the fussy Victorian parlor that was Lily's least-liked part of the house. ". . . probably quite late when we get home, so . . . yes, I'll tell her, but since we're coming up there Tuesday anyway . . . of course. *T'eius ven*, Walt." He disconnected.

"Walt again." She sighed. "I didn't hear the phone ring."

"It didn't. He called while I was talking to Scott. He'd like you to call at your convenience. I assured him we'd be home too late for "convenient" to mean tonight, but he didn't seem to think it could wait until Tuesday."

"What is it this time? Did he say?"

"Something about water rights."

"Do I look like I know anything about water rights? Walt's an attorney, for God's sake, even if he doesn't practice anymore. He's got to know ten times more than I do about water rights."

"It doesn't matter what you know. It matters what you carry."

She sighed. "I know." But this wasn't at all what she'd bargained for. She slung her purse on her shoulder. "So where's Scott? For that matter, where's José?"

"Scott was delayed by a traffic light that's not working. José is on the roof, filling in for Mark, who was injured during sparring today."

"Mark's okay?"

"The worst damage was to his pride, but José won't let him take a shift until he's fully healed." Rule's phone chimed once. He glanced at the screen. "Scott's out front."

"Let's go, then."

A lot had changed since last month.

The best and weirdest change was the sudden cessation of argument. The clans weren't bickering with each other. They'd stopped distrusting Nokolai and were grimly determined to hold the All-Clan some of them had been resisting for nearly a year. The Lady had told them to, after all. She'd spoken through the Rhejes, saying they were to come when "the two-mantled one calls"—and the lupi did not argue with their Lady. Ever. But the logistics and expense of assembling almost every lupus in the world in one place meant it couldn't happen overnight.

Every lupus in the world . . . Lily was beginning to feel uneasy about that. Wasn't holding an All-Clan a lot like issuing their enemies an irresistible invitation? "Here we are—come slaughter us." Last year, after they defeated Harlow and the Azá, an All-Clan hadn't been so much of a risk. The Great Bitch hadn't had agents who were ready to act. Now, though . . . now there was Friar and Humans First.

Of course, Robert Friar was supposed to be dead. Lily didn't buy it, but even if she was wrong, the organization he'd founded was very much alive and thriving. Their membership had jumped when Friar's death was reported—according to Humans First, he'd been martyred, killed by foul magic. Never mind that it was magic he'd brought in himself—that was government lies. Most of those members weren't likely to grab a gun and go lupus hunting, but some were hard-core.

She'd told Rule about her misgivings. He'd agreed . . . and said they had to hold the All-Clan anyway. There was something in the stories about it. Something the Lady had said three thousand years ago meant they had to have an All-Clan.

Lily did not understand.

Other changes were less boggling and more annoying. The basement of the row house was unfinished; a construction crew from Leidolf would arrive to finish it in a couple of weeks. They had guards now, ten of them, and Rule wanted those guards housed here, not at a hotel. He'd added an alarm system to the detached garage out back, and he wanted Lily's government-issue Ford in that garage. If she didn't want to park there, fine, he wasn't telling her what to do—but the garage would stay empty, because he wasn't going to use it. He'd rented space in a parking garage a few blocks away—the one where he kept a couple of vehicles for the guards' use. When Rule needed his car, he had one of the guards retrieve it. Since they were lupus, they'd smell it if anyone had tried to tamper with the car.

This focus on security was as necessary as it was unwelcome. But Lily's car was in the garage and Rule's Mercedes wasn't, so they left by the front door, watched over invisibly by José on the roof. Out back, she knew, Craig paced the perimeter of the small yard on four feet.

One up, watching the street; one down, watching the rear of the house; one with Rule. The Leidolf guards were blended with those from Nokolai now. At first they'd worked separate shifts, divided by clan, but Rule had recently changed that. They needed to work as a team, he said . . . which made sense, but Lily had expected it to cause problems, at least at first.

When she'd said something about that to Rule, his eyebrows had lifted. "A month ago, it might have. War changes things." He'd been right. The Leidolf and Nokolai guards were working together as smoothly as if their clans hadn't been enemies for a few hundred years.

"What did your ghost look like?" Rule asked as she locked the door. He stood with his back to her, scanning the street.

"Not my ghost." She dropped her keys in her purse and started for the car double-parked in front of the row house.

"The ghost that isn't yours, then."

"Five-ten, one sixty . . . or what might be one sixty if it had an actual body instead of the ectoplasmic suggestion of one. No distinguishing features. No features at all."

Rule's eyebrows lifted as he opened the car door for her. He was big on opening doors. "A faceless specter?"

She grinned. "In fact, it was." She slid inside and scooted over.

He followed. Scott clicked the locks.

This was the part Rule disliked most about the tightened security, she knew. He preferred to drive himself—but he also preferred to have his hands and attention free if they were attacked, so he used a driver now. Lily disliked pretty much every part, but she was adapting, dammit. Though the loss of privacy still grated.

She said hello to Scott and fastened her seat belt. "Married, I think."

"Yes, we will be," he said, claiming her hand. "Only five months now."

"And I'm not even hyperventilating." Marrying Rule was easy. Holding the wedding was another story, but she had a list, after all. Several of them. "But I meant that the ghost was married before the death-do-you-part clause got activated. He, she, or it wore a ring on the left hand."

"You saw a ring? No face, but a wedding ring?"

"When it reached for me, the hands got a lot clearer. The ring kind of glowed." She considered. "I should say he, not it. They looked like a man's hands. Not real young, not real old, and he wasn't a manual laborer." No, they'd been soft hands, she remembered. Clean and cared for. Narrow palms, long fingers, nicely trimmed nails.

"It reached for you?" Rule did not sound happy.

"Then wisped away." She squeezed his hand. "Relax. It— or he—didn't seem hostile, and even if he was pissed and was able to interact with the physical, what could he do? Lob a pencil at me?"

"I seem to recall a wraith who managed to do quite a lot."

"I couldn't see the wraith. I saw this, so it's unlikely he was a wraith." It was unlikely for other reasons, too, having to do with how wraiths were made.

"Hmm."

Rule didn't ask the obvious questions. He knew that whatever she'd seen, it hadn't been a trick of the light or a delusion. He also knew it couldn't have been an illusion. Lily was a touch sensitive. She felt magic tactically, but couldn't work it or be affected by it. Whatever she'd seen had been real.

Scott signaled for the turn. Lily tried to pretend he wasn't able to hear everything they said. Rule was better at that than she was. Ignoring their front-seat audience entirely, he played with her fingers. Especially the one with his ring on it. For a man who'd spent several decades morally opposed to marriage and all forms of sexual possessiveness, he sure was fascinated by that shiny token of his claim on her.

Maybe she should have gotten him an engagement ring, too.

"Something funny?" he asked.

"I was picturing your left hand with a diamond on the third finger."

He blinked. Went still. Then nodded. "That's a good idea. I wonder why it didn't occur to me that I needed an engagement ring."

He wasn't kidding. He honest-to-God meant it. She leaned in and kissed him lightly. "I love you, you know."

"I like hearing it." He switched his attention from her hand to her hair, running his fingers through it. "Shall we pick something out together?"

"Your engagement ring, you mean."

"We may have to go with something custom."

"Um . . . yeah, we might." Unless . . . "We might find something in San Francisco. Or in Massachusetts." Did gay guys buy each other engagement rings? Why didn't she know? The only XY married couple she knew personally had tied the knot in a big hurry, afraid their official permission to marry wouldn't last. They'd been right.

Rule smiled, following her thinking easily. "Perhaps I could ask Jasper."

"Jasper?"

"Your cousin Freddie's good friend. They recently moved in together."

"Oh, that Jasper." Lily's cousin Freddie—third cousin, really, but still a cousin—had started working for Rule last month. He was handling some of Leidolf's investments, which took a big load off Rule. Lily had mixed feelings about this. Freddie was indefatigably honest and good at what he did—at least Lily's father thought so, and he ought to know. But she'd built up a good head of Freddie-aversion over the years because he would not stop assuming that she was going to marry him. "I've only met Jasper a couple times. I didn't realize he was . . ." She sat straight up. "Wait a minute. You don't mean that Freddie—"

"You didn't know?"

"Freddie's gay?" Her voice rose in outrage. "He asked me to marry him a dozen times. Not because he wanted to, mind, but his mother wanted . . . so did mine. Are you telling me he's gay?"

Rule shrugged. "Define it how you like. He and Jasper—"

"Just because Jasper's gay doesn't mean Freddie is." Because it would really piss her off if Freddie had done his damnedest to marry her without mentioning that he preferred sexual partners who were outies instead of innies. "You can't be sure."

"I can't help but know when someone finds me attractive. Freddie might be bi rather than gay, but yes, I'm sure he finds men sexually appealing."

He smelled it. That's what he meant, and she'd known he could smell female arousal. She'd never thought about him smelling male arousal, too. Sidetracked, she asked, "Is that ever a problem for you? Knowing some guy is getting excited looking at you?"

"Why? I've never understood why human men get flustered or angry about that sort of thing. How is it offensive to be found attractive, even if you aren't able to return the compliment?"

"Hierarchy." Lily said that automatically, stopped to think about it, and decided it made sense. "That's part of it, maybe a big part. For a few centuries heterosexual males—white heterosexual males in particular, here in the West—have been at the top of the pecking order. Getting hit on by another guy would feel like an insult because someone was doubting your qualifications to be top dog."

"Ah. You're wise. Yes, that fits. What high-status group wants to give up their privileged position? It would explain the hysterical tenor of some of the anti-gay-marriage groups."

She snorted. "Fear and bigotry don't need explaining. They simply are, like traffic jams and taxes."

"That's one way of seeing it." He wound the bit of hair he'd been playing with around his finger. "Are you going to forgive your cousin?"

"Eventually. I may have to hit him first."

"Don't hit hard. He's doing a good job with Leidolf's finances."

"I'll bear that in mind. You were sure burning midnight oil for a while. If Nokolai hadn't been able to . . ." Her voice drifted off. He'd given the back of Scott's head a pointed glance. "Right." Two mantles, two clans, two sets of guards. Scott was one of the Leidolf bunch. Mustn't discuss Nokolai business in front of a Leidolf, even if the two sets of guards were playing nice together.

Rule let the strand of hair unwind. "About the ghost that isn't yours. What did you do after it wisped away?"

"Asked if anyone else had seen it, of course."

That amused him. "At a firing range for FBI agents."

"I needed to know, didn't I? Besides, everyone knows I'm part of the woo-woo crowd."

"And had anyone else seen it?"

"No." Which raised a number of questions, didn't it?

THREE

~

IF Lily had to be in D.C., she was glad it was October. Summers here sweated, winters were too damn cold, but October in D.C was nice. Almost as nice as in San Diego, if not as dependably pleasant. D.C. was also, she admitted, a lot greener. Water fell from the sky here on a regular basis. On her last sojourn in the capital, Lily had broken down and bought a pair of rain boots.

Not that she'd need them for the party. Trust a precog to pick the right weekend for perfect weather.

Ruben Brooks, head of Unit 12 of the FBI's Magical Crimes Division, wasn't just Gifted. His precognitive ability was off-the-charts. He lived in a Bethesda neighborhood that no FBI employee, however high up the ladder, should have been able to afford. But his wife came from money. Old money, not modern megabucks, the kind of wealth that, like river rocks, had been worn smooth by time into the polished detritus of trust funds and expectations. The Brookses' Bethesda home had been a wedding present from her parents.

The house itself had more bedrooms than Lily was used to and a fair helping of antiques, yet on the whole it was more comfortable than pretentious. Land and location—that's what pushed the price into the stratosphere. Bethesda was expensive to start with. The stone-and-timber home was a short subway ride from downtown D.C., yet sat on over three acres of land, nestled into a surviving patch of old-growth forest. The grounds immediately surrounding the house were beautiful—lush and imaginatively landscaped.

Backyard barbecue? Maybe, but not the sort of backyard Lily was used to.

There was enough space for the impromptu softball game they'd played while waiting on the food. As the day darkened into twilight, they sat down to eat at ten long picnic tables set up on the lawn to accommodate the guests. Those guests were an eclectic mix: Unit agents plus their partners, spouses, or dates; regular FBI; and plenty of non-Bureau guests, too. Lily had the chance to meet some of those spouses and dates—like Margarita Karonski, and wasn't that a mouthful? Karonski's wife was about forty, with big breasts, a big laugh, lustrous black hair, and a master's degree in electrical engineering.

It was all very egalitarian. Lily ate ribs and potato salad with Rule, a seventh-grade teacher, another Unit agent, the head of a small seminary, Ruben's secretary, and the director of the Census Bureau.

The director and the teacher turned out to be interesting people, even if they were wrongheaded about key issues. Like baseball. After dessert, the three of them lingered at the table, arguing about instant replay.

"Lily Yu!" boomed out behind her. "It's been too long!"

Lily turned. A man with Einstein hair, Ben Franklin glasses, and guileless brown eyes snared in a nest of wrinkles beneath bushy brows was beaming at her. He wore baggy shorts and Birkenstocks. A Hawaiian print shirt covered the decided paunch around his middle. "Dr. Fagin!"

"Fagin, my dear, simply Fagin, unless you wish to adopt Sherry's habit and call me Xavier. Otherwise I'll look like a patronizing ass when I call you Lily."

She grinned, swung her legs over the bench and stood. "Annette, Carl," she said to her fellow debaters, "do you know Dr. Xavier Fagin? He consults here sometimes, but he's at Harvard—"

"Ah, but I'm retired now. I moved to D.C. last month."

"I didn't know that. It's quite a change for you."

"Life is change, after all." He smiled his vague, dotty-old-professor smile, a gentle benediction meant to baffle all inquiries.

Lily took the hint and dropped the subject. "Fagin, this is Annette Broderick and Carl Rogers."

"I know Annette." Fagin turned that gentle smile on the Census director. "Delighted to see you again, my dear. And you're Carl? Good to meet you. I'm afraid I've come to rudely steal Lily away. A research matter."

Lily snorted. "Research, my—"

"A matter of personal research, we might say. Lily, I'm having a terrible time resisting the urge to tuck your hand in my arm and drag you delicately away. Men my age are allowed to get away with that sort of behavior. It's one of the few charms about growing old. But in your case—"

"Not a good idea."

Dr. Xavier Fagin—BA, MA, MFA, PhD, and for all she knew, DDT, LOL, and RAM as well—was one of the leading authorities on Pre-Purge magical history. He'd headed the Presidential Task Force that dealt with the aftermath of the Turning, which is how Lily knew him. He was also the only other touch sensitive she'd ever met. They'd discovered the hard way that it was best not to shake hands.

"Alas, it is not, so I must rely on curiosity to lure you away, rather than tolerance for an old man's peculiarities. You've seen a ghost."

Carl wanted to know all about it. Annette said that her cousin Sondra had a touch of a mediumistic Gift, so she saw ghosts occasionally. She hadn't realized Lily possessed that Gift, too.

"I don't," Lily said, "which is why it's so puzzling."

"And so," Fagin said to the other two, "I wish to ask Lily one or two terribly personal questions, which she will doubtless be inclined to brush off, but I believe if I can get her to myself for a few minutes, I can coax answers from her." He waggled bushy eyebrows at Lily. "I have a theory."

Lily allowed herself to be lured. She and Dr. Fagin meandered toward the tubs of beer and soft drinks set out on the deck. "You've been talking to Rule."

"I have. I've also been collecting data on non-mediums who see or profess to see ghosts."

Her own eyebrows went up. "It really is research."

He waved that away. "A personal interest. I doubt there's a paper in it. Too much of the data is anecdotal."

"Why are you personally interested in who sees ghosts?"

He heaved a windy sigh. "I suppose it's only fair to answer that, since I did promise to ask intrusive questions myself. Fifteen years ago, I saw my mother's ghost."

"Oh." They'd reached the tubs of drinks. Lily pulled out a Diet Coke and popped it open. "You're not a medium, so it must have been one of those intimate connection deals. I'm told that happens sometimes."

"She wasn't dead."

The can halted halfway to Lily's lips. Belatedly she took a sip. "Then would it be . . . I don't know. Astral travel, maybe? Was she Gifted?"

"No. I saw her ghost at five minutes after midnight—terribly appropriate time, isn't it?—and she died at 12:49 A.M."

That was a new twist.

"Of some interest," he went on, "is that she was in the last stages of Alzheimer's. She'd been at a nursing home in Cambridge for ten years, and hadn't spoken at all for the last year. That night I was here in Washington to speak with, um, a member of that administration, and I was sound asleep in my hotel room. I woke suddenly with the sense that someone was bending over me . . . and she was. She was wearing a pale blue nightgown and robe I remember from when I was small, and she smelled of White Shoulders. My father gave her White Shoulders every year at Christmas, and she wore the scent every day until he died. Never again after that. Her hair was brown and curly. She'd worn glasses for the last forty years of her life. They were gone. So were all the other accoutrements of aging . . . she tucked me in," he finished simply. "Gave me a kiss and smiled, then she was gone. I looked around and saw the clock. It changed to 12:06 at that moment."

"Wow."

"The scent of White Shoulders lingered for several minutes."

"That's incredible. It must have been . . ." Lily shook her head, unable to say what the experience had been like, other than powerful. "Did she physically tuck you in? Actually move the covers, I mean. Did you feel the kiss?"

"No and no. Her actions did not affect the physical world."

"But you smelled her favorite scent." Scent was physical, but scent memories could be triggered in the brain, so that didn't prove that she'd been physically present. "You mentioned the color of her hair and her nightgown. Did she look solid?"

"Almost." His voice turned dreamy. "She was unusually vivid, but not quite solid, no. I knew she was a ghost right away."

"And you're certain about the times."

"As I said, I saw the clock click over. As soon as she vanished, I called the nursing home and insisted that they check on her. They discovered her in respiratory distress, but still alive by all the measures we use to determine life. Medical personnel were in attendance from that point on. At 12:49, heartbeat and respiration ceased."

"A ghost that appears before death. I've never heard of that." She considered it. "Is such a visitor really a ghost? A woman I know—a highly Gifted medium—would probably say it depends on how we define *ghost*."

"Exactly." He broke into a smile like the merry gamin he must have been back when a woman in a pale blue nightgown and robe tucked him in routinely. "It started me on my little hobby of collecting ghost stories. At first I looked for those like mine—and I found a few—but I grew interested in the question of how and why some people without a mediumistic Gift see ghosts. You're wearing agate."

She blinked. "I am?"

"Your necklace. The white stones are agates. Were you wearing it when you saw your ghost?"

"It's not *my* ghost." Lily was already sick of that phrase. "And no, I wasn't."

"You donned it to protect you from the ghost?"

"I donned it because Rule gave it to me. This evening. Just before we came here."

He chuckled. "Perhaps I'm confusing causality with coincidence. White agate is said to enhance dreams and concentration. Because of its connection to the crown chakra, some consider it a way of enhancing spiritual communication, while others wear it for protection from malign or confused spiritual influences. Ghosts, in other words."

"Oh. Well, unless Rule has suddenly developed a precog Gift to rival Ruben's, me wearing agate tonight was a coincidence. You mentioned a theory."

"Also intrusive personal questions. This one, however, is not too intrusive. Tell me about the ghost you saw."

Lily described it briefly. ". . . so this wasn't like your experience. Misty form, no color, just a shape, and as far as I know, I've got no personal connection to the deceased."

"Hmm. Have you ever died?"

"I . . ." For several heartbeats Lily didn't know what to say. The story behind "yes" was both complicated and not for public consumption, since it involved the opening of a hellgate. "That's not a question I get asked every day. I'm going to say yes, but I can't give any details."

"Excellent." He beamed. "The stories of ghost sightings by non-mediums that I've collected fall into three categories. In one, there's an intimate connection between the corporeal person and the ghost. In the second, the ghost itself appears to be responsible, having acquired the ability to manifest itself visually. For whatever reason," he added, "English haunts seem to be especially adept at such manifestations. The third category, however, is composed of people who have had what is popularly called a near-death experience."

Lily took another swig of Diet Coke. She was uncomfortable, yet fascinated. "I have reason to believe that my, ah, my near-death experience . . ." She shook her head. *Near* was the wrong word. Part of her absolutely had died, but that part had been embodied separately from the rest of her at the time. "My own experience leaves me sort of open to spiritual stuff that—"

"Fagin, you're monopolizing . . . oh, dear." Deborah Brooks grimaced prettily. "I've interrupted."

"A beautiful woman is never an interruption."

Deborah was that. Her beauty was the classic English sort, with skin like milk and soft brown hair bobbed just above her shoulders. Her eyes were large and heavily lashed; her features were perfectly symmetrical in a heart-shaped face. Men wouldn't stop and stare when they saw her on the street. They'd hunt frantically for a puddle they could throw their cloaks over. Though given the scarcity of cloaks these days, they might have to settle for casting a T-shirt in the mud.

That perfectly symmetrical face produced a stiff little smile. "Thank you."

"Deborah!" Fagin swooped down upon her like a genial bear, seizing her shoulders and giving her a loud, smacking kiss on the lips. "Don't do that!"

A laugh startled itself out of Deborah. "You're impossible!"

"Merely highly unlikely. Your mother isn't here tonight. You can accept the compliment, punch me—not in the face, please—say, 'yes, I know,' tell me to stuff it, ask me to jet away to the Caribbean with you for days of sun-drenched pleasure and nights of madness—"

Deborah was laughing. "Oh, stop it. I'm too busy for the last, too inhibited to tell anyone to stuff it, and I couldn't possibly just agree with you!"

"I observe that you've kept open the option of punching me." He patted her arm. "Good girl. Lily, I cede you to our hostess for now, while reserving the right to pester you again later."

"So noted."

Fagin ambled off. Deborah's smile lingered as she turned to Lily. "I was sent to fetch you, actually. There's someone Rule would like you to meet."

Automatically Lily glanced over at the swimming pool fifty feet away. That was a tell, though Deborah wouldn't recognize it. Lily always knew where Rule was. That was one of the handiest things about the mate bond. At the moment, he was talking with two men—one tall and dark-skinned, wearing khakis and a yellow polo shirt; the other short, slim, and dark-haired with a trim little mustache. He wore jeans with a white shirt and a sports jacket. Lily was pretty sure he hadn't joined in the softball game.

It was odd for Rule to have her "fetched." Was there a sta-

tus thing going on? "I already know Croft, so it must be the
guy in the sports jacket."

"Dennis Parrott. He's Senator Bixton's chief of staff."

Lily grimaced.

"I know," Deborah said sympathetically, "but it can be useful to get to know your enemies socially."

Lily glanced at her, surprised. "You see Dennis Parrott as
an enemy?"

Rosy color washed over that soft, pale skin. "I shouldn't
have said that."

"Why not?"

Deborah pursed her lips. "I don't know, but I shouldn't.
Fagin has an absolute genius for getting me to let my guard
down, but once I do, there's no telling what might come out of
my mouth. Never mind. It's true that Rule would like you to
meet Mr. Parrott, but I had another reason for seeking you
out." She took a breath like she was about to jump from the
high dive. "I wanted to apologize."

"Apology accepted, but what are you apologizing for?"

"For the way I acted when we met. I . . ." That soft color
rose in her cheeks again. "I wouldn't shake your hand. I
wouldn't talk. I just nodded and hurried away. You must have
thought I was snubbing you."

That's pretty much what she'd thought, all right.

"I'm sorry." Deborah held her hand out.

Lily shook it, smiling at what she learned from that touch.
Also from relief. She hadn't wanted Ruben to be married to a
stuck-up bitch. "You weren't snubbing me. You're shy." Not
just wary or self-protective, which was learned behavior. Shyness seemed to be more innate.

"The experts are calling it social anxiety disorder these
days, but I like the old word better. Yes, I'm shy."

"That must be difficult for a teacher."

A sudden smile lit her face. "Teaching is different. It's
helped me get over myself to some extent. These days I bum-
ble along fairly well most of the time, but now and then I just
seize up, like I did with you. Then I torture myself about how
stupid or cold or awful I must have seemed. Shyness is really
very selfish, very inward."

"So's grief, but we don't blame people for feeling it."

Deborah blinked. "I like you," she said, as if startled by the notion. She tipped her head. "When we shook hands I expected you to say something about my, well . . . my little Gift."

"I don't speak of what I learn from touch unless there's a compelling reason, not unless I know it's okay. Some people dislike having others know." Earth magic always felt warm to Lily, warm and sandy and slow. A major Earth Gift felt weighty as well, as if the bones and boulders of the earth were pressing up from the sandy surface. Deborah's Gift wasn't major, but it was clear and vivid, the sign of someone who used a Gift regularly.

"I am a little uncomfortable discussing it," Deborah admitted as they started for the pool area. "It's not as if my parents were Orthodox. They aren't very religious at all, but I think they see magic as cheating. Certainly they consider it distasteful, not something one should speak of in public. I was raised to keep my ability secret."

"So was I." Lily had known Ruben was Jewish, but had the fuzzy notion he was a Jew by heritage more than belief— maybe because the subject of religion had never come up. She hadn't known that Deborah was Jewish in any sense. She looked so very English. "Back when I was with homicide, I never told anyone I was a sensitive. That was partly because I'd been raised not to speak of it, but also I worried about being used to out someone, you know?"

Deborah nodded. "Torquemada."

"Among others, yeah." Sensitives had been used before, during, and after the Purge to find those of the Blood as well as those "tainted" by magic, but Spain's Grand Inquisitor was the sensitive everyone had heard about. As mass murderers go, he was outranked by Hitler, Lenin, and Pol Pot, but he'd tortured way more than the nine or ten thousand he'd had burned at the stake. "It took a while to get used to being out, but I like it better this way. Lots better."

"I don't exactly keep my Gift secret. I just don't mention it."

Lily gave her a wry look.

Deborah grimaced. "I guess that amounts to the same thing. Does magic run in your family?"

"On my father's side, yes, though he isn't Gifted himself. Why?"

"Oh, I've gotten interested in the genetics of it. Particularly after we found out how Ruben's trace of sidhe blood affects him—first with that allergy problem, then by saving his life. Do you know Arjenie Fox?"

"Sure." Arjenie was newly mate-bonded to Rule's brother, Benedict—the only other Chosen in North America. That was a deep, dark secret, of course, but Lily had already known the woman. Arjenie was an FBI researcher.

"I was so surprised when she moved to California. But love does have its way with us, doesn't it? She's been helping me. Just as a favor, in her spare time," Deborah added hastily. "She isn't using government time or facilities."

Lily smothered a smile. She suspected Arjenie would use any facilities she wanted. She was highly ethical, but her ethics didn't run along the same lines as the bureaucracy's. "Now that I know about your Gift, I'm wondering how much of this"—Lily gestured at the grounds—"you did yourself. It's gorgeous. In my experience, most Earth-Gifted don't like to have other people mess in their dirt."

"I planted and tend every filthy inch," Deborah said with the particular smugness of a gardener.

So complimenting Deborah on her looks was out. That made her freeze. But compliment her on her gardens and she lit up. "I love this one," Lily said as they reached a round, tiered bed. "It looks like a wedding cake or a fountain of plants instead of water." She stopped, tilting her head. Most of the plants weren't blooming this late in the year, but . . . "Is it a white garden?"

"Oh, you must be a gardener! Yes, I love the way masses of white flowers seem to glow in the dusk. I wish you could have seen it a month ago. Even the summersweet is past its peak now, I'm afraid."

"Summersweet?" Lily asked. "I don't know much about your plants here, but I had the idea it was a summer bloomer. There's that "summer" in the name."

A dimple winked slyly in Deborah's left cheek. "I may have persuaded it to keep blooming longer than usual."

"Now that's a useful trick. Not one most Earth-Gifted can do, either."

"An elemental showed me how once."

Lily's eyebrows shot up. "An elemental?"

"They show up here from time to time. They're curious about me, I think."

"Ah." She didn't have to let herself be fetched, Lily decided, and she'd rather talk to Deborah than make up to Bixton's chief of staff. "I don't have my own garden, but my grandmother lets me muck around in her dirt. There's nothing like destroying a few square yards of weeds to set the mind at rest."

"Exactly. Though Bermuda grass—!" Deborah rolled her eyes. "The people who owned the place before us had planted it. After twenty years, I still find clumps I have to dig out."

"Nasty stuff. Roots that want to contribute to Chinese agriculture. Why anyone ever thought Bermuda grass was a good idea—"

"They'd never planted a garden, that's for sure. Talk about invasive. You have it out in California, then?"

"Oh, it's everywhere. I've heard," Lily said darkly, "it's been found at the bottom of the Grand Canyon. What kind of grass do you have? It's a turf grass, I can see that much, but it isn't like any we use out in California."

"Kentucky bluegrass. You have to mow it high, but if you do that, an established bluegrass lawn is almost weed-free."

Twenty minutes later, Lily and Deborah were studying a sad-looking rhododendron on the eastern edge of the lawn near the woods, talking about mulch and compost and black root rot.

". . . not much of a problem in my part of the country," Lily was saying, "but I know good drainage is key. But if you've already amended the soil and given it your own special boost, then switching to a different mulch—"

A clear tenor voice broke in wryly. "I should have known."

Deborah looked over her shoulder at her husband, that single dimple winking again. "Lily likes to garden."

Ruben Brooks didn't look like a man who'd recently had a heart attack . . . one that had nearly killed him and still had him on indefinite medical leave. A heart attack caused by a potion that, for reasons of timing and proximity, restricted suspects to those at FBI Headquarters. A potion administered by a traitor.

Tonight, though, Ruben looked healthy. Still on the skinny end of lean, he had a beak of a nose, messy hair, and glasses that said "geek" more than "power broker." But he wasn't wasted anymore. He wasn't in a wheelchair, either. When Lily first met him last November, he'd suffered from a mysterious condition that caused progressive weakness. The condition hadn't gone away. It was genetic and would be with him for life, but now he knew what triggered it and could avoid his triggers . . . mostly. You couldn't avoid iron and steel altogether.

He gave her a quizzical smile. "I didn't realize you were a gardener. You don't have one yourself."

"No, but like I told Deborah, I get to play in Grandmother's dirt." When she had time. When she was in San Diego instead of Washington.

"I'm glad you get a chance to get grubby. Lily, please try not to react visibly to what I tell you now. I'd like to have a word with you and Rule after the other guests leave. If you could linger without it being noticed . . . perhaps Deborah can show you the ficus that's trying to take over the sunroom. You can remain inside as the others depart."

Deborah sighed faintly. "Time, is it?"

"I'm afraid so."

Lily smiled and nodded as if Ruben had commented on the weather, but now that he'd brought it up, she noticed that the guests had thinned out while she was talking to Deborah. Half a dozen questions jostled in her mind. She suppressed them. If Ruben felt free to tell her what was up, he would have done so. "Okay."

He couldn't have read her mind and she didn't think her face gave her away, but he answered one of the questions anyway. "It's about the war."

FOUR

~

VERY few guests remained when Rule started making his way to the Brookses' back door. It was almost time. His main feeling was relief.

The next hour or so would be difficult. He didn't fool himself about that, but it would be hardest on Lily. First she'd be hit by Ruben's news, then . . . well, his *nadia* hated it when he kept secrets from her. He'd learned that he hated it, too, and was more than ready to lay that particular burden down.

He'd had no choice. She knew him well enough to understand that.

As he continued along the path, he felt the moon rise. He smiled.

Her song was always with him, but the bulk of the Earth muffled it until her orbit and the planet's slow turning brought her above the horizon once more. Tonight the song was quiet and pure, resonating inside him like a plucked harp string. Quiet and pure and sweet. Always it was sweet. The song and the pull would mount over the next week to the wondrous, full-throated call of full moon.

The Brookses' land would be a lovely place to spend full-moon night, he thought as he smiled and shook his head, declining an invitation to stop and chat with a couple of slow-to-leave guests. He'd love to sample the scents around him with a keener nose. Changing here would be easy. The earth itself welcomed him in a way he usually felt only at Clanhome. The Change was a matter of Earth communing with moonsong . . . and someone here worked Earth magic regularly.

Not Ruben, he thought as he went through the open French doors into a large, well-lit kitchen. Mainly because Ruben was not a practitioner, but also, Rule thought the welcome he felt suggested an Earth Gift, not spellwork. And Ruben's Gift was aligned with fire.

Deborah, then. Odd that Ruben had never mentioned his wife's Gift . . . or perhaps not. He seldom mentioned Deborah. Rule had wondered about that. He doubted that he'd gone half a day without speaking of Lily since he met her. But for all that he knew a good deal about human sexual customs, marriage remained a mystery to him.

It was a mystery he was growing eager to explore. Why had he thought it a good idea to wait until March for the ceremony?

He passed from the kitchen to a spacious, slightly cluttered den, then into a hall that gave access to the front of the house and to the stairs. Rule approved of Ruben's home. His own taste leaned more toward contemporary, but he had a love for old wood. Clearly, either Ruben or Deborah did, too, judging by the antiques sprinkled throughout their house.

The banister curving along the stairwell was old, too. He rested a hand on it as he climbed to the second floor. Smooth wood, polished by countless hands over the years. Had Ruben once dreamed that his children's hands would be among those polishing the wood? This was a large house for two people, yet he and Deborah had no children, either by birth or adoption. Rule wondered about that, too.

Of course, humans weren't as uniformly focused on children as lupi. There was a cultural assumption that everyone wanted children, but that wasn't always the case. Perhaps he was imagining a grief where none existed.

The stairwell opened into a hall with lovely wainscoting. Rule followed something that was not a tug, not a song, but was every bit as dear and certain to a door on the left. He knocked softly.

Lily opened it. She glanced behind him, confirming that he was alone, and sighed. "I've washed my hands, played with my hair, glossed up my lips . . . I'm running out of things to do in case someone comes up here and finds me hanging out in the bathroom. I take it Ruben asked you to wait around, too?"

"Your lips are beautifully glossy." He bent and kissed them lightly. "Apples. I like it. Almost everyone is gone. I believe we can wander downstairs now."

She started for the stairs with him. "Do you know where he wants us to wait? Deborah didn't say."

"In his study, I think. You and Deborah hit it off."

She slid him a grin. "You sent her to fetch me."

"I assure you I did not."

"Her word, not yours, maybe. But you wanted me to come meet Senator Bixton's chief of staff."

"Dennis Parrott. A smooth man. Like an iceberg, most of him remains hidden, and the exposed surface is cool and glossy. I'd like to hear your impression of him. Also, most people find it harder to accept killing if they know the victim."

She stopped moving. "You think Parrott wants me dead?"

"Not you specifically, perhaps, but he might privately use the term *collateral damage* if you were killed by one of the haters he and Bixton court. Publicly, of course, he would acknowledge no responsibility for the results of the inflammatory speeches he writes for Bixton."

"Doesn't the senator have a speechwriter?"

"He does, but Parrott handles speeches that deal with magical policy in all its many forms. He has ties to Humans First."

Her expression soured. "Is he going to be at the big rally?" The Humans Firsters had planned demonstrations to take place across the country. The big one would be here in D.C. at the Mall.

"Bixton's supposed to give a speech. Parrott will attend with him."

"Why in the world did Ruben invite him?"

"A better question might be, why did he come?"

She started down the stairs again. "I'll bite. Why did he?"

"I'm not sure. He despises Ruben, though he hides it well. Fears him, too, and hides that even better. If I weren't able to smell his fear, I wouldn't know."

"You're sure it wasn't you he was afraid of?"

"We've met before, and he's concluded I'm safe."

"Is he foolish about other things, too?"

Rule smiled. "Perhaps I should say that he knows I won't attack him physically. But he's known Ruben longer and better than he has me, and fears him more. I find that interesting."

"I'd guess that Ruben stands between him and something he wants. You don't."

That's why he'd wanted her to meet Parrott. She had a good mind, quick to cut through gristle and fat to the meat. "You may be right. Maybe Ruben can tell us what that something is."

"Do you have any idea why Ruben wanted to talk to us privately? The two of us." She frowned. "He said it was about the war, and that's just weird. He's not lupi."

"He's our ally."

"Yes, but first and foremost, he's FBI. Government. The U.S. government isn't at war. For the most part, it doesn't even know the Great Bitch exists."

War did not mean the same thing to humans as it did to lupi. Rule knew this. Most beings who knew anything about the Great War—and not many did—believed it had ended roughly three thousand years ago. Not lupi. To them, war ended only with the death or complete subjugation of the enemy, and their Lady's enemy was an Old One, as incapable of dying as she was of submission. Three thousand years might be a very long lull in the action, but lupi had been at war with *her* for all that time.

Recently the lull had ended.

"I think I understand what you mean," Rule said as they crossed the entry hall. The study door was almost directly opposite the staircase. It stood open. "For humans or lupi, war is a joint effort. An individual can only consider himself at war in a metaphorical sense, if his society isn't also at war. Perhaps Ruben spoke metaphorically."

"I don't think so," she said dryly. "Maybe he wanted me to

know it was about *her* without saying so directly. Deborah was right there."

"You think he hasn't told his wife about our enemy?"

"I don't know what he's told her. He carries a lot of secrets in his head. Some of them he isn't free to talk about. Some he may not want to talk about."

Rule considered that as they went into a room that, by day, would be sun-flooded from the tall windows on the north wall. Tonight the drapes were closed and the only light came from a floor lamp. It was an inviting room—dark cherry desk and file cabinets, chocolate drapes, cinnamon upholstery on the two armchairs, walls the color of an old chamois. The warm colors were likely Deborah's doing, since Ruben didn't take an interest in such things. But those chamois-colored walls held objects Ruben did take an interest in: books, framed photos, a tribal mask, what looked like a broken walking stick, and a magnificent abstract painting.

Lily, however, was looking at the floor, not the walls. "Is that for decoration, do you think?"

The floor here was the same warm hickory as on the rest of the ground floor, with one addition: a thin silvery inlay delineated a circle that included most of the room. "You can ask Ruben. I wonder if the need to keep secrets from Deborah is why . . ."

"Why what?"

"Ruben and Deborah seem to possess the kind of rapport that comes from intimacy. She's important to him, yet he seldom speaks of her. It seemed odd to me, but perhaps that's how he protects those secrets he holds. He doesn't speak often of his work to his wife. He doesn't speak often of his wife when he's working."

"A lot of cops do that. They want to keep the ugly shit they see from touching their families, so they don't talk about the job at home."

"You don't do that."

She snorted. "As if I'd ever had a chance to, with you."

That pleased him, so he moved close and kissed her.

A voice spoke from the doorway. "What a lovely reason to slip away from the party."

Lily jolted. Rule let go of her without looking away from her annoyed face. "Hello, Fagin."

"You heard him, didn't you?" Lily looked past him at the man who'd joined them. "You left an hour ago. I saw you leave."

The older man beamed at them. "It does my heart good to think I tricked such a clever and watchful woman."

"You didn't want anyone to know you'd stayed here."

"No more than you did, my dear." He lumbered into the room carrying a paper plate with goodies from the dessert bar. "If you have any electronics on you—phone or whatever— you need to put them on that table in the hall."

"Why?"

Fagin waggled his eyebrows at her. "Because you won't learn why you're here if you don't."

Rule retrieved his phone and held out his hand for Lily's phone. He could see the questions jostling around in her by the way her lips thinned with the effort of holding them back.

Funny. With the time rapidly shifting from "soon" to "now," he didn't feel so philosophical. His stomach was tight with worry. No, call it by its true name: fear. Taking their phones into the hall gave him a moment to get his face and body back under control.

Ruben arrived in the hall. Their eyes met. Ruben's voice was as relaxed as Rule wished to be. "Ah, you're placing your phones elsewhere. Good."

They went back in the study together.

"Ruben," Lily said, "what in the world is going on?"

"Paranoia is a common occupational hazard. I'm afraid mine has increased recently, since someone really is out to get me." Ruben glanced at Fagin. "I'll set the circle." He closed the study door, then crouched and put his hand flat on the floor, covering a section of the silvery inlay. After a moment he nodded. "It's up."

Lily's eyebrows lifted. "Learning some new tricks?"

"I can't set a circle, but I can activate one. It's best if we aren't overheard."

"Which this will make sure of." Fagin dug into his shorts pocket and pulled out a small, silk-wrapped object. He un- rolled the cloth to reveal a quartz crystal the size of Rule's thumb and held it up. "Quite a clever invention, this. The circle blocks magical eavesdropping. This will take care of the technical variety." He set the crystal on the leather-bound blotter on the desk, then patted his pockets. "I don't seem to have . . ."

Ruben moved to the other side of the desk, opened a drawer, and took out a hammer that he handed to Fagin.

"Ah, thank you." And he smashed the crystal.

Lily blinked. "That felt like node energy. A pretty good shot of it, too. I thought quartz didn't store power well."

Fagin handed Ruben the hammer and began dusting the smashed crystal into one large and chubby palm. "Not as well as gemstones, no, but that's what makes it work so well for this. A quartz matrix is a bit unstable, magically speaking. Overfill it too suddenly, or smash the crystal, and it releases the stored power all at once. Makes a nice little magic bomb for scrambling tech, even if one isn't a practitioner." Fagin looked at the bits in his palm. "Trash?" he said to Ruben.

Ruben gestured behind the desk and Fagin went to deposit the shards.

Lily watched. "You did that to disable any bugs?"

"That's right."

"What about directional mics? Or lasers? Will the glass and drapes keep those from working?"

Fagin's eyebrows slid up. "I have no idea."

Ruben moved behind his desk. "A directional mic won't work. The glass in the windows is too thick and the drapes are heavy. A laser device might—"

"Lasers?" Fagin asked.

"A laser beam is bounced off a window. The vibrations in the glass caused by sound in the room cause equivalent variations in the laser beam. Sophisticated equipment picks up and decodes the reflected beam to render any conversation in the room. With such thick glass, however, that's unlikely to work. Also, I believe Friar is biased toward magical means."

"Friar." Lily's voice was flat.

"He *is* a listener."

Who couldn't eavesdrop magically on conversations near Rule. Ruben knew that, though he didn't know why. And Lily didn't know Ruben knew. And Rule would be glad when he didn't have to make quite so many who-knows-what calculations.

"Just in case, however, Deborah is going to . . . ah, there it is."

The thrum of bass from a sound system started up outside. Rule nodded, appreciating the trick. The others might not hear it, but the windows were vibrating to the bass. "That should do it."

Ruben sat and gestured. "Please be seated, and I'll explain." He waited while they did—Rule took the wooden chair nearest the door—then lobbed his first bombshell. "I wanted you to know that I will be resigning from the Bureau due to my health."

FIVE

~

LILY'S stomach went tight. "I hate that. I hate it. I'd hoped . . . you look so well. Healthy. I guess the healer Nettie sent couldn't do as much as I'd thought."

Ruben's smile was small and wry, but as genuine as everything else about him. "He did a great deal, or I'd be dead. I'm told the damage was extensive. He was able to repair quite a bit—enough that I can hope to be around for a while yet. Not enough, unfortunately, to raise that from "hope" to "expect." The Unit can't be run by someone who could die in the middle of a crisis."

"Anyone can die. Isn't there some way to continue to share responsibility? Croft's good, but without your Gift . . ." She cut herself off in midquestion, glancing at Fagin with a small frown. Then she looked at Rule.

"You're wondering why Fagin is present. No, he is not my choice to run the Unit."

"Thank the Good Lord above," Fagin said. "Not that I'd accept if you did try to foist it on me."

"So why is he here? And Rule?"

Ruben ignored that question. "The news of my impending resignation is not to be spoken of outside this room. I'm delaying it because I believe strongly that it's best if the enemy behind the attack on me remains uncertain of my role for a while longer."

"Friar, you mean. You don't think he's dead."

"Officially, he died in the explosion. For now, we want him to think we have no suspicion of his continued role as *her* agent."

"We?"

Ruben smiled and ignored that question, too. So she offered him another one. "What about Croft? Does he—"

"I won't provide a list of those who know or those who don't. You might be tempted into unwarranted assumptions about those I haven't informed."

Lily nodded slowly. "So is this about the investigation? About finding the traitor? Or is it about *her*?"

"Both, since the existence of the traitor bears on another decision that I am asking you to not divulge. I'm establishing a clandestine organization I call the Shadow Unit to fight *her* and her agents and allies in our realm. This group consists of both Bureau and non-Bureau personnel and will operate without the knowledge or sanction of the government. I'd like you to be part of it."

Lily's stomach hollowed. Her hands went cold. She stared at him, unable to believe what she'd heard. "You can't be serious."

"I am entirely serious."

Anger washed through the shock, making her insides quiver. Her eyes narrowed. She twisted to look at Fagin. "You're in it? You're part of this—this Shadow Unit?"

"That I am." With his hands resting on his stomach, he looked like a badly dressed Buddha. Placid. Perhaps not really listening. "In an advisory capacity, primarily. I'm not one of the ghosts." He smiled at the look on her face. "That's my little nickname for those on the front lines in this war. Shadow agents, lacking any official existence. Ghosts."

She grimaced and faced Ruben. "No."

"You should listen before deciding."

"It may not be in your best interests to tell me more."

"You aren't thinking," he said crisply. "If I'm right, the Shadow Unit is essential to stopping an Old One from establishing her rule and worship in our nation and committing genocide along the way to creating a planetwide theocracy. If I'm wrong, I'm attempting to form a criminal conspiracy based on my delusions or lust for power, and you will need to stop me. In either case, you are obligated to learn everything you can."

"Damn it," she whispered. Then again, louder: "Damn it, damn it, damn it." Her stomach roiled. Her hands clenched and unclenched on the arms of her chair. She sucked in a breath, held it briefly, then let it out with a slow shudder. "Right. You're right. So tell me."

He leaned back slightly. "There has always been information I have not allowed into the record. You're aware of some of it—lupi secrets such as the mate bond. I assume there are additional lupi secrets you haven't told me about, and I suspect there are also events you haven't spoken of. I don't know the specifics, obviously, so I may be wrong in assuming that these matters sometimes involved extralegal actions on your part."

She started to speak, then shook her head—not denying his assumption, but refusing to comment on it.

"Now think about the fact that you are a single agent. One who has proved a nexus for the enemy's attempts, perhaps, but only one."

"You're saying *she*'s made more attempts than the ones I know about."

"Oh, yes. Think about it. There are one hundred seventy-nine full Unit agents, forty-one groups or individuals we contract with for their special skills, six hundred and five agents in the Magical Crimes Division, and just under fourteen thousand regular FBI agents. Did you think you were the only one who has had to deal with potentially explosive situations involving unusual magic or beings? Situations that could not be resolved through traditional law enforcement methods?"

"I haven't heard of any cases where our people were coloring outside the lines."

"Neither has the news media, fortunately." He paused. "Increasingly, I've seen a choice before me. If the enforcement of

the law remains my chief duty and highest priority, I will have
to accept a high rate of casualties—both in Unit agents and in
the civilian population. If protecting the people of this nation
is my greatest priority, I will be forced to allow and tacitly
encourage more and more extralegal activities on the part of
Unit agents."

"Every officer of the law faces that decision," Lily said.
"Would it be easier if we didn't have to read some murdering
asshole his rights? Sure. Would that protect some of his future
victims? Probably. That doesn't make it right. There's a reason
cops don't get to be the prosecutors and judges of the perps we
arrest."

He nodded. "You're right, of course. And yet for the last
several months I've had an increasingly strong feeling that
there needed to be an organization that was separate from the
legal institutions. I began thinking about how such an organization might be established, how it would function, what kind
of personnel it would need, how they would communicate,
how it could be kept secret. I didn't envision myself running
such an organization, but as helping establish it, then cooperating with and sometimes assisting it covertly."

Slowly Lily nodded. This wasn't as bad as she'd thought.
Ruben had no business organizing such a group while he was
head of the Unit, but at least he planned to step aside once it
was established. She could keep her mouth shut about that. "If
you want my word I won't speak of this—"

"Not yet. I may not have planned to run the Shadow Unit,
but three things happened to change my mind. First, Robert
Friar was given an immensely powerful Gift by the enemy.
Second, I began receiving calls from the Rhos of every lupi
clan in the world."

"Those calls—" She broke off and looked at Rule. One of
those calls had been from him. The clans had been told by
their Lady they were to ally with Ruben—with him personally, not with the U.S. government.

Rule wore his blank face, the one that gave her nothing
back. She hated his blank face. Was he shocked? Pleased? Determined not to influence her? Determined to hide his reaction
from Ruben? Whatever the hell that might be. She couldn't

tell, and he wasn't speaking. Lily faced Ruben again. "I know about the calls."

He nodded. "Originally I thought the clans would provide much of the manpower for the Shadow Unit, and therefore a lupus should lead it."

That made sense, actually. Lupi weren't exactly invested in the human legal structure. They were invested—hearts, minds, lives, clans, everything—in stopping *her*. Helping such an organization covertly . . . yeah, she could see that. Could even see herself doing just that. But for Ruben to go from there to establishing himself as the leader of a covert organization that operated outside the law while using agents and other resources of the Bureau . . . no. No and no and no. "You changed your mind."

"I consulted with the Rhos. With others, as well." He nodded at Fagin. "I had information you lack—a deficit I will partly make up tonight—but what the Rhos told me played a part. Their Lady's instruction was that they ally themselves with me. There was no compulsion that I offer alliance in return, but I needed to understand what it meant if I did so. Also, they provided a good deal of information about our common enemy. I realized that to go up against an Old One—even one unable to act directly in our realm—required assets and information only the government possesses."

"You consulted with the Rhos." Slowly she looked at Rule. "All of them?"

Rule spoke. "He consulted with me, yes."

"You've known about this—this Shadow Unit. For maybe a month, you've known. And didn't tell me. You made sure I didn't know."

"Because we knew you would react precisely as you have—with anger, a sense of betrayal, and the burning desire to arrest people."

Something was burning, all right. Her eyes were part of that heat. She couldn't look at him right now. She could not. She didn't want to look at Ruben, either, so she stared at her lap, fighting to get control.

"Lily," Fagin said gently, "consider the possibility that you're wrong. You know us. Me only slightly, I suppose, but you know Ruben fairly well. You certainly know Rule. Would they take this step if they weren't convinced it was absolutely necessary?"

Her hands clenched. He was too old to punch, but God, she wanted to hit someone. "Consider the possibility," she said through gritted teeth, "that a group of people who operate outside the law is going to abuse that. They won't mean to. They'll tell themselves they're only doing what they have to do, but that's just another version of the ends justifying the means. Sooner or later—especially when the stakes are so high—they'll be hurting people to protect themselves, because if they get exposed, why, that's going to strengthen the enemy, isn't it?"

Now she looked up, right into Ruben's eyes. "Power without accountability corrupts. Every damn time."

He looked tired. "Do you think I haven't considered this? Law enforcement in this country is designed to operate openly. We hold power over people's lives. That power must be tempered by accountability. By establishing a shadow organization, I eliminate that accountability, making abuse more likely. It's my hope that there won't be time for corruption to set in."

"If you think you can stop *her* in a month or two—"

"A month or two. Interesting that you chose that interval. Without the Shadow Unit, the United States has approximately two months left before it collapses."

He stopped there. Rule didn't speak. Neither did Fagin. Lily sat motionless, her mind skittering away from his words while her stomach clutched up tight, as if it could tie a knot in the silence, hold on to it, so she didn't have to hear . . .

It didn't work. She had to ask. "All right. All right. Tell me."

"The third thing that happened to change my mind was a series of visions."

Ruben's Gift meant he had the best hunches ever. He knew, without knowing why, that he needed to take a certain action, or avoid an action. He'd proved his accuracy time after time. But he didn't normally *see* the future. She knew of one occasion when he had, though. When a three- or four-thousand-year-old being who could not die was about to manifest herself and her power fully on Earth, dragging California and God only knew how much of the nation into chaos and nightmare.

Because of those visions, he'd been willing to hold back, to trust Lily, even when she couldn't tell him anything. Because he trusted her and his own hunches, in the end he'd exerted his authority in the only way that would help.

Now he wanted her to trust him—and his visions.

"Without the Shadow Unit," Ruben said quietly, "in approximately two months, perhaps one-third of the Gifted in the country will be dead. The Unit will be gone, its people dead or imprisoned or in hiding. The president and possibly the vice president will be dead. The nation will be in a panic, with mobs killing anyone suspected of magic. Some Gifted will strike back, killing large numbers of civilians and police alike. In one scenario, the surviving lupi retreat to Canada. In another, they pull back to their clanhomes, but after the military coup—"

"The *what*!?"

"I've seen five detailed scenarios. One of them results in an enormous physical cataclysm on the West Coast, the nature of which is unclear. Four of them end in a military coup a few months from now. It supplants civilian government in the West, Midwest, and Central U.S., and succeeds in restoring order at the cost of martial law and the end of elective government. The South descends into anarchy. Canada and Britain send troops to support the remaining fragment of U.S. government in the Northeast, but the world economy is in shambles due to the collapse of the United States. The dominant power that emerges in the new world order is the military dictatorship that arises from the coup, which is run by religious zealots who—some wittingly, some not—are *her* agents."

Lily's hands were cold. She wanted to disbelieve him. He was so certain, so damnably certain . . . "You said that's without your Shadow Unit. With it? What happens then?"

"We have a decent chance of averting the incidents that precipitate the crisis."

"What . . ." Lily's mouth was too dry. She had to pause and summon enough spit to speak. "What incidents?"

He shook his head.

He didn't know? No—if that were true, he would have said so. He meant that he wasn't going to tell her.

Fagin spoke, his voice dreamy. "We know what Gift Friar received from the enemy."

Dazed, Lily looked at the older man. Belatedly her mind caught up with what he'd said. Robert Friar had been imbued with some sort of Gift by the Old One he worshipped—the one Ruben referred to as their enemy. The one lupi often called the Great Bitch because it was dangerous to speak any of her names. Lily and Rule had been present for part of the ritual that invested Friar with his new power, but unable to stop it . . . Rule because he was in a cage. Lily because of all those elves trying to kill her. Soon after that, the node used to power the ritual turned unstable, bringing down half the mountain, burying Lily's SIG Sauer and presumably Robert Friar as well.

Lily had never believed that. "How could you know that?"

Fagin just smiled. "Patterning. Friar is a new and incredibly powerful patterner. Ruben discovered this soon after Friar supposedly died."

She looked at her boss. She'd placed her life on the line based on his hunches more than once. But to take his word—unsubstantiated, unsupported—for everything . . . he could be wrong. He was good, but he could still be wrong. "How do you know? Another hunch?"

"My knowledge is subjective, but not a hunch. Lily, you know that normally my Gift grants me knowledge of events in the near or very near future. More distant events are too fluid for a sense of them to emerge."

"But you've seen some pretty damn specific events this time. Events that are more than a month away."

He nodded. "That's what raised my suspicions. My visions started after the node collapsed."

"I don't see why—"

"If you'll stop asking, you'll get your answer faster. I have to explain a bit about how my Gift works. I seldom receive hunches, much less visions, about events more than a few days in the future. Even a week away, the future is usually too fluid for me to pick up much."

He'd spoken of this before. "Too many decision points, you told me once. Too many possibilities, choices, and people are involved in determining events, and the more distant a possible event is, the more these multiply, until it's all static."

He nodded. "Yet suddenly I was having explicit visions about events that were, at that point, three months distant, and some of them six months or more. I could only find one explanation for this abrupt explicitness. The future had been artificially constrained. I realized that an extremely strong patterner was manipulating events, forcing a single channel through which events flowed. Once I understood this, I consulted Sherry. You know that her coven observes node action throughout the nation through a simulacra map."

Lily did know that, even if she was fuzzy on what a "simulacra map" might be. She nodded.

"We'd hoped she could reconstruct what was done through the node used to imbue Friar with his Gift. So far she hasn't been able to. In the process, however, she discovered that virtually every node in the nation is being drawn upon by what appears to be a single, albeit untraceable, source."

"Every node? But that's not possible. That's . . . don't practitioners have to be in physical proximity to—"

"So we've always believed. But it would take a great deal of power for a single patterner to influence events across the entire country."

Fagin spoke up suddenly. "They call it the Gift of the gods, you know. Patterning is the most subtle and dangerous of Gifts. I think you encountered a patterner once."

Lily shot Ruben a hard glance. Apparently he'd been sharing a lot with Fagin, some of it highly classified. "I've run across a couple of them, actually."

"Oh?" Fagin's bushy brows shot up. "The one I was thinking of was named Jiri. You had some difficulty overcoming her."

"I didn't overcome her," Lily said dryly. "I managed to stay alive. She didn't, but that's because she only cared about one thing. And she got that." Her daughter's life. Jiri had not been a good guy by any means, but she'd given her life so her daughter would live. The child had been adopted by the Leidolf Lu Nuncio.

Fagin steepled his hands on his belly. "You have some understanding of the Gift, then. Patterners are rare, for which we can thank the good God. When the Gift does appear, it's almost always in the weak form. A weak patterner senses event patterns unconsciously. He may learn how to control his Gift so that his effect on events is less haphazard, but he doesn't sense the patterns directly. A strong patterner does. A strong and experienced patterner can manipulate those patterns in subtle ways to bring about what he or she wants."

"I thought all patterners did that."

"They all affect events, though the weak ones affect them only slightly and often unpredictably. A strong but inexperienced patterner . . . I descend into theory now," he said apologetically. "Strong patterners are so rare we have no hard data on how their Gift operates, but there is anecdotal and historical evidence. A strong but untrained or inexperienced patterner will generally be adept in one application of his Gift, but not others. Napoleon is a good example."

She blinked. "He is?"

"Certainly. He's often lauded as a military genius, but his real genius—and the way he used his Gift most effectively— lay in the social interplay of politics. He was eventually defeated on the battlefield, after all, but never politically. Had he taken the time to become more adept at patterning before plunging his nation into war, he might never have been defeated at all. I suspect Jiri was both a strong patterner and fairly experienced. She was not, however, a fraction as powerful as Friar now is."

That was so not good news.

Fagin smiled gently. "Patterning is called the Gift of the gods because we believe—and by 'we' I mean fusty old academics like me—that some of those who once were worshipped as gods were real beings, adept-level patterners of great power. They were able to influence such a multiplicity of events simultaneously that no single unraveling of their weaving could defeat them. Friar has power an adept would envy. He does not yet have the experience to wield it in a godlike way. That's one advantage for us. The other—"

"The Shadow Unit," she said wearily. "You're going to tell me it's needed to catch Friar."

"No, I'm going to tell you that Ruben is needed to run that Unit. There are two Gifts that can confound a patterner. One is ours. Sensitives can't be affected by the patterner's manipulations, which makes us the large rock in their artificial stream."

Rule spoke for the first time since admitting he'd deceived her. "As are lupi, at least as far as Friar is concerned."

Fagin nodded agreeably. "So you stipulate. Your fiancé," he added to Lily, "says that lupi are immune to *her* magic. Since we believe Friar's Gift comes from her, they would likewise be barriers to his patterning. You and I and the lupi form, ah . . . call us dead spots in his manipulations. He can mobilize events that affect us, but it takes more power because his magic can't touch us. But there's only one Gift that can truly act *against* a strong patterner. Precognition."

Lily frowned. "Because that's like patterning? A precog is sensing patterns, I guess, when he gets a hunch." Or sees visions of the Apocalypse.

Ruben shifted slightly in his chair. "I don't think so."

"No?"

"Fagin and I have discussed this." A smile flickered over Ruben's thin face. "At length. He would prefer to believe that my Gift picks up patterns from the future, much as a patterner senses patterns in the present. My input is subjective, of course, but it doesn't feel that way to me. I've discussed this with that young woman you sent me for training."

"Anna Sjorensen." The other patterner Lily had met.

"Yes. Her Gift is quite weak, so she doesn't sense patterns directly. This means her experience of her Gift should correspond to what I experience with my hunches if I'm also receiving patterns. Based on our conversation, this doesn't seem to be the case."

Fagin snorted. "Which could mean that the future's patterns are experienced differently than those from the present. Or that you're two different people and your minds interpret things differently."

Ruben's smile returned. "It could. But patterns are a spacetime construct. I have a strong feeling that the information my

Gift provides is not so bounded—that it comes from elsewhere and elsewhen, a state for which words are unsuited because it lies beyond space-time."

Rule spoke very politely. "I imagine Sam would enjoy discussing your ideas about time and precognition."

That widened Ruben's smile. "I've strayed from the topic, haven't I? Thank you for the reminder. Lily, the point is that I can act as a fulcrum, a way to leverage events away from the path Friar is establishing. To do so, I need the resources and cooperation of a great many people. Hence my leadership of the Shadow Unit."

She sat with that in silence for a long moment. "Earlier, you said 'the surviving lupi.' When you talked about your vision, you said that in one scenario the surviving lupi retreat to their clanhomes. What did you mean?"

Ruben answered carefully, like a man picking his way through a minefield where he knew the location of some—and only some—of the explosives. "There are elements I can't speak of at this time, but the greatest variation in the scenarios I saw involves the lupi. I believe that variation means that their very existence impedes her power. *She* has to destroy them to succeed."

No one moved. No one spoke. It was so quiet Lily could hear her own pulse in her ears, kind of like listening to the sea in a conch shell. Something chinked toward the back of the house. Maybe Deborah was washing dishes.

"All right," she said at last. "I'm willing to promise my silence about all this. I understand why you're doing it. I'm willing to offer some of that covert help you mentioned from time to time. But I'm not joining your ghosts."

SIX

‿⟋

IT must have rained while they were inside. The air was crisp with ozone, rich with the smell of damp earth. Wet grass glistened. But the sky was clear again and making a spectacle of itself, drifts of stars like spangled gauze swathing the darkness. As they walked to Rule's car along a path bordered by roses and baby's breath, Lily's stomach jittered while her mind jumped around like a hyperactive two-year-old.

She'd asked more questions before they left. Ruben had answered some of them. Not all.

"You turned him down," Rule said.

"This may be the right thing for him to do. That doesn't make it right for me."

"He didn't stop you from refusing. You aren't at risk because you know too much. Doesn't that prove that your fears about the Shadow Unit are misplaced?"

"I've got way too many fears at the moment for you to be sweeping them into a single pile and labeling them false. At least I'm restraining my burning urge to arrest people."

"For now," he said dryly.

"Look, let's stipulate Ruben's right and you're right and so is whoever else is part of this. I don't know. I haven't . . . it's going to take time for me to get my mind around everything, and we can't even talk about it! How am I supposed to think it through if I can't talk about it, or make notes, or . . . but even if you're all right, that doesn't mean I have to be part of it."

He was silent for several paces, then stopped just short of the car. "I hurt you with my silence. I'm sorry for that."

She stopped. Faced him. "It's not what you didn't say, it's how you pretended. For weeks—"

"Three weeks. Slightly less, to be specific."

She flung up a hand. "Okay. Fine. Be specific by all damn means. For three weeks you've acted like things are okay, but if you believe everything Ruben said, everything's going to hell—or could, pretty damn fast. How could you *pretend* with me?"

He looked baffled. "I haven't."

"When you first learned all that stuff I can't say out loud, it didn't just about blow off the top of your head? And you hid that from me!"

He answered slowly. "The timing came as a shock. *She* is moving much faster than I'd expected. The rest of it . . . no. We've known for nearly a year that *she* is active in our realm once more. Now we know some specifics about her plans. That's tremendously valuable, and learning that we—the clans—have strong allies against her is a great relief."

She stared at him. All this time, he'd been expecting something like this. When he proposed to her, he'd known they'd face some kind of Armageddon shit. When they planned their wedding, he'd known. He hadn't just thought there would be danger—he'd known it would be vast and powerful. World-toppling. All along, he'd known. "You're really okay with . . . with all this. You expected it. You're not freaked and hiding it. You're . . . okay."

A small frown tugged at his eyebrows. "My wolf helps. That I live more closely with him than I used to helps a lot. Fear is . . . an immediate thing for a wolf. What hasn't yet happened isn't real enough to trouble him."

"What about the man? How does that part of you stay so damn calm, and plan a wedding, and spend time picking out a necklace for me, and set up Toby's college fund, and—and look to the future as though things were going to be okay?"

"Lily." He took her arms gently. "How else could I live? It's helpful to know what our enemy intends, and while I take Ruben's visions very seriously, none of it is fated." He cocked his head as if listening to something she couldn't hear, then leaned in so close his lips brushed her ear as he whispered, "My Lady is also a patterner, and vastly more experienced than Friar."

"But . . ." She switched to a whisper so soft only he could hear. "But your Lady isn't able to act in our realm."

She felt his lips move in a smile and the breath of his next words. "Except through her agents, *nadia*. She acts through us."

Through lupi. Who she'd created, and who served her still, wholly and freely. She could act through them, and that was why the Great Bitch had to remove them. And instead of finding this terrifying, Rule took comfort in it.

Lily didn't answer with words. She took his hand. She was frowning as she did it, but knew he'd understand both the frown and the touch. "We should go home."

He tucked her hair behind her ear and smiled. "Yes. I love you."

Emotion burst out in a shaky laugh. "Don't I get to brood at all?"

"Later, perhaps."

LATER started as soon as they got in the car.

Ruben's street was quiet, but once they turned onto Bethesda Avenue the traffic picked up. Wet streets bounced light back from taillights, headlights, streetlights, bistros, clubs, and storefronts. If the brief rain had washed people inside for a time, they were back out now, wandering the pretty downtown area and sitting at tiny outdoor tables with frothy drinks or beer and nachos. It was only a little after eleven, and on a Saturday night.

All these people busy having lives . . . people mad at the boss, celebrating a raise, hunting for a hookup, getting busted, falling in love. People praying, partying, laughing, yelling, making up, breaking up . . . people helping a stranger or robbing one. People who expected tomorrow to arrive in about the same shape as today.

And maybe it would for most of them. And the day after, and the one after that. But next month was looking pretty damn iffy.

An Old One wanted to amputate the future all these people were building with whatever mix of altruism and cruelty, determination and thoughtlessness. The Great Bitch wanted to graft her version of the future onto the world. According to the lupi, *she* saw herself as humanity's benefactor. Sure, people would die on the way to her shiny utopia, but death was what mortals did, right? No real problem. She'd make it up to the survivors by making sure they didn't get to make bad choices anymore.

If the strongest precog on the planet—who also happened to be a good man, good all the way down—was convinced the only way to stop *her* lay in a shadowy, extralegal organization, Lily could accept the necessity. It didn't go down easily, but wasn't bullshit often easier to swallow than truth? She wouldn't be reporting Ruben to the federal attorney. She'd keep his secret, but she wouldn't be part of it.

She was a cop. She didn't know how to be anything else.

They left the downtown behind. Rule hadn't said a word since they got in the car, but he was holding her hand. He did that a lot. She looked at him. Light and shadow slid over his face, shifting as they passed this streetlight, that bar, a pocket of darker land anchored by oaks. "Did you know what Ruben had in mind for tonight?"

"I did."

She wanted to ask how he'd known. How did Ruben's Shadow agents communicate? Phones weren't safe. Neither was e-mail. Not if they wanted to be sure neither Friar nor the non-ghostly FBI caught them at it, but what other options were there? But if she wasn't going to be part of them, she couldn't ask. She couldn't ask who else was in the Shadow Unit, either, or who knew about it, or how it was organized, or what Rule's place was in it . . . other than as a coconspirator, that is.

This was deeply annoying.

As for the rest of it . . . the collapse of the nation, a military coup, "the surviving lupi" . . . her stomach churned. Contemplating Ruben's visions didn't help. Her mind kept trying to go there, but it didn't help. So what would? She drummed her fingers on her thigh and stared at the back of Scott's head.

Scott drew driving duty whenever Rule went out at night, partly because he looked so harmless. He was short and wore baggy clothes that turned his wiry frame skinny. His face was round and boyish with guileless blue eyes he framed in geek glasses—clear lenses, of course, since no lupus needed vision correction. He was adept in three martial arts, deadly with a blade, good with a gun and getting better.

From the back, she could see Scott's short, badly cut brown hair and the way his small ears hugged his head like they'd been superglued down. A small Bluetooth headset curled around his right ear like a question mark.

Questions. Lining up her questions always helped. Her fingers twitched with the need to jot them down, but she restrained herself. None of this could go on paper.

Okay, first question: why tonight? Why had Ruben tried to recruit her now instead of three weeks ago, or three weeks from now, or not at all?

That one almost answered itself. He had something he wanted her to do that hadn't needed doing earlier. Something he couldn't ask of her as an FBI agent. Maybe something he couldn't put on the record because the wrong person might learn about it? Something to do with the traitor.

Lily knew very little about the investigation into the attack on Ruben. Abel Karonski was lead, but if he'd turned up anything solid, he'd managed to keep it a big, fat secret. That was harder than a civilian might think. However tight-lipped FBI types were with outsiders, they were as prone to chatting with their colleagues as anyone else. Prone to speculating when they lacked information, too, but Lily hadn't heard any rumors. Everyone seemed to know that the perp was with the Bureau. No one knew anything else.

Lily's burning desire to arrest people flamed especially hot for the rat bastard who'd betrayed them all and nearly killed Ruben. If she could have a part in catching him or her, that was almost enough to get her to join the damned ghosts.

Almost.

Next question. This one, she realized, she had to ask out loud. "Have you told Ruben about, uh . . . the thing that's the Lady's secret?" Mantles, that is.

Mantle was a word whose meaning Lily could only approach obliquely. She knew it was a magical construct that unified a clan and granted unquestionable authority to the Rho who held it. She knew that lupi needed the mantles. But she couldn't say how they worked, how they felt, why the loss of that feeling could drive a lupus insane. She knew it could, but how and why were outside her experience.

"I haven't," Rule said. "Because that *is* the Lady's secret, and not up to me to disclose."

"But that thing you can't disclose keeps Friar from eavesdropping magically on us." Friar's power came from the Great Bitch. The mantles blocked *her* magic, so his clairaudience didn't work around Rule. "He can't listen in, and it's close to impossible for a directional mic to pick up anything from a moving vehicle. And if someone had planted a bug on the car, Scott would have smelled it, right?"

His eyebrows lifted. "We can speak more freely here than in other places, if that's what you mean." But his glance cut to their driver. Scott might seem professionally oblivious to their conversation, but he heard every word.

She nodded that she'd understood. No talking about Armageddon or Shadow Units in front of Scott. Or, technically, behind him. But Scott knew this part already. "I'm wondering about the Wythe mantle." She rested a hand on her stomach. "This has to be part of your Lady's plans."

"Of course."

And the Lady was a patterner. Lily hadn't thought of her in those terms before. It changed things . . . she couldn't say how, exactly, but since the Lady was an Old One, she'd be an adept. Maybe that meant that Lily was doing just what she was supposed to do.

Rule wasn't the only one in the car with a mantle. Lily had one, too. Sort of.

She wasn't a Rho. She wasn't lupi, could never be lupi, so she couldn't use the mantle in her gut. Couldn't do anything with it but get rid of it as soon as possible . . . which surely would happen on Tuesday, when they went to Wythe Clanhome in upper New York.

Last month, Lily and Rule had rescued his friend Brian from Friar, a sidhe lord, and a bunch of evil elf minions. But they'd been too late. The sidhe lord's experiments had damaged Brian so badly he was dying, and he lacked an heir. With his death, the mantle would be lost, and with it the clan. That meant death for some, insanity for others. Probably human deaths, too, because lupi did not deal well with being clanless.

Lily's Gift let her absorb magic the way dragons do. She'd breathed in the mantle as Brian died—and the lupi's Lady had somehow made it so she didn't just absorb the power. Instead the mantle resided inside her, intact and unreachable, a furry tickle that never went away.

Most of the time it felt like she needed to scratch her colon. Or burp.

She was caretaker of the mantle, not Rho. Wythe needed a Rho, but all they had right now were the clan elders. Normally they were an informal council of advisors to the Rho, men and the occasional woman who held positions of trust—as chief tender, for example, or head of security, or manager of an important business owned by the clan.

Walt McDonald was the most senior Wythe elder. He'd been an attorney for forty years before retiring to run Wythe's dairy farm, which he'd done for twelve years now. He was one hundred and seven years old, for God's sake, yet he consulted Lily over every little decision. As if she knew what to do with a twenty-year-old lupus who couldn't control the Change reliably! Or water rights. Or the dozen other things he'd called her about.

Not for much longer. Lily figured that if the Lady had stuffed a mantle into her, she could get it out again and put it where it belonged. They just had to find the right Wythe lupus to take it. The whole clan would be waiting for her Tuesday, so surely one of them would . . .

Rule turned her hand palm up, cradling it still in his left hand. With his right he gently opened her fingers.

She looked at him. It was darker along this stretch of road in spite of the headlights flashing up and past, up and past, but she saw the way his mouth turned up. The way his eyes locked on to hers.

Rule had hidden something from her. Something important. She hated that, but he hadn't hidden himself. Not on purpose. Shouldn't she have known, though? Shouldn't she have realized a secret lay between them? Had she been too wrapped up in everything else to see? In her wounded arm, her job, Friar's disappearance, the All-Clan that was finally scheduled, the muscle that might or might not regrow, the furry tickle in her gut and the complications it posed, their upcoming wedding, the . . .

Okay, yes, she should have noticed. But maybe she could give herself a pass this time.

With his thumb, Rule drew a circle lightly, lightly in the palm of her hand.

She knew his body very well. She knew the shapes of his mind . . . sometimes. Other times those shapes mystified her. It was like wandering through a fog, with shapes now emerging, now retreating into mist. How well could she know the mind of one who was only a part-time human, after all?

His thumb circled the pad at the base of her index finger. Every nerve ending in her hand woke up. Her breath did, too.

Slowly she smiled. Some shapes were easy to recognize.

For the next three-and-a-half miles Rule drew flesh-whispers in her palm. They were both silent, both still, except for the feathery brush of his thumb, over and over.

Somewhere Lily had read that there were around twenty-five hundred nerve receptors per square centimeter in the palm. Every one of them was bleeding sensation into the rest of her body by the time the Mercedes stopped in front of the Georgetown row house.

Rule thanked Scott gravely, as he always did. He and Lily got out on the sidewalk side, not touching now. Overhead, the sky was a dark, blank shield, its vastness muddied by D.C.'s reflected light. Their street contributed to the overall light pollution, but light made shadows, didn't it? Hard shadows, topped by the smoggy shield civilization raised between it and infinity. They were both watchful as they slipped between parked cars.

Lily unlocked the door. Even such minor details as this were scripted now. Rule's senses and reaction time were better than hers, so he kept watch while she opened the door and stepped into softer light. He closed the door behind them, muffling the city sounds of traffic and television, the distant wail of a siren, and someone's dog barking two streets away.

Rule moved to the foot of the stairs. He stood motionless, head up and nostrils flared. She waited until a subtle shift in his stance said he'd found no strange scents. Safety was a slippery state, but for now, they were as safe as they could be.

She didn't want to think about that. She didn't know how to stop. It wasn't as if she'd thought of safety as a constant—not since she was eight, anyway—but the dangers were so faceless and pervasive now that she—

"I hated it." Rule spun and stepped to her and gripped her arms, his eyes a dark blaze in his set face. "Do you understand? I hated keeping my word, keeping a secret from you, a place I couldn't let you in. I don't know how cops and Ruben and whoever else piles up such barricades of secrets can stand it."

She tilted her face up. His brows were drawn. His fingers clenched on her arm just below the wounded place, where muscle might grow back. Or not.

He needed something from her. Words? She hoped not. She didn't want words tonight. Words would open a gate to thinking and worry and fear, to the precipice gaping before them, a stony-toothed hole big enough to swallow a world, and her mind would skitter off to find means for a bridge, some way across or around or away from. And she'd do that, she had to, but not now. Now she slid her hands onto his shoulders, where cashmere slinked between his skin and hers. She went up on tiptoe.

She didn't kiss him. She bit his lower lip. Not hard, but hard enough. "Mine." She nipped again. "Secrets and all, you're mine. Don't do it again."

He lifted both hands to her face and ran his thumbs along the underside of her jaw. "Yours," he agreed, and touched the necklace he'd put around her throat earlier. "This. I want to see you in just this." He cocked a brow. "Upstairs?"

Yes.

Halfway up, a stair creaked beneath her foot. Otherwise the house was silent. To her, anyway. What did he hear? Three steps from the top he put his hand on the small of her back. Her heart stuttered.

"I'll get the lights," he said at the top of the stairs. Three were on, one in each bedroom. And the two downstairs, of course—parlor and kitchen—but they left those on all night. Security again. If anyone made it inside despite José and Craig, they'd show up great in the well-lit interior. Plus this gave them the option of suddenly shutting off the lights, blinding the intruder or intruders more thoroughly than it would Rule or the guards. If the guards had survived, that is.

And she was sick to death of thinking about security and survival. While Rule turned off lights, Lily went straight to their room at the back of the house. She left that light on.

"Catch up," she said when he joined her, and popped the button on her jeans. The wooden floor was decorated with her shoes, sweater, and bra.

He smiled and caught up—at lupi speed. Damn competitive man. She still wore her panties but he was entirely naked when he knelt in front of her, pressed his face to her belly . . . and blew raspberries.

She looked down at him, astonished. He looked up, grinning.

Oh, he wanted to play. She lifted her eyebrows. "Don't get full of yourself. I know your weak spots."

His hands slid up her thighs to her butt, clamped, and lifted—and sent her sailing onto the bed.

She landed in a whomp of tangled limbs and laughter, rolled onto hands and knees, and beckoned him. *Come on, big boy, I can take you . . .*

He dived onto the bed in a tackle that would have been far more effective if she'd been standing. And the tickle fight was on.

She was horribly ticklish on her sides at the waist. He knew it, damn him. He had two main points of vulnerability: his belly and his underarms. The belly was an iffy target because he could banish tickles by tightening his abs. Armpits, though—they worked every time, if she could get to them.

There was only one rule: no pinning. Otherwise the battle would be over too quickly; he could pin her about nine times oftener than she could him. She was agile, she was ruthless, but she was not lupus. So Lily was indignant when, with most of the covers on the floor and both of them breathless from involuntary laughter, he flipped her onto her back and held her down with the length of his body. "Hey!"

"I submit." His breath came fast. He was grinning in the way that melted her, open and happy. She didn't see it often enough. "I submit, I submit. You won."

"You're throwing the match."

"Oh, yes," he breathed, and lowered his face to her shoulder. This time he just inhaled, deep and luxurious. The inhale was to fill up on her scent, she knew. The exhale was her name, just that, warm and moist against her skin. "Lily."

Something in that soft exhale . . . she sifted a hand through his shaggy, too-long hair. "I'm here."

He pushed up on one elbow, raising his upper body, looking in her eyes. His were dark with need. "And here." He touched his chest.

She knew then, knew what his need was—not sex, or not just sex. He was only a man. He could take her scent inside him, but he couldn't take her body in, couldn't open to her as she did him. He had no portal, no cradle made to receive. Only skin, surfaces. And breath.

So she breathed on him. "And here," she whispered, letting her breath warm his shoulder before she licked it. "Here," she said, and blew on his throat, licked and nibbled, then blew again on the damp skin. He shivered. "And here." She drew her leg up along his, a slow slide of flesh, and ran her hand along his arm. He had long arms, tightly knit, smooth and firm with muscle. She kissed him in the hinge of his arm, the bent place, the tender skin in the crook of his elbow. *There is no place on you I can't love, and love grants me entry . . .*

She was following a familiar trail along his belly, heading for the part of him that bobbed, waving in its ever-friendly way, when he shuddered, seized her arms, and pulled her up. He kissed her thoroughly, tongues joining in a slippery duel, teeth nipping. He was breathing hard when he paused the kiss to say, "I mean to go slow tonight."

She smiled.

"Slow for now," he amended, and began showing her what he meant.

He wreaked shivers on her skin with his mouth, and he wouldn't let her rush him, rush them, so together they built the blaze one burn at a time . . . a touch here, on the smooth roundness of his butt, or here, where the skin of her inner thigh jumped at the flick of his tongue. She didn't notice when she lost the world of words and ideas, constructs too diverse for the need piled up in her.

So she didn't tell him "enough" or "now," but reached for his friendliest part, gripped firmly, and drew her hand up, knowing exactly how much to squeeze. His breath was a growl this time, long and guttural as he threw his head back, the clean line of his throat open, open to her.

She opened to him, and they made a new hinge, a place where the two of them bent, where *we* joined and bent and swung joyously up and up on the flat, level ground of their bed, flesh slapping flesh. Until she cracked at that hinge, cracked and broke open, calling his name as white fire rushed in.

After they caught their breaths, after they stroked and touched and smiled, he left to shut off the light. She almost dozed off. Darkness fell, then covers did—he'd tossed them over her before slipping back in bed. She told him, "Mmm," and snuggled close and put a hand on his chest, where his heart beat slow and strong.

Mine, she told the world outside their room, the top half of her mind muzzy with sleep, still mostly sundered from words. It made perfect sense, floating there in the dark, sated and sleepy and clean as a garden after it rains. *Mine.*

SEVEN

RUBEN'S eyes jerked open on darkness. His heart pounded out a sick, runaway rhythm. A heart attack. Another heart attack. He reached for his chest . . .

And realized that he didn't hurt. His mouth was gummy and sour with fear, his heart raced, but there was no monster crouched on his chest, cutting off air and life and possibilities.

There *had* been pain, though, huge and monstrous. Overwhelming. He remembered that, and the glimpse he'd had of his own familiar kitchen seen from the floor—the legs of the table, a shiny puddle next to a smashed coffee cup. But already the images and content of the dream were tattering under the focus of his waking mind, like dew evaporates under the regard of the rising sun.

Or like cockroaches scuttle into their cracks and crevices when you turn on the light.

Ruben drew in a shaky breath and listened to Deborah breathing beside him. She lay on her side faced away from him, but her rump crowded his hip. Her deliciously bare rump, he noted with a stir of interest. Her nightgown had ridden up the way it so often did.

The way he often helped it do . . . or used to. Not so much now, not with the doctor's warnings lying between them, stiff and rigid like an invisible bundling board. One could get around that unwelcome board with effort, but the sheer furtiveness of joining themselves according to the new rules left him sad afterward, and Deborah too often felt guilty.

Yet he was still here. In spite of a clever and determined enemy's efforts, he was alive this night. Tonight's death had been a dream.

Ruben glanced at the clock. 4:05. How appropriate. Four A.M. was the traditional dark time of the soul, wasn't it?

Slowly Ruben eased away from the woman at his side. Deborah slept on. He smiled at his sleeping lover, wife, dearest friend . . . Deb had always slept like a child, sunk so deep in dreams that the alarm seldom penetrated. Nor did other sounds. Touch her feet or her face, though, and she woke instantly. Other physical sensations could shift her up toward consciousness, bringing her close to awakening.

So he shifted carefully. He didn't want her to stir and ask what was wrong. He didn't intend to tell her, so there was no point. Deb knew about the other dreams, where he watched destruction and devastation rain down on so many all over the country. She didn't know about this one.

Ruben rose with nary a twinge of pain. That remained a wonder to him. After years of increasing weakness, of aching in every joint, he could stand so smoothly now, and walk. Even run, if only for a short distance and in a lumbering manner that ought to make any bystanders giggle.

It had been metal poisoning his body all along. Who could have guessed?

Most families had their little myths, stories passed down through generations that held a kernel of truth, if not a fistful. On his mother's side, the story was that some unknown ancestor had been sidhe—an elven lord gone walkabout, according to the tale, who'd encountered a young Jewish maiden drawing water at the family's well back in the Old Country.

The nut at the heart of this tale was true. The elven lord might not have been a lord. The maiden may not have been maidenly. And there was no saying if a well had been involved, or even if their meeting had taken place in Europe rather than after his people immigrated. But sometime, somewhere, an elf had dallied with one of Ruben's ancestors. He had a trace of sidhe blood.

Not enough to gift him with any of the wondrous abilities the sidhe possessed, but enough to have complicated his life tremendously. And saved it. If not for that smidge of elf in his makeup, the potion he'd been given last month would have killed him.

Folktales about the sidhe and cold iron possessed that kernel of truth family stories often do. Not all sidhe were allergic to metal; of those who were, sensitivity varied greatly. And not all metals affected them.

Iron was the most common allergen, however. The tales were right about that, but they never mentioned aluminum . . . the metal used in the wheelchair where he used to spend so much time. And which he turned out to be more sensitive to than iron. The gnomish healer who'd diagnosed his condition had tested him with various metals. They'd learned that, in addition to iron and aluminum, he needed to avoid tin and lead, though they weren't quite as toxic for him. Silver, gold, copper, nickel, and zinc were fine.

And so he used real silverware these days. They'd replaced doorknobs, switched out the bathroom fixtures to brass—an alloy of copper and zinc—and ate virtually no processed food. The cans weren't a problem, but he couldn't eat food cooked in steel or aluminum pots. Deb had doubled the size of her vegetable garden and switched to glass pans. Cars were unavoidable, but Ruben wore gloves when he left the house. Also when he used the computer. And Deborah had become preoccupied with finding out where on his family tree that trace of sidhe blood had flowed into his genetic stream.

Why did it matter? She didn't seem to know herself, yet matter it did. Perhaps her preoccupation was born of her own heritage. Old money, old bloodlines, an inbred interest in ancestry . . . or perhaps she just wanted to feel in control of something. Anything. The last month had been terribly hard on Deb.

Ruben moved away from the sleeping woman.

Their bedroom was at the back of the house. Ruben stood at one of the two tall windows on the back wall, looking out on their large, rolling lawn studded with flower beds and artfully placed outcroppings of rocks, trees, and shrubs that created subtle paths for the feet and the eyes, bounded at the rear and along the east by the dark sentinels of the woods. On the west side, moonlight glimmered off the long pool they'd put in when Ruben first began experiencing symptoms. He'd swum in that pool faithfully for years, until he grew too weak.

A fat moon peeked out from the branches of the enormous oak that anchored the east side of the yard. Nearly full, he noted. So near he couldn't pick out the difference by eye, but he knew when the full moon would arrive this month. That particular datum mattered these days.

Deb had poured so much of herself into their land. It was a mistake to see anyone wholly through the prism of their Gift, but there was no denying that Earth-Gifted tended to put down roots. He was not surprised she'd refused to leave her home, to go into hiding as he'd so urgently asked her to do.

And, he admitted in this four-in-the-morning privacy, he'd wanted her to refuse. However sternly he hid that from her, that's what he'd wanted. More time with Deb. Every moment he could steal.

This wasn't the first time he'd had that dream.

That trace of sidhe blood was responsible for more than his allergy to some metals. Though he had no proof, Ruben felt confident it was also responsible for his Gift. Not the existence of it, perhaps, but the strength. Precognition was actually very common. Accurate precognition was not. Accuracy such as he possessed was unheard of.

He was very, very good. Better than he'd allowed any tests to show. People were uncomfortable enough around someone who'd shown he could, at times, sense the future with seventy percent accuracy. They simply would not believe he was right ninety-eight percent of the time.

Deb knew, however. Deb knew almost everything there was to know about him.

Almost.

Precognition took many forms. Visual precogs—those who literally saw the future—were the rarest and statistically the most accurate, but they had almost no control over their Gift.

Visions either arrived or they didn't. Dream or trance precogs were less rare, but accuracy varied enormously because so often the dreams, voices, automatic writing, or symbolic images required interpretation.

Ruben's form of precognition was by far the most common—a simple, quiet knowing that arrived without fanfare and almost always concerned the near future. It was also generally the least accurate. "Hunch" precogs could easily mistake their own thoughts or projections for the working of their Gift. At least half the time, and usually more, that's what happened.

But not with him. Ruben always knew the difference. He didn't understand why others didn't. Sometimes the information his Gift provided was so muddled as to be useless—the specifics of the future were wonderfully malleable when a patterner wasn't meddling with the present—but he could always tell the difference between *knowing* and eavesdropping on the noise in his own head.

Two things were common to all precogs, however. They all occasionally experienced a different form of their Gift. A trance precog might have a strong hunch, or a huncher have a true dream. And—for reasons that were often debated, never proven—they were usually blind to their own futures.

Usually. Not always.

Behind him, his lady, the love of his life, rolled onto her back and began to snore softly.

Love and sorrow rose and swirled in him, leaving him giddy and filled with tears. He was alive *now*. Now was the time that truly mattered . . . an odd concept for a precog, he supposed, but true. He couldn't act, think, feel in the future or in the past. Only in this moment.

Was it terribly selfish of him to hold tight to this one secret? Probably. He had told one person about his recurring dream—his second-in-command in the Shadow Unit. But not Deb. Not his beautiful, wondrous Deb.

Twenty years ago Deb had asked him if he'd ever seen his own death. They'd just been dating then, but he'd known he would ask her to marry him. That hadn't been precognition, but the soaring dream of his heart. He'd told her "no" back then, quite truthfully . . . but added that if he ever did, he would tell no one. Not even her. Ruben marveled that his younger self—so often wrong about so much—had been so nearly right about that.

He'd had the practical discussions with her. Given his heart attack, that had been necessary. But those discussions came with a large and lustrous "if." He couldn't take that "if" away from her, though he knew it was wrong.

Four times now he'd dreamed of pain, terrible pain, the kind that eats thoughts and strength and life. He never remembered much about the dream, but his body did. When he'd had the heart attack, its kinetic memory had awakened, telling him this was the pain he'd previewed in a dream.

He'd expected to die. He hadn't.

He hadn't stopped having the dream, either.

Any dream he had that often, through so many changes of course, meant the events it depicted were not to be stopped by any conceivable branchings in the possibilities. His dream always ended the same way: in cessation. Not darkness or some version of the fabled tunnel, but a blankness his waking mind couldn't conjure or reconstruct.

Tomorrow or a month from tomorrow, his body would be crushed by pain. It would end. And Ruben would find out what lay on the other side of the small, dark door that everyone passes through alone.

He would miss her so much.

EIGHT

~

ON Sunday, Lily did not brood. Much. She called her parents because she was supposed to, and that was okay—she enjoyed talking to her dad—but it left her churned up. Ruben's scenarios would have her family living under some weird military dictatorship a year from now.

If they lived.

Rule called Toby and she talked to him awhile, too. Math still sucked, but quadratic equations were kinda cool. Toby was being homeschooled by a retired teacher, but Isen's cook/housekeeper, Carl, was teaching him quadratic equations. Which sounded like math to Lily, but not, apparently, to Toby.

He still couldn't decide on an instrument, but the oboe was okay, so he'd stick with it awhile. He and Johnny were going rock climbing—of course with an adult, and anyway Grand-dad wasn't really mad about the other day, but Toby did not want to be stuck with a bodyguard all the time, so he'd agreed he wouldn't do that anymore. And Dirty Harry was doing great. He'd established his territory in spite of the dogs that ran loose at Clanhome. He'd cowed several of them, but there was a German shepherd mix that gave him trouble. Or had until yesterday. Harry had figured out that the odd-smelling people he now lived with would back him up if the German shepherd gave him any trouble.

Being a cat, Harry had no issues about calling for backup. You used the tools available to you, right? He was pretty smug, Toby said.

Between phone calls, Lily cleaned while Rule did their laundry, a division of labor they'd settled on after a couple months. She was picky about cleaning—he didn't seem to even *see* dust bunnies—and he was picky about his clothes. That was part vanity, part necessity due to that whole "public face of his people" thing, and also because of his nose. Even unscented detergents left a scent, he said, and he wanted his clothes to smell one way and hers to smell another because of how those scents mingled with their personal scents.

She'd asked him once if he could actually smell himself.

His eyebrows had shot up. "You mean you can't?"

The rest of the day, Rule messed with his spreadsheets and financial wheelings and dealings while she studied up for the stupid damn committee hearing. They cooked supper together—salmon en papillote, which was a fancy way of saying you wrapped fish and vegetables and stuff in special paper and baked it.

When Rule first taught her how to make it, she was highly dubious. Surely paper in the oven wasn't a good idea. Apparently parchment paper was different. It hadn't caught on fire yet, anyway, and they fixed salmon en papillote pretty often.

She had a hard time getting to sleep that night, and when she finally did drift off, she didn't sleep well. Bad dreams, though they evaporated when she woke up.

ON a scale of one to firing squad, Monday was a five. First Lily put in a couple hours drone work at Headquarters— limited duty meant sitting on her butt a lot—then she went to PT, which was probably good for her soul even if she wasn't sure what it did for her body. Nettie had instructed Lily to continue her physical therapy while she was in D.C. and had given her the name of a therapist to use. Lily tried not to make

Dr. Nettie Two Horses mad, so she grunted and groaned her way through the session.

Then there was the stupid damn committee hearing.

The first couple hours went about like she'd expected. The senators wanted to know everything about the collapse of the node and what led up to it. They had the right clearance, so she gave it to them straight—well, except for leaving out a few things, like the mate bond and the tickly passenger in her gut. Some of them didn't believe her. Some did. Some even asked good questions.

The committee chair was Senator Bixton. He saved his pounce for the very end.

Bob Bixton must have watched Hal Holbrook do Mark Twain one time too many. He didn't go so far as to wear a white suit—his was pale gray—but he had the mustache and red tie, and his thick white hair was just as wavy. He had a great sense of theater, too.

"Special Agent Yu," he said, drawling her name and rank slowly as if they felt peculiar in his mouth. "I know I speak for my fellow committee members when I say we appreciate your traveling all the way across the country while you are, ah, recovering from an injury. You've been here about a week, I understand."

"Yes, sir. Six days."

"You came here with your, ah, fiancé." He leaned heavily on the first syllable and mangled the last one: FEE-ansee. "Rule Turner."

"Yes, sir. He testified, at your request, before another committee."

"I do recall that," he said dryly. "Now, you appear to have been wholly cooperative, answerin' our questions most patiently. But it is true, is it not, that you were coached by your superior in Unit 12 prior to speakin' with us?"

"No, sir."

The bushy eyebrows flew up. "No? You were at Ruben Brooks's home on Saturday night."

"With about fifty others, yes, sir. It was a social occasion."

"A social occasion. Yes, I believe it was, until the other

forty-eight people left around eleven. You and Mr. Turner stayed on, however. Are you telling this committee that Mr. Brooks did not take advantage of that to suggest to you anything about how to approach your testimony today?"

"Yes, sir, I am. We did not discuss my testimony or this committee at all."

"What did you discuss? For, ah . . ." He made a show of hunting through his papers before finding the one he sought. "For an hour and fifty-seven minutes."

Lily's heart began to pound. "That's a remarkably precise figure . . . sir. I'm afraid I can't confirm or deny the time frame you suggest. I wasn't paying attention."

"But I believe you can answer my question." The drawl was getting thicker, making that more like *Ah b'lieve you kin* . . .

"Yes, sir. We talked about Ruben's—ah, about Mr. Brooks's health—"

"For two hours?" Astonished eyebrows flew up.

"—and his plans. Also some personnel matters."

"Personnel matters? Would you care to clarify that for the committee?"

No, she really wouldn't. "You are aware that the investigation into the attack on Mr. Brooks suggests the perp was someone connected to the Bureau, possibly to the Unit itself."

"I am. I was not aware that you were part of that investigation."

"No, sir, I'm not. Nor did Mr. Brooks make me privy to any details." *Stay on track*, she told herself sternly. *He wants you to keep talking in the hope he'll get another hook he can tug on.* "More to the point, neither Mr. Brooks nor I mentioned this committee or my testimony before it."

"I see." He hung enough doubt on those two words to convict her of any number of unnamed crimes and proceeded to ask a series of questions about the investigation, to all of which she answered that she didn't know. "So you know nothing about this, ah, investigation, yet your superior wanted to discuss it with you. For two hours."

Lily allowed herself a very small smile. "Sir, when I'm in-

terviewing a witness or other source, it's not necessary for the
person I question to know anything about my investigation.
Often it's preferable if they don't."

"Hmm. So your Mr. Brooks questioned you about, ah . . .
personnel matters." The eyebrows sketched skepticism. "For
two hours. It seems a most roundabout way of attempting to
find this, ah, criminal."

"It was more informal than that, sir, and it's possible my
interpretation of his intent is faulty."

The senator on Bixton's right leaned closer to him and
murmured something Lily couldn't hear. Bixton chuckled.
"Well, Frank, if you want to make that motion out loud . . .
no? I thought not. But you do have a point." He went on to
thank Lily for her time and tell her to please remain in Washington, as he anticipated that the committee would have more
questions for her.

Lily left the senators and their stuffy, wainscoted room
with her palms damp and her stomach churning. What had just
happened?

She hadn't lied, but she'd sure as hell done her best to mis-
lead the U.S. Senate. That made her stomach hurt. But why
had the subject of Saturday night even come up? Lily knew the
rules. You couldn't tell a witness what to say, but you could
talk about what kind of questions to expect. Croft had done
that with her. Not Ruben.

Had that whole were-you-coached bit just been a way for
Bixton to bring up Saturday night? How had Bixton known
that she and Rule had stayed for an extra hour and fifty-
seven minutes? Had his chief of staff hung around after the
party, watching to see when they left? Why would he do
that?

Was it possible that Senator Bixton was one of *hers*?

TUESDAY she and Rule flew to New York State. Wednesday
they returned. Thursday morning at seven ten she was in the
kitchen, frowning at the muffin crumbs on her plate. "There
has to be a way."

"A way to what?" Rule entered the kitchen, sipping from a

mug. He was dressed and ready for the day in black slacks, black shirt unbuttoned at the neck, and a black jacket.

Lily put a hand on her stomach. "To make this thing go where it's supposed to." She eyed him. Those were "going out" clothes, plus she'd seen the wrapper from a frozen breakfast burrito. For Rule, a frozen burrito was not a meal. It was a snack to tide him over until he had real food. "Breakfast meeting?"

"Mmm-hmm. Followed by one that may extend into lunch, but I'll be free after that. You?"

"First an exciting round of paper shuffling at Headquarters, then a session with Mika." The committee hadn't released her. She and Rule were still stuck in Washington. "Who're you eating with?"

"The early meeting's with a venture capitalist and a Leidolf entrepreneur who needs capital to expand. Leidolf can't back him, but he's got a good business, a good plan for expansion. I'm introducing him to someone who might be interested."

"Nokolai isn't?" Rule's birth-clan was richer than Leidolf. A lot richer.

"Nokolai is not investing at the moment. Isen wants us to have greater fluidity."

"He wants more cash on hand."

"Quite a bit more. We'll be liquidating some assets. Financially it's not the best time for that, but tactically it's necessary."

War was expensive. "And your other meeting? Something secret you can't tell me about?"

He met her eyes steadily. "Not today."

Rule hadn't brought up the Shadow Unit once since Saturday night. Not in words, not with a strained silence or other indirection. That whole meeting with Ruben was beginning to take on the aspect of a dream. How could it have been real, yet Rule was busy arranging financing for a clansman as if the future held room for a business expansion?

Her lips thinned. She'd forfeited certain rights, hadn't she? When she refused to join the Shadow Unit, she'd given up the right to ask about it. "Who are you having lunch with, then?"

"Dennis Parrott wants to discuss the Species Citizenship Bill in more depth."

"Wants ammo for his boss, you mean. Or hopes to find out more about your strategy."

"I'm singularly lacking in strategy on that front at the moment, so there's a good chance I'll learn more than he will. My official slot with him is eleven, but I intend to invite him to lunch. Lily." He put a hand on her shoulder. "I didn't realize you were expecting to be able to force the mantle to go where you willed."

"I didn't exactly expect that, but . . ." She huffed a quick, impatient breath. "Eighty-nine Wythe lupi and the mantle never stirred, never gave a hint it wanted to go to one of them. But it *has* to. If your Lady won't or can't take the opportunity we gave her, it must be up to me. How do Rhos make a mantle do what they want?"

"Rather the way you make your fingers flex or grasp or release."

She drummed those fingers on the table. "A baby doesn't arrive knowing how to use its hands. Maybe I need to—to practice or something." But she didn't really possess the mantle. It hung inside her, impervious to her thoughts and will. She didn't *feel* it the way Rule felt the mantles he carried. Lily tilted her head to look up at him. "You could do it, right? If you wanted to, you could put the Leidolf mantle in someone from Leidolf."

"If he carried the founder's blood, yes. Apparently that's the problem with Wythe. Their founder's bloodline has grown thin."

"But it has to go to one of them." They knew that one Wythe clan member held plenty of the founder's blood—Brian's son. Lily had met him yesterday. He was three years old.

But there were six adult lupi descended from the previous Rho's great-grandfather, dammit. They had the bloodline—a bit diluted, yeah, but the mantle shouldn't be so damn picky. Aside from the sheer annoyance of the furry tickle in her gut, Wythe needed a Rho. Preserving the mantle might have kept the clan from an explosive death, but it didn't give them a leader.

Rule squeezed her shoulder and moved away, aiming for the coffeepot. "We'll begin looking outside Wythe."

"Lost ones?" she said dubiously. The potential for Change was carried as a recessive in clan daughters and their children. If two people with that recessive got together, they sometimes made a little lupus baby without either of them knowing it was possible. The clans kept records, though. Pretty good records. They kept track of their daughters' descendents. "That's a long shot."

"It would be, yes, but I was speaking of children born to a lupus of another clan whose mother is Wythe or descended from Wythe. We don't keep records of such pairings, so it may take a while."

"I can wait." She didn't have much choice. "I'm just hoping not to have to wait for little Charlie to grow up."

"If the Lady intends the mantle to go to a Wythe clan member anytime soon, then someone exists who can accept it. If so, we'll find him. I hope to have all such potential heirs located in time for the All-Clan." He filled his mug. "Ready for a refill?"

She sighed and pushed her chair back and stood. "I'd better grab a shower and get going. I may not be doing anything much at Headquarters, but I have to show up on . . ."

Rule's eyebrows snapped down. He took a quick step toward her. "What is it?"

An ice pick through my skull. "Headache."

"Do you want some . . ." He was in front of her now. She felt him, but didn't see him. Her eyes were closed against the pain. "That isn't an ibuprofen headache."

"I'm okay." But her voice came out wrong and her hands felt clammy. "Some ibuprofen, though, sure. That's a good . . ." Slowly her eyes opened. "Or maybe not. It's easing off on its own."

Rule took her arms. "You're pale."

"It hurts, but it's going away." No, not going away. Gone, between one heartbeat and the next. Though the departure of pain left her a bit shaky . . . she mustered a reassuring smile. "I really am okay."

His fingers tightened. "You'll cancel your session with Mika today."

Of course that's what he thought of. "I will not."

"Lily—"

"I'll tell Mika about the headache. If there is a connection—and honestly, I don't think there is. But if I'm wrong, he'd know, wouldn't he?"

"Sam probably would. I'm not sure about Mika. He's the youngest of them."

"Then he can ask Sam. Rule, it was just one of those weird pains everyone gets from time to time."

"I don't know what you mean."

"I guess not." She smiled wryly and went up on tiptoe to drop a kiss on his unsmiling mouth. "Everyone human, I should've said."

NINE

~

ROCK Creek Park was a welcome, woodsy sprawl sticking its unpaved finger up D.C.'s concrete butt. Portions of the park were tidied into bike trails, paths, bridges, a planetarium, a couple historic sites, and tennis courts. The wilder bits welcomed birds, raccoons, even the occasional deer or coyote.

And one dragon.

Not that Mika's lair had originally been one of the wild bits. It had started out as an amphitheater—the closest thing, Lily supposed, to a cave Mika had spotted when he arrived last December to take up his duties as a magic sponge. That lair was supposed to have been temporary, but Mika had decided he liked it here.

No one knew why, exactly. The park was a pretty place, but Lily wasn't sure dragons shared the aesthetic sensibilities of humans. Though she knew Mika liked trees. She walked along a cement path roofed by the interwoven branches of oaks beginning to don their fall colors . . . a path that was still intact because Mika hadn't wanted to damage the trees that hugged it so closely. He'd removed most of the cement in his domain.

It was the parking lot, she'd heard, that had pushed park authorities over the edge.

They wanted it back. They wanted their amphitheater back.

There wasn't much they could do about it—the Accords allowed dragons to choose from any publicly owned land. But city authorities were unhappy, too. Lily could see why. People can be remarkably stupid at times. You could post all the "Danger: Dragon Lair" signs you want. A few idiots are going to climb the fence anyway.

As far as Lily knew, Mika hadn't eaten any intruders. There had been a few incidents, however.

D.C. authorities had grown worried enough to approach Sam about it. Sam—otherwise known as Sun Mzao—was the largest, oldest, and most powerful of the dragons who'd returned to Earth after their long sojourn in the hell realm. It was he who'd sung the gate open wide enough, he who brought Lily and Rule with him . . . or they'd brought him, depending on how you looked at it.

Sam had been the one to descend from the night sky onto the White House lawn when he deemed it time to open negotiations. After the Turning, magic leaked into the world in quantities human tech couldn't handle. Dragons absorbed free magic—and needed it, too. They also needed a new home, hell having grown too hot for them after a certain demon lord devoured the Great Bitch's avatar and went wildly insane.

It wasn't surprising D.C.'s mayor thought Sam was the dragons' leader. Wrong, but not surprising. People really didn't understand dragons.

Sam had been—for him—quite polite to the people who'd flown across the country to speak with him. He hadn't allowed the mayoral party into his lair, but he had replied when they stood at the gate and talked to him.

Mika is young, Sam had said. *He will tire of his odd choice eventually.*

"But 'eventually' might mean years. Maybe decades, from what I understand. People use the park *now*. Children. It's an invitation to disaster, having him there."

Has Mika eaten anyone he shouldn't? A pet? Your government was anxious about pets, I recall.

"No, but the danger remains. He is—"

Not in violation of the Accords. If he violates the Accords, you may tell any of us and we will deal with it. Otherwise, it is none of my affair. Go away.

"If you don't wish to order him to move to the new lair, perhaps you could persuade him. Or just talk to him about it. He won't listen to us, but it's a very nice place, with a small lake and—"

At that point, the mayor and four of the five people with him had fallen asleep. The fifth—a husky National Park Service employee—had been told to remove the collapsed members of his party. He had. Quickly.

D.C.'s mayor was wonderfully persistent. That's why Lily knew about the exchange between him and Sam. After he woke up, he'd gone to Grandmother to ask her to intervene.

Grandmother had served him tea—not the full tea ceremony, simply the beverage—gotten the story from him, then told him the truth. "Mika has shown admirable restraint in the face of such rudeness. You will learn to live with his presence. You will stop pestering him, and you will not pester any of the other dragons about this. No one tells a dragon where to lair. Not even another dragon."

Lily smiled as she reached the end of the tree tunnel. Grandmother did enjoy telling that story.

Trees and path alike ended at a wall of earth and rock greened by uncut grass and an assortment of what gardeners optimistically refer to as volunteers or native plants. Weeds, to most people. Lily looked up. As hills go, this one was more abrupt than most. Lots of boulders, which was like the rocky jumble back home, but these were planted, not grown naturally from the earth's bones.

She'd been warned about this aspect of Mika's upgrades, so she'd dressed for it—jeans, Nikes, a tee, a light jacket that hid her weapon and had a secure inside pocket for her phone. After a moment, she spotted the faint trail off to her right and started climbing.

There were two ways into the heart of Mika's lair. One involved the lost parking lot, now a large livestock pen. Lily had been told not to approach through the dining room, so she toiled up the Mika-made slope. It was steep but not tricky; only one short stretch required handholds.

As she reached the top, magic buzzed faintly on her skin. Mika's ward, she assumed. She looked down. Farther down than she'd come up.

It didn't look much like an amphitheater anymore. Where rows of seats had stepped neatly down toward the stage, stone buttressed the earthen wall she'd climbed. Not solid stone, nor were the boulders arrayed with the tidy geometrics humans favored; it was thicker here, thinner there, with the occasional jut of a boulder clearly not native to this soil. An artistic choice, perhaps. At its foot was bare earth—Mika's landing pad and sun porch. Beyond that, the half dome where orchestras had played was partly obscured by hard-packed dirt built up to create a lip. The dome's roof was obscured by yet more heaped dirt. For a startled moment it made Lily think of an enormous sand crab burrowing down to safety.

Dragons always lair in earth and rock. They blocked the mental cacophony. "Hello, Mika," Lily said—and nearly jumped when a small, gray streak arrowed past her feet. A cat.

I named her Beelzebub, Mika said. His mental voice was different from Sam's—cool and precise, yes, but without the razorlike clarity, and with a whiff of flavor. It was like the difference between Arctic ice and a snow cone dribbled with a few drops of Bahama Mama. *She wanted more syllables at first, but I don't think her name should be longer than she is. Beelzebub is a use-name, of course.*

"Ah—do cats have real names?" Lily eyed the rocky jumble. This was going to be harder than the other side had been. Her bad arm twinged as if already protesting its role in the descent.

Your question is silly. I don't know all cats.

"I suppose not. Look, do I have to come down there for my lesson? Maybe we could do it with me up here."

No. Thirty feet below and twice that far horizontally, the shiny coils disposed on the sun porch began unwinding. Mika wasn't as large as Sam—no longer than a house, she thought, tail included, and dragons were eighty percent tail, neck, and wings. But he was ohmygod beautiful.

His scales were red. All shades of red, from ruby to magenta to crimson, shading into eye-popping orange on the wings currently folded along his back. He glistened and gleamed in the sunlight like every jewel men had ever coveted.

Sam said you had sustained damage to your limb. I perceive it has not healed. Humans heal poorly. This impedes you? Hold still. I'll fetch you.

"No, that's not necessary, I can—" But dragons can move fast when they want. Before Lily could finish telling him not to, Mika's bunched haunches had launched him into the air. He jumped most of the ninety feet between them to land in a blaze of brilliance, wings outstretched for balance. Landed lightly, too, his rear talons gripping a couple of those outthrust boulders.

His front talons gripped *her*. She made a deeply undignified noise more squeak than scream.

You are very loud, Mika told her disapprovingly. And shoved himself backward off the stone-strewn embankment.

The trip down was scary and uncomfortable—his talons were rough and gripped too tightly—but blessedly brief. They hit with a small jolt and a flurry of dust from his wings. He set her down and folded those wings back in place.

Lily's legs tried to buckle. She stiffened them. *I did not scream.*

You think loudly. Or you were. Your mindspeech isn't that bad. It's bad, just not as bad as I thought it would be.

Oh. She'd done it again—used mindspeech without meaning to. That had happened three times in the past month. Well, four now. The other three had all been with Rule, which was just as well. Some people would get upset if they found her thoughts in their heads all of a sudden.

You didn't intend to? Headshaking was not a dragon gesture, but Mika flavored his reply with something very like a disgusted headshake.

"Sam doesn't want me to practice on my own."

Of course not. At this stage, you would only acquire bad habits. Sit down and we will start.

She obeyed. "I know why Sam is teaching me. Why did you agree to do it, too?"

You know very little. It is not surprising you ask a great many questions. Mika's head darted to the right and swung back with a small branch in his mouth. He dropped it in front of her. It burst into flame. *Find me there.*

Great. She'd hoped a different teacher meant different methods. With a sigh, Lily looked at the small fire.

Her left ankle itched. The flames were too bright, making her squint. Why had she been determined to do this? Because Rule didn't want her to? Surely she had a better reason.

Oh, yeah. Because Sam told her to. But that reminded her . . . *I promised Rule I'd tell you about my headache.*

That was pathetic. You sent perhaps one word in three. If I weren't able to read your mind anyway, I'd have no idea what you said. What headache?

"Have you ever taught anyone?"

No. I thought it might be interesting. So far it isn't.

"You aren't supposed to tell your students they're pathetic." She went on to describe her brief pain-in-the-skull, ending with, ". . . since kinspeech hurt me in sort of the same way, Rule wants to be assured the headache has nothing to do with my mindspeech lessons."

Kinspeech is not mindspeech.

"Sam says they're related."

You're related to Beelzebub, since you are both mammals, but you are not Beelzebub. If mindspeech could damage you, Sam would have warned me. Find me in the flame.

When Mika called an end to the session, Lily had found him three times. She lost him again each time, but she was encouraged. She hadn't been sure how well her practice at finding Sam would translate to finding Mika. Turned out it was pretty much the same . . . a lot like groping in the dark with her hands tied behind her, trying to pick up a feather with her toes. Mostly she failed, but at least now she could tell what the feather felt like if she did come across it.

And her head didn't hurt. In spite of her insistence to Rule that her mindspeech lessons weren't the cause of that brief headache, she was relieved.

That was more interesting than I'd hoped.

"Oh?" Lily felt as wrung out as if she'd spent the past hour running.

Not your mindspeech. That remains pathetic. But human

brains are interesting—much more elastic than human minds, fortunately, which I suppose is necessary, given your brief allotment of time. You wouldn't otherwise have a chance to learn much of anything. Yours is forming new synaptic connections quite rapidly.

"You've been watching my brain?"

Perceiving is a better descriptive. I am uncommonly good at this.

"Is this perception like what a physical empath does?"

Closer to what one of your healers does. I need to observe that. I am not perfectly clear on the time frame, but since it will fall to me to—oh. You don't know about that yet.

"About what?"

If you don't know, I can't tell you. There was a broody feel to his thoughts. *This splintering of time can be disruptive. I am not accustomed to it.*

Alarmed, she sat up straighter. "What splintering? What are you—does this have anything to do with—"

The troubles foreseen by your Ruben Brooks? Of course. Oh. You are thinking I meant that time itself splinters. His breath huffed out, hot and smelling of metal and spice, in what might have been amusement. *No. I am newly arrived at . . . you lack a referent. It is the time when a dragon begins to grasp threads from not-now. It is a confusing period. Such threads are experienced much like memories, but they arrive tangled and before the events occur. Of course, "before" and "after" are poor constructs for out-time perception, but as usual, your language lacks more precise terms.*

Lily blinked. "Are you talking about precognition?"

No, I do not manifest those threads the same way Ruben Brooks does. Not that you have the slightest understanding what he does, either, so there is little point in discussing it. You need to bring me your healer. Oh, and someone who is injured, also, so I can observe the process.

"I don't happen to have a healer," Lily said dryly. "You know about Ruben's—"

I see. She is Rule Turner's healer. I will tell him I require her.

Rule didn't "have" a healer, either, but he had access to two. Nettie Two Horses was Rule's niece, Nokolai's healer, and on the other coast. The Leidolf Rhej was also a healer and was much closer. Leidolf's Clanhome was in Virginia.

That one will do. I believe my observation of your brain is helping me untangle your muddy thinking. A definite tinge of satisfaction coated that thought. *Why do humans all believe they are their thoughts?*

"I don't know. You know about Ruben's visions."

Why else would we ally with him? The wolves do not mistake their thinking for their selves, although they err this way when they are men. Li Lei, of course, has the advantage of having been dragon for a time, but I had thought that a human with a true name would know the difference. Yet you do not.

"Wait. Wait. You're allied with Ruben?"

A contemptuous snort. *We do not pass on his communications for the pleasure of reading your murky minds. If you could be a bit quicker to learn mindspeech . . . oh.* A whiff of chagrin. *You did not yet know that part. Not-now is very confusing.*

"You—you're how Ruben and his Shadow Unit communicate? You and the other dragons?" Of course. Dragons were the most undetectable communication device possible.

It is time for you to go.

"Mika—"

When a dragon says it's time to go, he can make it so whether you agree or not. Mika scooped Lily up in his front talons and hurled himself skyward. His wings snapped up and out. The jolt from their first massive buffeting of the air was huge. So was the second. And the third.

The jolt of terror and memory was pretty huge, too. Lily had been carried this way across the plains of hell, sundered from everything, even her name, hurt and lost and terrified, unable to do anything but endure . . .

You are loud!

"Put me down!" she screamed with mind and voice together.

He did. He landed about twenty yards from a teeming horde of fourth- or fifth-graders and the outnumbered adults trying desperately to corral them, set her on her feet, and leaped skyward again.

The shriek level was ear-numbing. She could not let her wobbly legs give out on her. She had to go calm down the miniature civilians and . . . oh, shit. Not all of the screaming was from fear, and here came . . .

"Tawny!" screamed one of the adults. "You come back here right now!"

The pigtailed sprinter had long legs for her age and a head start on the heavyset woman in pursuit. Lily could see how that was going to work out and started toward the girl, calling out, "It's okay. I'm, ah, a friend of Mika's. He didn't hurt me. It's okay, everyone."

The kid jolted to a halt in front of Lily. Her skin was dark. Her eyes were lit with urgent joy. "I want to meet him! Tell him to come back. I want to talk to him, to—to—he's your friend? You could introduce me. My name's Tawny. I *need* to meet the dragon!"

"Um, well, I don't think I can arrange that, but you got to see him from pretty close up. That's something, isn't it? I . . . uh-oh." Tawny's escape or her teacher's pursuit had stampeded the herd. Fifty or so kids were racing straight for her.

The teacher got there first. She was a tall woman, gray-haired and out of breath. "Tawny, you will go back to the class right now, you hear me?"

"The class is here, Miss Pearson." Tawny's eyes were limpid with innocence. "Mostly here, anyways."

Miss Pearson's skin flushed to a really deep chocolate. She glared at Lily. "I have no idea what you thought you were doing, flying that dragon so close to these children—"

"I didn't fly him. He flew me."

"But for every one like Tawny here who is overly fascinated by dragons, there's another child who was scared to death when it flew over us like that! It was shockingly irresponsible for you to—"

"Ma'am, a dragon is not a horse. I was not steering Mika."

The herd arrived. Everyone was shouting, wanting to know how to get a ride and if it had hurt and what if the dragon had dropped her and what did dragons eat and did his claws hurt and I don't see any blood and where did he go . . . although one voice, belonging to a young blond woman, did ask Lily if she was all right.

"I'm fine," she assured her sole well-wisher. "I'm sorry Mika scared some of you. He's not always very considerate. Oh. Sorry. I have to get that."

Lily had seldom been so glad to hear her phone buzz. She pulled it from her inside pocket. "Excuse me, I have to answer this, and I need to step away . . . no, ma'am, I realize that. Yes—" One of the teachers or aides had recognized her. "I'm Special Agent Yu. Move, please. Excuse me." She finally broke free of the horde and thumbed her phone on. "Lily Yu here."

It was Martin Croft, his smooth tenor voice utterly uninflected. "I need to know where you were from 8:30 until 12:30 today."

Her brain went blank. This was one hundred percent not what she'd expected. "Well. Okay. I arrived at headquarters at 8:00 and remained there until 11:05, when I left for Rock Creek Park to see Mika. I reached the park at approximately 11:15—the guard at the gate should be able to confirm—and was with Mika until"—she glanced at her watch; it was 1:00— "12:45 or 12:50."

"Mika." There was an odd note in Croft's voice. "I suppose that works, though I'd prefer not to be the one to depose him, should it be necessary."

"What's going on?"

"I'm taking you off limited duty, effective immediately. Report to Special Agent Drummond at 14321 Camber Lane in Georgetown. He's lead."

"Yes, sir. Lead on what?"

"Senator Robert Bixton has been murdered."

TEN

~~

LILY parked three blocks from 14321 Camber Lane. One block away and she started shoving. As she got closer, the elbow duel got vicious. The press was in feeding frenzy.

They didn't seem to know much yet, judging by the questions hurled at her. Well, neither did she. Croft hadn't told her much. He wanted Drummond to brief her.

Bixton's body had been found in his living room by the only person in the house at the time—the maid. His wife was visiting family in North Carolina. The maid's 9-1-1 call was logged at 12:01. Time of death not established, though Lily assumed they had reason to think it was between 8:30 and 12:30. The probable murder weapon was known. The killer had thoughtfully left the dagger in Bixton's body. No other visible wounds or trauma.

Left in his shoulder, that is. Not his chest, not near any vital organs. That's why Lily was here.

She saw three possibilities: one, the dagger had not caused Bixton's death, or had caused it indirectly, triggering a heart attack or other event. Two, the dagger had been dipped in a contact poison. Three, magic was involved.

Croft was betting on Door Number Three. So was Lily.

She accepted that she couldn't be lead on this one. The

reason made her stomach churn, but she understood, just as she knew why Croft had had to ask where she'd been when someone slid that knife into Bixton. Rule wasn't the only enemy Bixton had made in his political career. He wasn't the only lupus in the city, either. But the press would sure be looking at him . . . and whoever handled the case would have to, as well.

She hadn't called Rule. Croft had said the case was "need to know" at the moment. She wasn't to discuss it with anyone not part of the team Drummond was leading, so she hadn't called. But she'd been creative as hell in how she followed orders.

She'd been close to Mika's lair, after all. If she "shouted" at him that she wasn't allowed to tell him anything, well, he might have decided to snoop around in her head and find out what she wasn't telling him. He might even decide to tell someone else.

He might not, too. She hadn't heard from him, so she didn't know.

With luck, Rule would be alibied by the great man's top flunky. Lacking luck . . . *don't jump that creek yet*, she told herself. And don't assume the Great Bitch was behind this just because it looked so much like the frame *she* had arranged for Rule eleven months ago. A frame Lily had taken apart.

Less obvious was why the lead investigator was regular FBI. Murder by magical means was a crime for the Unit.

Magical means was not confirmed, she reminded herself, pushing a mic out of her face as she at last reached the barricade. They'd closed the street for a block around the senator's house. Things weren't quite as chaotic on the other side of the barrier. Close, but not quite.

"Special Agent Yu," she said to the uniform manning the barrier, holding out her badge.

He looked it over, checked his BlackBerry, and shook his head. "I'm sorry, ma'am. You're not on my list."

"Then there's a problem with your list. Get someone here who can—Crawford! Hey!"

A pale man with busy eyes and a bald head turned, frowning. Terry Crawford had thirty years with the Secret Service and a memory for faces no software could touch. She'd worked with him when she was briefly on loan to the Secret Service last winter. "Agent Yu. I wasn't told to admit you."

Her eyebrows lifted. The Secret Service was handling the perimeter? "You in charge of the scene?"

"I'm making sure we aren't flooded with help. If you're not officially assigned—"

"I'm officially assigned to Special Agent Drummond. Your list's wrong." A cameraman jostled her. She spared him a scowl.

Crawford's mouth thinned. "I'll need to confirm." He touched his headset.

Lily waited impatiently. She'd gotten spoiled, she supposed. Used to being in charge. Ever since the Turning, Unit agents had been spread too thin to team up, so she'd been lead on pretty much every investigation she'd been involved with. Plus Unit agents were pretty much top of the food chain, and she'd gotten used to that, too.

But it wasn't as if she didn't know how to be a subordinate. She was just out of practice. She'd be patient if it . . .

Crawford nodded at the patrol officer. "She's cleared."

Lily ducked under the barricade.

"Sorry about the delay," Crawford said under his breath when she reached him. "It's a goddamn circus. Every goddamn agency in town wants in. I turned away two agents from ATF, another from the DEA—" He broke off, shook his head. "I can see why they need you, though. Drummond's inside."

"Thanks. Where's the sign-in?"

"One of my people's handling it at the door."

The senator's Washington digs weren't all that different from hers, Lily thought as she approached the house. His place was bigger, sure, and stone rather than brick, plus the location was better—facing a small park rather than an identical row of conjoined homes. But from the outside it didn't look that much nicer than Nokolai's pied-à-terre in the capital.

Lily signed in at the bottom of the steps leading to the front porch, which held a couple of planters topped with profusely blooming yellow mums. The front door was open. She stepped inside.

Things took a turn for the grand on this side of the door. The foyer was large and floored with marble; the painting over the narrow console table looked old and expensive. The Bixton family had made their money from logging, if she remembered right, though they'd long since diversified. Rule had told her that the senator's personal wealth was held in a blind trust to avoid any possible conflict of interest. *Bixton's a bigot*, he'd added, *but an honest one*.

Facing the door was a short wall with a gleaming console table. It held a floral arrangement, a pair of silver candlesticks, and a cardboard box full of disposable booties. To her right, an arched entry led to the living room, where voices suggested the official presence was gathered. She couldn't see much of the room from here. To her left was a single closed door and a wide, sweeping staircase any forties movie star would have been delighted to descend on camera.

Lily bent and took off her Nikes and her socks. They went in the tote she'd retrieved from the trunk of her car.

"What the hell do you think you're doing?" someone asked in a deep, raspy voice.

Lily straightened. The man standing in the arched entry on her right was average height and on the thin side. He wore a navy blue off-the-rack suit and combed his thinning black hair straight back from a high, flat forehead. Plain gold wedding ring on his left hand, just like the ghost's. Disposable booties covered his scuffed black shoes. His eyes were dark and keen and pissed.

"It's the quickest way for me to check for traces of magic on the floor. I'm Special Agent Lily Yu." She held out her hand. "You are—?"

He scowled. "Al Drummond, but you can call me 'sir.' The floor didn't kill Bixton. A goddamn knife did. Put your damn shoes back on, grab some booties, and get in here." He turned and tramped back in the living room.

Lily obeyed one of those orders. She followed him into the living room . . . after digging out her baby wipes and giving her bare feet a thorough wipe-down. Her shoes stayed in her tote.

It was a long, narrow room, ending in French doors to the

backyard. Everything was capital-G gracious. The walls were pale gold, the silk drapes dark gold, the furnishings a mix of ivory and gold with splashes of red. Lily's mother would have loved it. There was a large oil painting over the mantle, a landscape in the pastoral style that had been big a hundred and fifty years ago. Ornate frame. More fresh flowers—in a vase on the mantle, floating in a bowl on the coffee table. No clutter. Everything was spotless . . . except for that messy body on the ivory carpet at the other end of the room.

Lily knew the small mob swarming the room by type, if not by name. One man was snapping still photos while another aimed a camcorder and an older woman took notes. Lily did know the woman. Hannah Kuruc was a topnotch Crime Scene Officer; the other two would be part of her crew. At the far end, a man in a dark suit stood in the open French doors with his back to the room, talking to someone Lily couldn't see. He turned his head briefly and Lily caught his profile.

The ME was on-scene himself. No flunkies for Senator Bixton.

Drummond was at this end of the room, talking to a short, sandy-haired man with a pug nose. He glanced at her. "This is . . . son of a bitch. What the hell did I tell you? You ever heard of contaminating a scene? Put the goddamn booties—"

"There are traces of death magic on the floor in the entry."

The sandy-haired man's eyebrows shot up. Everyone at the other end of the room looked their way except Hannah. Drummond's scowl didn't budge. "You're sure."

"Positive. Death magic has an unmistakable texture." Like ground glass and swamp goo. "It's faint, but it's there. I haven't picked up any traces on the carpet yet. I need to walk around."

"Hell, no. Your method doesn't get us anything admissible, and I don't want my scene contaminated."

"Such faint traces as I picked up are going to fade quickly, and I cleaned my feet thoroughly in the foyer."

"Climb down, Al," Hannah said, frowning at the carpet near the body. "It's my scene until I say you can have it. You said the maid vacuumed in here this morning?"

Drummond's mouth was tight. "That's what she said."

"Huh." Now she looked up. "Lily, you can come do your thing, but for God's sake—"

"Don't touch anything," Lily finished for her.

Hannah's mouth crooked up. "Right." She gestured at the man with the video cam. "Get her movements on record."

Drummond scowled at Lily. "You're here to check the knife. That's priority."

Lily held out her hand again. "You might as well shake hands. It'll save us both the embarrassment of me having to find some excuse to touch you."

He rolled his eyes, shoved his hand out, and took hers.

Firm grip, wide palm, long fingers, no magic. Lily nodded, dropped his hand, and walked slowly forward.

The quickest path to the other end was straight down the middle. She wandered from side to side . . . yes. "I'm finding something. A trail. Faint and spotty, but . . ." She dug in her tote, pulled out a pack of Popsicle sticks, and laid one on the carpet where she stood. Another went a foot back where she'd first picked up the trail. "I'll mark where I find death magic residue."

"Knife first, dammit. Do you in any way grasp the concept of taking orders?"

"It'll come back to me." She moved slowly, pausing now and then to place another Popsicle stick. About five feet from the body she stopped and put three sticks down. "Stronger here." Another step. Another, and another Popsicle stick. A couple more and she set down her tote and crouched, studying what was left of Bixton.

The senator had dressed for the day in a crisp white shirt and what looked like the same slacks he'd worn to question Lily, but without the vest and suit jacket. His tie was red again, but this one had little gold dots as well.

He lay on his back near an overstuffed hassock looking mildly offended. One hand rested at his side, palm up, fingers curled in. The other arm was flung out, the fingertips brushing the hassock's skirt. No visible defensive wounds. His eyes were glazed, his mouth open, his body slack with the peculiar stillness of death. That always struck Lily, how motionless the dead were. Dead people don't look like they're sleeping or unconscious. They look dead.

They often smell bad, too. All the muscles relax at death. Bixton had died with a full bladder, but without much in his bowels, judging by the smell.

The knife protruded from the fleshy place between the armpit and the top of the rib cage, just under the collarbone. Not much blood. The knife itself looked old, with a carved handle that might be bone or ivory or something like that. She could see about two inches of the blade.

Didn't get it all the way in, did you? No bone there to stop the blade. Either you aren't very strong or you didn't care how deep it went, didn't need the steel to kill him. It was just the means of delivery. Lily reached out a hand.

"Careful," Drummond snapped. "Don't get fingerprints on it."

Lily pressed the back of her hand to Bixton's palm. "Special Agent Drummond, *sir*, you aren't Unit." She checked Bixton's throat next, paused there briefly, then pressed the back of her hand to his face. "You haven't worked with a sensitive before. But you might try pretending you think I'm a professional."

"Are you going to professionally check the damn knife anytime soon?"

Anger prickled over her skin almost as tangibly as magic. She clamped down on it. Truly she was out of practice at the subordinate thing . . . oh, yes, she'd grown unaccustomed to assholes giving her orders. "If Bixton was killed by magic, some residue may still be in his body. Where the magic lingers and how much is present makes a difference in determining the type of spell used."

"Does it matter what kind of spell it was? Killed by magical means is a capital crime. Doesn't matter what kind of chanting went into it."

"If he'd been shot, would you want to find the bullet? Maybe—I don't know—run some ballistics tests?"

He grunted. "So what did you find?"

"Nothing in his hand or face. A very small trace on his

throat. I'll need to loosen his clothing to check elsewhere, but I'll do the knife first." Now she pressed the back of her hand to the knife's hilt. And grimaced. Ugly. "Death magic and lots of it. This won't fade anytime soon. You'll be able to get confirmation from the coven." The only magically produced evidence that was admissible in court was that obtained by a certified Wiccan coven. The coven couldn't do what Lily did—Gifts were stronger and more accurate than spells—but with that pretty dagger loaded with so much death magic, coven spells would do the job just fine. "Have you contacted Ms. O'Shaunessy, or shall I?"

"Your man Croft's supposed to be handling that. Go ahead and check for lingering magic elsewhere."

Maybe the asshole was capable of learning. Lily glanced at Hannah.

Her mouth tipped down unhappily. "Okay, but I'll unbutton him. You got more of those baby wipes?"

While Lily cleaned her hand, Hannah knelt on the other side of the body and bent low, studying the starched landscape of Bixton's shirt. After a moment she grunted, motioned to one of the other techs, and got tweezers and an evidence bag from him. "Looks like one of Bixton's," she said, depositing a single short, white hair in the Baggie, "but you never know."

After that, Hannah undid four buttons—enough for Lily to slide her hand in between cloth and cool, clammy flesh. Bixton turned out to have a hairy chest. That surprised her, somehow.

"One spot where the death magic is concentrated," she said after a careful grope. "Over the heart. It thins out evenly as I move my hand away from the center of the chest. I didn't touch the wound, but did touch about two inches from it." She withdrew her hand and twisted to grab her tote.

"What does that tell you?" Drummond demanded. "Where the magic is and isn't. What does that mean?"

Lily scrubbed her hands with another wipe as she stood. It wasn't touching a DB that made her feel unclean. It was the death magic. "First, that he wasn't killed by death magic directly. It was used to power the spell that killed him, not as a sort of blunt force trauma all on its own."

"You can do that?" His eyebrows lifted in surprise and for a brief moment he didn't sound pissed. "Just blast someone with death magic and it kills them?"

"I can't," she said dryly, and started back toward him, avoiding the trail she'd marked with Popsicle sticks. "And I'm really damn glad to find out this perp can't, either." The only time she'd run up against that kind of killing, it had been done by a madwoman using an ancient staff created by the Great Bitch. The woman was dead, the staff destroyed, but presumably *she* could make another one if she wanted. "That the magic was heaviest over his heart suggests the spell targeted his heart specifically."

Drummond rubbed his jaw, eyebrows down. "Brooks's heart attack was caused by a potion, not a spell. Never heard that death magic was involved, either."

"As far as I know it wasn't, but I'm not part of that investigation. The heart is a popular target for killing spells. I had a perp a couple months ago who used a heart-stopping spell delivered by a blade." She frowned, slid her foot a few feet to one side. She wasn't finding a second trail of death magic. Shouldn't the perp have leaked it coming and going?

Not necessarily, she realized. Once the spell was discharged, there probably hadn't been anything to leak. The odd thing was that it had leaked in the first place. Could be the perp had charged himself or herself with death magic rather than charging the blade, sending the power through the dagger when he or she struck.

Was that likely? She needed to call Cullen.

"Huh. Guess that's why you're here. You've dealt with this crap before." He looked past her. "Hannah, it's all yours. I've got people to talk to. Let me know what you find. Doug, Agent Yu, with me."

He led her and the sandy-haired man into the foyer and from there through the door on the left. Turned out that wasn't the coat closet, like she'd thought, but a small study. Lots of books, a single small window. Desk with the usual computer stuff and tidy stacks of files and papers.

He stopped, turned, faced her. "I do not like having my direct orders ignored."

"Yeah? I don't like being treated like an idiot."

"The difference here is that I'm in charge. You aren't. This is Doug Mullins. He's second-up as far as I'm concerned. You'll take orders from him, too."

Mullins was a squat little man with pale skin, pale eyes, and a wide mouth that probably altered his face a lot when he smiled. If he ever smiled. Or spoke. So far she hadn't heard one word from him. "Fine," she said, and held out her hand. "Good to meet you, Agent Mullins."

He studied her outstretched hand about the way he'd examine a wad of gum stuck to his shoe.

Drummond snorted. "Don't be a pussy, Doug. Shake the nice agent's hand so she knows you aren't a big, bad witch."

Reluctantly he did. Damp palm, short fingers, no magic. Wedding ring on the left hand, plain gold. Lily looked at Drummond. "Do you ignore the expertise of everyone on your team? Or is it just the women you discount? Or the ones with a Gift?"

Drummond rubbed his jaw again. After a moment he nodded. "Point. I should've asked what the hell you were doing before I told you to stop doing it. But from here on in, if I say hop on one foot, you start hopping and keep one damn foot off the damn floor. Or I'll get someone else from the woo-woo side to handle that part of the investigation."

Lily didn't buy the threat. Croft had assigned her to the case. Drummond couldn't unassign her . . . but he could make it hard to do her job. "I'll follow orders. Sir. But I'm not good at hopping for no damn reason."

"Tough. Tell me about death magic. Tell it like I don't know a damn thing. You won't be far off."

"It's magic sourced through ritual killing." He had to know that much. Every cop in the country knew that much. "The practitioners use the power of the transition—"

"What do you mean, practitioners?"

"It takes more than one person to perform the ritual. The only known exception is a wraith, which both creates and subsists on death magic, no ritual needed."

"Any chance we've got a wraith on our hands?"

"How much detail do you want?"

"Put the detail in your report. Give me a yes or no now."

"There's a chance, but it's extremely slim." First because wraiths were really, really hard to make. Second because a wraith wouldn't have left so much tasty death magic behind on that dagger. Wraiths ate the stuff.

"We've got a human perp, then."

"Perps. Five is considered the minimum necessary for a death magic ritual. One for each of the four compass points, and one to direct the ritual and do the actual killing. In all of the known rituals, the killer uses a blade, usually to cut the victim's throat. The ritual allows the person in charge to absorb or contain the power released when a soul transitions from life to whatever comes next."

Turned out Mullins did have a voice—a gravelly baritone at odds with his size. "Soul?" He loaded plenty of scorn into the word. "You believe in souls?"

"You don't like the word, pick another one. Something persists after the body dies. We don't know how long it persists or what happens to it, not in any definitive way, but souls are fact, not belief."

Mullins's chin jutted pugnaciously. "You can't prove that."

"Death magic itself proves something other than the purely physical exists."

"All that crap about transitions! You sound like a TV psychic. Obviously death magic uses the life energy of the victims, not some holy-baloney transition."

"What's life energy?"

"The energy it takes to keep a body alive."

She snorted. "Talk about an undefinable term! If you stick to the purely physical, a subsistence diet consists of twelve hundred calories. That's the equivalent of about five Btus. If all a death magic practitioner could access was the purely physical, he'd do a hell of a lot better figuring out how to eat the energy from a blow-dryer."

Drummond broke in impatiently. "Enough metaphysics. To make death magic, someone's got to kill someone else. That's where we start."

"It's still death magic when the sacrifice is an animal," Lily said, "but people give the bigger bang. I suspect our perps needed a human death, but . . ." She drummed her fingers on her thigh. "I need to consult an expert."

"You're supposed to be the damn expert."

"You wouldn't ask a blood splatter specialist to analyze fiber. I'm a touch sensitive. I can't work magic, so I've never learned spellcasting. I need to talk to someone who knows it all—casting, theory, history."

"You got someone in mind? One of your Unit people?"

"No, he's a consultant." Cullen Seabourne, lupus and sorcerer. Sorcerers were rare enough that some people didn't think they existed. A lupus sorcerer was supposed to be impossible.

Cullen did like to break the rules. "He's got clearance," Lily added. "The Unit uses him often. I'll need you to approve his fee."

He grunted. "I need your request in writing—name, contact information, fee scale. Did Croft tell you—" His phone buzzed. He took the call, said he'd be right there, and told Mullins, "You brief her. I need to talk to Armistead."

"All of it?"

"Hell, yeah. She has to know why she can't shoot her mouth off." He left, closing the door behind him.

Mullins looked at her. "I hear you've got homicide experience."

"That's right."

"Don't let it go to your head." He pulled a small pad from an inside pocket on his jacket and looked over his notes. "Bixton was a man of regular habits. Up at seven every weekday, according to the maid. Name's Sheila Navarette—unmarried, thirty-two, lives in. She has his breakfast ready at seven thirty every weekday, and that's when he arrived to eat it today. Eggs and toast, coffee, apple juice. While he ate, she ran the vacuum downstairs—she does that every damn day—then went to wash up the breakfast things. Passed him on her way to the kitchen about eight fifteen. She thinks he went to his office then because that was his routine, but she didn't actually see.

"So she cleaned up the kitchen and went upstairs, where she made the bed, tidied up, and collected the laundry. She took that down to the basement. That's where she was at between nine thirty and ten when the doorbell rang. The doorbell rings on all three floors—basement, first floor, and second floor. She answered the door and showed the visitor in to the senator here in the living room. After determining that they didn't want coffee or tea, she returned to the basement, where she remained, ironing the senator's shirts, until she went upstairs to fix lunch around noon and discovered the body."

He looked up from his notes. There was an odd, mocking gleam in his eyes. "That's the only visitor the senator had this morning."

"Are you saying we already have a suspect? Or at least a witness. You have a description? A name?"

"Both." He consulted his notes again ostentatiously. "Thin, average height, wore a dark gray suit with a white shirt. Pale blue tie. He was not carrying a briefcase or laptop or other object. She estimates his age as between forty and fifty. Dark hair and eyes, large nose, glasses. She hadn't seen him there before and he didn't have an appointment, but the senator saw him anyway."

"And the name?"

Mullins smiled thinly. "Ruben Brooks."

ELEVEN

~

AT eight twenty that night Rule heard a car in the alley, followed by the sound of the garage door opening out back. He was in the kitchen, his laptop on the table, his ass in one chair, his feet in another, wearing his headset. "Okay, Andor, thanks. I appreciate your not asking us to wait for the All-Clan."

"Chad is unemployed at the moment. It is no difficulty for him to fly to D.C."

"He'll stay here, of course, and Wythe will pay his airfare."

The Rho of Szøs clan snorted. "You speak for Wythe now as well as Leidolf and Nokolai?"

"My father speaks for Nokolai," Rule said mildly. He listened to the car pull into the garage, glad that Lily hadn't worked too late. She'd texted him a couple hours ago not to wait supper on her, which could have meant she'd be home at eight or at midnight. Or later. "No one speaks for Wythe at the moment, but my *nadia* and the Wythe Council agree that the clan will reimburse others for expenses incurred in this search. Let Walt know how much and who the check should go to— you or your young man—and he'll send it immediately. You have Walt's number?"

"Szøs will pay Chad's expenses," Andor said gruffly. "It is not good for a clan to be without a Rho. This would be true at any time, but in time of war, we do not bicker over a few dollars." Andor paused. "Of course, if Chad does turn out to be capable of holding the Wythe mantle, he will no longer be Szøs. Wythe will owe us reparation for the loss of a clan member."

Rule's mouth twisted in wry amusement. "A matter you can discuss with the new Rho, if that happens."

"So I can. *T'eius ven*, Rule."

"*T'eius ven*." Rule removed the headset and went to unlock the back door for Lily. He swung it open.

She had her key out—because, of course, she never let the guards unlock the door for her. She claimed this was so they'd be free to do their job. He suspected she preferred to pretend they weren't there. She looked up at him, her eyes narrowed. "You are not a suspect."

Amusement lifted his eyebrows. "I don't think so, no."

"Even if Croft were willing to put me on an investigation where you were a suspect, Drummond wouldn't let that stand. But I'd really like to know if it was Dennis Parrott who alibied you."

"It is, though it seems, since you *are* part of the investigation, that you should know this already. Come in. I saved you some supper." He turned to get it. "Shepherd's pie. It's keeping warm in the oven."

"I'm probably hungry, but I'm too tired to tell." She followed, closing the door behind her. He heard the dead bolt click. Lily cultivated useful habits such as locking doors automatically, squeezing the toothpaste tube from the bottom, and cleaning her weapon every time she used it.

"Wine first, then." He'd opened a nice Syrah to go with his own supper, so he retrieved the bottle from the cooler.

"Wine sounds good, but I'd better follow it with coffee after the meal or I'll fall asleep." She set her laptop on the table next to his and sat down. "I didn't ask Drummond about your status in the investigation and he didn't volunteer anything. He isn't completely shutting me out, but he isn't treating me like a colleague, either."

"Drummond is the one in charge of the investigation into Bixton's death?" He set the glass he'd poured near her elbow.

She nodded and sipped without, he thought, noticing the bouquet at all. "Special Agent Al Drummond considers me an unfortunate necessity. He has to have someone from the Unit on his team, given the nature of the crime. But that's a problem, given the identity of his chief suspect." She slid him a glance. "Funny, you don't look at all curious about who that is."

"It's difficult to keep secrets from a dragon."

"Mika did hear me, then? I mindspoke to him, but didn't know if he'd peeked inside my head to find out what I couldn't tell him." She sighed. "I shouldn't have done that, but—"

"Lily." He rested a hand on her shoulder. "You didn't violate your orders or do any damage to the investigation. Unless you've decided there really is a chance that Ruben is guilty?"

She snorted. "Of killing Bixton after making abso-damn-lutely sure he'd be IDed as the senator's only visitor? Not hardly."

"Well, then." He gave her shoulder a squeeze and went to get the shepherd's pie from the oven. "What do you think of Special Agent Drummond?"

"Intense, angry, irritating. A control freak, but that's not unusual in a good cop. I called Steve Timms."

"Oh?"

"Looking for gossip. Steve's MCD, which isn't exactly regular Bureau, but he knows the people on that side of things a lot better than I do. Turns out Drummond's sort of a rock star, but with a rep as a maverick. Steve says he'd have advanced a lot further, but he kept getting held back because he slithers around the rules so often. Which makes it damned odd that he's using the rules to block me, doesn't it?"

"How so?" He set the warm casserole on a place mat on the table and sat across from her.

"Maybe he's not really blocking me. We'll see. He's sure slowing me down. I had to send him a request in writing to consult with Cullen. In *writing*." She shook her head and scooped out a serving of the meaty stew topped by mashed potatoes. "His minion can't stand me. That's Doug Mullins," she added, taking a bite. She paused, looked at her plate. "This is pretty good."

"I thought so. I was talking to Andor just before you arrived."

"Andor? Oh, you mean the Szøs Rho."

"He's got a possible candidate for the position you're longing to see filled."

Her eyebrows shot up. "Someone with Wythe founder's blood?"

"His mother was Edgar's granddaughter."

It took her a moment to unpack the genealogy of that statement—proof, if she'd needed it, that she was tired. Edgar had been Rho before Brian. "I guess his father was Szøs. What's he like?"

"He's a dominant, of course. Andor says he's bright, self-assured, and cocky as only a very young man can be. Unemployed at the moment, but he has a degree in telecommunications. He'll be here Saturday. Tell me about the minion."

She grimaced. "At first I thought Mullins was pissed because I didn't kowtow properly to the boss—he thinks the sun shines out of Drummond's ass—but I think it's mostly because I'm Unit. Mullins is one of those who are deeply, personally offended by magic."

"A religious zealot?"

"You could say that. A devout atheist."

"Atheism and the magic aren't antithetical."

"You missed the devout part. With Mullins it's a creed: thou shalt not partake of the irrational, with *irrational* defined as anything he can't sense directly. Magic screws with his worldview. Aren't you going to have some wine?"

"In a moment." He'd poured himself a glass, but left it on the counter to breathe. Lily didn't object to red wine straight from the wine cooler, but Lily had very little nose.

Silence fell for a few minutes. Lily ate. Rule thought about how foolish he'd been. He'd thought that once Lily knew about the Shadow Unit, he wouldn't have to hide things from her anymore.

Being wrong was a bitch.

Mika was not Sam. He couldn't screen hundreds of minds simultaneously, looking for a particular one, nor could he read the minds of those distant from him. Even those close to him were difficult for him to decipher. He could, however, pick up and understand Lily's thoughts better than most. He'd flown close enough to do that several times today so he could keep Rule and Ruben informed. He'd also passed word back and forth between Rule and Ruben.

Ruben had spent a wearying afternoon being questioned. He'd denied leaving his house that morning. Deborah confirmed that, but neither prosecutors nor juries took a wife's word as gospel. At the moment, Ruben's best defense was the sheer stupidity it would have required for him to commit murder in such a way.

He had one more defense. At the moment, he didn't intend to use it. Rule wasn't sure that was wise, but it wasn't his call.

Lily was nearly finished eating. He stood and retrieved his glass of wine, holding it close to savor the rich, complex scents of the wine before sipping. Time to probe a bit. "I'm wondering if I should tell you something, or if it will just complicate the dilemma you find yourself in."

She frowned. "What do you mean?"

He sat across from her once more. "You've talked about your superior on this case. About this Mullins person. You haven't said anything about the investigation itself. Were you told not to discuss it with me, or is there some question in your mind about whether you can, given my connection to the Shadow Unit?"

She put her fork down. "I hope to hell this place isn't bugged."

"It isn't. You'd know better than I if someone could eavesdrop with one of those long-distance devices."

She glanced at the kitchen window. "Probably not. They'd have to park in the alley, and I suspect José would notice that and check them out."

"He would."

She sighed. "I was told not to discuss the investigation with anyone not on the team. That came from Croft, not Drummond. It's a reasonable order, under the circumstances." She drummed her fingers once on the table. "I'm going to violate it."

"I don't have to—"

"This is about what I need. What the investigation needs. I don't know what the deal is with Drummond. Maybe he's obstructing me because he doesn't trust me, given my connection to Ruben. Maybe he's going all regulation because it's such a high-profile case and he's nervous. Maybe he's the damn traitor in the Bureau. Although," she added with a sigh, possibly regretful, "that's unlikely."

"Oh?"

"I talked to Croft, too. He says Drummond was in D.C. on the day of the attempt on Ruben's life, but not in Headquarters, and I'm to take that as definite. So unless Drummond's part of a greater conspiracy within the Bureau, he's out as a suspect. Most likely he's a control freak who doesn't trust me." Her fingers drummed again. "Do you know what he had me doing most of the day?"

"Mika didn't go into that kind of detail."

"Knocking on doors. And it's not that I think I'm too important for that sort of—"

"Was it Mullins who said that or Drummond?"

"Mullins." She grimaced. "I know, I know. I shouldn't let the little shit get to me. *He* was in Wyoming when someone dosed Ruben with that potion. Never mind. What happened today was that I followed the perp's trail—"

"There was a trail?"

"That's one of the things I need to discuss with Cullen. The perp seems to have leaked quite a bit of magic on his or her way into the house. The trail stops at Bixton's body. I traced it the other direction and ended up at the little park across the street. The trail went right up to a bench, then stopped. That doesn't make sense. If the perp was loaded up so much he leaked, why would he only start leaking at that bench? Anyway, Drummond decided that once I'd done that, I'd served my main function. He had me knock on doors the rest of the damn day. It's not like finding wits isn't important, but it's a poor use of my time. He doesn't have anyone other than me who knows shit about tracking down a death magic coven—"

Rule's eyebrows shot up. "A coven?"

"Not a Wiccan coven. A group of practitioners who used ritual killing to create death magic. Um. The 'death magic' part should be news to you, but I guess it isn't. I should ask what you know from Mika."

"I know Senator Bixton was killed sometime after 9:30 with a dagger imbued with death magic. His maid believes she admitted Ruben at that time. Ruben says he never left his house. Ah . . . that's the detail I was considering telling you. Ruben has a witness who can testify to that. Two, actually."

"What? Why hasn't he said so? Or has he, and Drummond didn't tell me?"

"Ruben is holding them in reserve. They're lupi."

Her mouth opened. Closed. Then thinned. "I should've guessed. He's been attacked once. When that failed, he should've had bodyguards at home as well as at Headquarters. I wasn't thinking. But why lupi instead of Bureau body-guards?"

"Budgetary constraints," Rule said dryly. "Croft had guards at Ruben's house at first, but he was told by the director to remove them two weeks ago. Given how important our Lady considers Ruben, the clans were willing to share the duty of protecting him and Deborah. Today's team was Cynyr."

Her eyebrows lifted. "From Wales. They came all the way from Wales. You couldn't handle it among the U.S. clans?"

"The Lady named Ruben our ally. Guarding him is an hon-ored duty. No one could be left out without giving offense."

"So why hasn't Ruben mentioned his alibi?"

"He doesn't want to draw attention to his unique relation-ship with the clans. Had today's guards been Nokolai or Lei-dolf, we could say I sent them out of concern for a friend. It's more difficult to explain why a Welsh clan would send body-guards to protect a man they've never met and shouldn't even know exists. We can't explain it, not without speaking of the Lady's instructions to us. And we do not want to make that public."

"I suppose not." Her frown deepened. "Besides, lupi don't make the best witnesses. No offense, but everyone assumes a lupus will say whatever his Rho wants him to say, so all the prosecution would have to do is establish some reason their Rho might have told them to alibi Ruben. Given that most lupi could be expected to hate Bixton, that shouldn't be hard."

"I gather Ruben thought much the same thing. How much danger is he in?" Rule asked quietly.

"The only reason he hasn't been arrested yet is that Drummond's annoying, but he's not an idiot. Hard to believe Ruben could be stupid enough to give his name to the maid, then walk in and kill Bixton." Her jaw tightened. "*She's* behind this. Her first attempt failed, so she's coming after Ruben a different way. I have to call Cullen. I've got questions I need answered."

"I thought Drummond hadn't approved that."

"And I thought you might lean on Cullen for some pro bono work."

"Actually, I already spoke with him. He'll be here . . ." The sudden wincing around her eyes, the draining of blood from her face, had him on his feet. "Lily."

"It's that damn headache again."

"That's twice today," he said grimly.

"Yeah. This one doesn't seem to be going away as fast as the other two." Her voice was thin. She touched the air near the back of her head. "Is this what a migraine feels like? I swear I'm never going to . . ." Her eyes closed.

"That's it. You're getting checked out by—" He leaped and caught her as she toppled out of the chair.

He went to the floor with her spread across his lap, his heart pounding in fear. Her eyes were rolled back in her head. Her pulse was rapid when he pressed his fingers to her throat. She was so damn pale. "You've got five seconds to wake up, then I call the ambulance. One—"

"Didn't faint," she whispered, her eyes still closed.

His own eyes closed briefly in relief. "You gave a damn fine impression of it."

"I'm okay. Headache's gone." He could see the effort it took to force her eyes open. "When the pain shut off, I went dizzy. Now . . . just tired. No ambulance."

"You've got to be checked out."

"No doctors. They'd look at my arm, figure out something was going on with it. Can't tell 'em what, so better not provoke them."

He wasn't sure a regular doctor would be much help, or

he'd bundle her in the car over her objections and take her to the ER right now. Fortunately, there was an alternative. "The Leidolf Rhej will be here tomorrow."

She blinked. "Oh. Mika told you."

"Mika? What does he . . ." He scowled. "If you suffered a reaction at your mindspeech lesson and didn't tell me—"

"No, no." Her hand flopped vaguely in denial. "He wants to watch a healer work. He wanted you to bring him one." Her eyes closed. "Rhejes don't jump when their Rho says hop."

"She'll come. For this, she'll come."

"'Kay. I'm so damn tired. Did you make coffee?"

He gathered her in his arms and stood. "I'll put some on. You might as well rest while it's brewing."

She was asleep before he was halfway up the stairs.

TWELVE

~

LILY woke to the sound of voices downstairs. She knew before opening her eyes Rule wasn't beside her, so no surprise that one of those voices was his. The other was familiar, but unexpected.

She glanced at the clock—6:22. A normal time to wake up, but those glowing numbers said she'd slept for nearly ten hours. She never slept that long. But then, she didn't usually pass out from exhaustion.

Her head didn't hurt. She felt fine . . . in a "gibbering in fear" sort of way.

What was wrong with her?

She wasn't going to figure that out by pulling the covers over her head, even if that sounded good at the moment. Might as well get her day started.

Fifteen minutes later she headed downstairs with her hair still wet from the shower. Rule met her on the staircase and handed her a mug of coffee without speaking . . . at least, not out loud. His eyes said plenty.

She sipped. Rule made incredible coffee. "I feel fine. I don't know what's wrong. Something is, but until we have more facts, I don't see any point in thinking about it."

His mouth crooked up in spite of the worry in his eyes. "Qualified denial?"

"It isn't denial if I admit something's wrong."

"I spoke with the Leidolf Rhej. She'll be here by noon."

The muscles across her shoulders loosened in relief. "Good. It's probably some sort of weird migraine."

"You won't use the investigation as an excuse to delay seeing the Rhej."

"You need to stop pulling mantle on me. It doesn't work, and it annoys me. But yes, I'll make time for her. I'll come home for lunch. I'm not an idiot." She started down the stairs again. "Cullen's here."

"I asked him to come yesterday."

"You said something about that just before I got the headache we aren't talking about. Is Cullen, uh . . . is he part of Ruben's group?"

"I've briefed him on what I know about Bixton's death."

In other words, she wasn't part of their secret club, so he couldn't tell her who was. Lily kept moving. "I smell sausage."

"There should be some left. I threatened Cullen's life if he ate all of it."

The only lupus sorcerer in the history of the planet sat at their kitchen table, finishing up a plate of French toast. He was a bit shorter than Rule, his hair a bit lighter brown—more spice than mink—and his face stopped people in their tracks. The spectacular face went well with a supernally graceful body.

This morning that face was unshaven, the expression surly, and the body dressed in disreputable jeans. He wore a small diamond in one ear, a larger one on a chain around his neck, and his T-shirt bore a cartoon of what seemed to be a Sasquatch in a ninja costume.

Sometimes Lily did not get Cullen's sense of humor. "A ninja Sasquatch?"

"Cool, isn't it?"

"Sit," Rule said. "I'll fix you some French toast."

Lily wasn't going to argue with French toast. She sat. "What time did you get in?" she asked Cullen.

"Plane landed at one. Traffic sucked. Got here about two. Napped for a couple hours." He dragged the last bite of battered bread through a puddle of maple syrup. "You going to eat your sausage?"

"Yes. How—"

"Don't know yet, but you've got a minimum of five perps."

"So I assumed. What I was about to ask is, how are Cynna and the baby?"

Surly vanished, eclipsed by what Lily could only call a glow. Cullen's phone was on the table. He shoved it at her, tapped the screen a couple times, and said, "Beautiful. See? They're both ungodly beautiful. She's smiling in some of these pics. I don't care what they say—that's a real smile."

"She" meant Ryder, Lily assumed, the six-pound, seven-ounce explosion that had rocked the clans' world. Cullen and Cynna had a daughter. And she was lupus.

That was impossible. There had never been a female lupus and there never would be. Lupi had daughters sometimes, sure, but only their sons could Change. Only their sons were lupi. Yet according to Cullen, who could see the magical energy around his daughter, little Ryder would someday turn wolf. According to the Rhejes, Cullen was right.

A lot of lupi were dealing with this knockout punch to their worldview in the time-honored way: selective denial. Yes, the Lady said that the arrival of a female lupus meant that war had resumed with their ancient enemy. War was fine. They understood war. They did not understand the concept of a female lupus, so they refused to talk about it.

Lily had started scrolling through a few hundred lovely if incredibly repetitive photos of the mother and baby stored on Cullen's phone when Rule set a plate of French toast in front of her. As she ate, Cullen talked about cloth diapers, tiny fingernails, Cynna's breasts—she was breast-feeding, as about a hundred of the photos testified—infant massage, and gas.

It was surprisingly comforting. Not interesting, no. She couldn't say she found a lecture on various ways to burp a baby interesting. But comforting. By the time Rule joined them with his own plate, Lily had almost finished thumbing through the photos and Cullen was discussing the potential problems of seeing a daughter through First Change.

". . . one of the biggies, of course, being contraceptives." He brooded on that a moment. "We have to assume the pill won't work. As soon as she goes through the Change, her body will reject any drugs in her system. So we'll have to rely on mechanical methods, but fourteen- and fifteen-year-olds aren't noted for their skill at planning ahead. Telling the boys I'll kill them if they forget to use a condom won't work."

Lily didn't quite choke on the food in her mouth, but it was a near thing. She swallowed. "You don't think abstinence is a possibility?"

Cullen snorted. "Not with lupi boys—and not, I'm guessing, with a lupus girl. Normally we control availability. New wolves simply aren't around potential sex partners at *terra tradis*. But the only way to control availability with Ryder would be to separate her from the other new wolves. I won't do that to her."

Puberty arrived a bit later for most lupi than for humans, typically around age fourteen. When it did, it triggered First Change. At that point the boy—or, as the lupi usually said, the new wolf—was sequestered with other adolescents at the *terra tradis*, a private area where new wolves could be closely supervised and trained. It took a young lupus several years to learn to control the Change and his wolf. "I guess new wolves want to be around their age-mates."

"It's more need than want," Rule said. "The two years following First Change are critical to integrating our dual natures. Lupi who are deprived of age-mates in that period can be forever at war with themselves."

Cullen didn't look happy. "So limiting availability is off the table. Chemical and mechanical means won't work. I'm going to have to find a magical method."

"Is there such a thing?" Lily asked, startled. "A magical contraceptive?"

"By the time my daughter turns thirteen, there will be."

"I guess that'll be complicated, since, uh . . . I mean . . ." This was not an easy subject. "It'll have to be a flexible method, won't it? There aren't condoms for wolves. And they couldn't put them on if there were."

"Oh, you're talking about when she's wolf." Cullen said. "That shouldn't be as much of a problem. We'll have to wait and see to be sure, but it's unlikely she'll be in perpetual heat the way human females are."

Lily opened her mouth. Closed it.

"Biologically speaking," Rule said apologetically, "being in heat means being fertile. Human females don't have heat cycles because they remain potentially fertile. Female wolves generally go into heat only once a year, in the winter."

Cullen nodded. "We may have to segregate Ryder when her wolf's in heat, but the jury's still out on that. We can only speculate based on the behavior of wild wolves, but abstinence might work for her wolf form. Most female wolves refuse to mate with non-dominants, and the dominants Ryder will be around will be adults and able to control themselves."

"Out of charity for Mason," Rule said dryly, referring to the Nokolai elder who had charge of the youngsters at *terra tradis*, "segregating her during her cycle might be best."

Cullen chuckled. "Maybe so."

Lily sighed. "I'm really, deeply uncomfortable talking about fourteen-year-old kids having sex."

Two uncomprehending male faces turned toward her.

"It doesn't feel icky to you? Never mind." Clearly it didn't. Lupi were deeply protective of their children. Lily knew that. No pedophile who preyed on—or tried to prey on—a clan child had to worry about arrest. He'd be way too dead to worry about anything. And kids having sex with kids was not the same thing at all, and there'd been a time when fourteen-year-olds married, but . . . *not now*, she told herself firmly. "Let's talk about something simpler, like illusion spells."

"They don't exist," Cullen said promptly. "Not in any meaningful way. Not in our realm."

"And yet someone who looked like Ruben killed Senator Bixton. Wait, wait," she said, shoving her chair back. "I need my pad." Taking notes was how she thought.

Rule put his fork down, reached out one long arm to the

nearby counter, and retrieved the little spiral she knew damn well she'd left in her jacket pocket.

She accepted it from him. "When you stay three jumps ahead of me, I start feeling inadequate."

"You're welcome." He handed her a pen, too.

She flipped to the page where she'd jotted down the questions she wanted to be sure she asked Cullen. "Okay. Illusion spells don't exist in our realm, but the Great Enemy isn't from our realm, isn't human, and doesn't have a lot of limits on what she can do. One of the limits she does face is contacting someone here directly. She'd need a telepath on this end to do that, right?"

"For the kind of clear communication it takes to teach someone a spell, yes," Cullen said. "At least *she* did three thousand years ago. If she's learned any new tricks since then, she didn't use them when she was getting the Azá to open that gate for her. Friar probably dreams about her." He shoved his chair back and headed for the coffeepot. "I mean that both ways. He's smitten, plus she probably contacts him in dreams."

"But it would be somewhere between unlikely and impossible for her to teach him an illusion spell in a dream, right?"

"In my opinion, yes. But I'm not an Old One." Cullen refilled his mug and leaned against the counter to sip from it. "Still, what little I know about illusion spells suggests that they're mage-level, if not adept. Friar's got a gazillion oomphs of power now, but even if *she* managed to convey the details of such a spell in a dream, he lacks the training and experience to execute it."

"You're sure."

"Spellwork isn't just saying some fancy words while you stir together eyes of newt and toes of frog. You have to know what you're doing in blood, body, and brain, and the only way to get that kind of knowledge is through practice and lots of it. It's like the difference between watching football and playing it. Armchair quarterbacks might be able to analyze the hell out of a play, but they couldn't execute it."

"The Great Bitch is an Old One. Couldn't she just inject that kind of knowledge into Friar when she gave him his Gift?"

"Not according to my sources—whose names wouldn't mean much to you, so you'll have to take my word for it." He sipped again. "But that's why she gave Friar a Gift, not a lot of fancy spells. He won't be able to use any but very basic spells for a good, long time."

"Bring that pot over here, would you? I wonder why mindspeech doesn't work across realms." She made a note to ask Mika about that.

"You're sure that it doesn't?" Rule asked.

"Based on the fact that *she* hasn't been doing it all along, yeah, that seems a good bet." She frowned at her notebook. "If illusion is out, what does that leave us?"

Cullen carried the pot back to the table with him. "I didn't say illusion was out. I said an illusion spell was extremely unlikely. There's still the possibility of an illusion Gift." He set the pot by her elbow and sat down. "That Gift has never appeared in a human, but elven lords often develop it. I suspect illusion is the mature form of their innate ability to cast a glamour."

Lily drummed her fingers. She truly and deeply did not want to be dealing with another sidhe lord. The one they'd encountered last month had been more than enough. Still, she noted the possibility . . . and caught a glimpse of her watch. "Shit. I'm going to have to rush through the rest of the questions, or leave some for later. You'll be here later?"

"I'll be around." For some reason, that amused him. "You have a time clock to punch?"

"Drummond wants me at Headquarters at eight. I'm supposed to vet every agent on the team—make sure none of them are tainted by death magic. Which takes me to my next question. How long would the taint linger in someone who took part in a death magic ritual?"

"There's an easy one to answer. I don't know."

"If you could give me some idea—"

"Anything I tell you is likely to be wrong. Your Gift is going to find traces that non-sensitives can't, but I don't know how long those traces linger—too damn little to go on and too many variables. Some people are more"—he gestured vaguely—"more porous than others. They'd soak up more.

Plus it would depend on how many participants were at the ritual, whether the sacrifice was animal or human, and how many were sacrificed."

"How many? You mean there could be more than one victim at a single ritual?"

"Sure. Theoretically, the only limit comes from how much power the chief celebrant can absorb or channel. The old Aztecs managed to do at least a thousand people a day when they consecrated their temple."

"A thousand a day."

"Some experts put it much higher. I suspect they wasted most of the power, but you've got to give them points for enthusiasm."

"No," she said, "I don't. You think it could have been animal sacrifice?"

"Could be. The Azá used animal sacrifice."

"That's not what they had in mind when they grabbed me."

"Human sacrifice is needed for a major working, sure, if you're powering that working through death magic. But the real question is why they used death magic at all."

Lily frowned. "What do you mean?"

"Spells that kill don't need mega-oomphs of power. How much depends on the precision of the spell and the skill of the caster, but anyone with a strong Gift should have enough power on his own to enspell a knife to kill. So why involve at least four more people? Why use death magic?"

"Could it be someone with a weak Gift? Or someone who doesn't know what he's doing? Maybe he or she thought they had to use death magic to kill."

"That's . . ." Cullen stopped. Scowled. "Never underestimate the power of ignorance. Yeah, that's possible. There is so much hogwash out there masquerading as fact."

Progress. Lily jotted a few things down. "For whatever reason, the perp used a lot of power. That's why I assumed human sacrifice. The dagger was still loaded with the nasty stuff over an hour after doing its job."

"If you've got an ignorant asshole in charge, that would make sense. Overloading the power, I mean. I need to see that knife."

"I'll try to arrange it, but so far Drummond isn't cooperating."

"Yeah, Rule told me I'm not getting paid."

"Speaking of ignorant assholes, Drummond may yet approve the consult, which would let me get this on the record. So do you think we're talking about Friar as the perp? He lacks experience."

He shook his head, looking frustrated. "I don't know. It doesn't fit for me. If *she* passed a killing spell to him in a dream, she did a pisspoor job."

"Maybe he had to find one on his own. Maybe he used some flunky. It's a place to start, anyway. Next question. Why would someone suddenly leak death magic?"

He frowned. "You'd better explain."

She told him about the trail she'd found and followed to a bench in the park.

"That doesn't make sense."

"That's what I said."

"I don't . . . wait." He sat up straighter. "If your perp didn't do the deed himself—if he gave the knife to a null—"

"A null? Someone unGifted could use the spell on the knife?"

"Sure. Remember those sleep charms I made? A death spell on a dagger is a charm, basically. More difficult to shape than a sleep charm, and it takes more power, which is why I assumed . . . but they've got the power. That would explain why they used death magic. Blades will take a killing spell readily, but they don't store magic well. It can be done, but then it would take magic to trigger the spell. A null couldn't do it."

"And this makes you think a null used the knife? Because he couldn't?"

Cullen rolled his eyes. "Let me take you by the hand and lead you step by step. We'll call the guy who did the actual killing Perp Number One. He's null. Perp Number Two, who probably was part of the death magic ritual, is Gifted. Perp Number Two meets Perp Number One at that bench. Number Two activates the spell on the dagger and hands it to Number One. It doesn't start leaking until it's activated."

It fit. It fit really well, and yet it bothered Lily. She couldn't put her finger on why. Maybe it was the sheer complication. "Why have a null do the killing? What's the advantage? You're talking about a pretty elaborate conspiracy."

Rule spoke. "We've been talking about a conspiracy all along."

She looked at him. His mouth was grim. His eyes were dark and clear. "Yeah, I guess we have been. But I—shit." She'd caught a glimpse of the clock on the stove. She shoved her chair back. "I have to go."

Cullen shoved his chair back, too. "Okay."

Suspicion dawned. "Why are you agreeing with me?"

"I'm going with you."

"Drummond isn't going to let you—"

"Lily." Rule stood. "You can't drive, so Cullen will. You passed out last night. It could happen again at any time."

Her lips thinned.

"You could take one of the guards instead, but there are advantages to having someone with you who can see and work magic. And answer questions about it."

"I hate it when you're right." She looked at Cullen. "You'll have to wait in the car, maybe for hours. You're going to be bored." Cullen hated being bored.

He snagged his phone from the table. "Got a new app. I'll play while I wait."

THIRTEEN

~~~

LILY did ask her driver a few questions on the way to Head-quarters. No pain gods sent lightning bolts through her skull as he parked in the underground garage. She thought about Aunt Mequi as she rode up in the elevator.

Her aunt had migraines. Serious migraines. A couple times she'd ended up at the ER with one, though no one was supposed to mention that. Aunt Mequi's dignity was much affronted that she'd been unable to endure the pain without help. Of course, Mequi's migraines lasted for hours, not the few moments Lily's bolts-from-the-blue had occupied so far. But there were bound to be different types of migraines, right?

Rule feared that Lily's malady was rooted in some terrible malfunction, either physical or magical, but Rule was lupus. He'd never had a headache without a concussion. Lily could see plenty of other possibilities.

There was a small crowd in the hall near the designated conference room. Lily recognized two of them: Doug Mullins and Sherry O'Shaunessy. Everyone glanced her way. Mullins frowned. Sherry smiled.

Sherry O'Shaunessy looked like a young, upscale grandmother, except for her hair. That was gray and reached past her hips when down; today she wore it in a braid coiled on top of her head. Her cheeks were chubby, her smile contagious, and her Gift was Water. She was one of the most powerful witches in the country, and the High Priestess of the Wiccan coven the Unit kept under contract.

This morning, she looked tired. Lily went to her. "Good to see you. You didn't pull an all-nighter, did you?"

"I'm afraid so. That's not as easy as it once was. Did you—"

Mullins interrupted. "He wants you inside, Yu."

In Mullins's world, "he" had to mean Drummond. Lily nodded at him and said to Sherry, "I'll see you inside, I guess."

Sherry took Lily's hand and gave a little squeeze. Water magic felt like the element it drew upon, but there were variations. Sherry's magic evoked the ocean for Lily rather than rain or brooks or deep pools. She could almost smell the salty spray. "I'm glad you're working on this one, dear."

"Inside," Mullins repeated, scowling.

Sherry smiled at him. "Your name is Doug, I think?"

Mullins blinked and looked conflicted, no doubt trying to resist the urge to smile back. Satan himself would find it hard to resist Sherry's smile. "Doug Mullins, yes, ma'am."

She patted his arm. "Not everyone is able to offer the proverbial spoonful of sugar, but we can at least avoid pouring vinegar over everything." She looked at Lily. "Doug is guarding the door. I'm afraid he's been a bit abrasive, but he does have orders."

"I guess I do, too." Lily gave her a nod and headed for the closed door.

The conference room was large enough for a table that could seat up to thirty people. At the moment it held four: Drummond, a senior MCD agent named Mike Brassard whom Lily knew slightly, and two others who were strangers to her. There was a whiteboard with crime scene pics tacked up and a console table with a coffeepot, cups, and fixings.

Lily headed for the coffee.

Drummond stopped talking to the woman beside him—brown and blue, pale skin, glasses, five-five, one sixty, wrinkled gray suit. She looked to be on the far side of forty. "You're late," he told Lily.

"It's 8:01, so yes, I am." She poured herself a cup. It smelled fresh.

"I want you to check everyone in this room in your own special way. Do it now."

Lily sighed, put down her coffee, and walked up to the dumpy woman beside Drummond. A quick handshake confirmed her lack of a Gift or any trace of death magic. She did the same with a bright-eyed Asian man of around thirty and with Brassard, the MCD agent.

"Well?" Drummond said.

"No death magic. I should check Ruben Brooks."

"No."

"It wouldn't prove anything, but it would be information."

"You aren't just his subordinate. You went to his damn party Saturday. You won't go anywhere near him during the course of this investigation."

Her lips tightened. She went to retrieve her coffee.

"Feed your caffeine jones later. We're going to be working with a large team. I want them all cleared before we start. Doug will send 'em in one at a time. Stand by the door and check them out. If you find death magic, don't say anything. Signal by rubbing your hands together. Nguyen, stand by to take anyone down who doesn't pass."

It was a good plan, minimizing the confusion if she did find anything suspicious. Lily nodded but said, "My clearing someone this way only means they haven't worked death magic recently. I can't even say how recently."

"It's information."

Hard to argue with what she'd just said, but she wanted to. Drummond affected her that way. "I've got a theory about one of the perps. The one who stuck the knife in Bixton."

"Make it quick."

She explained Cullen's idea about the killer being a null—though she didn't use that term, which some considered derogatory.

He grunted in what might have been surprise. "I'll call on you to repeat that later. Right now, get started at the door. I want to get this thing under way."

Lily shook nineteen hands. No death magic. One agent had

a minor Gift—physical empathy—which surprised Lily. It
was an unusual Gift and not one the man could have remained
unaware of, as it essentially provided him with another sense.
Physical empathy, unlike true empathy, allowed someone to
sense physical objects directly in a way that had no clear ana-
logue to the usual senses.

The agent met her gaze when she shook his hand and said
nothing. Lily didn't, either. She refused to out people. But she
made a mental note of his name and face: Don Richardson,
European ancestry, early forties, five-ten, brown and brown,
with a small scar just under his right ear.

Lily knew some of the people, like Paul from Research and
Hannah from CSI. And she knew the last person in, who had a
minor patterning Gift. Lily already knew about that. She'd
recommended Anna Sjorensen for training when they met last
month. Sjorensen had been delegated to Headquarters recently
so she could receive that training; she'd be transferred to the
Unit once she'd completed it.

Working in the Unit was Anna Sjorensen's dream. Lily
gave her a smile. "Good to be working with you."

Sjorensen nodded back, very serious. She was always very
serious. "This is a bad business. I'm not sure why I'm here,
though."

"If I say to fetch coffee, someone'll file a damn suit against
me," Drummond said sourly, "and Erin will bean me. You're
here to do as you're told. Sit down and let's start."

Drummond introduced Mullins and the three people who'd
been in the room first, calling them Team One: Mike Brassard,
Erin Hoffsteader, and Sam Nguyen. Each of the three would
be in charge of a different aspect of the investigation. He said
he'd summarize the status of the investigation and call on
some of them for reports after Ms. O'Shaunessy gave them
her findings. She would take questions, but he wanted to let
her get some sleep, so "keep the questions pertinent."

Maybe the man wasn't always an asshole.

Sherry gave a quick précis of what her coven had learned.
Yes, the dagger held considerable death magic, and there were
traces on Bixton's body as well. They had also confirmed the

presence of a spell, but hadn't been able to identify the spell. "It may take weeks, even months, to deconstruct the spell," she concluded, "if we can do so at all. There are no visual components, so it's a matter of trial and error."

Lily had already figured out that she was the only Unit agent in the room. The questions that flew after Sherry's report made it clear that most of the others knew diddly about magic. They weren't stupid questions. Just ignorant. A couple people seemed skeptical about the validity of magically derived evidence. One guy was downright hostile.

". . . scientific method means the results can be duplicated. You can't say that about dancing around naked all night then coming up with—"

"Mayhew," Drummond said, "shut up. She's the expert. You aren't. If you can't flex that steel-trap mind of yours enough to accept that, you don't belong on this team."

Mayhew shut up. Lily didn't think his mind had flexed, but he did shut up. She took advantage of the brief silence to say quietly to Sherry, "About IDing that spell . . . Cullen's in town."

"Excellent! He's just what we need."

Drummond had good ears. He zeroed right in on that. "Are you talking about Cullen Seabourne? That damn consultant you wanted?"

"That's right. He arrived last night."

"And you thought it was somehow okay to bring him in when I haven't authorized—"

"He's working pro bono for now."

Sherry's eyebrows shot up. "Cullen?"

Lily flashed her a grin. "Amazing, isn't it?" She looked at Drummond. "We need to know more about the spell on that knife as quickly as possible. For example, if we know what tradition it's drawn from, that may limit our suspect pool."

"Explain."

Sherry fielded that one. "With a few exceptions, practitioners can only work spells derived from or couched in their own tradition. A Vodun priest wouldn't be able to cast a Nordic rune spell, for example, or an Egyptian *zoan*. There's more overlap among the so-called pagan traditions, but even there, variations in symbology and sourcing make it difficult for a North American shaman to use most Wiccan spells without altering the spell."

The MCD guy—Brassard—spoke up. "But there are exceptions."

"Sorcerers are said to be able to work in multiple traditions."

He snorted. "They're also said to be rare. As in, there aren't any."

"You're confusing sorcerers with adepts. Sorcery is a Gift, not a level of ability. We have no adepts in our realm anymore. Sorcerers are extremely rare, but that Gift does still appear from time to time. Also, we know very little about the non-human traditions, such as gnomish or elven magic, so I have to consider them possible exceptions."

Sjorensen spoke up gravely. "You said something about adjusting spells. What does that mean?"

Sherry blessed her with a smile. "Advanced practitioners can often adapt a spell from a foreign tradition to their needs. But that would be information, too. If this spell shows signs of drawing on multiple traditions, you'll know you are looking for an advanced practitioner."

The woman directly across from Lily frowned. "Don't we already know that? They harvested death magic and used it to kill Bixton. That sounds pretty advanced."

Sherry shook her head. "Unfortunately, death magic can be harvested by someone with only a moderate understanding of magic if they get hold of an accurate rite. Your suspect may be quite advanced, or only the equivalent of a bright middle-schooler willing to put out a lot of effort."

"Which is why," Lily added, "once someone starts down that path, they usually practice with animals at first. That's a possible way to track our perps, or to provide corroboratory evidence. And only one guy has to be skilled. The others involved in the rite may be completely ignorant. There's some disagreement," she added with a glance at Sherry, "about whether they even have to be Gifted." The disagreement she knew about was between Sherry and Cullen.

Sherry's eyes twinkled. "True. I personally believe all the participants must possess some trace of magic, but that's a theoretical preference on my part. Obviously I can't test it."

Erin Hoffsteader said, "What about the spell on the knife? That has to be pretty advanced."

"We don't know that," Sherry said calmly. "Not yet."

"In fact," Lily put in, paraphrasing Cullen again, "for all we know, our perps didn't enspell the knife themselves. They could have found it or bought it. It's even possible—not likely, but possible—they got hold of a pre-Purge artifact with an intact spell." She looked at Sherry. "If the knife's old enough, that is."

"I don't know. The most accurate spell to determine age must be performed in two parts—at new moon, then at full moon."

"Pre-Purge?" Drummond was skeptical. "That would make it over three hundred years old. Is it possible for a spell to survive that long?"

"Oh, yes," Sherry said, "if it was cast by an adept. I know of three such artifacts with intact spells. Two of them are in museums."

Now that was interesting. Lily didn't want to get side-tracked, though. "All of which explains why I want my expert to have a look at that dagger. We need information, even if it isn't admissible."

Sherry smiled. "There's a good chance my coven can corroborate anything Cullen learns, and our results *would* be admissible."

Drummond looked like he'd bitten into the proverbial lemon, but he agreed, with the provision that Sherry be present when Cullen examined the dagger. Drummond then thanked Sherry brusquely for her time and dismissed her. The he told them sourly to "get some coffee if you want, but make it quick."

Lily didn't hesitate. She had her foam cup in hand and was sipping when he began the briefing. "You've all heard shit about this one already. Most of it's wrong. Listen up to what we actually know." He went on to hit all the basic points concisely without leaving anything important out, covering when, where, and what they knew of how the senator had been killed. Then he called on Hannah to describe what CSI had found.

That turned out to be not much, except for an oddly damp spot on the carpet near the body. They were running tests on fibers from that spot. Results not in yet.

Drummond told Hannah she could go if she wanted. She did. He looked around the table. "This next part is going to stay in this room. Anyone leaks it, I'll find out, and I'll bury you. We've got a wit—the maid—who places someone on the scene with the senator at the right time. Someone who identified himself to her as Ruben Brooks."

A chorus of exclamations was summed up by Brassard from MCD: "What the hell?"

Drummond spoke over them. "None of us likes having one of our own fingered, and why would a lifetime cop commit murder after announcing himself to the damn maid? Doesn't make sense. But trust me—we're taking it seriously. We have to. He's got motive enough, given the senator's opposition to his Unit." He paused. "For the record, Brooks denies it. Says he was home all morning. His wife says the same. Special Agent Yu here has a theory that supports Brooks's innocence."

Nearly two dozen pairs of eyes fixed on Lily. The scowliest pair belonged to Mayhew, the one Drummond had told to shut up earlier. "She's Unit. Brooks is her boss."

"He is," Lily said evenly. "I won't give you my opinion of him, because that wouldn't mean shit to you. Or to this investigation. But aside from my opinion, there's reason to think he isn't the perp." She went on to explain why the trail of death magic she'd followed suggested that the knife had been intended for use by someone without magic. "Brooks, of course, is Gifted. There's no reason he would need a weapon fueled by death magic."

Mayhew wasn't giving up. "Unless he wanted us to think it couldn't be him."

Lily's eyebrows rose. "So he announced himself to the maid? Which is he—a devious mastermind, or a bloody idiot?"

"Enough," Drummond said. "You've got the basics. Now you get assignments. Each of you will work with at least one partner. I want every interview, every shred of evidence, sub-stantiated by two people."

Drummond was thorough. He had teams checking public transport, looking into Ruben's activities the past month, ob-taining financial information on Bixton, his wife, and his fam-ily. One team would head into North Carolina to look into associations in the senator's hometown. Another—the one Sjorensen ended up on—would try to trace the dagger. Drum-mond would handle the interviews with Bixton's wife and im-mediate family himself. He assigned Lily the job of digging into Bixton's political enemies, starting with an interview with his chief of staff.

Her partner was Doug Mullins.

WHEN Drummond dismissed them, Lily had to swim up-stream through the mass of people leaving the room. Mullins was in his usual spot next to his idol, who was talking to Nguyen.

"Come on," Mullins told her.

"In a minute." She waited until Nguyen finished and turned away. "Two things," she said to Drummond. "First, I need to let you know I've got a medical appointment today. Second—"

"What the hell?" His eyebrows snapped down. "I was told you were good to go."

"I am. There's some lingering weakness in my right arm, but otherwise I'm fit. But I was moved from light duty to ac-tive without a doctor signing off on it." Let him assume her appointment was for dotting those bureaucratic *i*'s.

He waved that aside. "Don't bother with your second thing. I've already heard it from Doug." His smile was slow and sour. "The two of you are stuck with each other."

She glanced at Mullins, who scowled. "No, the other thing is that I want to dig into the death magic angle."

"How?"

"Homeless shelters. Missing persons reports. At least one person and possibly more were killed to charge that dagger. There's a good chance that wasn't the first time our perps killed, either. They probably had to practice."

His eyes narrowed. He gave a brief nod. "Good enough. You'll give your assignment priority, though. If you—" His brows snapped down. "What is it?"

Her heart was pounding, but unlike Rule, he wouldn't be able to hear that. Maybe her eyes had widened for a split second before it vanished. "What do you mean?"

"You look like you've seen a ghost."

She had. It had hovered in the air between Drummond and Mullins for a second, a pale blur in the air . . . one hand outstretched, just as at the shooting range. A wedding ring on one finger.

No way in hell was she telling Drummond and Mullins about it. "I'm fine." She turned to Mullins. "Let's go."

FOURTEEN

THE wolf wanted more time to sniff at the base of that oak, to trot along leafy paths flavored with scents of deer and raccoon. He wanted to chase his clanmate through the trees, romp with him in a tumble of nips and pounces on that wide, grassy lawn. But the man was needed now. He allowed himself one gusty sigh, then reached for the song.

Moonlight flooded him, blinded him, ruptured his heart and flung him into the abyss where leaf-crunch and fire-crackle melded with inky black, a silent tsunami of song and pain rending him, rendering him . . .

Whole. Reformed, two-footed, his breathing unruffled, Rule lingered in the fringe of trees long enough to pull on the jean shorts he'd carried in his mouth.

He'd been right. Ruben and Deborah's land welcomed the Change. He strode out of the lovely little scrap of forest into their backyard.

Deborah stood near one of the rear flower beds, a dirty trowel in one hand. She wore a faded blue sweatshirt and jeans. She was staring at him.

"I hope I didn't startle you," he said as he drew near. "I'm afraid I'm a trifle underdressed, but it's difficult to carry much in the way of clothing when I'm four-footed."

She had an odd, stunned expression on her face. "What did you do? I . . . felt it. Something moved through the earth. I've never felt anything like it."

"The Change calls earth to dance with moonsong. I imagine it would feel peculiar to one touching Earth at the time."

"Peculiar. Yes." She smiled suddenly. "And incredibly lovely. I was encouraging my rhododendron, you see. You're here to see Ruben?"

"I am, yes."

"I'll take you to him. "

"I don't like to interrupt you."

"I'll take you to him," she repeated, and started for the house. Rule perforce walked with her. "You didn't want to be seen coming to the house. That's why you came through the woods in, ah, your other form."

"It seemed best."

Silence fell. He didn't try to fill it, sensing something was brewing in her. Halfway across the yard, it boiled over into words. "I hate this. I hate it."

Her voice, low but throbbing with emotion, told him to step carefully. "This?"

"This, them . . . the people who tried to kill him. The way we're living now, with guards lurking around. Ruben almost died, but he didn't, so now they're trying to strip him of everything else—honor, freedom, his reputation, his work. He didn't even want me to work outside today. He wishes I weren't here at all, but he especially wishes I wouldn't go into our own yard. He wants me to hide. Did you know that?" It was demand as much as question. "He wants me to go into hiding."

Rule knew. He'd suggested it to Ruben last week . . . but it had already occurred to Ruben that their enemies might try to grab Deborah, to use her against him. She refused to leave her home and her husband. "You've every right to be angry."

"Oh, that's fine, then. I'm entitled to my anger, so that's fine." She stopped, faced him. "He doesn't get visions about himself. He doesn't even get hunches, usually, not about his own welfare."

"I know." It was a common blind spot for precogs. They

were much more likely to get hunches about others, or about the grand sweep of events. Now and then a precog might have a feeling he shouldn't cross a certain street at a certain time, but most of the time a precog was as likely as anyone else to step blithely into the path of an out-of-control car.

Deborah shook her head as if to shake off some troublesome thought. "How do you do it? Lily was injured last month, just like Ruben. She's a target still. You have to live with that. How do you do it?"

What could he say? That his wolf wasn't prone to worry? That the man was, so he wrapped as much protection around Lily as she'd allow? Neither of those options was available to Deborah. "I fell in love with a cop. She's always been a target. The danger is greater now, but she hasn't changed. I can't ask her to." He paused. "It helps when I can run as wolf. Does digging in the earth help you?"

"Sometimes. Lately it hasn't been enough." She started walking again, her head down. "You and Lily are partners in this—this secret war. You aren't pushed to the sidelines, to the sit-home-and-wait role."

Rule was uneasily aware of being drawn too close to the explosive intimacies of someone else's marriage. Probably he should shut up. He didn't. Her distress was too real. "Have you been pushed?"

"No." She brushed her hair back impatiently. "I opted for the sidelines years ago, as far as Ruben's job goes. I didn't see a place for me there, and I had my own place. Teaching matters to me. That way worked for both of us for a long time. It isn't working now."

"Hmm."

"Not that I know what I can do. I'm not a cop, not a lupus or a trained witch or a spy or—or anything useful."

"You don't have to be a warrior to be part of this fight. You do have to want and intend to oppose *her*. You can't join the Shadow Unit as a form of marital therapy."

"Is that what you think I'm doing?"

"I don't know."

"I'm making you uncomfortable."

"This is a conversation you should have with Ruben, not me."

Her sudden smile woke the dimple in her cheek. "I'm making you uncomfortable."

He had to smile back. "Yes, you are. You seem pleased by that."

"I feel quite daring. I'm used to worrying about what others think, or what I think they might think, or what I think about what I think they think. That doesn't seem to matter right now. I wonder why?"

"Perhaps because it doesn't matter what I think."

"That might be it." She was quietly delighted. "That might just be it. Would you like some coffee? Or something else to drink?"

They'd reached the back door. "Coffee would be lovely." He knew from previous visits that Deborah made excellent coffee.

"I'll bring some in. It will just take a few minutes. Ruben should be in his study."

Apparently she no longer felt the need to escort him personally to her husband. Rule smiled wryly as he made his way to the book-lined room. He spoke before he reached the open door so Ruben would know it was him. Humans could seldom identify someone from the sound of their footsteps. "Deborah let me in. She's going to bring us some coffee."

"Ah. Good." Ruben was at his desk with his laptop in front of him. He moved it to one side, but didn't rise, which meant he wasn't feeling well. "Thank you for coming. Do sit down. I was just reading an interesting article about a new synthetic polymer they believe may make a good insulator against magic."

"Really? I thought plastic was transparent to magic—as are most synthetics."

"Apparently this is more akin to rubber than plastic, but has different properties than rubber."

"Cullen will want to hear about that." They continued to discuss the various approaches different corporations were taking toward developing an inexpensive magical insulator for tech. It made an interesting and innocuous topic while they waited.

Deborah arrived with a tray holding two steaming mugs

and a sugar bowl. Ruben took his coffee sweet. She reminded Ruben of a doctor's appointment that afternoon. He grimaced. "Cardiologist," he said briefly to Rule, rising as soon as Deborah left. He went to the inset circle on the floor, crouched, and activated it. "I think we won't bother with the magic bomb this time," he said as he straightened and returned to his desk. "Your presence should be sufficient. Mika said you have news. About the Bixton investigation?"

"No. I should have made that clear—sorry. Though I can update you on what Lily knows." He felt a twinge of guilt, but it was probably not called for. Lily must suspect he'd keep Ruben informed. She'd made a point of informing Mika, after all, even if she had done it in a roundabout way.

Ruben waved that away. "I'd better hear what brought you here first."

"It requires discussion, which is why I didn't pass the details through Mika." Mika could "speak" to anyone within the metro area without leaving his lair, and he checked in with Ruben frequently. For the rest of the ghosts, however, it wasn't so easy. Unless the sender had mindspeech—which none of them did—Mika had to be fairly close to read his or her mind. Even then, the amount of mental noise in the city made it difficult for him to focus in on a single thought, so they'd been told to use a nonsense word to get Mika's attention—a string of syllables that no one else on the planet would be concentrating on.

Fortunately, Mika was keeping to a schedule on his overflights of the city, which limited the amount of time Rule had to spend saying, "nininfalaha" to get Mika's attention. "We lost Chittenden."

"What happened?"

"He went to the mall. My men followed him, but lost visual contact. His scent led to an exit, but he was gone. That was four days ago, and he hasn't returned to his condo. His car is still at the mall parking lot."

"Ah." Ruben tented his fingers. "I'll have flights and car rentals checked. He may not travel under his own name, of course, but we'll see what we can find out. Anything new about Jones?"

"He's been on the move a lot, but my people have been able to keep up with him. James is in place in L.A., if you decide we should take Jones out."

"I prefer not to use that option."

"So do I."

Neither of them wanted to kill Friar's two lieutenants. Rule had no moral qualms about it; assassination was surely one of the most moral tactics one could employ in war, assuming it was done so innocent bystanders weren't harmed. He suspected Ruben didn't share his view, but the man would do what was necessary. However, at the moment Chittenden and Jones were more valuable to them alive. They hoped to find Friar through the two men closest to him in Humans First.

The aspect Rule had needed to discuss was their "throw-away"—a lupus who would attempt to infiltrate Paul Chittenden's network, ostensibly as a spy, but really to see if Chittenden had some means of identifying lupi. If so, it would increase the difficulty for the assassins. Normally there was no way for humans to tell if a man was human or lupus without a blood test, but Friar had been allied with a sidhe lord until last month. They didn't know what he might have acquired from the elf before Rethna's death. It was possible Friar's lieutenants had charms to detect lupi.

Their throwaway was a young Nokolai named James. Rule had watched him grow up. James's job was extremely dangerous, and Rule wanted to give him every chance to complete it without dying. Benedict was handling that part of the operation, but needed to know what, if any, resources he could draw upon from the Shadow Unit. They discussed backup, communication, and extrication methods, then touched on other aspects of the war, including money. Finances were a key component of the battle on both sides. Then they switched to the investigation into Bixton's death.

It didn't take long for Rule to relay what he knew about it. When he finished, he glanced at his watch. "I need to get back."

"Before you leave, I need to tell you that Humans First has applied for and received a permit to demonstrate near the capitol building in Albany."

"Damn." Rule's lips tightened. "That moves it from 'maybe' to 'almost certainly.' "

He referred to their suspicion that the hate group knew where the main clanhomes were in the United States—and intended to make them known to the public. Nokolai's clanhome was already widely known, of course, but the others weren't. At first they'd hoped that planned demonstrations in San Diego and Albuquerque was coincidence. Though there were clanhomes near those cities, there were none near the other places where rallies would be held. But Albany was only about eighty miles from Wythe Clanhome. Adding it to the mix suggested intent, not coincidence.

"I'm afraid so." Ruben stood. "Rule, you can't discuss our plans with Lily, but I won't ask you to keep this visit from her unless you feel it's necessary."

Rule hesitated. "I think she suspects I'll communicate with you, but would rather not have her nose rubbed in it."

Ruben nodded. "How do you think she's dealing with my revelations from Saturday? She seemed to accept the need for the Shadow Unit, but that's several steps away from joining us."

"I wish I could say I was optimistic, but understanding why we've chosen to act outside the law isn't the same as doing so herself. It's not like bending a regulation or overlooking a minor crime in order to prevent a major one. We're asking her to give her allegiance to something other than the law."

"To something in addition to the law."

"I'm not sure she can see it that way."

"I'll continue to hope you're wrong."

So would he. Because he hated keeping secrets from his *nadia*, yes, but also because Ruben said they needed Lily. Needed her to go beyond tolerating the existence of the ghosts. Needed her to be one of them. This certainty came from Ruben's visions, though Rule didn't know the details. When asked, Ruben waved a vague hand and said sometimes disclosure altered the course of events. He also said they had to at all costs avoid putting too much pressure on Lily, that she had to come to this commitment on her own.

Ruben Brooks didn't use language carelessly. When he said "at all costs," that was what he meant. So Rule couldn't tell Lily that unless she joined the Shadow Unit, the chances were excellent that over half the lupi in the country would be dead within three months.

FIFTEEN

DENNIS Parrott lived up to his name—lots of pretty feathers, and now and then something he said was actually pertinent. He was in his early fifties but looked younger—a slim man with a narrow face, perfect haircut, rimless glasses, pleasant voice, pleasant smile. Interviewing him was like talking to a magazine ad.

Glossy, Rule had called him. So far Lily hadn't gotten so much as a peek beneath the polish. "But you don't know anything about any of those crank letters the senator received."

"I'm sorry, no. We never discussed that sort of thing. But you have copies, you said."

"Of those that were turned over to the Secret Service, yes. There could be more."

"You'd need to ask Nan about that. I'm afraid this is all the time I can give you today, but Nan will have passed on my request that the staff cooperate with you fully."

Nan was Nanette Beresford, the senator's secretary, a handsome older woman with a thick drawl and the proverbial steel-trap mind. She was arranging for Lily and Mullins to use a small conference room to question staffers.

"Just one more question." Mullins smiled vacuously at the glossy Parrott. "Won't take but a moment. I know you're busy—very important job, and with the senator's passing, you must be buried in work as well as grieving the loss of a friend. I really appreciate the time you've given us."

"Of course." The pleasant smile made a brief appearance on Parrott's thin face. "I'm very eager for you to catch whoever did this terrible thing. But we do have to make it quick."

Mullins had seriously surprised Lily. As they rode up in the elevator to see Parrott, he'd transformed into a snub-nosed Colombo with a whiff of Andy Griffith. The funny thing was, he was good at it. His bashful, bumbling version of a TV detective set Parrott at ease.

"I just wondered . . . couldn't help wondering, really, it's the way this job gets you thinking, you pick up on any little discrepancy, even though it's probably meaningless. When we were talking about the senator's work, his campaign against the misuse of magic, you said you weren't Gifted yourself. I wondered why you said that."

"Because I'm not."

Mullins looked confused. He glanced at Lily. "But you gave me the sign—when we all shook hands, you signaled that he . . . but he says he isn't."

"A minor Gift, I think," she said, "though the charm he's wearing to conceal it does a pretty good job, so he might have more power than I think. A Water Gift, I believe. Isn't that right, Mr. Parrott?"

No smile now, and at last Lily got that peek beneath the surface. Way down deep in those pleasant brown eyes lurked a predator who was not happy with Lily. "I don't know what you mean."

She shook her head sadly. "That's not going to work. Sometimes people don't know they have a touch of magic. When it's not a strong Gift, it's not that hard to suppress without knowing you're doing it. But people who are unaware of their Gift don't make or obtain a charm intended to hide it."

Mullins blinked, looking stupider than ever. "I didn't know you could do that. Make a charm like that, I mean."

"I didn't, either. It's quite a remarkable thing for someone who opposes magic to possess."

The pleasant expression stayed stuck to Parrott's face like

gum to the sole of a shoe, but he ran a hand over the perfectly styled hair. One with a plain gold wedding ring, again like the one the ghost had worn. Did all men's wedding rings look identical? "This could ruin me. I'm asking you not to say anything, anything at all, about it."

"I don't out anyone unless I have to. Unless it's essential to the investigation, whatever Gift or trace of the Blood people are concealing is their own—"

"I am *not* of the Blood." His lip curled in disgust. "As for my Gift . . . yes, it's quite minor. But I am not a hypocrite, Special Agent. Magic is wrong, an essential weakening of the tie between humans and our Creator. I had the charm made years ago for religious reasons. I wanted to suppress my Gift. Not to hide it, but to suppress it."

That was . . . entirely possible. Maybe. When she'd shaken Parrott's hand, she'd felt . . . not his magic, exactly, but the pressure of it, as if buried magic coursed beneath a null skin. The sensation of something flowing beneath an artificial skin was why she'd guessed at a Water Gift—a hidden one. But it was possible to suppress a Gift. Lily knew an empath who did just that with a spell. Parrott's magic hadn't felt the way the empath's did, but maybe his charm operated differently. "You'd have to have the charm renewed from time to time."

He grimaced. "Unfortunately, yes. I dislike it intensely, but I . . . I don't feel I have much choice. I've been told there is no way to rid me of magic entirely, so I have to renew the charm."

Mullins shook his head. "That's tough. And working here with the senator, who disliked magic as much as you, maybe more . . . shoot, I bet he'd have fired you in a heartbeat if he found out."

"He knew."

Lily's eyebrows climbed. "You're claiming Senator Bixton knew about your Gift and kept you as his chief of staff?"

"I've been with him for fifteen years. Of course he knew. I confessed it to him years ago. He also knew about the charm. Bob is—was—a compassionate man. He respected the choice I'd made to suppress the trace of magic I'm cursed with."

Naturally Lily tried to convince him to let them take the charm with them and have it tested. She wasn't surprised when he refused. Either he was lying and it didn't do what he said, or he was telling the truth and was worried about the state of his soul if he were parted from the charm.

He wouldn't tell them where he went to have the charm renewed. That was a tad more suspicious, but he might not want to provide additional evidence of his Gift. He might even be protecting the practitioner he used the way he claimed. Lots of practitioners were wary of authority.

Lily left that interview unsatisfied. They let Bixton's secretary know they were ready for the space she'd cleared for them, and she showed them to a small conference room. No windows, but it did have a pot of coffee. Lily headed there first. "Want a cup?"

"Never touch the stuff. What do you think?" Mullins pulled out a chair and sat. "He really tell Bixton his nasty little secret?"

"Maybe. If he didn't and Bixton found out, it would make a dandy motive. Especially if he isn't as suppressed as he claims."

"How'd you know about the charm?"

"I guessed, based on experience. It could've been a spell—"

"Isn't a charm a spell?"

"They look a lot the same to the rest of us," she agreed, "but practitioners consider them quite different. A charm is the product of a spell, and not all practitioners can make them. I'm told the main difference is temporal, whatever that means. For me personally, charms and spells don't feel the same. Charms are usually weaker, and their texture is, uh . . . more repetitive, maybe." She shrugged. "Different, anyway. I thought you were going to say, 'aw, shucks' any minute there."

He pulled a pack of gum from his jacket pocket. "I'm good." He nodded, agreeing with himself. "You weren't completely idiotic yourself. Picked up my pass right on time."

"Better watch it with the compliments. I'll get all fluttery."

He unwrapped his gum slowly, looking as dour and dull as ever. "You going to have trouble working with me now that you've discovered my massive intellect, charm, and sex appeal?"

"My God. You've got a sense of humor."

"All part of the package." He put the gum in his mouth. "Have to fight you women off with a stick sometimes."

SENATOR Bixton had a large staff. They talked to four of them before Lily had to leave to get checked out by the Leidolf Rhej.

She was thinking about appearances and first impressions as Cullen pulled into the garage behind the row house. Doug Mullins wasn't the unthinking, self-important prick she'd thought. Oh, he was a bit of a prick, but he was not stupid, and he was self-aware enough to know that people underestimated him and use that. He was damn good in interview.

Was she making assumptions about Dennis Parrott the way she had Mullins, based on dislike?

"Tell me more about the difference between charms and spells," she said to Cullen as she got out of the car. "It's something to do with time, right?"

He shut his door. "A charm is a spell held in stasis."

"Like a ward? Wards don't do anything until they're activated, either."

"Not exactly. A ward doesn't act until it's triggered, but then the action is immediate and complete. With a charm, part of the spell remains suspended even when the charm is activated. If it didn't, the charm would work only for a split second." He glanced at her as they started for the house. "Spells act in the now. In the moment. Charms can act over a period of hours or days or weeks, depending on the skill and intent of their maker."

"Weeks? The sleep charms you made last month lasted a couple hours."

"I made those in a hurry, and they needed to knock someone out immediately. I've got sleep charms that would keep someone asleep for a week, but they'd doze off gradually, which was not what we needed at the time."

True. "What's the upper limit on how long a charm can work?"

"Theoretically there isn't one. Practically, it depends on what kind of charm you're making, how it's powered, and how good you are. But for reasons we don't understand, charms don't last beyond a single moon cycle. You'd have to be an adept to make one that lasted longer, and then what you'd have would be called an artifact."

Startled, she paused just short of the deck Rule had added at the back of the house before Lily met him. "So an artifact is like a charm on steroids?"

"Pretty much, yeah. Or so I think. Since no one knows how to make an artifact anymore, I can't prove it."

"You'll get a peek at the dagger used on Bixton this afternoon. Will you be able to tell right away if it's an artifact or a . . . I guess a charm, though that doesn't sound right when its purpose was death."

"A charm that kills or wounds is often called a curse, but that's poor nomenclature. Curses can also be spoken spells. I prefer to call a cursed object a *maluuni*. That's from Swahili, though the original derivation is Arabic, and it means—"

"Back to my question," she said firmly, stepping onto the deck.

"One glance will tell me that much. If I don't see the spell and can't call it up into my vision, then it's an artifact."

"Wait a minute. What does that mean? If you don't see it—"

"I've got a spell that brings up the details of other spells so I can see them."

"Your magnifying spell, yeah."

"It doesn't work on artifacts. At least not the ones I've seen. I've seen five objects we'd call magical artifacts. With four of them, the details of the spell—the construction of it, the girders and wiring and plumbing—were hidden when it wasn't being used. The only part that showed was the trigger, the part designed to interact with the user. Adepts didn't like to give away their tricks, and they knew how to hide what they wanted hidden. And no, I don't know how they did it." He brooded on that a moment. "If I ever get that damn elfstone figured out, I'll be able to tell you more."

"The gem you snatched off Rethna, you mean? It's an artifact?" It had made bullets bounce off the elf lord. Or maybe they'd poofed out of existence. She didn't know how the gem worked, but she knew it worked. She'd shot Rethna several times at close range. Didn't hit him once.

"Oh, yeah. Tricky bugger. I haven't figured out how to activate it or get the rest of the spell to show, but the trigger shows, and I can see the power, so I know the charm didn't evaporate with Rethna's death."

"Which makes it an artifact." She opened the back door. No one in the kitchen, but Rule was upstairs. Maybe the Leidolf Rhej was with him. "And the fifth magical artifact you've seen? What about it?"

"With that one, nothing showed but power, even when it was used." He followed her inside. "Which ought to be impossible, because the trigger has to show. Otherwise there's nothing for the user to connect with."

"But you're sure it was an artifact?"

He slid her a grim smile. "Oh, yeah. But that one wasn't an adept's work. That was the staff *she* made."

ALL Rhejes were Gifted, but their Gifts varied. Two were healers. The Leidolf Rhej was one of those two, a statuesque woman with skin the color of hot chocolate made with plenty of milk. Her hair was a tight cap of mixed gray and black that showed off a high, round forehead and the pair of huge gold hoops in her ears. Lily didn't know her name. It was custom to not refer to a Rhej by name unless the Rhej gifted you with her name personally.

"No need to cram your lunch down so quick," she told Lily, leaning comfortably on her forearms, crossed on the round kitchen table. "I'm not going anywhere."

"I'm supposed to, though." Lily finished the corned beef sandwich she'd thrown together and reached for her glass of milk. She was usually a Diet Coke girl, but corned beef demanded milk. "Tell me something. Your Gift doesn't work on me, so why is it you can peek inside my body?"

"Same reason Mr. Gorgeous here can see your magic," she said promptly. "It's not vision I use, but it's a way of sensin'." She flashed Cullen an amused smile. He looked all twitchy with the need to interrupt . . . but she was a Rhej. Even Cullen managed a modicum of respect with a Rhej. "An' he's just dyin' to argue with me and explain it all real pretty, but you don't need all that talk. Does the Nokolai Rhej sense where you are, even though she can't see a thing?"

"Well . . . yes. But she's a physical empath."

"But your magic doesn't keep her from sensing you. The way I see it, physical empathy's a lot like healing, but a physical empath has all her Gift sittin' on the sensing side of things. A healer has a bit of that sensing, only we have to lay on hands to do it, and then we can look under the skin, not just on the top. But it's a sense, not that different from when Cullen here senses the shape of your magic." She smiled. "You 'bout ready to begin?"

Lily's stomach jittered unhappily. She didn't think it was the corned beef. "I guess so. Do I need to do anything?" The only healer who'd worked on Lily before was Nettie. This woman's methods might be different. Probably were, because she wasn't a shaman like Nettie was. Same Gift, different practice.

"Just a few questions first. Tell me about these headaches of yours. You've had three of them?"

"Yeah. They hurt pretty bad, but didn't last long. The first was just for seconds. A minute or less the second time. I'm not sure about the third."

"Just over a minute," Rule said. "I didn't time it, but it was probably between one and two minutes."

"Okay," the Rhej said. "Where'd it hurt?"

"Here." Lily rubbed the back of her head. "Um . . . the third time it happened, I was exhausted afterward. I couldn't stay awake."

"Any dizziness? Nausea? Weakness in one place more'n another? Any change in vision?"

"You mean like a migraine aura?"

"Any kind of change."

Lily shook her head. "I felt dizzy after it happened the third time. Exhausted. No nausea, though. I thought it might be some kind of migraine. My aunt has migraines."

"Let's find out. Give me your hands." The older woman stretched her hands across the table to Lily.

The Rhej had warm hands with wide palms and long fingers . . . and lots of magic. Healing magic, yes, and Lily loved to touch a healer's magic. If air could experience touch, it would feel like this beneath the slow stir of the summer sun, with new-grown grass blades brushing against it like a friendly cat. But there was more. Lily felt that more, banked and waiting and massive—the fur-and-pine prickle of lupi magic.

A Rhej could, at need, draw upon the magic of the entire clan. Lily had no idea how. The Rhej was fully human. She didn't hold the mantle, couldn't affect it, wasn't part of it. But she could use it to do what the Rho could not.

The Rhej's face smoothed out, her eyes losing focus. She hummed softly . . . "Amazing Grace," Lily realized. Maybe she did work with spiritual energy like Nettie did. Lily didn't feel anything. No wave of seeking magic touched her skin. She didn't get sleepy the way she usually did when Nettie examined her, but Nettie almost always ended up putting her in sleep, so . . .

"Cullen," the woman said in a low, soft voice, "I want you to look at that passenger of hers. Look real close and careful."

Rule frowned. "What is it?"

The Rhej shook her head without replying. Cullen slipped out of his chair and knelt on one knee beside Lily. "Push away from the table so I can see."

"I can't . . ." But the Rhej let go of Lily's hands so she could. She scooted her chair back and tried not to fidget while Cullen moved in front of her and stared intently at her abdomen. After a bit he frowned. He started muttering under his breath—it sounded like an unholy mix of Hawaiian and Norwegian—while he sketched signs in the air. He put his palms together as if he were praying, then drew them apart slowly, stopping when they framed about twenty inches of space.

He moved that space slowly up to Lily's neck, peering at it intently for several moments, then shifted so he could move behind Lily, holding his hands steady. She couldn't see what he did for several way-too-long moments. Her heart pounded.

Finally he moved back in front of her. His hands were only about ten inches apart now. He dragged those ten inches of empty space back down her trunk, pausing now and then, passing her stomach to study her pelvis. He snapped his fingers, releasing what Lily guessed was a magnifying spell.

Slowly he stood. "That . . . doesn't make sense."

"What did you see?" the Rhej asked.

"Roots. That's what they look like, tiny tendrils finer than a hair, too small to see without magnification. I found seven of them. They go from the mantle into her spinal cord. Four of them seem to stay there. Three of them . . ." He stopped, looked at Lily, then at Rule. "Three extend through the brain stem to the cerebellum and are tangled up in her brain."

"In my brain?" Lily's voice came out too high. "The mantle's doing something to me? It shouldn't be able to. My Gift wouldn't let it."

Rule clasped her hand tightly. "Even without your Gift, it shouldn't be doing that. Mantles don't root in their holder. They don't work that way." He looked sharply over his shoulder at Cullen. "You've never seen that with another mantle."

Cullen shook his head. He looked from Lily to Rule and back. Not at their faces, but their middles, as if he were comparing Rule's mantles to the one Lily harbored.

"I'm sorry," the Rhej said. "I can't say what's going on, but the mantle seems to be . . . changin' things in your body. Not in a way that makes sense to me. Not in a way that's good for you."

"Is it trying to make me lupi?" Lily's voice was still too high. She couldn't make it sound normal.

The Rhej shook her head slowly, her eyebrows drawn in a hard frown. "I don't know what it's doin'. Oh, it's healing that arm of yours—that's part of it—but the rest . . . maybe it is tryin' to turn you lupi and can't, but I've seen plenty of youngsters right close to First Change. There are neurological changes that occur then. But the changes I sense in you aren't what I sensed then. Maybe it's tryin' to heal you in a way your system isn't set up for. I don't know."

She met Lily's eyes. Her gaze was steady, but Lily saw trouble in those dark eyes. "But whatever the mantle's doin', it's not good for you. You've had two mini-strokes in the last few days. The mantle's healing that damage, but what else it's doin' . . . I don't have the medical words to describe that, but you need to get it out of you and where it belongs. You need to do that real soon."

"It's not all one way," Cullen said.

"What?" Lily craned her head to look up at him. "What do you mean?"

He gestured at her stomach. "The Wythe mantle is still purple, but it's the wrong shade of purple. It may be doing something to you, but you're doing something to it, too."

SIXTEEN

LILY reached the conference room she and Mullins were using a little after two thirty. Craig drove her, not Cullen. That pissed her off. She didn't know Craig well and hated the idea of having one of her headache fits in front of him. But Cullen needed to keep his afternoon free to go take a look at the dagger, and that was exactly what she wanted him to do. She had no damn reason to be angry.

Maybe her anger wasn't about Cullen.

She shoved the door open. Mullins looked up from a scatter of papers. "About time you got back."

The air was redolent with hamburger and onions. Lily could see the remains of Mullins's lunch pushed to one end of the table. She headed for the coffeepot. "You ever get in to see a doctor exactly on time?"

"Guess not. I want to take the secretary first."

"Nanette Beresford? Sure." Lily poured a cup of coffee.

The Rhej hadn't told her to avoid caffeine. She'd said Lily should "avoid exertion." No running. No late nights. Not that the healer knew for certain those things would hurt Lily. She was just guessing.

Mini-strokes. Dear God.

"The doctor gave you a green light?"

"I'm supposed to avoid strenuous exercise."

"Guess you'd better not chase me round the table, then. You were going to talk to your expert. Find out anything useful?"

"Parrott must be having his charm renewed every four weeks at the very least. Whether or not it does what he says, it would need renewal at least that often."

He grunted. "Doesn't tell us much. You sure you're okay? You look like crap."

"Headache. It won't interfere with the job." Except that her head didn't hurt right now, and it would interfere. She was lying and would keep on lying. She couldn't tell anyone about mantles, and she didn't see any way of explaining that a healer considered her life in danger without mentioning why. If she tried, she'd be pulled from the investigation and stuck in a hospital and they'd run tests, which wouldn't help because the doctors couldn't fix the mantle even if they knew about it.

She poured herself some coffee. Her arm shook ever so slightly. "We need to find out who made Parrott's charm. Who's renewing it. Maybe he's doing it himself, maybe he knows a really good practitioner—because it would take a real expert to make a strong, sophisticated charm like that." She sipped. It was this morning's brew, old and bitter. "Someone who can make a charm like that might be able to make a cursed dagger, too."

"Huh." He made a note on the paper in front of him. "I'll pass that on to Al. Worth looking into. Here's who we still need to talk to." He read a list of names.

Lily listened and sipped at the bitter sludge in her cup and tried so damn hard to think about the case, and not about ticking time bombs and Old Ones who used you for their own purposes and didn't care if it killed you or not. Not about Rule and the wild fear in his eyes, or how many people her dying would hurt, or how in the hell she could keep that from happening.

She went to get their first witness for the afternoon. And managed to focus on the case, on what the senator's secretary had to say, fairly well. But as soon as the interview was over, her attention splintered as needs nudged and shoved and yelled inside her. As she asked Nan to send in the next staffer—a young man with the interesting name of Kemo Maddon—one of those needs reared up and spoke clearly.

She wanted her mother.

How could she not smile at that thought? It was funny, it really was. Lily's mother drove her crazy, but she wanted her, wanted to be home, back in San Diego, maybe back in her narrow childhood bed, with the covers drawn up and her mother fussing at her.

Sometimes being a grown-up sucked.

THE wolf skidded to a stop atop the rock and earth dam that arced around this side of Mika's lair, his sides heaving. The air reeked of dragon. Beneath that smell were a thousand others—oak, rabbit, dirt, a hundred variations on green—the complex mix unique to this place at this time of the year. Added to that was a hint of approaching rain. And cat.

He hadn't known he was coming here. He'd just run flat out and this is where he ended up. Good. Sometimes instinct worked better than all that thinking the man was so fond of.

He turned to face the gray and black wolf scrambling up the slope behind him, lifting his lip in a silent snarl. Deliberately he pawed the ground three times—*back off and wait*.

José took Rule's signal literally. He stopped and began backing up.

Rule turned and picked his way down the rough slope more carefully than he'd shot up the other side. He didn't see Mika, and the wind was blowing the wrong way for his nose to tell him if the dragon was here. If not, he would be soon. Rule had crossed the dragon's wards. That was not allowed, not without an invitation. Mika would come, and quickly.

Good. Rule snarled at the empty, dragon-scented air. He would have answers.

He reached the level ground at the base of the slope. Stopped. *Mika!*

Rule put all the roil of intent and emotion he felt into that call. It wasn't mindspeech, but the dragon would hear. *Mika, I will speak with you!*

From the sunken place beneath the dome that used to shelter symphonies, a head lifted over the earthen rampart. That head was about the size of Rule's desk and resembled a seahorse's as much as it did a lizard's, with a narrow snout and domed skull and large eyes set on each side, eyes as brightly yellow as flame. Against the crimson scales an orange frill rippled along the dragon's jaws like fire teased by wind.

You annoy me, little wolf. You trespass and you yell. You are not usually such a fool. I do not have to kill to punish.

Words came harder in this form—even harder when emotion had him in its jaws, shaking him like a terrier shakes a rat. Instead of words, Rule remembered as hard as he could—remembered Lily falling from her chair, then announcing that she hadn't passed out; remembered Cullen speaking of roots sent out by the mantle, the Rhej saying that the mantle was harming Lily.

Peculiar, Mika said then. *I cannot see any reason your Lady would wish to damage Lily. Can you? Oh, do calm down. You can't attack me, and why should you? I am not the cause. Why are you here?*

Rule shook with the storm of rage-fear-attack surging through him. This was not good. He couldn't allow himself to be mastered by the storm in his gut. He dropped his jaw and breathed slowly, reaching for the place of icy clarity where thought and action merged, untroubled by the roil of emotion.

Certa was a battle state. But there was more than one sort of battle, wasn't there? *I would speak with Sam.*

I will pass your information to him when next I report.

I would speak to Sam directly. It was possible. Sam had told him so. Sam could mindspeak through Mika or any of the others if they gave permission to be used in this way.

That is absurd. Such sending takes far too much power. It is only for emergencies or—

I will speak with Sam through you, or I will withdraw Leidolf from the alliance.

You can't . . . you would? Sheer astonishment tinged that thought as Mika absorbed the truth of Rule's intentions. Slowly he oozed up out of the pit beneath the dome to end up standing on all four feet, his head raised high on that long, muscular neck. He looked down at Rule, yellow eyes glowing, orange frill spreading in agitation. *I ought to eat one of your legs to discourage such stubborn stupidity.*

Rule tipped his head back and bared his teeth. *Even if I do withdraw Leidolf, Nokolai is still allied with you, and I am still Nokolai. You can't attack me. You are bound by your word.*

Silence, both mental and physical, followed. Slowly Mika's frill subsided. He knew as well as Rule that Sam would not be happy if he refused and Rule did withdraw Leidolf. He probably understood the consequences better than Rule did. *I will see if Sam is willing to speak with you.*

Good.

Humans are very foolish.

I am not human.

Mika snorted. *You are certainly acting like one.*

"**ALL** right, Ella," Cullen said crisply, taking the Rhej's arm and turning her to face him. Lily was gone. Rule was gone. Time for some answers. "Tell me whatever it is you didn't want to tell them, and don't bother with that 'aw, shucks, I don't know them big medical words' shit. I know better."

Her smile came easily, but it was belied by the strain in her eyes. "I guess you do."

"TIAs can cause intense headaches, but they don't go away in seconds. And there should be other symptoms—vision changes, weakness, slurred speech. Something."

"That's true. But she's got damage in the cerebellum consistent with at least two transient ischemic attacks. Could've been a third that's already healed. Those two I found are nearly healed, much better'n I could do. Seems like that has to be the mantle fixin' what it's breakin'. Her tiredness afterward, that's likely the healing. It drains a person."

Cullen frowned hard to keep from tightening his grip on her arm. Or screaming. "Dizziness. She was dizzy the third time, toppled out of her chair, Rule said. You say there's damage in her cerebellum. Those damn roots come out through the cerebellum right next to the carotid artery."

She nodded wearily. "I checked the carotid. Didn't find a problem. I'm guessin' it's not occlusion TIAs she's having, but low-flow. Somehow every now an' then, those roots just shut down blood flow in the carotid artery."

"You could have told Rule and Lily any of this. There's something you aren't saying."

"Not a fact. Not somethin' I found."

"Something you believe or suspect."

Ella tugged against his hold, reminding him he still gripped her arm. He let go. "I'm reluctant to talk guesses."

"You're talking to me now. Not Lily. Not Rule. You'll feel better if you share it with someone."

Her smile tilted wryly. "I see that some things don't change. You are still one manipulative son of a bitch."

"She matters to me. They both matter to me. I need to help, but I can't if I don't have all the facts, guesses, wild-ass crazy notions."

"All right, then. What I suspect is happenin' is that the mantle keeps healing her . . . only she isn't lupus. Her body can't handle the kind of magic it uses. It's been healing her arm, but that's slow. It took a while for that kind of healing to strain things so much she had the first TIA. But if the mantle works like regular lupi healing, it prioritizes—and the brain is its first priority. So that TIA created a rush job."

"TIAs are by definition temporary. They don't cause lasting damage."

"The *symptoms* of a TIA are temporary. That don't mean there's no damage. Now, that damage is minor enough that the brain establishes a workaround pretty quick, but it's there. But the kind of healing you lupi do wants to make everything perfect, and it's her brain, so it heals her as fast as it can, only fast healin' is harder on Lily than the slow kind. She has another TIA. More rushed healing. Another TIA."

Fear tightened his throat. It made way too much sense. For four weeks after Lily accepted the job of host to Wythe's mantle the only thing that happened was the gradual healing of her arm. Then one very brief but blinding headache. The next day, two headaches—and they lasted a bit longer, weakened her more. "It won't stop. She'll keep having TIAs until one of them causes too much damage for the mantle to heal. It will try. And it will kill her."

SEVENTEEN

⁓

THE sky was dreary with pending rain when Lily slid her key into the lock, turned it, and shoved open the back door. She wanted Rule and he was not here. About ten miles to the northeast, she thought.

She could ask one of the guards where he'd gone. They'd probably know.

Hell with that. She shut the door, locked it, and dropped her purse. And stood there, clenching and unclenching her left hand, staring at a hole in the wall next to the pantry. A fist-sized hole.

Rule had needed to run, he'd said. When she left to go back to the job, he'd said he needed to run, and with the way his eyes had kept trying to bleed to black, she'd thought that was a good plan.

Apparently he'd also needed to put his fist through something. She could relate. Lily set her laptop on the table. "Cullen? You here?"

She heard footsteps on the stairs. "Quiet," he said as he got closer. "The Rhej is asleep. I was about to order pizza."

"No anchovies." The tight band around her shoulders eased slightly. Maybe it was just as well Cullen was here and Rule wasn't. Some things might be easier to talk about with him.

"And let the guards know about the delivery. Order plenty. Rule's headed this way." She hadn't noticed that at first, but now that she was paying attention she knew he was in motion, headed this way.

"Rule likes anchovies."

"I don't." She took out the coffee grinder. She used her left hand. It gripped the grinder just fine. "Maybe the Rhej doesn't. Did you ask?"

He snorted as he reached the kitchen. "Did you miss the part where I said she's asleep?"

"You could have asked before she fell asleep."

"I didn't. Rule called the Szøs Rho. That candidate he found for the Wythe mantle will be here tomorrow morning."

"He texted me about it."

"Huh." He tipped his head. "It isn't five o'clock yet."

"No. It isn't." She opened the canister where Rule kept his special-order, fresh-roasted coffee beans. "Did you get a look at the dagger?"

"I called Sherry and asked to put it off until tonight. We'll meet up there about eight. You're taking a coffee break?"

"I got sent home. One of those damn pain bolts hit me in front of Mullins, and he banished me."

Cullen's eyebrows climbed. "This Mullins guy told you to go home . . . and you did?"

"I didn't pass out." She brooded on that a moment. "I must've looked bad, though. I, uh, told him it was a migraine. He gave me a choice. Either I go home or he tells Drummond about my little problem." Unstated but clear was that Drummond would pull her if she couldn't pass a medical. The surprising part was that Mullins would cover for her at all.

Maybe he'd lied. Maybe he'd told Drummond anyway. She'd find out, she supposed. "This one was different."

"Different how?"

"I didn't get nearly as dizzy, and while I'm tired now, I'm nowhere near passing out. Only . . ."

"Keep going."

"It lasted longer, my vision went blurry, and my hand . . ." She held it out, studying it as if it didn't belong to her. "It went numb. I dropped my notebook, dropped the damn thing right in front of Mullins, and"—her brows snapped down—"and you're happy about that?"

"I am." He patted her shoulder. "That's excellent news. At least I think it is. Assuming your hand and vision are okay now—"

"They're fine." Automatically she squeezed her hand into a fist, proving once again that she could.

"Then it's good news. Probably. Sit down and I'll tell you what the Rhej told me. How long did the attack last?"

"Less than ten minutes. More than five. What did she tell you?"

"You aren't sitting down."

"Your keen powers of observation are a wonder to all of us." She spooned beans into the grinder. "I'll sit when I need to. Start talking."

He leaned against the counter, arms crossed, and wisely decided to accept that. "Consider what I tell you hemmed in by all sorts of qualifications about it being speculation. That's why the Rhej didn't pass it on to you and Rule earlier. First the part we're sure of. The mantle's been healing your arm."

"Slowly, yes."

"It looks like slowly is better than quickly for you. We—the Rhej and I—think the healing the mantle has been doing on your arm caused you to have that first TIA. The Rhej says that any TIA causes damage. Minor damage, so small that the long-term effects are close to nil, but the mantle doesn't seem to know that. Lupi healing sets priorities, and the brain's number one, so the mantle tried to heal that damage quick-quick. But that quick healing was too hard on you, so you had another TIA, which kept the cycle going."

"Shit." She slapped the button and the grinder buzzed away. "Double shit. Stupid damn mantle. Can't it tell it's screwing with me?"

"No. The mantle is a magical construct. It isn't sentient."

"That's what Rule always says, but it's not an artifact like that damn staff you burned. I don't care what you say." She rested a hand on her stomach, frowning. "It's . . . it feels like it's alive."

"Oh, yes."

"But you said—"

"I said it's a magical construct. I didn't say it lacked life. Artifacts are charms on steroids. Constructs are—pay attention here, this gets complicated—*constructed*. And *sentient* means—"

"Capable of thought and reason. Which, okay, I'm not doing so hot with right now." She scraped the newly ground coffee into the insulated French press she'd bought Rule a couple months ago. "So the mantle's alive, but it doesn't think."

"Let's not try to define *thinking* right now. Suffice it to say that mantles can't be reasoned with and give no signs of reasoning on their own, which is why it's doing the wrong damn thing with you. But living things are capable of learning or adapting. Some more than others. Plants pretty much suck at learning, but they can adapt to some extent."

"So what kind of living thing is a mantle? Plant, virus, bacteria, cute little kitten?"

"The immortal kind."

She stared. "But they can die. That's why I've got the Wythe mantle in here causing all these problems—to keep it from dying."

"If the holder of a mantle dies without an heir to receive the mantle, the mantle is lost, not dead. The constructed part is destroyed. The living part goes back where it came from. Back to the Lady. Mantles hold a bit of the Lady's life within them."

It made a weird kind of sense. The mantles were what kept lupi from being beast-lost. They imbued Rhos with authority that was literally inarguable . . . and the lupi's Lady was the one authority lupi would not or could not deny. "Why didn't I know this?" she demanded. "I've asked Rule questions about the mantles dozens of times. I've talked with the Nokolai Rhej about them. Why didn't I already know this?"

Cullen's mouth quirked up. "Because it's a secret."

"Ninety-five percent of everything about you people is a secret!"

"This one is secret from pretty much everyone. Only the Rhejes and the mantle-holders know."

"Then how did you . . . oh." Cullen had been born to Etorri, not Nokolai. Etorri was a very small clan, steeped in honor, and—for complicated historical reasons—the heir's portion of their mantle was shared among all Etorri lupi, not just the one their Rho named heir. Which was—natch—a secret, and meant that Cullen had been a mantle-holder once. Only a small bit of a mantle, but he'd been there, done that, and had apparently been given both the T-shirt and the secret hand-shake. "You're breaking the rules by telling me this."

"Technically, you're carrying a mantle now yourself. And you need to understand why Rule's control is splintering."

She glanced at the hole in the wall. "That's not hard to un-derstand."

"If all he does is put his fist through a wall now and then, we'll be lucky. Rule believes the Lady has betrayed him."

"Because she shoved this thing into me without clueing us in about the consequences? That pisses me off, too." Lily had had to give permission, but apparently Old Ones didn't worry about informed consent.

"Lily." He sighed. "The Wythe mantle is doing something it should not be able to do. Mantles don't send out little roots. They are controlled by their holders—within limits for the heirs, and entirely by the Rhos. There's only one exception, one way the mantles can act without direction by a Rho. They are of the Lady. If a mantle starts doing something wholly new, we have to think that she's directing it."

"*She's* making it try to kill me?"

"That's unlikely," the Leidolf Rhej said.

Lily damn near dropped the coffeepot. "Dammit, how did you do that? You're not lupus. You shouldn't be able to come down those stairs that quietly."

The woman smiled wearily. "Maybe you're a little preoc-cupied."

Maybe so. "Why do you think the Lady isn't trying to kill me?"

"If you die, the Wythe mantle is lost."

Oh. That was a lot better answer than the sort of "have faith" argument Lily had been expecting. "Then maybe she's just not very good at whatever she's doing."

"Could be. We don't have any idea what she is doin'. As far as we know, she hasn't fiddled with a mantle since she changed

Etorri's, but Cullen says she's doin' something to this one. Whatever she has in mind, though, I'm sure she doesn't want you to die, which is why I agreed with Mr. Gorgeous here about what we might do to help a bit."

"What do you mean?"

"I hadn't told her that part," Cullen said.

"Good. You makin' coffee, honey? I could sure use some." She headed for the table, moving as if her body was twice as heavy as it had been earlier.

Lily suppressed her impatience and grabbed the kettle. "Coffee's coming. What did you do that left you so tired?"

"Made some phone calls, then spent some time in the memories." She sat at the big, round table with a sigh.

When the Rhej said she'd spent time "in the memories," she meant she'd essentially relived certain events. The memories were just that—actual memories magically preserved and passed from Rhej to Rhej. A lot of them were from the Great War. All of them involved key events, which meant heaping doses of disaster, death, betrayal, battle, pain, tragedy . . . and, now and then, triumph.

Also—now and then—spells. Spells such as hadn't been cast since the Purge. Spells that had been lost centuries *before* the Purge. Adept-level spells, some of them. Which was one reason Cullen was so damn twitchy about Rhejes. They knew things he desperately wanted to learn, and they weren't talking.

Maybe there was a spell that would help Lily now. She put the kettle on the stove, glanced toward the front of the house, then at the Rhej. "I hope it was worth it. You learned something?"

"A technique that hasn't been used for a very long time. The Wythe Rhej—she was one of those phone calls—agreed to try it. The idea is to pull enough power out of the mantle that it has to slow down on healin' you. Slower healin' should mean less damage. In addition to that, I want you to stay close to Rule. Physically close. The mate bond may be able to help."

Lily's eyebrows shot up. "She can pull power from the mantle? I knew she could pull power from the clan as a whole, but to take it directly from the mantle . . . that seems like a different deal."

"It is," the Rhej said grimly. "And it is not recommended. It makes the mantle vulnerable. Lily, you're Lady-touched, so it's okay for you to know about this, but you can't speak of it to anyone. Neither of you can." She fixed Cullen with a firm stare. "Rhej's seal."

"I have no objection to secrets," he said, "as long as I'm the one keeping them." He made a graceful gesture with one hand, touching his lips then his heart. "It is sealed, serra."

The kettle started whistling as the Rhej turned that imperative stare on Lily.

"Sure," Lily said, retrieving the kettle. "Except for Rule, of course."

The Rhej shook her head. "Especially not Rule."

"Serra—" Cullen began.

"No. None of the Rhos are to know about this."

Too late. "I can't agree to that."

"Nor can I," Rule said from the doorway.

"Good timing." Lily poured steaming water into the French press. "Coffee's almost ready."

RULE breathed deeply of the kitchen's smells—the richness of coffee blended with undertones from last night's shepherd's pie, the spicy-sharp meatiness of corned beef, notes of lupus from Cullen . . . and Lily. It smelled of Lily. "I gather you found a way to drain power from the mantle."

The Rhej frowned unhappily. "I gather you were eavesdropping."

"I overheard, yes, but how is it eavesdropping to walk into my own home?" He walked up behind Lily and put his arms around her from behind. She leaned back into him. He closed his eyes, wishing they could stand here, just stand here like this, for an hour or two. "If it makes you feel better, I will honor the Rhej's seal you have declared on this knowledge."

"Not much," she said dryly, "but it's something. We're hopin' that draining the mantle some might help Lily."

"Did help," Cullen corrected, "or so it seems."

Rule stood quietly, holding Lily while the coffee steeped and the others told him about Lily's latest brain-bolt—that was her term—her temporary banishment from the investigation, and about what Cullen and the Rhej had discussed . . . a discussion they'd purposefully left him out of. He didn't bother being angry about that. His anger had more important targets.

". . . basically, we hoped slowin' the healing would slow the occurrence of the TIAs," the Rhej finished. "And drainin' the mantle was the one way we could think of to slow things down."

"That seems clear, yes," he said, sipping the coffee Lily had handed him. She was taking her own mug over to the table. He sent her a smile. "You've gotten good at coffee."

"It's a matter of priorities." She sat beside the Rhej. "Coffee's important."

Priorities. Yes, he'd learned something about his this day. He sat beside her. "I also heard something about us staying physically close. It seems a good idea. The mate bond has sometimes helped."

The Rhej's eyebrows lifted. "You figured that out on your own, Rule? That the healing was causing the problem?"

"Once I'd run a few miles I did, or suspected it, at least. Sam agrees."

"Sam?" This time it was Lily's eyebrows that shot up. "I'm pretty sure he doesn't have phone service."

"Sam is able to mindspeak through any of the other dragons, if they agree to allow it. I persuaded Mika this was important enough to make such a contact. The three of us, ah . . . discussed your condition." Before they could talk about Lily's condition, Mika had briefed Sam about what he'd observed during his training session with Lily.

If *briefed* was the right word. That communication hadn't involved anything Rule recognized as words, thoughts, or images. Rule had damn near passed out. Mika had forgotten to separate that channel from the link the three of them were sharing, and wolf brains weren't physically able to handle that form of communication.

Rule was glad he could heal quickly. He'd still had a headache for a while. "Sam says the mantle's actions are affecting Lily's Gift."

"The roots?" Cullen said, sitting up straighter.

Rule wobbled his hand in a yes-and-no way. "We don't know what the roots are doing. Maybe they're healing her. Maybe they're doing something else."

"Like what?"

"I don't know. Sam declined to guess. Specifically, he said he does not 'presume to guess what purpose an Old One holds, nor to meddle with that purpose.' I gather that means he doesn't know what the Lady is doing, but he agrees that she's up to something."

"Nothing that involves Lily's death," the Rhej said firmly. "The Lady does not want to lose that mantle."

"I never heard that the mantle-holder's brain had to be firing on all cylinders," Lily said, "and Leidolf's last Rho pretty much proved otherwise. So the fact that the Lady wants to keep me alive isn't as reassuring as it might be."

"Yes." Rule's voice was desert-dry, as bleached of emotion as a cow skull. The mantle would be fine as long as it was in a living host. It didn't matter if the host's brain was damaged. "So I concluded also."

"Rule—"

"I'm all right. Let me finish this the way Sam told it. We knew the Lady had done something to allow the Wythe mantle to rest within Lily without Lily's Gift absorbing it. Sam says the Lady persuaded Lily's magic that the mantle is part of Lily. This should have kept the two magics from interacting. The problem arises from the healing, but also because of the nature of Lily's Gift. Very young dragons can't control their healing, so—"

Cullen's eyebrows shot up. "Adult dragons control their healing?"

"Apparently. If a dragon who hasn't yet learned this control is seriously injured, he's subject to a condition called *netha* in which his natural immunity to magic is set askew by the large amount of power needed for healing. What Lily is experiencing is similar to *netha*."

Lily shook her head. "My Gift seems to be working fine."

"It wouldn't affect the way your Gift works. Sam likened *netha* to an allergic reaction in which the body's immune system becomes hypersensitive or confused and overreacts to some substance. Your Gift is overreacting to the healing."

"You're telling me it's my own Gift that's causing the TIAs."

"Boiled down, yes."

Lily scowled and drummed her fingers once on the table. "If Sam can figure all this out from over two thousand miles away, seems like your Lady should've been able to guess it could happen when she first stuck this mantle in me. Old One, vast amounts of knowledge—they go together, don't they?"

Oh, yes. Yes, the Lady must have known. The wild rage surged up like a sandstorm, tattering thought, fraying his control—

"Rule." Lily closed her hand firmly over his.

He took a slow breath. Looked down at the table, at her hand on his. *I am not whole.* "I would speak with my *nadia* privately."

"Sure." Cullen shoved his chair back.

"That," Lily said, "was a very Rho way to handle it."

He looked at her, puzzled.

She squeezed his hand. "You didn't excuse us so we could go to another room. You just let everyone know what you wanted."

He didn't understand her point. "I was courteous."

Her mouth tipped wryly. "Yes, you were. Never mind." She looked at Cullen. "About those pizzas . . . is ten large enough, if we're including the guards?"

Six guards plus the four of them in the room. . . . "Better make it a dozen." Rule lifted up so he could retrieve his wallet.

"I've got it," Cullen said.

It was for him to feed his people. "No."

"Yes. I've got your card number."

Of course he did. Rule nodded.

The Rhej had stood, too, and moved behind Lily, placing her hands on Lily's shoulders. "I won't tell you to have faith. Faith is for God, not the Lady. But she's good people. She'll do right by you."

Lily looked uncomfortable. That was probably more because the Rhej had brought God into the conversation than because she didn't agree with the Rhej. She took a swallow of coffee to hide her discomfort. "I'll bear that in mind. So how do you feel about anchovies?"

"Nasty little . . ." The Rhej stopped. Stilled. "Do that again."

"What?" Lily craned her head around to look up at the woman. "Talk about anchovies?"

"Take another swig of coffee. A nice big one."

"Uh . . . okay." Lily did just that.

For a long moment no one spoke or moved. Then the Rhej nodded slowly. "Honey, I think you're going to like this prescription. I want you to drink lots of coffee."

"I always thought coffee affected you." Lily refilled her mug.

Rule was leaning against the counter, frowning into his own mug. "I'm still not sure about it."

Lily smiled and shook her head. Stubborn man. "The Rhej can sense what happens when a lupus drinks coffee. If she says it affects you, that's good enough for me."

"It's what she said about it affecting the mantle I have trouble with. Nothing affects the mantles."

Rule had always maintained that he enjoyed coffee purely for the scent and flavor. Caffeine couldn't affect him any more than any other drug. His healing eliminated the effects too quickly. Lily had suspected he was fooling himself.

Turned out she was right . . . if, that is, you believed the expert.

That shouldn't be much of a stretch. There weren't many things that affected lupi, but a few herbs did, like wolfbane. According to the Leidolf Rhej, coffee acted like both stimulant and sedative on lupi, heightening concentration while calming them. The mechanism was different than for humans. It was the scent—the vaporized brew—that did it. Drinking coffee increased the effect, but not because of what was swallowed. Vapors travel from the mouth up the sinuses to scent receptors in the nasal passages, so drinking it increased exposure to the vapors.

For lupi, it was all about the smell.

The Rhej believed coffee acted on the mantle itself because the effects were strongest in mantle-holders. She couldn't be sure. She sensed the physical, and the mantle was all power, no substance, so she couldn't monitor what happened directly. But she was sure of the effect.

She was also sure of what coffee did for Lily. She'd sensed that clearly when she was touching Lily while she sipped from her mug. Whether because it affected the Wythe mantle or for some other reason, coffee did good things for the blood supply to Lily's brain. Things that made a TIA less likely.

"The Rhej treated Victor with coffee," Lily said. "It made him calmer, she said."

"I am not Victor Frey."

"Thank God." The man who'd been Rho of Leidolf before Rule had been vicious and unprincipled . . . and that was before he went batwing nuts. Lily took a thoughtful swallow of coffee.

Had she been craving the stuff more than usual? Maybe. Probably, she admitted as she counted up the cups she'd drunk today. The Rhej had asked her that. She thought Lily had been unconsciously reaching for something that helped.

The Rhej and Cullen were in the living room, banished ever so politely because Rule needed to talk to her. So far, he wasn't saying much. Lily walked up to him, set her mug on the counter, and slid her arms around his waist. "I know you'd rather that the mantles were invulnerable, but I'd just as soon believe the Rhej is right."

His mug joined hers on the counter. He put his arms around her and rested his cheek on the top of her head. "I want coffee to work. To help. I want that so badly I don't dare believe it." He paused. His breath was warm on her hair. "I asked Sam to remove the mantle from you."

She jerked her head up. "You what? You did what? Sam couldn't . . . could he?"

"He can't. Or won't. I'm not sure which. He called me a fool and said it was as well that he wasn't one, also. I asked if he could help you in some other way. That's when he said he doesn't tamper in the plans of Old Ones. Lily." He ran both hands into her hair. "I understand better now why it's so hard for you to consider joining the Shadow Unit."

His eyes were dark and focused intensely on her. She rested a hand on his chest. His heart beat steady and slow. "Okay. Why?"

"You don't know who you are if you aren't first a cop. I knew that, but I didn't . . ." He sifted her hair with his fingers as if he might find words there. "I didn't understand in my gut. Now I do. I learned that I'm not . . . I'm no longer the Lady's first. I still serve her, but she's not first. If I must choose between you and her—"

"Don't. Don't try to choose."

He placed his hand over hers. "Too late. I already have."

EIGHTEEN

⟋

LILY bent over the young man sitting in one of the kitchen chairs and breathed into his mouth.

Nothing. Stupid damn mantle. She sighed and straightened. "That was awkward."

"Hey, I enjoyed it." Chad Emerson of Szøs had light brown hair, baby blue eyes, and a brash grin he knew very well was charming. "Maybe we should try a kiss."

"It wouldn't help, and it would annoy me."

"That's not the usual reaction."

She could believe that. Chad looked a bit like Harrison Ford circa Han Solo. "Let me rephrase that. It would annoy me if you kept flirting with me."

"That's also not the usual—"

"Chad," Rule said, "did Andor tell you why we asked you to fly here sooner than we'd originally planned?"

"He said something had come up. He didn't say what."

"The mantle is affecting Lily's health. It's become urgent that we find a lupus who can carry it."

"Shit, I'm sorry." He drooped like a scolded puppy. "I didn't mean . . . to tell the truth, I don't really want to leave Szøs. Nothing against Wythe, but I've been Szøs all my life. I'm not sure about becoming a Rho, either. It's a huge respon-

sibility, and being Rho to a clan other than mine . . . I know it
would become mine, but it isn't now. I'm not sure I'm up to it.
But, well, I gave permission before like you said I should, but
maybe my doubts kept me from meaning it all the way." He
leaned forward. "I'd mean it now. Maybe we should start over
with the permission part."

Lily glanced at Rule. He shrugged—why not?—so they
tried again. Chad agreed very sincerely to accept the mantle,
should the Lady be willing to bestow it on him.

The results didn't change. The mantle never twitched.

Chad was troubled. Lily was tired—drinking umpteen cups
of coffee did not make for a restful night's sleep. Rule was
impassive. He thanked the young man and took out his phone
to call a cab. Between Cullen and the Rhej, they were out of
bedrooms, so Rule had booked Chad into a hotel. Lily thanked
Chad, too, and Rule walked him to the door. She could hear
Rule assuring him he could linger in D.C. a day or two on
Nokolai's dime, if he wished.

Lily refilled her coffee, then stood quietly, frowning at
her mug.

Chad was young and cocky. More to the point, he was a
dominant. Lily was still working out exactly what that term
meant to lupi, but the dominant package definitely included a
take-charge attitude. Chad was also bright enough to realize
that there was a huge dose of sacrifice that came with the status and power of being Rho, and honest enough to be unsure
he was ready for the responsibility. He was also generous
enough to "mean it all the way" once he knew Lily was being
harmed by her stewardship of Wythe's mantle.

If he wasn't good enough for the mantle, who would be?

She sipped her coffee and moved to look out the back window. It was early still. Last night's rain hadn't cleared out the
cloud cover; whatever nudges the sun might be making toward
rising hadn't yet penetrated the gloom. She couldn't see whoever had guard duty . . . but then, she seldom did.

Overhead, the pipes rattled as someone turned on the
shower. The Leidolf Rhej was up. Lily knew it must be her
because Cullen had woken a couple hours ago. He'd picked
Chad up at the airport, fed him breakfast someplace, then

dropped him off here before leaving on some mysterious errand.

Maybe something to do with the dagger? He'd been awfully quiet about what he'd seen after inspecting it with Sherry last night. Lily shook her head, trying to shake her thoughts back on track.

The thing was, Lily had never met Chad before today. He didn't know her, but he'd been ready to upend his life to help her. Maybe that was, in part, a sense of fairness, of responsibility; the mantle belonged with a lupus, not an all-too-human Chosen. It also arose from the lupi's deep-seated need to protect women . . . and, she thought, from his personal need to do the right thing.

She understood that need. Rule said he understood now why joining the Shadow Unit would be hard for her. He was right, but there was more to it.

If she wasn't a cop *first*, how would she know the right thing to do? What metric would she use? When you were up against such powerful forces, when the stakes were so ungodly high, it could seem downright immoral to choose ethics over expediency. "Whatever works" becomes the default if you don't have clear and compelling reasons to handle things otherwise.

Lily was pretty sure that was the answer the Great Bitch had come up with a couple eons ago: whatever works.

Yet that hadn't really worked for the Great Bitch, had it? She'd been defeated once, forced to withdraw from this realm and lick her wounds. Whatever she'd been doing for the last three thousand years, she'd had to do it because "whatever works" hadn't worked.

Did the lupi's Lady understand that "whatever works" was a failed metric?

The front door closed. Lily didn't hear Rule heading back to the kitchen, but she felt him moving her way. She turned away from the window. They had to hope the Lady understood, or they were all screwed—Lily in an immediate way, but everyone else, too. If the Old One on their side was as "anything goes" as the one they opposed, they were in deep shit.

"We haven't exhausted the possibilities," Rule said as he entered the kitchen. "I called my father while Chad and I waited for the cab. He'll be urging the other Rhos to step up the pace in their search."

She nodded. They were doing all they could. They had to hope it would be enough . . . and in the meantime, she'd be drinking a lot of coffee. And the Wythe Rhej, presumably, would continue to keep the mantle turned down to "low." "I haven't had a pain bolt since yesterday afternoon."

"True." His smile looked effortless. It would be easy to think he was as unworried as he looked. Wrong, but easy.

It was a gift, that smile. He wanted her not to worry, to be confident, so he suppressed everything he was feeling to project that confidence. Lily knew what he was doing, and still it helped. "I love you."

He blinked. "Ah . . . yes?"

She laughed. It was rare for him to be flustered. "Just that. I love you. You're doing everything possible, and so are others, and we're going to kick this thing's ass." Might as well believe that. What was the good in thinking otherwise? She went to him, put a hand on his shoulder, and went up on tiptoe so she could touch his lips with hers. "No, don't grab me. I need to get my weapon and get going."

"It's barely seven."

"I need to get to Headquarters early." She started for the stairs. Her shoulder harness was in their bedroom.

He followed. "You haven't eaten."

"I'll eat in the car. Since I have to be chauffeured, that'll be easy. I want one of those enormous muffins from that bakery on Jefferson."

The argument that followed was brief and mild and comfortingly familiar. Rule might know in his head that she couldn't eat the way a lupus did, but the irrational underneath part of his mind couldn't believe a muffin was a meal for anyone.

"The muffin will be plenty," she repeated as she buckled her shoulder harness. "What's your schedule like today? Are you up for a change of plans?"

"I could be. Why?"

"I thought you might go with me."

His eyebrows shot up. "You want me to meet the minion?"

"I'm going to talk to Croft. It's Saturday, but he'll be there. I checked. I ought to tell Drummond myself," she admitted, "but I can't bring myself to do it. Besides, Croft will accept the 'clan secrets' deal and not press me for more than I can tell him."

"Lily, you haven't explained anything."

She sighed. Sometimes doing the right thing was a bitch. "I'm not dependable right now. I've gone sixteen hours without an episode, but I could get zapped again at any time. Right in the middle of an interview, maybe. Or shit, who knows—in the middle of an arrest, or a chase, or . . . I can't even say what the next pain bolt will do. Make me drop things or drool or fall down or all of the above. Or something new. I have to tell Croft so he can have someone else from the Unit take over."

"You're removing yourself from the investigation."

"Officially, yeah."

He was silent for several heartbeats. "And unofficially?"

"That's why I'd like you along. Rule . . ." She moved closer so she could take his hand. "Chad knew the mantle wouldn't go to him unless the Lady wanted him to have it, right?"

"Yes, we explained that the Lady may have to move the mantle herself. This isn't the normal way of transferring it."

Lily nodded. "So Chad knew that if the mantle did come to him, that would be the Lady's doing. And he wanted to be willing to accept the Lady's decision. He wanted to . . . but he didn't become wholly willing until he knew I needed it to happen. That I was being endangered by hosting the mantle."

"Yes." His eyes were puzzled. "Of course he wanted to help you."

"Because I'm a woman." She smiled wryly. "That's how you're all wired—protect the woman. Your Lady knows you pretty well. I guess she made you that way. That choice you said you made? She can't be upset about it. She knew you'd choose to protect me. It may take a while for you to come to terms with what it means, but don't think your Lady is surprised or disappointed."

"Lily."

She tipped her head.

He lifted the hand she'd clasped his with to his lips and kissed it. "I love you."

RULE had been to FBI Headquarters many times. In the past, the man seated at the large, scuffed desk in this windowless office had been Ruben Brooks. Today it was a lean man with skin the color of the coffee in Lily's thermos.

Martin Croft looked more like a Harvard don than a cop. His gray-spattered hair was staging a strategic withdrawal from his high forehead, and he dressed too well to fit any cop stereotype. His shirt was impeccably pressed, his tie silk, and while his suit might be off the rack, it was of excellent quality and fit. Rule suspected he'd had it tailored. All in all, Croft didn't look like a man who'd wrestled many a suspect to the ground.

In that much, appearances were deceiving. But he was every bit as bright as he looked—and completely unGifted, though he knew more about magic than most practicing witches.

Croft listened gravely as Lily told him why she'd needed to see him so early and so urgently. She looked tired.

No surprise. She'd had an attack—a TIA—as soon as they left the house. It had lasted longer than the other one he'd witnessed, which was supposed to be a good thing, indicating the healing was being slowed. He wasn't able to see it that way.

Rule had taken her home, of course. And of course she'd protested. The Leidolf Rhej had checked her out, but there was nothing more she could do save assure them both that so far there was no lasting brain damage.

Lily finished her highly edited explanation. Croft said, "How serious is your condition?"

"Potentially serious, but we have a healer staying with us. She's confident she can help. She already has, but my condition is still, ah, unresolved."

"And your condition is related in some way you can't specify to a clan matter you're unable to discuss."

"That's right."

"And you're certain that conventional medicine can't help."

"Quite certain."

"Why did you bring Rule with you?"

"You're aware of the mate bond."

He nodded. Croft knew about the mate bond because he was *ospi* to Wythe. His mother was the daughter of a Wythe lupus, and either she or his grandfather had passed on a bit more about clan secrets than they should have.

"We believe it mitigates my symptoms if Rule stays close to me."

"Hmm." He steepled his fingers together in a way that was disconcertingly like Ruben. Had he consciously copied his boss, or was it unconscious mimicry? "You need to be pulled from active duty."

She sighed. "I'm afraid so."

"Very well. I'll contact Drummond."

"Who will you replace me—"

But he was shaking his head. "If you aren't part of the investigation, you aren't privy to anything about it anymore. I certainly can't speak of it in front of Rule. I'm sorry."

Lily's lips tightened, but she didn't argue. Rule wanted to take her hand, to assure her she'd done the right thing, but he knew better. No hand-holding in front of her boss. She would consider it unprofessional. Rule understood, though he'd put it differently. Being professional in this sense meant "don't show your belly."

"I'll tell Drummond this is related to your wound," Croft said. "There's little point in telling him it's due to something I'm unable to discuss because you can't discuss it. The man's got an attitude where magic's concerned as it is. No point in raising his hackles."

"What kind of an attitude? Is it magic itself he dislikes or—"

"Enough." But Croft grinned. It was a tired grin but real enough, the first sign Rule had seen of the man rather than the man's position this morning. Professionalism again. "I'm not going to gossip with you. Lily, you're worrying me. Off the record, can you tell me anything else?"

She couldn't, of course. Croft's mother or grandfather

might have shared more than was strictly allowed, but hadn't gone so far as to speak about mantles. So Lily refused as tactfully as possible and stood. "I won't take any more of your time. I know you're jammed."

Croft rose as well, which should have signified the end to a meeting Rule knew had been hard on Lily. But he walked around his desk and touched Lily's arm. "I'll see that you have the leave you need. Take care of yourself." His dark eyes were worried. He turned to Rule. "I'm sure I can count on you to see that she gets all the help possible."

"You can." Rule decided to step them all back from all this careful professionalism. "You look tired, Martin."

Croft shrugged. "I'm hoping Ruben can come back soon. For his sake, of course, but also selfishly. I miss fieldwork."

"You're very much needed here."

"I'm a decent administrator, but I was a damn good investigator. I want to get back to what I'm best at, but . . ."

"But if you weren't doing this job, someone with less understanding of the Unit would be. Or one of the Gifted agents would be promoted to a desk, and they're needed in the field."

"Exactly." He ran a hand over his hair. "With your people, Rhos face the same problem, don't you? There has to be distance between the Rho and everyone else, plus they have to stay denned up at their clanhomes. Except that you don't. Stay denned up, I mean. How do you pull that off?"

"Two clans," Rule said. "Two sets of duties. And I can't be the public face for my people if I never leave Clanhome."

"Hmm. Rule, I won't ask if Lily has told you anything about the investigation she's been on. I do need to make it clear that the order for silence on this one came from the director himself."

"I see." That was a clear enough signal for him to stay out of it . . . which wasn't what Lily had in mind. "If one of my people just happened to be in the park across the street from the senator's house, would you be interested in hearing about any unusual smells that he notices?"

Martin shook his head. "You're as stubborn as she is, but more diplomatic. Hypothetically speaking, yes, I would."

"I'll keep that in mind. I hope to see you again soon, Martin, when things are less difficult for all of us."

Croft walked out with them, stopping at Ida's desk to give her instructions for the form he needed to sign concerning Lily's leave.

Rule and Lily started down the long hall. "That's a good idea," she said, "having someone sniff along that trail I followed."

"I thought of it while we were headed here." He glanced at her. "You look relieved. Glad to get that over with?"

"Oh, yes." She lowered her voice so only he would be able to hear. There were others in the hall. "And damn glad Croft isn't going to be too upset when he finds out what we're about to get up to."

"And yet he made a point of bringing up the order for silence."

"He made a point of it being the director's order. That means he doesn't agree with it. He has to enforce it, but he doesn't like it, and maybe he suspects I'm not going to spend the rest of the day in my sickbed."

"Ah." Was this convoluted, don't-say-it method a purely human style of communication? One common to cops? Or one used by bureaucrats in any large organization? "How would he have signaled that he supported the director's order wholeheartedly?"

"He'd have said it to me, not you. And he would have restated it as his order. If he . . . later," she muttered. "We'll talk about it later."

They'd reached the elevator. Three others were waiting: a tall woman with rimless glasses, a short Asian man, and a bald, middle-aged man, possibly Pakistani. Lily greeted the bald man and pushed the down button. Quite unnecessarily, since it was already glowing, but if you provide humans with a button, they will push it.

The doors opened. A short blond woman in red-framed glasses and a severely tailored black suit got out. Her mouth was a perfect cupid's bow. "Lily!" Anna Sjorensen's delight was obvious. "I haven't had a chance to thank you properly. I guess you don't have time to chat now."

"A minute or two, maybe. We need to make time later to grab coffee or something." Lily smothered whatever impatience she felt and stepped aside, letting the others enter the elevator. It was a kind move, especially because Rule was sure she didn't realize Sjorensen had a bad case of hero worship. "But no thanks are necessary. You needed training."

"Which I would never have gotten if not for you." Sjorensen paused and said civilly, if coolly, "Hello, Mr. Turner."

"Make it Rule, please." He doubted that she would, but that wouldn't matter, because she didn't want to talk to him anyway.

Sure enough, Sjorensen's attention zipped right back to Lily. Rule listened as the two talked about the training the younger woman was receiving for her minor patterning Gift. He listened, but that wasn't the only sense he used, and he had the satisfaction of solving a small puzzle.

The elevator came and went and another small crowd had gathered when Lily glanced at her watch. "It's ten till eight. I'm going to have to take the next elevator. It was good running into you, Anna."

"Oh, yes. And I do have to thank you, whether you like it or not. If you hadn't gotten me here for training, I wouldn't be part of the investigation." She leaned closer to add softly, "We've got a lead on the dagger."

"Oh?" Lily didn't bat an eye. "Maybe you can tell me about it later."

"Later would be best." Sjorensen grimaced prettily. The poor woman did everything prettily, which was why she wore severe suits and kept her hair so short. "I have to go, too. I'm supposed to be in Croft's office in ten. See you soon, I hope."

Lily frowned as she got on the elevator with Rule and three others. "She's not Unit."

"Croft could transfer her now, if he wanted."

"I know. And she's bright enough, but . . ."

"Inexperienced."

Lily nodded, her expression abstracted. They got off on the ground floor and turned left. There were four entrances to Headquarters; one for freight; two for Bureau personnel; and one for the public. Lily usually avoided the one the public used because it meant passing two checkpoints, but Rule had to turn in his visitor's badge.

In a low voice he said, "You didn't mention to Anna that you weren't part of the team anymore."

"If you're thinking I should have—"

"I'm glad you're being your usual inquisitive self. If Croft wants to be sure no one talks to you, he'll tell them so. As for Sjorensen . . . she's bi, you know."

"What?"

"Bisexual."

"What are you talking about? Why are you telling me this?"

"That's why she doesn't like me. Not because I'm lupus, as we had suspected. She has a major crush on you, so she's jealous, not bigoted. Possibly she thinks of herself as lesbian, which would make her attraction to me both unwelcome and suspicious. She may think I'm putting out some mysterious, magical sexual juju on purpose."

"I cannot imagine why you're telling me this."

"You need to understand the people who are your allies. If you . . . Lily?" He stopped, taking her arm. "Are you—"

"You don't see it." She was staring at the checkpoint where people were admitted to the secure area they were in. A guard made sure that everyone passing that point had an ID or visitor's badge. The IDs were scanned; visitors had to sign in and out. "Of course you don't see it."

"What?"

"The ghost. He ran his ID through the scanner, nodded at the guard as he walked passed, and vanished."

NINETEEN

~~

"NONE?" Lily said. "Okay, okay. I'm not arguing, I just . . . yeah, go ahead. Might as well be sure. Thanks, Arjenie." She disconnected and frowned at her phone.

"Arjenie couldn't find anyone recently deceased who fits your ghost's profile?" Rule asked.

She looked over at him. Rule was behind the wheel himself for once. Not that they'd gotten away without any guards, but they were in Lily's government vehicle because Cullen was AWOL in Rule's, and Lily refused to sit in her own backseat. Rule refused to sit back there by himself, so Scott was.

Lily shook her head. "Not an agent, not a secretary or a clerk or researcher or janitor. No male working at Headquarters has died lately." And Arjenie would be able to find out. She might be living in California now to be close to Rule's brother Benedict, but she was still a Bureau researcher, with access to pretty much any database her little heart desired. "She's going to expand the search to include frequent visitors to Headquarters."

"Someone who visited often enough to make going through the checkpoint routine."

"Yeah." She drummed her fingers on her thigh. "He wasn't looking at me this time, just going through the motions, so maybe it wasn't the same ghost. Some ghosts are more like habits than people—they go through the same shtick over and over until they fade. This could have been that type, and not the same one I saw before. I didn't see a face. But I did see the wedding ring. It's got a bit of color, even with the rest of him all filmy and white, so I spotted it." She paused, frowning. "Though I guess more than one ghost could have a glowy gold wedding ring."

"You could call the Etorri Rhej and ask her."

"Maybe." Rhejes were always Gifted. The Etorri Rhej was a powerful medium, though you'd never guess it to look at her. She was a very medium sort of woman in the unspooky ways—medium young, medium brown hair, medium build, pleasant but unremarkable face. Very Canadian. "I probably will, but not now. Ghosts happen. I'd like to know why I'm suddenly seeing them, but that's not a priority. I need to finish briefing you about our next move."

"You got a tip from one of what you refer to as the locals. Something about a missing homeless man, which is why we're headed for a soup kitchen."

She flashed him a grin. "You're cute when you try to use cop talk. Yeah, though it wasn't so much getting a tip as tracking down someone and wringing a resounding 'maybe' from him." Lily didn't have any contacts in the local PD, but Cynna did. So she'd gotten a name from Cynna and talked to that lieutenant, who'd passed her to a sergeant in the precinct where they were headed. She in turn had passed Lily to a patrol cop, who'd admitted he was worried about a particular homeless guy who seemed to have disappeared.

"Not that any of 'em can't up and do that at any time," the man had said. "But Birdie's . . . well, if I say he's different you'll laugh. He's a friendly little bugger, and he's like clockwork. Always at the same corner trying to sell his little pictures from eight to noon. Heads to Twelfth Street Kitchen for lunch. Never goes to any of the others, it's always Twelfth Street, though there's another one closer. Heads to the park on Madison after that, where he draws more little pictures. Gets in line at Good Shepherd's before five. Only he isn't anymore, and hasn't for the last couple weeks."

"Coffee," Rule said firmly as he signaled for a turn.

Lily grimaced but took out the thermos she'd brought. Who'd have thought she could get tired of coffee? But she sipped because that was the right thing to do. Just as telling Croft about her problem had been right, however much she hated it. The pain bolt she'd been hit with in the car earlier had underscored that.

But this was right, too. Against the rules, and maybe there'd be a price to pay. But she knew how to investigate, dammit, and Drummond was ignoring the bigger picture. Who had the death magic crowd used for practice before moving up to the big leagues?

Lily looked at the buildings around them. More Laundromats in this part of town. Skin joints. Pawn shops. More people other people could overlook, ignore. Nameless people who didn't smell right, look right, act right. "His name is Birdie," she said suddenly.

"What?"

"The homeless guy. Well, his real name is James Johnson, but he went by—or goes by—Birdie. He likes to draw pictures of birds." He had a name. A life. Even if it wasn't much of a life by most people's standards, it was his . . . or had been. No one had the right to take it away from him.

CULLEN didn't know much about real estate, but he knew northwest D.C. was pricey. This particular street was all leafy residential—lots of beautifully restored or maintained Craftsman homes with big front porches, well-groomed lawns, and a mix of Mercedes and minivans parked out front. Rule's car blended right in.

Fagin's house did not. It was pink. Pink with lilac trim. It had probably started life as turn-of-the-century Craftsman like its neighbors, but somewhere along the line someone had craved a touch of Tudor, adding bulky crosshatched beams in the oddest places. Beams some later owner had painted lilac.

What an odd little wart of a place. Fagin's neighbors were probably praying he planned to paint really soon. Cullen was grinning as he entered the small front yard . . . and paused, raising one eyebrow. Interesting. Then he mounted the steps and pressed the doorbell.

Nothing happened. He rang again. This time he heard floorboards creak, then—slowly—footsteps coming toward the door. It opened. Dr. Xavier Fagin blinked at him sleepily, his bright orange robe drooping around what looked like a woman's scarf knotted around his middle in lieu of a belt. His hair was more awake than the rest of him, bursting out frenziedly in all directions. "I know you."

"Of course you do. Cullen Seabourne. We met when you headed that task force. We've e-mailed a few times since. You said I could use your library."

Fagin's eyes opened wider in mild astonishment. "I believe I did. My library, like myself, was in Cambridge at the time."

"You moved. I didn't think that revoked the invitation."

"I can see why you would think that." But he didn't move.

Cullen rolled his eyes, dug in his pocket, and took out a smooth black pebble. For a second it lay in his palm—then began to glow like a firefly. The glow faded quickly and he stuffed it back in his pocket.

"Ah, well, then, come in." At last Fagin stood aside.

"Who did you think made those things?" Cullen asked crossly as he followed.

"Either you or your wife or both, but that's an assumption, not something I've been told as fact. I dislike acting on assumptions."

"Huh. Good guess. I make the blanks; Cynna personalizes them. Have I interrupted something?"

"Alas, no. Poor Merry had to leave for work at some horribly early hour. I went back to sleep, naturally. A man my age needs rest after prolonged exertion." He frowned faintly. "What time is it, anyway?"

"Ten-ish, I think." Not that he'd paid attention, but the sun had been up awhile. Cullen looked around curiously.

The entry hall was small, giving access to a narrow staircase and the front parlor. The fireplace in the parlor was clearly original, with a beautifully carved mantel no one had desecrated with paint. The faded rose-colored wallpaper might be original, too. The carpet was newer—avocado green seventies shag. Fortunately you didn't see much of it. The room was buried in packing boxes, some opened, most not. "Prolonged exertion?"

Fagin sighed happily. "Merry is a delightful woman. Do you know how to make coffee?"

"Everyone knows how to make coffee."

"Without a coffeepot, I should add. I can't locate mine. I've tried simply boiling the grounds, but the results are less than satisfactory." This sigh was windier and filled with regret. "I do miss Martha."

Cullen knew Fagin was a widower, but he was pretty sure the man's wife had died a decade or two ago. It seemed ample time to learn how to make coffee. "I can probably figure something out. Martha was your wife?"

"My housekeeper. She refused to leave Cambridge, unfortunately. I miss Janie, too, but not for her coffee. She made terrible coffee. Brilliant woman, but her coffee was even worse than mine, and that's saying something. The kitchen's this way."

The kitchen was narrow and made narrower by more packing boxes. Most of these had at least been opened. "How long did you say you'd been here?"

"Priorities, dear boy, priorities. I had to work on the library first. Ah, here's the coffee." Fagin beamed and held out a foil package from Starbucks. "There's a pan on the stove that I used to boil previous attempts."

So there was. Surprisingly, it looked clean. Cullen handed it to Fagin. "Fill it halfway with water. Filters?"

"With the coffeepot, I imagine, wherever that may be."

Paper towels would do, and Cullen saw a roll of those. "I need a strainer or a funnel and something to decant the brew into. Did you know there's an earth elemental lurking beneath your porch?"

"A very small one, yes. It took some negotiating, which Sherry was kind enough to handle for me, but it agreed to keep an eye on the place in exchange for the traditional offerings. Will this do?"

Cullen accepted the large mesh strainer Fagin held out and tore off a couple paper towels. "Get the water boiling."

"That much I know how to do. Why are you here?"

"That damn dagger. The one someone left in Senator Bixton." Cullen dumped grounds into the paper-lined strainer.
"Do you have another pot? A big one?"

"Hmm, yes, I think . . . here." After clattering around in
one of the boxes, he tried to hand the pot to Cullen.

"Put it in the sink. This goes on top." Cullen followed and
balanced the strainer over the pot. "Part of the spell on the
dagger is Vodun. Part of it is something that . . . well, it sounds
crazy, so I need to check. I went to see a Vodun priestess I
know, but she wasn't helpful." Celeste had been royally pissed,
in fact, when she learned he'd meant those marriage vows he
took a few months ago. The offer of cash hadn't eased her
troubled spirit. "You told me you had a journal by Papa Araignée."

"Oh, yes. It's not long, but it is quite remarkable. So few
Vodun priests write things down, and Araignée was . . . hmm.
Twisted, but very bright. Do you read French? Are you sure
that's enough coffee?"

"Yes and yes. Do you have anything by Knoblauch or
Czypsser?"

"Just that treatise Armand wrote on Knoblauch, which, as
I'm sure you know, is mostly hogwash. However, I've got a
copy of Czypsser's *Ars Magicka* that was supposedly made
from the original."

A thrill went through Cullen. "The entire thing?"

"Alas, only fifty-two of what is reputed to have been eighty
pages, and some of them are damaged."

Fifty-two pages. Fifty-two pages of one of the most sought-
after grimoires in the world. Czypsser hadn't been an adept,
but he'd studied under one as a youth. Five years ago, Cullen
had paid five thousand dollars for a blurred copy of two pages
from Czypsser's *Ars Magicka*.

And Fagin was going to let him see fifty-two pages? Cullen
twitched all over just thinking about it. "Do those pages include his list of elven runes?"

"Oh, yes. Most of them are legible, and some have brief
definitions or notes on congruencies. Do you read medieval
German?"

"No, but you do."

"I'm fairly fluent. That doesn't look like enough coffee. I've been using at least twice as much."

"And drinking it?"

"I take your point."

IT wasn't the best coffee Cullen had ever had, but it wasn't bad. He sipped from the mug Fagin had washed while they were waiting for the coffee to drip through its makeshift filter and nodded acceptance of Fagin's grateful praise. Once the man paused Cullen said, "About that journal and the Czypsser manuscript . . ."

"Oh, yes. The library's right through here." Fagin headed for a door on the far end of the kitchen.

Cullen followed . . . and stepped into a room that bore no resemblance to the rest of the place.

Large, airy, and orderly, it ran the length of the house. The floor was wood. An area rug marked a reading zone at the far end, where two comfortable armchairs and a square table invited you to sit and browse in front of a bow window. Cable lighting zigzagged over the entire ceiling, but it wasn't needed now. In addition to the bow window, two tall windows interrupted the floor-to-ceiling bookshelves along the west wall.

In the center of the room rested a huge, battered desk flanked by a pair of low bookcases. It held the usual sort of detritus, both electronic and traditional: computer, printer, calendar, a small scattering of papers. And at this end, a long library table held court. A single, half-empty packing box sat on it.

There was even a card catalogue. An honest-to-God, old-fashioned wooden card catalog claimed pride of place in a section of wall clearly reserved for it. "Priorities," Cullen murmured. "Yes. You're a man after my own heart, Fagin."

Fagin beamed proudly at his domain. "I had the wall removed and the shelves added. It started out as a bedroom and dining room, you see. This suits me better." He lumbered into motion. "I don't have my entire collection in here, but I think I unpacked Papa Araignée's journal. It should be in the Vodun section . . . ah, yes. Here it is." He held out a tattered, leather-bound journal. "You can take it with you, if you like."

Cullen's eyebrows lifted. That was an unusual degree of trust—but then, Fagin wasn't a practitioner himself. He tucked the slim journal carefully inside his jacket. "Thank you. And the *Ars Magicka*?"

"You're drooling."

"Hardly at all," Cullen said repressively. "I have tremendous self-control."

Fagin chuckled. "The original is in my safety-deposit box back in Cambridge. I recently acquired a safety-deposit box here, but I haven't made the trip to Cambridge to retrieve the items from my Cambridge box. But perhaps my translation will work better for you anyway, since you have some difficulty with medieval German."

"I've never seen anyone actually twinkle before, but damned if you aren't doing it. An English translation, I take it?"

"Of course." Fagin headed for his desk. "It's a work in progress, mind, not finished, but I have a decent rough draft you can see. I'll burn you a disc so—"

The front window shattered.

Without blinking or thinking or any of the things there was no time for, Cullen flexed into a deep crouch. A shiny glass shower cascaded into the room. He sprang. A second projectile followed the first as he slammed into Fagin, grabbing him and twisting so momentum would spin them sideways as they fell—*the desk, the desk, it will shield us*—

The ground reached up and smacked them as the air ignited in a wall of stink, heat, and flame.

TWENTY

THE woman's gray hair frizzed around her face in an untidy halo. Her eyes were small and suspicious, her skin as scuffed and worn as an old suitcase. She smelled of baby powder, sweat, and the chicken concoction she shoveled into a small, pursed mouth with all the dainty greed of a cat enjoying a dish of tuna. Her hands were small and immaculately clean, even under the nails he suspected she trimmed with her teeth. They looked chapped.

She did not smell of alcohol, unlike the man on Rule's right. He gave off fumes that should have robbed everyone in a nine-yard radius of their appetites. "But you do know Birdie, I think," Rule said. He didn't say the woman's name because he didn't know it. She wouldn't give it to him.

"Everyone knows Birdie," she said without looking up. "I ain't seen him lately, but that don't mean he ain't around."

"How long do you think it's been since you saw him?"

"Well, now let's see." She stopped eating and mimed patting her pockets. "Sumbitch. I think I done lost my PDA, where I jots down all that important shit."

Rule wasn't sure why he didn't give up and move on to someone else. She didn't want to talk to him, and he couldn't make her. But she was enjoying giving him a hard time. Why not let her have a few more minutes of it? "It's hard to know who to trust, isn't it?"

She snorted. "That's easy. Don't trust nobody. Do I know you from someplace?"

"I've been on TV now and then. I'm the Lu Nuncio of my clan."

"Of your . . . shit, you're that prince guy. The werewolf." Her eyes narrowed even more and she pointed at him with her fork. "You're a ce-le-britty." The last two syllables sounded more like "bratty."

Rule grinned. He was beginning to like her. "Of sorts, yes."

"How come you're here without the cameras? Ever' time you goddamn ce-le-britties come around to feed the homeless, there's a camera someplace. Marianne says it's good publicity. Brings in donations. I say it's a pain in the ass."

"But I'm not here to feed the homeless. I'm looking for Birdie."

"He ain't here."

"True. Is there anyone else who's usually here who you haven't seen lately?"

"Tom Cruise. That man plumb loves the chicken and noodles. Can't figure why he ain't been around lately."

"Perhaps he's on a diet. Us celebrities have to watch our waistlines."

"Ha!" In high good humor, she slapped the table. "P'raps he is. Watchin' your waistline, are you? Why you wanna know all this, anyway?"

He glanced across the noisy room. It wasn't as crowded now. The line of people to be fed was gone; there was a shorter line now leading to the trash cans. Patrons were encouraged to scrape their cafeteria-style trays before turning them in.

Lily was talking to a tall man in a spattered white apron—one of the servers. She had instructed Rule firmly not to divulge why they were here. Some of these people were not screwed down tight, and all lived a precarious existence. It would not be helpful to tell them that someone might be snatching homeless people and killing them to power their magic. "I'm not supposed to tell you," he said at last.

Her mouth twisted in scorn. "But I'm supposed to tell you stuff?"

"I can't think why you would," he admitted. "I may not be here for a photo op, but I do want something from you. Why should you care what I want?"

She stuck a forkful of chicken-whatever in her mouth and chewed in silence for a moment. "She's a cop. That woman you came with."

"Yes. Federal, not local."

"Why's she want Birdie?"

"She thinks someone may have harmed him."

"You 'spect me to believe some big-shot federal cop cares what happens to Birdie?"

"She cares." Rule looked at the nameless woman who smelled of baby powder, whom life had taught a great deal about survival and very little about trust. "You have no reason to believe that, but it's the truest thing I know. She cares what happened to Birdie."

"Hmph." The sound was scornful, but after another bite the woman put her fork down. "You wait here. I'm gonna turn in my plate, then maybe I'll tell you." She heaved herself to her feet.

Rule waited. Why not? While she was gone the pungent man on his right got up. The two who'd sat across from him had already left. By the time the woman who wouldn't share her name returned, they were alone at that end of the table.

"Better get up. They don't mind if'n we talk awhile, but they don't want us camping out once we're done eating."

He pushed back the folding chair and stood.

She was shorter than he'd realized and wide in the hips, wide through the shoulders, with heavy breasts restrained by a dark green tee. The flannel shirt she wore over that was thick, frayed at the cuffs, with the buttons on the right—a man's shirt. Her jeans might have been meant for a man as well. They were cuffed up several times at the ankles and none too clean. She had dainty feet tucked into tattered athletic shoes smaller than the ones Rule had recently bought his ten-year-old son.

Was there any way he could get her new shoes and a dozen

pairs of socks? The homeless had to take care of their feet, he knew. One of the hardest parts of living on the street was finding a way to wash clothes, but socks could be washed in the sink at a public restroom. Maybe some lotion for the hands she kept so scrupulously clean? A nail clipper—no, a small pair of scissors would be better, useful for more tasks. Or even a Swiss Army knife.

She tipped her head back and fixed him with a belligerent look. "I'll tell you. You won't b'lieve me, but I'll tell you what happened to Birdie. Them aliens took him."

"Hmm."

"Don't believe me, do you? Think I'm a crazy old bat."

"I think you saw something. Did you see the aliens take Birdie?"

"Hell, no. But I seen 'em take poor Meggie, and now Birdie's missing, so I knows what happened to Birdie."

"Tell me what you saw."

"Meggie, she allus tries for a spot at the shelter, but she drinks too much to know what time it is, so she gets there late a lot. They was full up by the time she showed up that night, so she comes around whinin' at me about how I could let her stay at my place just this once. She allus says that—'just this once.' I likes my privacy, see? I don't share my place with no one. I don't like anyone knowin' where it is, but Meggie . . . well, I made a mistake with her one time when it was real cold an' let her stay with me. But it weren't cold that night, and she smelled pretty damn ripe, so I tells her to move on." She scowled. "Wasn't like I knew what would happen, was it?"

"Of course not. And you're entitled to your privacy."

"I am." She said that forcefully. "So I tells her to move on, an' after a while she does. Now, my place . . ." She slid him a suspicious look. "I ain't telling you where it is, but it's close to the street, so I heard it when she starts talking to someone. I wanted to know who that was, 'cause Meggie's too scared to speak to a shadow if'n she don't know 'em. 'Specially a male shadow. So I'm thinkin' it's someone I know, and I don't want her telling anyone where my place is, so I went to see."

"You saw her taken?"

"Big old black car. Not a flying saucer, nothin' like that.

They was in a big old black car, real nice. And Meggie . . . she just stood there." For a moment the woman stared into space, her face slack, her eyes holding a touch of real horror. "She weren't right. I saw her face, and she weren't right. They used their mind powers on her, I guess. That one of 'em who'd got out of the car took her arm and told her to come along, and she did. She just did what he said." She shuddered. "That's how I knew they was aliens. Meggie wouldn't never get in a car with someone that way. 'Specially not a man."

"They didn't look like aliens, then?"

"Only saw that one. The other was driving the car, or mebbe there was a bunch of 'em in the car. I couldn't see. But that one, he looked just like anyone."

"He was disguised."

"That's right!" His suggestion unlocked a fierce series of nods. "That's absodamnlutely right! I figure they can be anyone, those aliens. But you're a werewolf. They can't turn themselves into werewolves."

"I don't think so, no. This one you saw . . . was he fat or skinny or in between?"

"Kinda skinny, I guess. Dressed nice, but not fancy. Not in a suit or anything." She squinted, thinking. "Not jeans, though. Businessman pants."

"Dark skin? Pale?"

"Oh, he was white."

Further questions revealed that the alien who snatched Meggie was neither "real old or real young." His hair had been dark and short, and he hadn't worn glasses or facial hair. He'd been a lot taller than "poor Meggie," but Meggie was such a teeny dab of a thing, that wasn't saying much. Mebbe six foot?

The alien abduction had happened about three weeks ago, and she hadn't seen Meggie since. She didn't know what time the men in the black car showed up, but it had been full dark for "a couple–three hours." She had no idea what the make or model of the car was. She wouldn't tell Rule where it had happened. She refused to talk to Lily—"Mebbe you ain't an alien, but how do I know about her?"—and she still wouldn't tell him her name. When he asked again, she stepped back. "I got somewhere to be."

"All right. I'd like to pay you for your time."

"Yeah? Well, I charges a hundred an hour."

His lips tugged up. "I believe we spoke less than an hour." He moved so his body blocked them from any prying eyes before slipping his wallet from his pocket. Some of those here wouldn't hesitate to mug an old woman. He took out three twenties—and his card. One of the ones with his cell number. "Will you call me if you see them again?"

"Mebbe."

"I'm glad you're cautious. Don't tell anyone else about these men. Who, ah, only look like men. You don't want them to know you've seen them."

She stuck the bills in her jeans pocket and gave him a sly smile. "Seen who?"

He could probably find out what name she went by, he thought as he angled across the room toward Lily, who'd finished with the servers and was talking to a shriveled little man in an incredibly bright blue sweater. Someone here probably knew that much. He wasn't sure he wanted to. She liked her privacy, and who was he to take that away?

Lily might not see it that way. Probably wouldn't. If . . .

His phone rattled through a drumroll. That was Cullen. About time. He wanted his car back. Rule unhitched the phone from his belt. "Yes?"

Cullen's voice was breathy, strained, and urgent. "Get here quick. 1125 West Brewster. I'm hurt. So's Fagin."

LILY never understood why they weren't stopped on that mad ride. They damn sure should have been. Rule's reflexes meant he could drive faster than a human without increasing the risk, but there were limits.

There'd been a bomb. A firebomb, according to Cullen— not much bang, lots of heat. He'd refused to stay on the phone for more than a moment, and hadn't answered when Rule tried to call him back. "He needs his Lu Nuncio," Rule had said as the car skidded around a corner.

"He told you that?"

"Not in words, but I could hear it."

If Cullen needed his Lu Nuncio, it meant he was hurt enough to threaten his control—bad for him and for anyone who tried to help him. Cullen had superb control, better than most lupi, control forged in the dreadful furnace of living so long as a lone wolf.

So Rule hurried. Halfway there Lily got a call from Cynna, who'd received a text from Cullen telling her not to worry, that he wasn't hurt bad. Somehow it didn't have that effect, especially because he didn't answer her, either, so Lily spent the next few careening turns telling Cynna they didn't know anything yet. Her lips as well as her knuckles were white by the time they screeched to a halt a block away from 1125 West Brewster.

In spite of Rule's heavy foot, the emergency responders had been closer and arrived first. At least most of them did. A second ambulance wailed to a stop as Rule slammed his door shut.

They set off at a quick lope—her, Rule, and Scott. Most of these homes were two stories. Lily scanned rooflines. If someone wanted to pick her or Rule off, there were plenty of spots to shoot from. By the time they reached the tangle of cop cars blocking the street, her heart was pounding as if she'd run a mile.

She couldn't see the house from here. A pumper truck blocked her view. No smoke, though. Surely that was good.

Lily flashed her shield at one of the patrol officers. "They're with me," she told him when he frowned at Rule and Scott. "They're needed. Where's the—no, I see him. Captain!" she called, hurrying forward.

She'd taken a guess about the rank. From the rear, she could only see that one firefighter's helmet was black, which meant an officer. When he turned, she saw she'd guessed right. His helmet bore a captain's bugles.

He was a blunt-featured man, Hispanic, midway between her height and Rule's. Probably midway between their ages, too. And scowling. "What the hell do—wait a minute," he said as his gaze shifted up and to Lily's right. "You're Rule Turner. Are you Rule Turner?"

"I am."

"He's asking for you, and by God, you'd better tell him to quit with his tricks and let us get some water on the building. Come on." He turned and marched for the pumper truck's high snub nose.

Lily and Rule exchanged one quick, startled glance and hurried to catch up. "Captain," Rule said, "are you talking about Cullen Seabourne? He won't let your men put out the fire?"

"Says he got rid of the fire himself and we should go away. He put the other victim on the porch. On the damn porch, like we were FedEx picking up a package. He did let the EMTs approach to take care of the man, but—"

"The other victim?" Lily said quickly. "Dr. Xavier Fagin? Is he—"

"In pain," said a weak but familiar voice on the other side of the pumper. "A great deal of pain, but that's"—this was interrupted by a long, wheezy breath—"encouraging, since it means the nerve endings weren't destroyed. I—no, no, I don't want that. I want drugs. Strong drugs."

A stiff female voice said, "They can give you some at the ER, sir, but you need oxygen now."

Lily rounded the nose of the pumper truck and saw Fagin. He was sitting up, leaning against his own front door and coughing as he swatted at the EMT who was trying to pull the oxygen mask back up. The other EMT was positioning a gurney.

She saw Cullen, too. On the roof.

The front of Fagin's house was a mess, but it wasn't in pieces. The porch was blackened. The bay window was broken, but the ones on the other side of the door were intact. The roof looked sound, too—which was just as well, because that's where Cullen sat, his feet dangling over the edge. His jeans were burned partway up the calves. His lower calves and feet were black and oozy. He sat there and swayed as if there were a high wind.

A pair of firefighters stood on this side of the pumper truck aiming their own scowls at the wobbly man on the roof. It looked as if they'd started uncoiling a hose, but hadn't gotten far.

Lily exchanged a quick glance with Rule. "I'll take Fagin."

"I'll take Cullen. Scott, call Cynna. Keep her updated."

They split up—Scott staying behind, Rule stopping short of the porch, and Lily hurrying up the porch steps.

"Lily." Fagin's smile was a shaky facsimile of his usual beaming welcome. "My feet are a mess, but . . ." Another short coughing fit. "My new best friend kept it from being worse. He threw me to the floor behind my desk and covered my body with his own. But my feet are broadcasting enough pain for two of me."

"Then let them put that mask on and take you to the ER," she said firmly.

"I don't need—"

"If it gets you to those painkillers quicker, why are you arguing?"

"Ah. Hmm."

Behind her Rule said, "How bad are you hurt?"

Cullen's voice was strong enough, though the words were a bit slurred. "Tell 'em to—"

"Cullen," Rule repeated with a new note in his voice, "how bad are you hurt?"

A second's silence, then: "Feet, ankles, lower calves. That would be roughly nine percent of my body, so it's not too bad. Third degree on my feet. I can't feel 'em. I sucked down some smoke, but that's pretty much cleared up."

Lily caught Scott's voice, quietly repeating that to Cynna.

"All right," Rule said. "Why didn't you answer your phone?"

"Battery's dead. I need you to stop them."

"Stop who from what?"

"No water. Water ruins books. And the elemental doesn't like it. Fire doesn't bother it, but it hates water. That's why it—*you* stay back." He pointed.

Lily looked over her shoulder in time to see a thin stream of fire dance on the ground in front of the captain. The man backed up. Quickly.

"We're going to have to shoot your sorry ass if you don't quit that," the captain growled. "You're in enough trouble already. You're hurt. Let us help you down."

"No."

The EMTs were loading Fagin onto the gurney. He hissed and muttered as he was shifted, but didn't seem to be in shock. Lily moved off the porch so she could see Cullen with his dangling, blackened feet glowering down at Rule. "No firemen," he said. "No water."

Rule said, "You put out the fire?"

"Fagin's elemental isn't fast enough. Earth elemental, y'know. Not quick. So I did it."

"And you're sure there is no ember, no tiny trace of anything smoldering?"

Cullen was scornful. "'Course I'm sure. It's Fagin's *library*. The bastards firebombed his bloody *library*. Bloody damned irreplaceable shit in Fagin's library." He scowled in contemplation of the magnitude of this offense, then added as an afterthought, "And there's the elemental. Doesn't like water. Might hurt someone. Can't let it hurt them, can I?"

Fagin—who'd finally allowed them to put the oxygen mask on and was being wheeled away to the nearest ambulance—pulled the mask down again. "No hosing the house," he ordered, then coughed some more.

Lily glanced back at him. "I'll take care of it. Keep your oxygen mask on and behave." She pulled out her ID once more. "Captain, may I have a word with you?"

It helped that the captain was basically a reasonable man. He was royally pissed at Cullen, of course, but when Lily explained who Fagin was and that his library might contain documents vital to national security, he was willing to listen. When she told him Cullen was Fire-Gifted and able to put out much larger fires than this had been, he snorted, but kept listening.

It helped even more when the elemental chimed in.

She was talking to the captain when she felt it—a vibration groaning up through the soles of her feet. She grabbed the man's arm. "What the—"

"Son of a—"

The rest of the captain's exclamation was lost in a sudden *crack!* like a muffled gunshot. The sidewalk near the street buckled. "What the hell?" He glared at Cullen. "I've had it with you. Officer—"

Cullen peered down. "Not me. The elemental. Uh . . . you might want to get your men to back up. Maybe move the truck."

Along the street the earth began to crumble *up*, clods of concrete and dirt clumping together in gravity-defying cohesiveness. Firefighters scrambled back, exclaiming.

"Is that thing emerging?" Rule asked sharply.

"Don't think so," Cullen said, watching the slow heave of earth with bleary eyes. "But you should get on the porch. Ought to be okay there. It agreed to protect the house. Porch is part of the house."

Rule grabbed Lily's hand and the two of them scrambled up the steps. A second later, Scott landed beside them. He'd jumped.

"Cullen," Rule called, "What's it doing?"

Cullen's voice came from above, mixed with the deep grinding of earth as a wall continued to rise along Fagin's property line. "Not sure. But I was wrong about one thing."

"What's that?"

"It's not a *small* elemental."

TWENTY-ONE

~~

THE problem with earth elementals was that they were very literal.

A warded wall of dirt and stone, concrete and grass, sticks and boards from the fence that used to divide Fagin's yard from his neighbor's now encircled the property. It was roughly four feet wide at the base and nine feet tall. The ward extended above the wall, Cullen had said. It was unlike anything he'd seen.

The good news was that they didn't need to worry about firefighters increasing the damage to Fagin's library with water. They didn't need to worry about subsequent attacks, either. Nothing was getting across that property line.

That was also the bad news. Cullen was pretty sure the ward went both ways—keeping things out and keeping them in. He was also pretty sure he didn't want to test it to find out. He'd said so when Rule retrieved him from the roof—just before he passed out.

"The Rhej will meet us at Memorial in Bethesda," Rule said, putting up his phone, "once we're able to leave."

"Bethesda? You've got to be kidding. There must be closer hospitals."

"All of which consider their facilities inadequate to treat a lupus patient."

"Assholes." Lily leaned her head back against a chunky post holding up the roof over the porch and let her eyes close.

The air was still and sullen and smelled of burned things: ash and smoke and a whiff of chemical nastiness mixed with the singed-pork stink from Cullen's burned flesh. The temperature had dropped enough to make her glad for her jacket. Clouds had moved in to dull the day, hanging low as if working themselves up to rain. Three days in a row now it had rained. Surely it couldn't do it again?

Against those clouds a red and white mechanical dragonfly darted. Lily could hear the whomp-whomp-whomp of the news helicopter as it dipped closer. She resisted the urge to shoot the bird at the reporters. Not a good image for the six o'clock news.

There were four of them on this side of the wall: her, Rule, Cullen, and Scott, who'd leaped it before it finished growing, unwilling to leave his Rho without protection. Scott sat on the bottom step frowning at the earthen rampart enclosing them. Rule sat across from Lily near the other pillar. Cullen lay between them in a nest of blankets and pillows that Scott had found in the house.

Damn them. Whoever they were. Lily didn't know, couldn't even guess. Friar's people were staying so many jumps ahead she was dizzy, furious with her own consistency. Again and again she failed to keep up, much less catch up. Why had they attacked Fagin? Had Fagin even been their target? Why a firebomb, of all things?

She was just so damn tired. It felt like she'd been up all night or tried to run for miles after fasting. No reserves. "What did you mean when you asked Cullen if the elemental was emerging?" she asked Rule.

"You know that each type of elemental has a preferred form they take sometimes?"

"Yeah, I guess. Salamanders, sylphs . . . I can't remember the other two."

"Earth elementals emerge as giant worms or snakes when they want to do battle."

"Oh." She made an effort and got her eyes open. "Guess we should be glad it didn't emerge, then."

She glanced at Cullen, but he hadn't shifted. When she looked at Rule, she frowned. His eyes looked funny.

"Are you holding up okay?" he asked.

"I'm tired, pissed, but my head doesn't hurt. How about you?"

"Me?" His eyebrows lifted. "I'm fine."

He sounded fine. His body looked loose and relaxed. But his eyes . . . there was too much black in his eyes, she realized. Not a big difference. If you didn't look closely, you'd think his pupils were slightly enlarged, but she knew better. Black was trying to eat the irises and spread itself out over his eyes.

The Change. That's what that meant. When black swallowed Rule's eyes, he was fighting the Change. But why? They weren't in immediate danger. And maybe *why* wasn't as important as doing something about it. She got up and went to sit beside him. His arm came around her, and she leaned into him.

If this felt as much better to him as it did to her . . . "Full moon tomorrow night," she said casually.

"I'm okay, Lily."

When she looked at his eyes, they were normal again. So maybe he was okay, now. She wasn't sure he had been a minute ago.

At the moment, he literally had his hands full—one arm around Lily, the other hand resting on Cullen's shoulder. It allowed Cullen to relax, he'd said. Lily wasn't sure *relax* was the right word, but she knew what Rule meant. The contact let Cullen know all the way down that his Lu Nuncio was with him. He didn't have to fight to retain control of himself or cling to consciousness. He was safe.

They were, too—as long as they didn't try to leave. Fortunately, Cullen had told them what to do before unconsciousness claimed him. Call Sherry. Get some of Fagin's blood.

Sherry was on her way. Lily was on hold. She put her phone on speaker so she'd hear it when Croft returned and set it in her lap.

"You think they were after Fagin or Cullen or the library?" she asked. "Cullen thought it was the library."

"Hard to guess until we know what Cullen was doing here."

"True."

Rule never had trouble controlling the Change as full moon drew near. Even on the night of the full moon when, he said, moonsong was so pure and sweet it made a mountain spring seem tainted, he could refuse the Change if he needed to. But it was taking effort for him to hold it off now, with a day still to go. "Rule—"

"Sorry that took so long," said a voice from her lap.

It was Croft. She picked up the phone and took it off speaker. Not that it mattered—Rule would hear both sides of the conversation anyway. "No problem. I'm here."

"I've got people heading for the hospital to guard Dr. Fagin. One of them will bring you the vial of blood, assuming Fagin gives consent—either Matthew Cates or Royce Richards. Do you know them?"

"I don't know Richards. Cates is . . ." She searched her memory. "Late twenties, shaggy hair, very slight charisma Gift?"

"That's him. Richards is in his early fifties, brown and black, mustache, small half-moon scar on his jaw. Wiccan with a teleport Gift. Ida is sending you their phone numbers so you can get in touch if you need to."

"Any word on Fagin's condition?"

"Just that he's reached the hospital. Do you think Sherry can get you out without Fagin's presence?"

"Cullen thought so. Sherry does, too. She knows the specifics of the bargain Fagin has with the elemental. She knows how to contact it."

"For which she needs Fagin's blood."

"Apparently."

"How's Seabourne doing?"

Lily glanced at the pale face of the unconscious man stretched out between her and Rule. Rule had used the pillows to get Cullen's feet higher than his head. While it was rare for a lupus to go into shock, taking steps to prevent it kept his healing from having to work on that as well as the burns. "Second- and third-degree burns over an estimated nine percent of his body. Breathing shallow, but not labored. He's hurting, he needs fluids, but he's lupi. He should be okay."

"Good. You're cleared to collect evidence. Ida is setting up the expert consult you requested."

Evidence collection was not Lily's job. Sure, she'd had training, but a patrol cop's job was to secure the scene, not wander around picking up cigarette butts. Homicide cops and FBI agents didn't play CSI, either. There were specialists for that. At the moment, though, Lily was all they had. She wanted help, advice, questions answered. "Thanks."

"You should get a call soon about that. Oh, and I'll have someone waiting to take custody of whatever you collect once you're able to leave. Hannah, probably. The press is out in force."

As if to underline that thought, the news copter dipped close enough for her to see faces and a camera behind the glass bubble. No doubt there were plenty of the earthbound version of the press waiting to pounce on the other side of the barricades the police had set up on Fagin's street. "You need to tell them to keep their damn helicopter higher. No saying what the elemental might do if it decides they're a threat."

"They've been warned. I'll repeat it. When the press descends on you—"

"I'm good at ignoring them."

"I don't want you to. Tell them that the elemental is not dangerous as long as it isn't disturbed. Emphasize the need to keep back. Emphasize that it hasn't harmed anyone. You can add that we're pursuing all leads regarding the bombing, and I'll be giving a press conference at three thirty."

"Bless you."

"You're welcome." He sighed. "What the hell was Fagin thinking, dealing with an elemental?"

Lily didn't try to answer that one. It was a good question, though, so after she disconnected she repeated it. "What the hell was Fagin thinking?"

The unconscious man spoke. "Thought it was little."

Lily jumped. "You're awake."

"Unfortunately. Thirsty."

"I've got water," Rule said. "No, hold still." He lifted Cullen's head and shoulders with one arm and held a glass to his lips.

Cullen drank the entire glassful without opening his eyes. "Ah. Good. That's good." Rule lowered him back to flat. "Fagin thought the elemental was little. Sherry probably told him that. I thought so, too. Looked small, not much power. Turns out most of it was asleep. They don't sleep here."

Lily frowned. "Here . . . you mean in our realm?"

"Yeah. We need Fagin's computer. I've got the journal, but we need the other one. The book."

Rule spoke. "What book?"

"*Ars Magicka.* A grimoire. By Eberhardus Czypsser."

"Gesundheit," Lily said.

"It's in medieval German. The translation's on Fagin's computer."

"The one on his desk?"

"Yeah, it . . . shit. Fire's probably not good for computers."

"I'm guessing it isn't. But—"

"Original's in his safety-deposit box. Cambridge. You can get a warrant or something." His eyes came open, burning blue in his pale face. "I need that book."

"I was about to say that Fagin is not an idiot. He's bound to have backed up his work. Even if he didn't, it may be possible to recover the data from his hard drive."

"Get everything. I need . . ." He winced. His eyes closed again. "Dammit," he muttered. "Think some of the nerve endings are coming back online."

Lily glanced at Rule, who shook his head. "He needs to shut up and rest."

"I need," Cullen said, his voice faint but adamant, "to see that damn grimoire."

"Does this have something to do with the dagger?"

Blue eyes popped open. "That's mostly Vodun work. I've got the reference I need for that. But there's something else."

She waited. When he didn't continue, she prodded. "What?"

"Don't know. It looks almost like elf work, though."

"Elf? As in Rethna?"

"I'm probably wrong. I need to see that grimoire." His eyes closed again.

"We'll work on that," Lily said. "You called it a bomb. You didn't see any magic involved?"

"No. Purely physical stuff."

"Okay. Did you see or smell anything I need to know before things went boom?"

"Two projectiles, one right after the other. First one broke the window. Second one lit everything on fire. Lots of nasty smoke. Smelled . . . sweet, for a second. Then nasty. Uh . . . like garlic, matches, and smog. Don't know what else. I was busy."

A raspy baritone called from the other side of the wall. "Agent Yu! Ms. O'Shaunessy's here."

The baritone belonged to the police sergeant who was handling crowd control. Lily shoved to her feet. If only she wasn't so tired . . . tired of trying to do unofficially what she should be investigating with the full force of the Bureau. Tired of keeping secrets from her boss, from everyone. Tired of people she cared about being attacked, hurt, killed. Tired of clandestine organizations and war—God! The war had barely begun and she was so sick of it! Sick as hell, too, of mantles—stupid damn mantles that did what some stupid damn Old One wanted them to do, and never mind who got used up in the process and what that did to Rule.

Anger smoldered in her at that last thought. It gave her the energy to head for the stupid damn wall.

"Hey, Sherry," she called as she drew near the earthen rampart. "Do you have what you'll need for contacting it?"

"Except for what only Fagin can provide, yes. I understand that's on its way."

"Should be."

"Emily and Kirk are with me. Emily's a strong Earth-Gifted. Kirk's Earth Gift is minor, but he's very skilled. They'll be handling the contact under my supervision."

"Why—oh. Right." Sherry's Gift was Water. "The elemental isn't crazy about water."

"I should never have been the one to deal with it in the first place," Sherry said grimly. "Hubris and stupidity are a bad combination. Can you climb over the wall? Rule said Cullen's out of commission, but I have some questions you might be able to help with. It would be better if I didn't have to shout them where prying microphones might hear."

"Uh, the ward can't affect me, but if the elemental decided to drop me in a pit and fling big rocks at me—well, my Gift doesn't stop rocks."

"Of course. Sorry. I'm shook up," Sherry admitted. "I can't believe I missed how big this one is."

"Cullen missed it, too. He says most of it was asleep, and they—earth elementals—don't sleep in our realm."

"He's sure of that?" she called, her voice sharp.

"Cullen's always sure. He isn't always right, but he's always sure."

Sherry's mutter was barely audible with all that dirt separating them. "He's right a disagreeable amount of the time."

Lily had to grin. "We'd better talk over the phone," she said, and took hers out. As soon as Sherry answered she went on, "I'm not sure what help I can be. Mostly I can only repeat what Cullen told me before . . ." She caught a glimpse of movement and turned. "Or maybe you can ask him your questions after all. Looks like the stubborn son of a bitch has talked Rule into bringing him over here for some reason. You'll still need to talk to him by phone so he doesn't have to raise his voice." She paused. "I have some questions, too."

"I do need to talk to Cullen, but if you can make your questions quick, go ahead."

"You said you might have to negotiate a separate agreement to get us out of here. Why's that?"

Sherry's voice was dry. "That's not a quick question—or not one I can answer quickly. Basically, all I can do is remind the elemental of its agreement with Fagin, using his blood. The problem is that the agreement uses words, but earth elementals are nonverbal."

"Not making sense yet."

"Elementals can use words, but only in the most literal way. They think spatially rather than verbally. The agreement is both spatial and verbal. Fagin's blood . . . um, you might say it activates the spatial portion of the agreement. That's why the elemental erected the wall and wards—because Fagin bled. There are two ways the elemental is allowed or required to act: first, if Fagin specifically invokes its protection. Second, if Fagin's blood is spilled within the defended space."

Lily chewed that over a moment. Scott had brought Cullen's nesting materials out; she watched as he made Cullen a pallet several feet back from the wall. "So if Fagin had cut himself shaving, the elemental would have closed down the property?"

"It's literal, not stupid. It knows the difference between an attack and an accident. Accidents don't invoke it. But if it had been invoked in error, Fagin could ask it to remove its protections."

"He didn't do that."

"So I noticed. Since he hasn't, we have to negotiate a second agreement to get all of you out. First we remind the elemental of the original agreement, which does not require it to keep you inside the defended space. Then we persuade it that allowing you to leave will benefit it."

Rule settled Cullen on his new nesting spot. Cullen frowned at Lily briefly, then turned his head to study the earthen wall. "What does an earth elemental consider a benefit?"

"Power or love."

"It wants love?"

"The stories say that Earth elementals have sometimes formed a loving bond with a human and will go to great effort on their behalf. But love can't be arranged or bartered, which is why blood is the usual initial offering."

Yuck. "Initial? And whose blood are we talking about?"

"Possibly a small amount from each of you, with additional non-blood offerings at subsequent full moons for an agreed-upon period. At least that's what we'll try for. Which reminds me—Fagin probably won't be able to make his offering tomorrow. Tell him one of my people will take care of that for him."

"Will do. How long do you think this negotiation will take?"

"Anywhere from an hour to the rest of the day and into the night. And now I need to talk to Cullen."

"Wait—one last question. This one really is quick."

She asked, Sherry answered, and Lily got off the phone with a real sense of relief. Sherry was willing to speak to the press about elementals. After Lily gave the piranhas of the press her brief spiel and promised them a press conference with Croft, she could hand them off to Sherry. Which was really mean, but Sherry wanted to do it. She was sort of the Wiccan equivalent of Rule: the public face of her people. She considered it her duty to educate people about her faith and about magic in general—preferably in ways that made it all less scary.

Lily wasn't sure how she'd explain an ancient and powerful elemental in a way that made it less scary, but if anyone could, it would be Sherry.

Lily went to stand beside Rule and looked down at Cullen. "He looks terrible. Why is he out here instead of decently unconscious?"

"He wants to study the ward while it's still up."

Of course he did. Lily looked at the pale and strained face of Rule's obsessive friend. Her friend. Who could have died, but hadn't. "The elemental won't be taking down its ward anytime soon. You can study it later."

"You sure about that? If the original bargain was done right, there should be a mechanism for terminating—"

"There's a problem with that," she said firmly, then subvocalized so those on the other side of the wall wouldn't hear: *"If the ward stays up, Fagin's library stays safe. Sherry knows we want that, for now."* In a normal voice she added, "Sherry wants to talk to you, if you're up to—"

On cue, Cullen's phone beeped. He fumbled it from his jeans pocket, touched the screen, and said to it, "I'm here. Hold on a sec." He looked at Lily. "Go see if Fagin's computer got crisped and if he has DVDs or whatever for backup. If you can't find them, or if they're cooked—"

"Cullen, shut up." Lily knelt beside him, bent, and smacked a quick kiss on his forehead. "I am deeply, completely glad you're going to be okay, but you're not okay now. You need to rest. You need to let me do my job." She looked at Rule. His eyes were almost normal. Almost.

She stood and went to him and touched his arm. "Time for me to work the scene." A bombing wasn't a Unit case, not unless they found magic involved, but she was here and no other investigator would be, not anytime soon.

"Of course. I need to stay with Cullen."

"I know. It's harder to be the support system, to worry about others, than it is to be the one out there risking yourself."

He didn't say anything for a long moment. Darkness flickered once around his pupils, then they returned to normal. Or almost normal. "That has always been true. Would Scott be any help to you?"

Rule wasn't going to talk to her about it right now. Whatever "it" was. She looked at the bespectacled wolf in geek's clothing. "Sure. I might be able to use his nose."

First, though, Lily sent Scott to scrounge for some items she needed. She had her purse but not her evidence kit, so she'd be improvising. While he was on his scavenger hunt, she made a phone call.

Maybe she'd find some DVDs or a flash drive in Fagin's library. Maybe the data on the hard drive would be recoverable. But there was another possibility that might be even faster. Fagin might have backed up online. He was probably used to doing that at Harvard, which might still have his files. Or he could've used one of the commercial online backup services. She called one of the agents Croft had sent to guard Fagin at the hospital.

Turned out Cates was on his way here with the vial of blood and Fagin was in treatment, but Richards would ask him about backup once the doctors let him.

Time to get to work. While she waited to hear from whatever expert Ida found, she took her phone to the porch and set it to camera mode.

The porch was compromised from being occupied by many sets of feet, but she took a couple photos of it anyway, then a few more of the bay window. She moved closer so she could shoot inside the library.

The rear of the room looked untouched. The center was blackened. The desk Cullen and Fagin had sheltered behind was a charred hulk. Lily assumed the plastic blob on top of it had been a computer a couple hours ago.

The fire had melted the computer before Cullen could put it out. She didn't know exactly how long it took Cullen to do that, but she was guessing no more than a fistful of seconds. How did a fire get that hot that fast? Some kind of accelerant, obviously, but she didn't know much about the makeup of fire-bombs.

Lily got pictures of the window frame, then of the floor. The burn pattern was clear even to her ignorant eyes—roughly circular, originating five to nine feet this side of the desk that had shielded Cullen and Fagin. She got some pics of that from the window, then headed for the door. She'd enter the library from its undamaged rear. Even if Scott hadn't found any Baggies yet, she could start making sketches and notes, but—

Her phone chimed. After a quick glance at the number, she answered it. "Special Agent Yu here."

"This is former CSO Rod Uddley," a hearty male voice announced. "Retired now, but I've worked more bombings than anyone in the country, living or dead. The Bureau likes me so much they let me teach the babies now and then, and now and then they pay me big bucks to consult. I understand you want a consult."

"I do. Did Ida brief you on my situation?"

Captain Uddley said she had indeed and congratulated Lily on having the good sense to ask for help.

"I need help establishing priorities. I may only have an hour to work the scene. I may have all afternoon and part of the evening. It depends on how long it takes to get the elemental to agree to let us out. I need to know what to do in that first hour."

He asked a few questions. Lily paused just inside the front door to answer, sent him the pictures she'd already taken, and then told him what Cullen had reported about the smell of the explosion. "I've got another lupus standing by in case his nose might be of use."

"Ah! Yes, that might help. That might indeed help. They're supposed to have a very keen sense of smell."

"It's strongest when they're in wolf form, so I'll ask Scott to Change."

"Excellent. First I need to look over those pictures you sent me. Hold on a moment."

Scott came out of the back of the house, carrying a plastic grocery sack. "Baggies, trash bags, Sharpie, masking tape, paper towels." He held it out. "I couldn't find paper bags or a ruler."

"Thanks." She took the sack and reported to the hearty Uddley on what kind of crime scene equipment she had. "I've got my spiral, so I can take notes, make some sketches. I don't have anything to measure with, but I can estimate shorter distances pretty well. My spread hand is eight inches from thumb to little finger, so . . . just a sec." Scott still stood there, waiting. "Yes?"

"Is it okay if I scrounge for sandwich fixings or something? For all of us, I mean, but especially Cullen. Healing burns a lot of calories."

And lupi shouldn't get too hungry. "Sure, go ahead. I won't need you right away, but eat quick, just in case."

He headed for the back of the house. Lily did, too, stopping at the doorway into the library. "We're going to do this bass-ackwards," Uddley boomed cheerfully in her ear. "Could all blow up in our faces, but we'll go for it anyway."

"I'm not following you."

"When you work a scene, you never start with a theory and look for evidence to support it—but that's what we're going to do. It gives us a clear set of priorities, you see, in case you run out of time. Now, we know we've got an incendiary device, not a true bomb—not much blast, plenty of burn. According to your witness, there were two projectiles."

"According to one of them, yes. The other—Dr. Fagin—I haven't interviewed him yet. His injuries needed attention."

"Two projectiles fits my theory. They wanted to break the window first so they could get their incendiary device well into the room before it broke and started burning everything. The witness you interviewed is a lupus, yes?"

She agreed that he was.

"Excellent. It's his description of the smells that all but clinches it. Good man. Observant. I'm betting someone tossed an SIP."

"Okaaay."

A quick, booming laugh. "Jargon's a bitch. Sorry. SIP stands for self-igniting phosphorus. The original SIPs were made during World War II by the British, but were never used in combat. Too dangerous to the user. They're a take on the good old Molotov cocktail, though more sophisticated chemically. Easy to make. You put white or yellow phosphorus—that's the garlic smell—mixed with benzene, water, and a bit of rubber into a glass bottle. Benzene smells sweet, see? Like your lupus reported. You throw your bottle at a hard surface. It breaks, the ingredients ignite, and you get a quick, hot fire, caustic smoke, and fumes from phosphorous pentoxide and sulfur dioxide. Sulfur dioxide—that and phosphorus make a burned match smell, and it's also a key ingredient in smog. It all fits. So here's what we'll do."

Uddley went on to give her a quick précis of what she would do in the first hour and what would come later, if she had more time. He assured her he could stay on the phone with her all day, if necessary—"No need to rush on my account! It's all billable hours!" They'd keep the line open, but she'd need both hands to work the scene, so she put her phone on speaker and clipped it to her waistband.

Thirty-eight minutes later she'd taken dozens of pictures, completed a rough sketch, and had begun collecting trace evidence. She'd scraped burned crud from walls and floor, carefully marking each Baggie with the precise location, and sticking each location with a bit of masking tape, then taking a picture of the marked location. She'd also taken into evidence one larger item—a big chunk from a concrete block. Probably the first projectile.

Now it was time to collect glass. Unfortunately, there was glass everywhere from the window. What they wanted was glass that might have come from a bottle filled with phosphorus, benzene, and a bit of rubber.

Time for less conventional means. Lily straightened. Her

right arm, the weak one, was aching. She'd been leaning on it a lot. Absently she rubbed it. "Scott? I'm ready for you to Change."

A tinny voice came from near her waist. "I'd like to brief him myself, if you don't mind."

"Sure. Hold on a minute, Scott," she said, heading for the door to the kitchen. She reached for her phone with her left hand and unclipped it.

And dropped it when her hand tingled, then turned numb and useless.

TWENTY-TWO

⇝

"YOU should've told him," Scott said.

They were in Rule's car, headed for Bethesda. Scott was driving, of course. Lily had turned the heater on. The sun was down and the temperature kept dropping. Surely it was too early in the year for snow? She hoped so. She hadn't brought a heavy coat with her.

Rule was in the ambulance with Cullen. Her mate-sense told her they were still in motion, so they hadn't reached the hospital yet. But they'd get there well ahead of her and Scott, having left first. Before Lily could wade through the surging sea of reporters to the car, she'd needed to hand off evidence and get a bandage on her arm so it didn't bleed onto her jacket.

Sherry had been right about the type of offering the elemental would require. The cut was small and tidy, on the inside of her elbow . . . her left elbow. That hand was working again. Not quite normally, but headed there. "I'm going to tell him. I want privacy for it."

She hadn't had that at Fagin's place. Once the elemental agreed to release them, things had moved quickly. They'd had a brief window of time to seal the deal with blood, then scramble or be passed over the earthen wall. Then they'd been surrounded by cops of both local and federal flavors, with the press just the other side of the barricades.

"When are you going to tell him?"

"At the hospital, probably. You don't argue like this with Rule."

"You're not my Rho. And I do get to argue with Rule if I think it's important. Not during, but afterward."

She sighed and shoved back her hair with her left hand. Those fingers still felt thick and clumsy, but she felt them. She could use them.

No pain bolt this time. Just a hand that forgot it was part of her body, or a brain that forgot how to talk to the hand. The paralysis hadn't lasted long, but for a few minutes Lily had been scared shitless. She'd had Scott find her some coffee— old stuff that he'd heated up in the microwave. Maybe it had helped.

Lily let her hand drop to her lap. She closed the fingers in a loose fist. Opened them. Closed them. "Thank you for giving me time to tell him myself. I am going to. I'm not quite stupid enough to think I could keep this from him." Or that she had any right to. But God, she was dreading it.

Rule was teetering on some unholy edge. She might not understand what that edge was, exactly, but she recognized it. She'd seen his eyes bleeding toward black like that before— when she was threatened, when he was locked up, when the first of the power winds blew shortly before the Turning.

She'd never seen the wildness try to take over, try to force the Change on him, when things were calm. He was angry that Cullen had been hurt, sure. But anger, even rage, didn't threaten his control.

Maybe he'd felt trapped because of the ward? That plus the imminence of the full moon . . . yeah, that might do it.

Relief loosened the muscles across her neck. Much as he hated it, Rule did suffer from claustrophobia. Though it was usually triggered by small, enclosed spaces, and Fagin's yard wasn't small. Not like an elevator, which Rule hated but consistently used. Not like the cramped seating on a plane . . . which he also hated but consistently used. His eyes didn't bleed to black when they flew across the country.

But he *had* been trapped. Until the elemental agreed to let them out, Rule had been well and truly trapped. "Did it bother you?" she asked Scott. "Being trapped inside the elemental's wards, I mean."

"I didn't like it, but I knew we'd get out sooner or later. Why?"

"Some lupi have a touch of claustrophobia."

"A touch of it, yeah, and that would be true for just about all of us. But there was plenty of room and, like I said, I knew we'd get out. I guess if we'd been stuck there a couple days I'd have started getting the willies, but we were only there a couple hours."

Two hours and twenty minutes, to be specific. Time enough for Lily to get quite a bit of glass bagged and tagged, with Scott's help. With the help, maybe, of the coffee she'd drunk. Lily looked at the fist she kept clenching and opening. It was getting better.

She could have gone to Rule right away, right when it happened, and told him. That's what Scott had wanted her to do. She'd finished collecting evidence instead. Maybe that was wrong. No doubt Rule would be angry that she'd waited. But she didn't have these spells because she'd been exerting herself. She had them because the Lady was messing with the stupid damn mantle.

And that, she feared, was why Rule hovered on that precarious edge. It was rage unbalancing him, yes, but rage born of betrayal. Not something she could discuss with Scott. With Cullen, yeah, if he hadn't been hurt, she could've asked him. But Rule was Scott's Rho. Lupi needed to know their Rho was in control.

And he was, Lily told herself. Maybe Rule was having to work for control, but he hadn't lost it. But she hoped they got to the damn hospital soon. Absently she rubbed the crook of her elbow.

"Your arm hurting?" Scott asked.

"Stings a bit. Not bad. I suppose yours is all healed up."

He sounded apologetic. "It wasn't very deep."

There had been very little ceremony involved in the blood offering. She and Cullen had only had to donate a token amount, no more than a medical vampire would extract for a blood test. Scott and Rule had donated quite a bit more. The elemental had been especially interested in the lupus blood. That was new to it.

Blood offerings themselves were not. One reason the negotiations had taken so little time, Sherry said, was that the elemental was both old and familiar with human concepts. English was new to it, but it understood the ideas behind the words with relatively little explanation. The humans it used to deal with had spoken another language, calling themselves the Acolhuas, the Tepanecs, and the Mexica. Nowadays, those people were usually named collectively: the Aztecs.

They'd been a waste-not, want-not sort of people, it seemed. They'd harvested death magic from their ritual slayings and given a portion of the blood that flowed from their altars to earth elementals. Or at least to this one.

Surely it was a mistake to trust an elemental grown old and powerful on so much human blood. Sherry assured Lily the creature would not break the restrictions the agreement placed on it, but it made Lily nervous to have such power lurking beneath a populous D.C. neighborhood. And if it made her nervous, how would everyone else react? She needed to—

Her phone chimed. She dug it out of her pocket, glancing at the display. Getting pretty low on juice. She'd better plug it in. "Agent Yu here," she said, digging in her purse for the cable.

"It's Anna. Anna Sjorensen."

Her voice sounded tight. Unhappy. "What's up?"

"You remember I told you we had a possible lead on the dagger? Well, it played out. I guess it did, anyway, but I just can't believe it. Something's screwed up, though I don't see what, but I'm not a computer whiz, so maybe—"

"Anna, what's happened?"

Lily heard the young woman take a deep breath. "We traced the dagger to a dealer. It was a credit card transaction, and it's been confirmed, checked, and rechecked. The credit card—the address the dagger was mailed to—they both belong to Ruben Brooks. Drummond is getting a warrant for his arrest."

*   *   *

RULE hated the ambulance.

Cullen didn't seem to mind how close and cramped it was, though he did wince when they turned the siren on. But Cullen wasn't entirely present. He'd dealt with the pain extremely well, but it had gone on too long. He was running out of whatever mix of willpower and curiosity had kept him focused.

Normally, EMTs did not allow passengers to clutter up their tiny mobile domain, but Rule had explained that he could keep Cullen calm. That had nearly delayed them. Only one of the EMTs had known his patient was lupus; the redheaded one got a bit panicky when he found out. Rule had been soothing. Cullen had roused himself to joke with the young man.

Humor worked. Humans were odd that way. They tended to trust those who made them laugh, as if humor and danger couldn't reside within the same person. But the young man had relaxed and they'd gotten Cullen loaded.

They broke with procedure another way. Both EMTs had elected to ride up front as soon as the IV was hooked up. That was practical. It was cramped enough back here without them. It was also easier for Cullen to remain calm.

Burns were incredibly painful . . . and the moon was almost full. If Rule hadn't traveled with Cullen, the EMTs might have arrived at the ER with a wolf on their gurney instead of a man.

Because of his injuries, because of the moon, Cullen's wolf was rising. He watched Rule in silence for the first part of their wailing ride, and Rule saw more wolf prowling behind those glittering eyes than man. Cullen's wolf would not like the smells or the sounds of the ER. He wouldn't like having so many strangers near when he was weak and hurt and unable to defend himself properly. He wouldn't like being touched, handled. He wouldn't want to go into the hospital at all.

Rule's wolf certainly didn't. Or perhaps it was the man who wanted to scream at the driver to stop.

Rule's wolf, too, was trying to rise, called by moonsong and propelled by rage. Deep within Rule, a hard and bloody knot of silence tightened. That place had no words, only

teeth . . . but Rule knew the words. His wolf wanted—
needed—the hot spurt of blood spewing from his enemy's
throat as his teeth ripped through the jugular. The spill of guts
from their fleshy pouch.

Friar's guts. Friar's blood.

Best if he didn't think of that now. Not when they would
soon be immersed in the smell of blood and illness. It might be
Friar's blood his wolf craved, but that craving could spin out
into a more general hunger. Rule had spent way too much time
in hospitals, but he'd never walked into one when his wolf was
this . . . eager.

Had he made the right decision? Rule looked down at his
friend. His clansman. Cullen's eyes were closed now. His
breathing was even and shallow enough that he might have
been asleep, though Rule knew he wasn't. His heart beat
steadily.

Cullen would heal with or without a doctor's attention.
He'd heal faster if the burned skin were debrided, if fluids
were replaced with the speedy efficiency of an IV. But neither was essential, especially with the Leidolf Rhej available.

Rule did not have to take his friend to the ER. But if he
didn't, he would have to lie—either directly or by misdirection. He would be breaking from expectation. Leidolf might
not have been in the habit of seeking human help for their
wounded. Nokolai, however, did. And as Lu Nuncio to Nokolai, as Rho to Leidolf, Rule *could not look weak.*

None of the lupi around him—not even Cullen, as good a
friend as he was—could be allowed to suspect that Rule's control was less than flawless. That was duty, not politics. A Rho's
first duty to his clan was to be strong enough to control both
his own wolf and all the wolves of the clan, if necessary. Even
Victor Frey, a cruel and crazy bastard of a Rho, had possessed
that cardinal virtue: his control was absolute. Or it had always
appeared to be so.

According to Isen, the second was almost as good as the
first. No Rho possessed perfect control, so it was best to strive
always for the first, but accept the necessity of the second on
rare occasions.

According to Isen, a Rho could deceive his clan in other ways, too.

For him to lie outright to them dishonored both Rho and clan, causing a terrible sundering of trust . . . unless it was necessary. If a lie was essential to the clan's well-being, if all other choices meant worse harm, then a Rho should lie. He must do it brilliantly, so that his clan never suspected. Never for convenience. Never to avoid something you dreaded, or in support of any but the most vital goal. And chances were, if a Rho found himself in the position of having to speak a bald-faced lie to his clan, he had bungled things badly.

Rule had asked, of course. When his father gave him this advice shortly after naming him Lu Nuncio, Rule had asked. Twice, Isen had said. Twice in the fifty-some years he'd been Rho, he had lied to the clan. And no, he would not tell Rule what those lies were.

Rule supposed that two lies in over five decades was a fairly strong vote in favor of honesty.

Misdirection, now . . . the lie by omission, the partial truth, the subtle weaving of expression, gesture, and words to either deceive or confuse . . . Isen had a rather higher opinion of misdirection. He considered it acceptable over a fairly broad range. This was no surprise, coming as it did from a grand master of that slippery art.

But always, always, the compass must be pointed at the welfare of the clan.

Rule didn't even consider lying today. He could simply say they would not go to the hospital. He didn't have to explain. But his people, both Nokolai and Leidolf, would speculate. Why not get Cullen treated? What did Rule know? Was it no longer safe to be publicly lupus? Did he fear a specific attack by their enemy? Was Rule's control unequal to spending a few hours at an ER?

Such speculation did not serve the clan. Either clan. And so Rule arrived back where he'd started. He had to take Cullen to the ER.

He emerged from his thoughts to find Cullen's eyes, burning blue, fixed on his face again. He found a smile and squeezed Cullen's shoulder. "Nearly there."

"And then it really gets fun."

"I'm afraid so." Cullen still had language. Good. Rule hadn't been sure. Most lupi this far into the wolf would already be four-footed . . . but that's why Rule was here. He continued to draw on the Nokolai mantle, projecting calm. "The Leidolf Rhej will be there. She'll help. Will you be able to use the pain-blocking spell during the debridement?"

"If they're quick."

The spell was one Cynna had found or devised. It worked extremely well. Unfortunately, it didn't just shut down pain—it shut down healing. The body forgot it was injured.

First and worst, blood didn't clot. Even when blood loss wasn't an issue, the spell caused damage. The entire complex dance of healing was disrupted—fibroblasts didn't form; white cells and other immune agents didn't speed to the wound; the endocrine system grew confused; hormonal signals were missed or went unsent. Lupi healing could quickly right such imbalances, yet the spell was as dangerous for them as for humans. It was a power hog, a vampire. Even when employed as a charm—the only way most lupi could use a spell—it would somehow drain a lupus's healing power itself.

Still, used for very brief intervals, the spell could be a boon, and Cullen could use it more safely than most of them. Not that Rule entirely trusted Cullen's notion of safety. He studied his friend's face and sighed. "You've already tapped into it, haven't you?"

"Some."

"Cullen—"

"Not stupid. Made sure it drew from my diamond, not me. Had to talk to Cynna, didn't I? Didn't want to scare her."

"You also had to study the damned ward. And confer with Sherry. And—"

"You're tense."

Rule snorted. "I hate hospitals." That much he could say. Cullen would accept it, even expect it.

"You need Lily. She'll help."

"She's following in the car."

"You need her," Cullen repeated, and closed his eyes.

Cullen—or his wolf—was much too observant. Rule did need Lily. Her touch would help greatly . . . because of the mate bond. The bond Lily had first cursed, then accepted, and finally come to value for the gifts it brought them.

The mate bond. The Lady's gift.

The bloody knot inside Rule tightened.

Man and wolf alike feared for Lily, were frantic at the separation, desperate to fix what they had no power to fix. But it was the man who felt betrayed . . . and who knew that betrayal pointed within as well as toward the Lady. It was the man who was riven by guilt.

"Consent is necessary," he'd told Lily. As they knelt beside Brian where he lay dying, he'd told her the Lady could do nothing without her consent. He hadn't urged her to play host to Wythe's mantle, no, but he'd aided and abetted. He'd known when he asked that she didn't believe it was possible. A hypothetical, that's how she'd seen it when she gave permission.

He hadn't warned her of danger. He hadn't thought there was any.

Fool, fool, fool . . .

They slowed, turned, and slowed even more. The siren cut off. Rule glanced over his shoulder to look out the bit of windshield he could see. He caught a glimpse of the ER doors before the ambulance angled to the right, then started backing up. "We're there," he told Cullen, squeezing his shoulder.

Cullen's eyes flew open. Vivid eyes, clearly awake and aware . . . but with no trace of the man. Wolf eyes. He didn't speak or move.

"Good," Rule said softly. "You're keeping still. That's good." He made the sign for "hold" to reinforce that. Cullen-wolf understood English just fine, but physical language carried more meaning to a wolf.

They stopped. The driver opened his door and hopped out. The other EMT joined Rule in the back; Rule had to move forward to give him room. Cullen tilted his head to keep his gaze fixed on Rule, so Rule made the sign for "hold" again.

Obediently he lay still. The ambulance doors were flung open. The driver gripped the foot of the gurney and, with the redhead at its foot, slid it out. Rule followed. He jumped down lightly . . . and froze.

Three guns were pointed at him. Three guns held by three uniformed guards fanned out between them and the open ER doors. No—they were aiming at the goddamn patient. At Cullen.

A growl tried to rise in Rule's chest.

The EMTs stopped dead. "What the hell!"

"Just a precaution," one guard said. His hair was gray, his arms thin, his belly taking over what his chest had lost through the years. He wore bifocals. He held his .45 straight out in both hands. "You've got a lupus patient. We're here to make sure he doesn't hurt anyone."

"I know he's a lupus. That's what *he's* here for," the red-headed EMT said, a jerk of his head indicating Rule.

The guard's gaze flicked to Rule. "He's lupus, too?"

"Yeah, but he's been—"

"Don't move, you." The guard's gun fixed on Rule now. "Manny, cover Joe while he gets those cuffs on the one on the gurney. I'll keep this one from interfering."

"That's illegal, you know," Rule said pleasantly. He would not growl. He would not grab. He would not slap that fool's face so hard it slid right off his empty head. "You have no need for your weapons, no reason to draw on us, and you can't shoot me for accompanying my friend."

"I can make sure you don't cause trouble. That's what I'm doing. Move away from the gurney."

"No." Rule inhaled slowly. He was in control, dammit. "I'm going to put my hand on my friend's shoulder. If you shoot me, you'll have two patients and one hell of a lawsuit." He started to do just that, but his phone interrupted with an electronic version of a gypsy violin—several bars from Oleg Ponomarev's "Smelka."

Lily's ring tone.

TWENTY-THREE

﹏

"... BE there in about five minutes." Lily finished leaving a message for Rule and disconnected.

"He didn't answer?" Scott said.

"Maybe they've got a phone Nazi in charge at the ER." Her fingers were tingling. An odd sensation was rising in her, as if she had bubbles in her brain. Which was a deeply scary thought. She clenched both hands. They worked fine. "Turn right at the light."

"GPS says to go straight."

"And I say to turn right."

"Okay. You want me to park a couple blocks away or out back or something?"

"No time." Her toes were tingling now, too. Was she hyperventilating? Lily tried holding her breath. "I'll deliver the news and we'll clear out." She should have time. Sjorensen had called Lily when Drummond left to talk to the federal attorney. There was a possibility the attorney wouldn't want to go to a judge—but that was slim.

"Okay. Pretty nice acreage along here. Lots of room between the houses."

She let her breath out so she could talk. It hadn't helped, anyway. "Yeah. The Brookses' place will be on the right about a mile, just past a scrap of woods. Old brick, two stories, circular drive." Would Ruben run? Was that what he should do—what she wanted him to do?

She didn't know. He might choose to sit tight, let them arrest him, let the system work. A couple weeks ago, she would have known that was the right thing to do. But he had this whole Shadow Unit thing going. In his visions, the country fell apart, riven into bloody chunks, part of it falling into anarchy, part into dictatorship. Lupi dead, Gifted dead . . . maybe Ruben had foreseen his own arrest and was expecting her. Maybe he was already gone. Maybe he knew exactly what he must do to keep his visions from becoming reality.

One thing was crystal clear. Ruben's arrest was part of *her* plan.

"You trust this woman who called," Scott said. "You believe her about Brooks getting arrested."

Of course he'd heard both sides of that phone call. "Ninety-five percent trust, I guess." Not that Lily knew Anna Sjorensen all that well, but what reason would she have to lie? Other than getting Lily to expose herself by racing to Ruben's house to give him a chance to evade arrest. "Maybe eighty-five percent," she corrected herself as Scott turned where she'd told him to. She clenched both hands again. They worked, but they didn't feel right. Her head didn't feel right. "But we'll play the odds."

THREE to one was not bad odds, not with only one gun aimed directly at him—and that by a man only ten feet away.

Ten feet increased the chance that Rule would catch a bullet if he leaped, but a head shot was highly unlikely—and it would take a head shot to stop him. There was a good chance he wouldn't be injured at all. Most people couldn't hit a moving target even at this range. *There are humans here*, he reminded himself. Bullets that missed him could hit the more fragile humans around him. Or Cullen. Best not to give idiots with guns a reason to start shooting.

He fought to appear calm and gripped Cullen's shoulder.

"Hold," he said soothingly, feeling the wire-tight readiness in his friend. "Hold."

"Get your hands back up!" the guard barked.

"I'm not going to do that. Do you have a dog, Officer?"

A fine tremor went down the guard's arms. He reeked of fear. "Don't talk shit. You people don't turn into dogs. I worked MCD back when they rounded y'all up. I know what you're capable of."

Rule doubted that. Not when the man thought ten feet was a safe distance.

One of the other guards kept his gun trained on Cullen, while the third had holstered his and was reaching for the cuffs clipped to his duty belt.

Rule's voice roughened. "Handcuffs are a very bad idea. My friend is seriously injured. He might panic if someone attempts to restrain him."

"Cuff him," the gray-haired guard said hoarsely. "Do it."

Rule looked at the EMT standing closest to him. He reminded Rule a bit of LeBron—tall, muscular, with dark skin and a shaved head. LeBron, who'd been killed last month. "I don't want anyone hurt," he said quietly. "I can keep Cullen calm, but I've failed miserably to calm your gun-wielding associate. You and your friend should move away from the gurney."

"Like hell they will," said a raspy female voice from within the ER. "Their contract says they deliver 'em inside the doors. They'll wheel him in here like good boys. That your man?"

"They both are," said a second woman in a thick, warm drawl. The Rhej, Rule realized with a rush of relief as two women stepped out through the ER doors. "But I'll share the one on the gurney with you soon as we get him moving again." She came toward Rule. "I can take Cullen in while you get things straightened out with these boys. They're scared," she said, her voice balanced nicely between sympathy and scorn. "You might try looking a little less like you plan to rip out their throats."

He'd thought he was. "I'll stay with Cullen. He isn't in any shape to be around so many strangers at the moment."

"Ma'am," said the guard with the cuffs, "you have to get back right now."

The Rhej ignored him and looked down at Cullen, who lay motionless, his eyes bright and intent and not at all human. She nodded. "I see what you mean. You know me, though," she told Cullen reassuringly. "I won't leave you with strangers, no more than Rule will. Belle? We need Rule to stay with our patient."

The other woman wore scrubs. She was shorter, heavier, and older than the Rhej, with skin a half shade darker and a face whose lines mapped out weary cynicism. She was light on her feet, though, as she came forward. "Harold, put up the damn gun."

"Get back, Belle! You don't know what they're capable of."

"I know what you're capable of, and it don't include putting a bullet in me just 'cause you're feeling twitchy." So saying, the woman put her broad body between the guard and the gurney. "Take him in, boys."

"LILY!" Deborah's pretty eyes widened. "Is it—is Fagin—"

"Fagin?" It took Lily a second to figure out what Deborah meant. Of course—she'd have seen it on the news. "No, he's fine. Or he will be, I guess. I haven't heard anything lately. I need to see Ruben. It's urgent." The wind had picked up. Lily wished for a heavier jacket and tried not to shiver.

"Of course." Deborah's gaze flicked to Scott, who stood behind Lily. He'd insisted on going in with her. Couldn't guard her from the car, he'd said. It wasn't important enough to argue about, so Lily hadn't. "This is Scott. Scott, Deborah Brooks."

"Ma'am," he said.

Deborah opened the door wider. "Come in."

Lily walked into warm air that smelled like chocolate chip cookies.

"He's in the kitchen," Deborah said, and started down the hall. Her low-heeled shoes clicked on the hardwood floor. "What's going on?"

"Trouble. I need to tell him about it quickly."

"I see. I've got a fresh pot of coffee, and cookies in the oven. You take your coffee black, I think?"

"I do, but I haven't got time. But thanks."

"I'll pour a cup. You can ignore it, if you like."

Hinting wasn't working. "I need to talk to Ruben alone."

"We don't always get what we think we need, do we?" Deborah's voice remained pleasant. She didn't turn around.

Should she insist? God knew her news would affect Deborah as well as Ruben, so maybe the woman had the right to hear it. But Lily didn't know Deborah well. She didn't know how she'd act or react, especially if Ruben did run. She'd be questioned relentlessly. If she gave Lily up . . .

"We have company," Deborah announced in an overly bright way as she entered the kitchen.

Lily began to think she'd interrupted an argument.

"Lily!" Ruben sat at the breakfast nook at the west end of the room. A built-in banquette curved around the table; two chairs were tucked in at the front. He looked tired.

A timer dinged. "Ah, that's the cookies." Deborah veered for the oven, grabbed a hot pad, and opened the oven door. Scent washed out. "She says she comes bearing trouble. I'm going to pour her and her friend some coffee." She smiled at Scott as she set the cookie sheet on a cooling rack. "Do you like cream or sugar?"

"Nothing for me, thanks," Scott said.

"You'll have cookies, at least."

"Deb," Ruben said as he eased out of the banquette and stood. "They're not here for cookies. Ah—Scott, is it?"

Lily nodded. "Scott White. He's one of Rule's people. Ruben . . ." Lily glanced at Deborah, who was pouring the coffee she was so determined to offer. "I got a call from Anna Sjorensen ten or fifteen minutes ago. They traced the dagger used on Bixton."

"That ought to be good news. I'm guessing it isn't."

"They traced it to you."

Ruben's face went blank. Deborah dropped the cup she'd just filled. It smashed loudly.

Ruben spoke slowly. "I assume there's a warrant for my arrest. Are you serving it?"

"No! No, I came to warn you because, ah—because of everything we discussed the night of the barbeque."

He nodded. "Deborah knows about my visions."

"They can't arrest you," Deborah said blankly. "That doesn't make sense. They can't think you could do such a thing. Not unless one of them is one of the bad guys."

Ruben rubbed his face with one hand. Tired, yes—maybe beyond tired. He looked halfway beaten. "With sufficiently damning evidence, they'll have little choice. Someone has seen to it that such evidence exists."

Deborah bit her lip. Straightened her shoulders. And spoke firmly. "You'll do what you have to, of course."

He looked across the kitchen at her. Their gazes held for a long moment. "I love you," he said. "Beyond reason or measure, I love you."

A small smile played over her mouth. "And I love you. But I would really like to have some clue just what you're going to do."

He gave a half laugh. "So would I. Lily." He looked at her with the oddest expression—puzzlement and dismay mingled with a peculiar, hard focus. "Why are you here?"

She blinked. Shock had rendered Ruben stupid? "To warn you. Like I said. I don't know what you'll do, what you should do. I was hoping you'd seen this. Foreseen it, I mean, or something like it, and maybe had plans to . . . but I guess not."

He shook his head. "Why are you here? My phone works."

"Your . . ." A cascade of shocks swept through her like electricity—pop! pop! pop!—no, it was magic, magic fizzing on the inside, not on her skin, magic like a hundred bottles of Coke shaken and spewing and that's all she saw, too—magic cascading behind her eyes, a phosphorescent explosion smearing a rainbow of whites across her eyeballs.

The floor reached up and smacked her in the back. She felt that, felt her breath whoop out at the blow, felt her legs twitching and her arms jerking and heard voices calling her name . . .

No, only one voice, a beautiful voice, compelling as starlight. A woman's voice. She called Lily's *name*, the name only Sam knew, the one the black dragon had sung to her once. Only once. Her true name. Stillness flowed from that calling like spilled ink seeping into the rug, staining the frenzy of magic with quiet.

"Okay," she said, or maybe she didn't, because she didn't hear herself. The white was bleeding out of her vision, leaving a face hovering above hers—fuzzy for a second, but turning sharp and clear. Ruben's face. His eyes were dark and worried. His hair had fallen onto his forehead. His mouth was moving. Dimly she heard his voice, but she didn't know what he was saying.

Okay, she said again, but this time she knew she hadn't said it with her mouth, hadn't said it to those who heard with their ears, and she knew what she agreed to—knew without hearing or sight or senses or words, knew in a way that didn't impinge on her physical self at all, that would leave no trace behind on her brain to be later retrieved through memory.

She reached up, gripped the back of Ruben's neck with one hand. Pushed herself up with her other arm. And breathed into his mouth.

Magic moved through her, a smooth, tickly, tingling wave of pine and fur and midnight and song—song she could taste but not hear as it rolled out of her gut, up her throat, into her mouth . . . and out. Into Ruben.

Who jerked back, eyes wide, mouth a round *oh!* of amazement before it stretched, contorting along with the rest of his face in a grimace of pain, then froze in that contortion for a second, two, three . . .

He clutched at his chest. Tried to shove to his feet, but fell over, screaming. A scream cut off as the reality he'd been born to and lived in all his life splintered—reality contorting as his face had, a sundering of flesh and form that shuffled rules and shapes and meaning into Other.

As he began to Change.

TWENTY-FOUR

~

LILY had watched the Change many times. She had never truly seen it. Her eyes couldn't track or her brain process events that were only partway of her space. But she recognized it, oh yes, and scrambled back. Away from the place where a man was being ripped apart.

"What the hell!"

That was Scott, clearly audible over Deborah's panting, wordless exclamation as she reached for Ruben.

Lily knocked her hand away. "Stay back. Stay back."

"What have you done!" Deborah screamed. "What did you do to him?"

It was taking Ruben so long. The Change didn't drag on for this long. Or it never had when Lily saw it, but she'd never seen First Change.

Dear God. First Change.

"Lily," Scott cried, "I can't—I can't fight it."

Lily's head jerked around. Scott's eyes were almost wholly black, with only tiny triangles of white tucked into the corners. Ruben was dragging him into the Change. He was a mantle-holder. He could do that—would do that, willy-nilly, since he had no control himself.

"Let go!" she cried. Let it happen. It couldn't be stopped,

so don't fight it, and maybe if Scott stopped fighting, Ruben's Change could complete itself.

Reality went tap-dancing where Scott stood, folding and twisting itself like a Möbius strip on speed. Scott's clothes fell to the floor, unsupported by a body that briefly failed to conform to the usual dimensions. Then a large gray wolf panted in Deborah's kitchen.

And a large black wolf lay on her floor.

The black wolf's sides heaved as if he'd been running. He raised his head, gave it a little shake. Tried to rise, but fell back. Slowly gathered himself for another try.

"Ruben," Deborah whispered, and started forward.

Lily stepped in front of her. "Stay back. It's First Change. He's not safe."

As if her voice loosed some spurt of energy or focus in the wolf, he heaved to his feet, then stood with his head hanging.

"Scott," Lily said softly, "how much danger are we in?"

The gray wolf answered by moving between the women and the other wolf . . . who raised his head to look at them. His eyes were bright and fierce and yellow. A low growl rumbled up from his chest. His hackles rose.

"But it's Ruben." Deborah sounded numb and baffled. "Whatever you did to him, it's still Ruben." She tried to move around Lily.

The wolf's lips peeled back from a fearsome set of teeth, and the growl grew louder.

Lily seized Deborah's arm and pulled her back. "He doesn't know you because he doesn't know himself. He doesn't remember being a man. He's beast-lost, and he's scared, and you—"

Clumsy but fast, the black wolf charged.

The gray wolf blocked him and the two of them fell to the floor in a tangle of fur and snapping jaws. Scott twisted free and placed himself in front of the women again, his own hackles raised, teeth exposed. Dominance posture.

"Back," Lily hissed, pulling Deborah with her. The woman's breath came in scared little pants.

Ruben should have been intimidated by the confident adult wolf. Instead he charged.

Lily bumped into one of the chairs at the table. No place to go. She looked around quickly for a weapon. She wasn't about to start shooting, but she had to get Deborah away from the snapping, surging clangor of wolves on the kitchen floor.

No weapons. "Scott, we're going to head for the back door along the rear wall. Try to—"

Deborah jerked out of Lily's hold and grabbed her shoulders. "Change him *back*! Whatever you did, you have to undo it!" She shook Lily's shoulders. "Undo it!"

Lily brought both hands up and spread them quickly to break Deborah's hold. "I didn't—" But she had. Or rather, she'd agreed to it. She knew that much, even if she couldn't quite remember what she'd known when she said *okay*. "I can't change him back. He'll have to do that himself, but he won't be able to for a while. He's a new wolf, Deborah. That means that for now he's *all* wolf."

A crash had her spinning back to face the two struggling wolves. They'd knocked into the wheeled island in the center of the kitchen, sending it smashing into the cabinets. In three quick seconds the tangle of fur resolved into two wolves once more . . . with the black wolf looming over the gray one, looking down with teeth bared, that ominous growl rumbling up his throat.

The gray wolf lay still. Breathing, not visibly harmed, but motionless.

He was submitting. Scott was submitting to Ruben. It made no sense. Mature wolves simply did not submit to new wolves. Scott was a canny and experienced fighter. Better on two feet than four, according to Rule, but good in either form. He should have been easily able to subdue a wolf so new to four legs that he'd had to relearn walking.

But the black wolf held a mantle.

A new wolf with a mantle. Dear God. A terrified, confused, and no doubt *hungry* new wolf with a mantle.

"Deborah," she whispered. Both wolves would hear her, but maybe a whisper was less threatening. "Do you have meat? Something defrosted. It needs to smell like meat."

Deborah shook her head, staring at the wolves in her kitchen. "Some chicken. We were going to have chicken and dumplings for supper. I think . . . he didn't hurt him. See? Ruben isn't hurting the—the other wolf. He's not as dangerous as you—"

The black wolf's head shot forward. In an eye-blink he'd seized Scott's foreleg in his jaws. Lily heard the crack of bone clearly in spite of Scott's single, high yelp.

Deborah made a small, choked sound. Scott was utterly silent. Utterly still.

The black wolf moved slowly, turning to face them, head down, eyes intent.

"Okay," Lily said, thinking fast. "I'm going to head for your refrigerator. He'll track me because I'm moving. See if you can make it to the back door. Scott will do what he can." Even three-legged, Scott could fight. Surely whatever mantle mojo Ruben had pulled wouldn't hold Scott frozen if Ruben attacked one of them. It was the wrong mantle, wasn't it? Scott was Leidolf, not Wythe. Ruben might be able to force Scott to submit, but he shouldn't be able to truly control him.

She thought. She hoped. "He needs to eat. I'll feed him. Scott, I know you heard me. Wag your tail or something to confirm."

Scott's tail twitched once.

"I will not."

Lily looked at the stupid, stubborn woman beside her. "You will do this."

"I'm not running away."

Lily took a deep breath. "He broke Scott's leg because he's a threat. We aren't. We're food."

"Then we'd better feed him something else. And fast."

"Then—" Lily's shoulders tensed as she sensed something. Thank God. Oh, thank God. They only had to hold Ruben off a little longer. "Better take a chair."

"What?"

The black wolf settled back slightly on his haunches.

Lily shoved Deborah hard, reached behind her for the chair she'd backed up against—and swung it with all her strength. It connected squarely with the leaping wolf.

He fell, skidded, then staggered to his feet. Scott had gotten himself erect and once more placed himself between the other wolf and the women. "Rule!" Lily yelled. "Hurry!"

Something smashed at the front of the house. The black wolf shook his head once . . . and came in low. And fast, faster than he'd moved before. He was learning this form way too quickly. He knocked into Scott, shoving him aside. Lily held him off with the chair—but he seized one of the legs in his jaws and pulled.

The chair went flying.

Rule raced into the room—leaped—and Changed—and was wolf by the time he collided with the black wolf.

"It's Ruben!" Lily called out. "I don't know what he smells like, but it's Ruben, only he's a new wolf."

The fight was brief. Ruben couldn't use the mantle on Rule, couldn't intimidate or slow him, and Rule *knew* this form. In moments, Rule had the black wolf by the neck. The other wolf sank to the floor. Rule released him and the wolf rolled onto his back, belly up. Rule moved to stand over him, opened his jaws, and seized Ruben by the muzzle.

"Oh, God, oh, God, oh, God," Deborah whispered.

"It's okay. He's just saying it like he means it. Ruben has to mean it, too."

For several heartbeats the two wolves didn't move. Finally Ruben whined faintly.

Rule lifted his head and looked at Lily. As clearly as if he'd said it, she read the "What the hell?" in his eyes.

"I don't know. I don't know, but he's the one the Lady picked." She gestured at the black wolf, still lying submissively quiet. "When I got here . . . I'll tell you later, but he's got the mantle now."

Rule's gaze went to Deborah, who'd gripped Lily's arm again and held on tight. Back to Lily. He growled once.

"Tough. If the Lady didn't want Deborah to know about mantles, she shouldn't have stuck one in her husband. Are you okay?"

He nodded once, looking at her intently. After a second she guessed what his question must be. "I'm fine. Actually . . ." She paused, lifted both arms. Flexed her biceps. "I'm all the way fine." No pain. No weakness in her right arm. None. She twisted that arm to look. There was a scar still, but no dent. The muscle had grown back. "Jesus, that's weird. Scott? You okay?"

The gray wolf nodded slowly. Not fine, maybe, but as okay as he could be with a broken leg.

Rule moved off the black wolf, who rolled so his belly wasn't exposed but stayed down, watching Rule intently. Tentatively he stretched up his head so he could lick Rule's muzzle: wolf-speak for *You're in charge. Let's be friends.* Rule allowed that for a moment, then licked him back once. The black wolf wriggled like a puppy.

Deborah was still breathing too fast. Still on the edge of panic. "I don't know what's going on. What happened to Ruben? What did you do? He'll be himself again, won't he?"

"Eventually. I think. I, ah . . ." Lily struggled for words to explain the inexplicable. "The CliffsNotes version is that I've been babysitting a mantle—that's a magical construct that Rhos use to unite their clans, and you need to not tell anyone, anyone at all, about mantles, okay?"

"That will be easy. I don't know anything to tell."

"Details later. I had to babysit this mantle for a while because the Rho of that clan died without an heir. For some God-only-knows-what reason, today the Lady decided to put the mantle into Ruben. Somehow that triggered him into going into First Change. I don't know how. It sure didn't do that to me, and he's not lupus either, so—"

Rule yipped.

"You mean he is? He smells lupus?"

He nodded.

Deborah looked more baffled than ever. "Is he—is Ruben okay now?"

Lily looked at Rule. "Is Ruben going to obey you? Because you need to clear out. I need to clear out. I came here because they're going to arrest him. Did you get my message?"

Rule yipped again, glanced at Scott, and made a little circle in the air with his muzzle.

Lily frowned. "Why do you want Scott to Change instead of you doing it?"

Scott wasn't as blindingly quick as Rule, but fast enough.

In a few seconds he stood there, entirely naked, cradling his broken arm. "Where's the chicken?"

"What?"

"The chicken. Rule needs to feed him."

"The refrigerator," Deborah said quickly and hurried to it. The black wolf shivered as if her movement excited or frightened him, but a glance from Rule kept him still. Deborah took out a package of chicken breasts. "Do I—"

"No, I do." Scott snatched the package, ripped off the plastic, and advanced a couple steps before going to his knees and scrunching down, his head bent low, to set the foam tray on the floor. He shoved it toward the wolves.

He was underscoring Rule's dominance, Lily realized. Baring his nape, submitting to Rule, showing the black wolf that all the other wolves in the room let Rule boss them around, too.

Rule stepped away from the black wolf, who started to rise—until Rule's head swung around, teeth bared. He went flat again. Rule then inspected the offering in a leisurely way, sniffing it thoroughly. The black wolf quivered but didn't move.

Rule-wolf selected one breast, crunched a couple times, then gulped it down. Then he used his nose to push the tray toward the other wolf—who looked at him as if asking permission. Rule stepped back. *It's all yours.*

The black wolf was on his feet and devouring the chicken like he was on fast-forward.

Rule made a single, low noise, sort of a grunt. He looked at Scott. Scott frowned, then his eyes widened. "A car. I hear it now. It's out front."

Drummond? Maybe. Probably. "Quick," Lily said, turning to Deborah. "Go see who it is. Don't let them in. See who it is and let me know."

For once the woman didn't argue. She ran. Lily spun back to Rule. "You have to get Ruben out of here. They're going to arrest him. If they find him here like that"—she waved at the black wolf, who'd polished off the chicken and was licking the wrappings—"he won't be able to control himself at all. He won't understand what's happening. God. You'll need clothes."

She flung the next words at Scott as she hurried to the back door. "Can you go with them? With your arm?"

He was already bending, scooping up piles of fallen clothing with his good arm. "Of course."

Rule nudged Ruben with his nose. The black wolf snarled but stopped hunting for another scrap of chicken.

Lily fumbled with the lock, then flung the door open. "Make sure you've got Rule's wallet and phone. Hurry."

Rule gave Lily a single glance, then shoved at Ruben with his whole body before loping out the door. The black wolf followed as if he'd been told to. Scott was a few seconds behind with one arm circling their bundled clothing, the other one propped uncertainly on top of it. He hadn't taken time for clothes, but he'd slipped on his shoes.

Lily shut the door, grabbed the tray the chicken had been in, and jammed it in the trash. She raced to the sink, turned on the water, and yanked at the roll of paper towels.

"There's four of them," Deborah said, slightly breathless as she ran back into the room. "I don't know the other three, but I know Al Drummond. He interviewed me. They're almost—"

The doorbell rang.

"Pour you and me some coffee." Lily thrust a wad of paper towels under the tap. "Not full—as if we've been sipping awhile. Put the cups on the table. Pick the chairs up. I dropped by unexpectedly," she went on quickly as Deborah hurried to the coffeepot. She bent and started wiping blood smears from the floors. "Ruben wasn't here. He left to take a walk about an hour ago, shortly before I arrived." Neither of the wolves had bled badly, but they'd smeared it all over, dammit. Lily went for more paper towels.

"But you'll be in trouble." Deborah set two half-full mugs on the table and a plate of cookies. Good touch. She broke off a corner of one the cookies and crushed it to leave crumbs on the table then righted one of the chairs. "You aren't supposed to be here."

"No choice." Rule's car was in front of the house. If she skipped out the back door, they'd look for him. She couldn't let that happen. "We haven't talked about the investigation or the events at Fagin's house. Mostly about you—how you're holding up, that sort of thing."

Deborah was carrying the other chair across the kitchen. "My parents are giving me a hard time. You can tell them that. The leg on this one's broken." She opened a door to what seemed to be a pantry and took the chair inside. "Where will Rule take Ruben? What's going to happen to him?"

The doorbell rang again.

"Questions later. Better let them in." Lily tossed her towels in the trash, then cast a quick glance over the kitchen. No visible blood. Even if she missed some and Drummond was psychic enough to run lab tests on it, the tests wouldn't tell them much. Not with lupi blood.

The kitchen island still rested against the cabinets. Lily hurried over to it as Deborah emerged from the pantry. "Get the door. Hurry."

Deborah's face was pale but composed. Or maybe she'd just shut down. Either would work for now. "The cup. The one I dropped. There're pieces by the table."

"I'll get it." Lily shoved at the island. "Go."

Deborah did, her shoes clicking firmly on the floor. Lily left the island roughly where she remembered it being, hurried to the table, and bent to snatch up bits of broken coffee cup. Should have seen this when she was mopping up blood.

Voices at the front of the house. No time. She crammed the pottery shards behind a spring green throw pillow on the banquette, sat in the only remaining chair, and took a bite of a cookie.

"I told you," Deborah was saying, her voice growing closer, "he went for a walk."

"Was that before or after someone smashed your window?" Drummond asked.

"I didn't know it had been broken until you asked me about it just now. I haven't been at the front of the house."

Lily washed down the bite with a sip of cold coffee just as Drummond strode into the room with Deborah a pace behind. Three more men followed behind the two of them—two she didn't know, plus Mullins, who was looking especially dense and dull.

"I'm sure Ruben will be back soon," Deborah said. "I don't know what else to tell you."

Drummond stopped when he saw Lily—but not like he was surprised. He smiled, cold and nasty, his eyes glittering with anger. "Look who beat me here. What a coincidence. You dropped by to chat with a suspect just before I came to arrest him."

"You're arresting Ruben?"

"He doesn't seem to be here, does he? You know anything about that?"

Lily looked at those glittering eyes and her stomach lurched as if she were in an elevator headed down way too fast.

That wasn't anger she saw. That was triumph. Drummond had just gotten exactly what he wanted. "How could I? I'm not part of the investigation anymore."

"You got the last part right. Special Agent Lily Yu, you are under arrest."

TWENTY-FIVE

~~

IN the cold darkness beneath the oaks and hawthorns and elms, the world was moist and fragrant. Two wolves walked under those trees. Leaves crunched and released their mélange of scent-messages with every footfall. Impossible even for Rule to walk silently here, much less the raw new wolf who trailed him.

Enough leafy canopy remained above them to hide the stars . . . though not the moon, not entirely. Fat and pale and so nearly full Rule's eyes could barely limn the missing sliver, she lit their way and flooded them with moonsong. Behind him the new one paused as he had from time to time, so intoxicated by the scent-torrent the world poured upon him in shimmering abundance that he had to stop and smell. Just smell.

Rule paused patiently with him.

Tomorrow was full moon. The three days and nights leading up to full moon were the normal period for First Change. And that was the only normal thing about this particular First Change.

Rule didn't think of the wolf who followed him as Ruben Brooks because he wasn't. Surely he would be again. This First Change couldn't be that different. But it would be a few days, perhaps a week, before memories and thoughts of his other form began to surface; another week before he was able to resume his original form for a time. That would happen at the new moon following First Change. Brand-new wolves often needed help with that Change, or at least strong encouragement.

Those first two weeks were a heady time, each moment brimming with newness and delight. Or they should be. The wolf keeping pace with Rule had known all too much confusion and fear. It boded ill for how man and wolf would weave their joint life in days to come.

Of course, until now, no lupi had ever been a forty-six-year-old man when First Change hit. They could hope that would make a difference.

Rule and the wolf who used to be Ruben Brooks wound through the trees along the west side of Dumbarton Oaks Park, roughly forty acres of woodlands in the middle of Georgetown. It had taken them hours to get this far. Some of that was due to the careful, roundabout way two wolves must travel in a populous city, but some had to do with the new wolf's need to play.

Normally new wolves were born at First Change into bodies as gangly and unfinished as the boys they were before that moment—not puppies, no, but not fully adult, and with a youngster's need to play and explore. This wolf needed that, too, though his body was fully mature. He and Rule had romped in Rock Creek Park—Mika was away from his lair, unfortunately, but Rule made sure they left their scent near it—and rolled in the creek as they followed it south. Once they reached Dumbarton, they'd snapped at scampering field mice near the Naval Observatory, then flushed a rabbit in the wooded area between the embassies of Denmark and Italy.

The new wolf had been very excited about the rabbit. He'd lost him quickly, of course—rabbits were fast and agile, and this wolf was still unused to his body. But he'd had a marvelous time making the attempt.

Rule rather regretted that rabbit now, though. He was hungry and getting hungrier by the minute.

It wouldn't be long now. Immediately in front of them lay

the Citibank parking lot. Rule approached close enough to
watch the lot while remaining hidden himself, covered by the
shadow of a large elm. With the wind at their backs, they'd
have scent to alert them of intruders from behind.

He lay down—not curled up for sleep, but keeping his head
erect. The other wolf settled close to him, their sides touching,
and licked his muzzle. Rule allowed that for a moment, then
sniffed along the other wolf's muzzle and jaw and gave his ear
a single lick: *You're safe. You're not alone. You've done well.
I will look out for you.*

The new wolf wagged his tail once, then rested his head on
his forelegs with a tired sigh, relaxing.

He needed the physical contact. He needed a great deal
more. A new wolf should be surrounded by clan—by their
scent, the feel of their bodies, with even their pulses coursing
in time with his.

Rule could give this wolf only a small taste of that comfort.
He'd done what he could. He'd defeated him, dominated him,
and fed him, so the wolf trusted him now. But instinctively, the
new wolf would be longing for many, and Rule was only one.
One who did not smell like Wythe.

Rule had hoped the new wolf might accept non-Wythe
wolves. No luck with that. When Rule had paused in the scrap
of woods near Ruben's house to contact his guards stationed
there, the new wolf had snapped and snarled at them. In spite
of that, Rule had signaled the others to circle the new one,
knowing what would happen when he Changed so he could
give them instructions. Sure enough, when the only wolf he
trusted turned into a man, the new wolf had tried to flee. The
others hadn't let him, but it had been a near thing. Rule had
given his instructions, sending Scott to the house to relay
some of them, and Changed back quickly.

Three Changes in close succession, and only a single,
gulped chicken breast to eat. No wonder he felt half-starved.
Rule continued to wait upon the company that would arrive
soon.

That company would please him more than his charge.
Wolves who were not-Wythe did not comfort this wolf—who
instinctively tried to gather them under his own dominion, and

never mind how bad an idea that was. The new wolf didn't know that, didn't know much of anything yet, but a new wolf *had* to be controlled. Not only because he was dangerous, being all power and instinct and no control, but because he needed the security of knowing he was guided by one able to dominate him.

Very few could dominate this wolf. Only those with a mantle.

A new wolf with a full mantle—what was the Lady *thinking?*

Rule wasn't surprised Scott had submitted. The surprise was that the black wolf had chosen to cripple rather than kill. That was remarkable restraint in a wolf fresh from First Change.

But then, Ruben the man was highly dominant. As a wolf he had the same instincts, even without memory's guide.

Lily, he thought, wouldn't understand the connection. She didn't understand dominance. It frustrated Rule. How could she not understand, when she herself was so clearly dominant? But she confused dominance with the need to control others—and that was part of it, yes, yet naming the whole for the part distorted meaning into incoherence.

He suspected she saw dominance and submission in vaguely sexual terms. She considered submission a surrender of autonomy. But *autonomy* as humans used the term seemed absurdly artificial to Rule. He understood personal responsibility. He also understood that "no man is an island." He did not understand why so many humans embraced the myth that individuals could and should stand alone. It was as if they thought *everyone* should be dominant.

No, at its heart, submission simply acknowledged fact: the other had the skill and power to kill you . . . and the skill and power to defend you. The two were inseparable. When you submitted, you placed your life in the other's jaws. If the other was truly dominant, he accepted this. And would then defend that life as if it were his own.

That's what he must tell Lily, Rule realized. A dominant wolf controlled, yes—but the need to control arose from the need to protect.

Lily.

His heart bunched itself up tight in his chest, sending a tremor of hurt and fear rippling through him. The hurt was the wolf's. It was good Lily wasn't here. Necessary. She was much too human to be around such a new one, who would know her only as threat or prey. But he knew she was distressed, in trouble, and he ached for her, ached to be with her.

The man was more frantic. Words, always words, for the man, but fewer than usual this time: What had happened to her? Did they know she'd tipped Ruben off? They would guess, surely. She wasn't supposed to be at Ruben's house. What would the authorities—her own Bureau—do to her?

The new wolf raised his head, rumbling deep in his throat. There are as many kinds of growls for a wolf as there are smiles for a human; this one betokened anxiety, not anger or challenge. Muscle by muscle, Rule denied his fear. He was used to this discipline, to the need to physically mask his emotions, but doing so came hard tonight. He wanted to howl, to run. To Change and go to Lily.

He did what he had to do. Slowly the other relaxed as well, even falling into a light doze.

The moon climbed a handspan higher. Rule waited.

At last headlights wheeled across the pavement on the other side of the screening oaks. Rule stood, keeping his muscles loose and his stance alert. The other wolf rose with him, hackles raised slightly, but holding himself still and quiet.

Perhaps the age of the wolf's submerged other self did make a difference. The other was following Rule's signals unusually well for one so raw: *Be alert. Be silent. Watch.*

The vehicle pulled to the rear of the lot. It was an old panel truck, slightly scabrous with peeling paint, but the motor sounded good. Not one of the vehicles Rule kept for the guards' use. It stopped about thirty feet away. The engine shut off. The driver's door swung open.

It wasn't who Rule had been expecting. Though he probably should have. He yipped once, softly, to announce his location. He looked at the other wolf, then at the ground.

The other either didn't understand or didn't want to. Rule lay down again to show him. Slowly the other did, too. Rule stood, but this time when the other tried to rise, Rule shoved him back down. He looked directly in the other's eyes.

The black wolf sighed and dropped his head to his paws. When Rule trotted to the edge of the pavement, he stayed put.

Cullen limped toward them carrying a plastic grocery sack and a small duffle bag. His gauze-wrapped feet were thrust into soft house slippers. Stubborn ass. Skin healed faster than bone or muscle, but not this fast.

Rule had sent word to José about where to meet and what was needed. He hadn't said Cullen should be the one to bring those supplies. He hadn't specifically forbidden it, either. He should have known Cullen would take that for permission. He should have known Cullen would be here. That his friend would know he needed him.

Behind him, the other wolf stirred. Rule gave him one sharp stare and he subsided. Rule faced Cullen and looked him in the eye.

"What?" Cullen stopped. "Oh, right. I forgot." He ducked his head to expose his nape—a clear statement that he was subordinate to Rule. The new wolf would be confused by this. Cullen wasn't wolf, but his posture announced his claim on Rule.

Now Rule had to announce his own claim on Cullen. Rule stepped forward and made a show of greeting him by sniffing his face—then, pointedly, his feet. He looked at Cullen.

"Not a problem," his friend lied breezily. "The Rhej sped things up a lot."

He was walking on them, so the Rhej must have done him some good. Not as much as he was pretending. Rule snorted.

Cullen ignored that. "Scott's doing fine. It'll be a couple days before he's healed enough to go back on duty, but he's fine. The house is being watched. Had a bitch of a time getting away without being seen, then I had to get a panel truck, which is why I'm so late. Ready for dinner?" He opened the grocery sack and tossed a raw brisket on the pavement.

Rule heard the other wolf rise. He turned his head, growled—*You do not eat before I do*—then bent to rip off a bite. "Dessert's in the back of the truck," Cullen said, backing away quickly. "Hot bratwurst."

Hunger gnawed, but as soon as Rule swallowed that token mouthful, he stopped. Later he'd make the new wolf wait until he was truly finished eating—it was good discipline—but not yet. He stepped back, looked from the meat to the black wolf. *I have provided for you. Eat.*

The other was on the raw meat in a flash. Cullen set a second brisket on the pavement and sat down beside it.

That one was Rule's. He trotted over and ate while Cullen talked.

"I talked with Walt and a couple of the other Wythe elders. Officially, Wythe is elated to have a Rho again. Unofficially, they're almost as scared as they are relieved. He's not just a new wolf—he's never been lupi before. He doesn't know our ways, our history, et cetera, et cetera. I pointed out that Wythe was already allied with Ruben per the Lady's command, and now she's given him to them as Rho. She must have special plans for Wythe. That puffed out their chests. They're still nervous, but excited, too."

Rule wagged his tail once as he gulped down a chunk of warm beef: *Good work.*

"About the rendezvous. Walt's bringing Mac Sutherland—he works with their new ones—and three others, like you wanted. You said for him to pick the spot. He suggested Bald Eagle State Park in Pennsylvania. You know it?"

Rule shook his head and ripped off another bite.

"It's about six thousand acres, a lot of that forest, which works for us. Unfortunately, it's always open season on coyotes in Pennsylvania, but otherwise not much hunting's going on right now. The park's between four and five hours from Wythe Clanhome, maybe three and a half from here. That's assuming you can get your new wolf into the panel truck and he doesn't freak. If he does, well, everything will take a lot longer. I brought a map and some other gear."

Cullen pulled a folded map from his jacket pocket and spread it on the ground. He glanced at the new wolf, who kept interrupting his meal to growl at Cullen—warning growls, not seriously aggressive, so Rule ignored it. "I talked to Mason," Cullen said, naming the Nokolai who had charge of the new

wolves at the *terra tradis*, "so I'd have some idea how to act.
I've never worked with brand-new wolves. You did, though."

Rule nodded. That experience was coming in handy now.
Rule had spent one season working with Mason. It had been
frustrating, exhilarating, funny, infuriating, and at times great
fun—new wolves were teenagers, after all.

Or had been until this one arrived. Rule glanced at the
other, then polished off his meal and shifted to study the map.

"This is Bald Eagle," Cullen said, pointing, "just north of
I-80. We'll look for Walter south of the lake. You think the new
one will tolerate four hours in the van with me so close?"

Rule couldn't shrug in this form, so he snorted. How could
he know? New wolves were introduced to clan members' two-
legged forms early on, but not in the cramped confines of a
panel truck, not for hours at a time, and always with older
adolescents around to demonstrate proper behavior and adults
to enforce it. But it was worth trying. So far, the wolf that had
been Ruben Brooks was handling himself very well.

Rule looked pointedly at the duffel bag.

"Right. Guess we'll find out." Cullen pulled a collapsible
water bowl out of the duffle bag, then a gallon jug of water. He
filled the bowl. "José didn't think I should take a vehicle registered in your name, so I bought the panel truck for cash from
a guy who'd advertised in the paper. Your cash, of course. You
didn't get a very good deal, but I was in a hurry."

Rule nodded and went to the water bowl.

Cullen waited until he finished, refilled the bowl, then
backed off again, but only ten feet. There was a brief clash of
wills as the new wolf tried to get Cullen to go away and Rule
insisted that Cullen was his to direct, not the new wolf's.
Eventually the new wolf accepted that and drank.

This didn't mean he'd accept it the next time. Or the next.
The wolf had no instinctive understanding of Cullen except as
threat or prey, and it took time and repetition to create a new
role—*lupi, one of us, never mind the form*—in the wolf's
mind. Once he began remembering being a man himself,
though, that lesson would stick better. Once he'd Changed a
few times, it would be solid.

It took much longer for a wolf to stop seeing humans as potential prey. Four or five years, usually. Oh, most new wolves were able to restrain themselves long before that, but forbidden food is still food. They were kept away from humans except in controlled circumstances until their first response to the smell of humanity was *people*, not *meat*.

How long would it be before Ruben could live with his beautiful Deborah again?

Rule shook that thought off. Worrying about things he couldn't change was foolish.

The other wolf had finished drinking. He stood still and taut, sniffing the air warily, glancing frequently at Rule. That wasn't typical. With a full belly and no immediate danger, most new wolves would be looking for sleep or play or some interesting scent to track. Was the difference a matter of this one being older? Or was it the way he'd been brought into this form, unprepared and surrounded from the first with what he considered threats instead of clan?

No way of knowing. Rule collected the new wolf with a glance, and the two of them trotted into the trees. They relieved themselves, then Rule had a good roll in the leaves. It felt good, it smelled good, and he wanted to take some of the scents of the forest with him into the metal cage-on-wheels Cullen would be driving.

The plan was to get the other wolf to follow Rule into the back of the panel truck. The bratwurst should help. Rule didn't know a wolf who wouldn't salivate over that smell. Cullen would close the door quickly, then wait.

Rule hoped the other wolf would not turn out to be as sensitive to small places as he was. Even so, there would be a period of panic and adjustment. Assuming Rule could get the new wolf to settle down, Cullen would drive them to Bald Eagle Park—Rule had let Walt pick the rendezvous point—where Walt and several Wythe wolves would meet them.

Being surrounded by wolves who smelled right should help the new wolf adjust. It would be great if, at that point, Rule could turn his charge over to his clan. That wasn't going to happen. The new wolf didn't really know how to use the mantle he carried, but no Wythe wolf was going to be able to dominate his own Rho. On foot or in a mobile cage, Rule would be continuing with the others to Wythe Clanhome . . . nearly three hundred miles away from Washington.

If the mate bond allowed it.

Rule snarled silently at the empty air. The mate bond was the Lady's gift.

Hadn't the Lady contrived to land him—and Ruben, and Lily, and the entire Wythe clan—in precisely this position? Rule didn't understand it. How could Ruben have been turned into a lupus? One with founder's blood, no less, able to carry the mantle. It made no sense. But somehow the Lady had done just that. She'd tinkered with the mantle while it resided within Lily.

She could damn well tinker with the mate bond, too.

She'd better. If Rule crossed that invisible boundary at highway speeds and passed out, it meant that here in D.C. Lily would probably pass out, too. Wherever she was. Whatever she was doing.

Lily.

Cullen hadn't spoken of her. Rule hadn't forced him to, though he could have, even in this wordless form. Silently, tacitly, they'd agreed to put off the moment of bad news . . . because it would be bad news.

Enough of that. Rule shook himself and glanced to his left. The other wolf had relaxed once they were surrounded by trees again and was happily digging at an abandoned rabbit burrow. Rule left him to that and trotted up to Cullen. He sat and looked at his friend.

For a long moment Cullen met his gaze without speaking. He sighed. "Lily. Yes. I haven't talked to her myself, but . . . well, Drummond charged her with interfering with an investigation. She's in jail."

TWENTY-SIX

THEY don't turn the lights off in holding cells.

The heavy woman with dreads and a blood-spattered orange shirt rocked and muttered to herself. She'd kept that up all night. A Hispanic woman argued with a brittle-looking blonde with a puffy lip and torn shirt. Up near the bars, a tall, skinny woman hooted with laughter at something one of her friends said. Prostitutes, those three, and Lily's most relaxed roommates . . . unless you counted the ones who were passed out. Like the white-haired woman in a Dior suit who'd vomited all over herself and the floor about thirty minutes ago. Lily had had to get up and turn the woman's head to make sure she didn't aspirate the vomit and choke to death. At the rear of the cell a sad but sober-looking young black woman with some kind of stomach problem sat on the toilet, ignoring the rest of them.

When Lily first arrived, a muscular fortyish woman with bad teeth and biker tats had tried to charge admittance to the toilet—"I'll keep them black bitches from messing with you, an' you'll owe me a favor, see?" Bad Teeth hadn't taken "go away" for an answer, probably because Lily looked too little to be a threat. Lily had put her on the floor quick enough that the guards either didn't notice or hadn't felt a need to intervene.

Turnover was high here. Bad Teeth was long gone. So was everyone else who'd been here when the cell door shut behind Lily.

Lily had one of the prime spots. She sat on the floor and leaned against the wall near the front of the cell, where the air was a bit better. Three feet from her face were the torn jeans of a girl who probably wasn't eighteen yet. She was clearly coming off something, shifting from foot to foot, staring out the bars with wild eyes. "I gotta get out of here. I gotta get out."

It could have been worse. Lily had seen worse. At no point had the cell been too crowded to sit down, and she'd been able to lie down part of the time, until she got too sleepy. She hadn't dared fall asleep, which might be good sense or sheer paranoia.

She was here because she'd screwed up, yeah. Also because she'd been manipulated by the Lady to carry that damn mantle to Ruben. But she was certain, deep in her gut, that she was also here because this is where someone wanted her.

She'd been set up. And she'd fallen for it.

Not that she could prove it. Her thoughts circled round that lack of proof yet again, trying to fit it to her conviction, testing this person and that one as suspects. Drummond? Sjorensen? Mullins? She had nothing to go on.

Almost nothing. She'd had nothing to do but think since they locked her up, and some of that had been productive. She had a mental list of questions and some ideas about what to check out if she ever got out of here.

Lily shifted, sick of sitting. But there was nowhere to go. Nothing to do. Lily had been in for nearly a full day. She'd been allowed her one phone call, but was beginning to think she'd called the wrong damn person. None of the others had been here as long as she had. She shouldn't have been kept here this long, either.

She shouldn't have been here at all. And not just in the *oh-mygod* sense.

Drummond had delegated her custody to his favorite flunky. Doug Mullins had brought her here, not to Headquarters or another federal facility, not to an interrogation room. She hadn't been questioned at all.

That was either sheer spite or something more ominous. If they questioned her and she refused to answer without an attorney present, they'd have to process her into a regular cell, not the smelly hell of a holding cell at a county jail. So they wanted her here, but was that because they wanted her to have a really bad night? Or did they have some other reason for keeping her tucked away, in the system but not where anyone would expect to find her?

Some of the reasons she came up with were probably nutty. She still hadn't dared sleep.

Once she'd told Rule she wondered what it would be like to miss him. The mate bond had made that unlikely, she thought. They always played it safe. Sometimes it allowed them to put plenty of space between them, sometimes it didn't, so they stayed within the same city.

He was miles and miles away now. Two hundred? Three? She couldn't tell. Why so far? Where was he, and where was he going? There hadn't been time to talk about what he'd do—and he hadn't been shaped for talking.

But surely the distance meant he and Ruben had gotten away. At least Rule wasn't locked up in a reeking cell. And Ruben . . . dear God. The Lady wanted him for Rho of Wythe? He was lupi? Only he couldn't be. You had to be born lupi. You had to have founder's blood to carry the mantle.

Start with what is and work back, she told herself. Ruben had gone through First Change. He smelled lupus. He hadn't before, but he did now. Those added up to a big, fat yes—whatever had happened to him, he was now lupi. Second fact. He carried the Wythe mantle, and not the way Lily had, as a passive passenger. It was active in him. Scott had been unable to stand against him, unable to fight him effectively. Did that mean he did have some of the founder's bloodline in him? Did she know anything to contradict that?

She didn't know anything, period. But it was something to check out . . . if she ever got out of here. If she ever . . . her head jerked. She'd dozed off. Only for a second, but she couldn't stay awake forever. She should get up and move around, do some stretches or sit-ups or something, wake herself up.

She would in just a minute. Even though she was probably

crazy to think she was in danger. The only threat in the fifteen hours she'd been here had been Bad Teeth, and she'd been after "favors," not murder. But she'd get up and move around and . . .

Her head jerked again.

One of the guards, a heavyset woman who hadn't smiled in at least thirty years, came up to the door. "Lily Yu."

Lily blinked and stood slowly. "Yes?"

"Guess you've got a good lawyer." The woman unlocked the cell door.

The guard didn't have handcuffs out. "I'm . . . being released?"

"Own recognizance. Follow me, please."

She hadn't been arraigned, which was when bail would be set, or the judge could decide to let her out on her own recognizance. Yet they were releasing her. Lily shook her head, trying to clear it, and walked out of the cell.

Being released was nowhere near as humiliating and time-consuming as being admitted to the facilities, but it still took a while. She had to confirm receipt of everything that was returned—her shoes, jacket, necklace, and engagement ring. Her phone. Her purse and all its contents. Her shoulder holster. Her weapon. She got it all back.

Everything except what mattered most. They couldn't hand her life back. But then, they hadn't taken it. She'd tossed it away of her own free will.

Lily didn't know if she'd actually serve jail time beyond this one day. Interfering with an investigation was a serious charge, but could be hard and costly to prove; few federal attorneys would be interested in prosecuting any but the most egregious cases. And unless they'd gotten Deborah to change her story, they couldn't prove Lily had tipped Ruben off. They could strongly suggest it, sure, but a good lawyer could probably keep her out of jail. Any halfway decent prosecutor would know that. Even if Friar was behind this, even if he had a prosecutor in his pocket and was frothing at the mouth to get Lily locked up, odds were she wouldn't be convicted.

She didn't have to be. The fact of her presence at Ruben's house was enough to get her kicked out of the Bureau.

She wasn't a cop anymore.

Lily walked down the hall a few steps ahead of the heavy-set guard, her head light with exhaustion, and felt no relief at all. She tried to at least be curious about her release, but it didn't seem important. In a minute she'd meet with whatever lawyer had arranged it and he or she would tell her what the situation was.

She emerged into a small, bare room where another guard waited . . . and another man. The one she'd called, but she'd never expected him to come here. A burly man in dark slacks, a pressed shirt, no tie. With his beard, rusty brown hair, and blacksmith's chest and shoulders, he looked like a minor forest god in disguise.

Isen Turner. Rule's father. The Nokolai Rho. Isen, who almost never left Nokolai Clanhome, and absolutely never left California. Yet here he was, crossing the ugly little room to grab her up in a hug.

"Lily." He squeezed her firmly, patted her back, then pulled back enough to smile at her, still holding her arms. "You smell awful. Come. Let's get out of here."

A fondness for Mercedes-Benz must run in the family. That's what Isen had waiting for them in the parking lot. Waiting right outside the courthouse door was a stringy, six-foot-eight-inch giant named Pete Murkowski, second-in-command of security at Clanhome. Pete had baby-fine hair the color of old ivory and long, ropy muscles. He looked funny in clothes, Lily thought. She was used to seeing him in cutoffs.

"Rule," she said to Rule's father. "Have you heard from him? Where is he?"

"He's remaining wolf, so no. I have talked to Cullen, who's with Rule and the new wolf. They're doing well and have arrived at Wythe Clanhome. We'll discuss that later, when there's no chance of anyone eavesdropping. It's unlikely here, but not impossible. You have a nine o'clock appointment tomorrow with your lawyer."

"The arraignment." Lily's stomach knotted.

"That's tomorrow afternoon." They'd reached the car. Pete

gave Lily a nod and a smile as he opened the door for them. "Your lawyer is Miriam Stockard. Perhaps you've heard of her? She regrets that she was unable to meet you this morning, but she had to be in court. Still, her associate seems to have done well by us."

"Stockard. Yeah, I've heard of her. Hi, Pete." Lily felt a bit dazed as she slid into the backseat. Miriam Stockard was one of the top defense attorneys in the country, the bane of prosecutors on both coasts.

Automatically she scooted over so Isen could slide in beside her. He did. Pete went around to the driver's side, climbed in, and got them moving. Lily fastened her seatbelt, turned to Isen, and let the question erupt. "What are you *doing* here?"

Isen's bushy eyebrows rose. He was relaxed, pleased with himself, as if he'd had a wonderful day so far and anticipated plenty of treats to come. "Aside from getting you out of jail, you mean?"

"The lawyer did that. I mean . . . I appreciate you hiring her. I really do. And I'd like to find out how she got me sprung before the arraignment, but she didn't do anything differently because you flew across the country." Lily paused. "I hate to think about what she's costing."

Isen squeezed Lily's shoulder. "Nokolai can afford it."

"I didn't mean for Nokolai to—"

"You called on your Rho for help. Of course Nokolai is paying Ms. Stockard's bill."

Lily fell silent. Naturally Isen would think of it that way. But had she? When she called him, who had she called? Rule's father or . . .

It was disconcerting as hell, but Isen was right. Given one phone call and knowing she couldn't reach Rule, she'd picked Isen. Not because he was Rule's father. Because she trusted him. She trusted him not just to get her a lawyer, but to know what to do, how to do it, who should be told, what the repercussions might be, how to minimize them. She'd trusted him because he was wily and wise, cynical and kind, underhanded and openhanded. Most of all, she'd trusted him to handle things because that's what he did. Because he was Rho. "I guess you've had experience getting your people out of jails."

He chuckled. "That I have, though we prefer to avoid it."

"I'm surprised Stockard took the case. It's small potatoes for her."

"Ah, well, she owed one of the clan a rather large favor. We called it in. Our opponents need to be aware that we can pull out the big guns if they force the issue."

She exchanged a long look with him. Isen had realized the same thing she had—the arrest might ruin her in other ways, but there was a good chance she'd never go to trial. Especially now that the prosecutor knew he'd be dealing with Ms. Miriam Stockard. "Have you ever practiced law?"

"That would create a conflict of interest."

Because he couldn't be sworn in as an officer of the court without lying? Probably. Isen didn't share her respect for the law, but he considered his word binding. He wouldn't want to swear to something he didn't intend to back up. Even now he avoided speaking a deliberate untruth, didn't he? "I guess you called my parents."

"I regret that I didn't follow your request precisely. I called your grandmother. Such news might come best from her, I thought."

"What did she say?"

"She was very angry." He patted Lily's hand. "Not with you. I can't repeat what she said at first. Chinese is not one of my languages. But I do believe our enemies have been well and truly cursed. After we spoke a bit more—in English, for my sake—she gave me instructions for you. You are not to act precipitously, particularly when it comes to killing people."

Lily choked on a laugh. "It's not a habit of mine."

"She may have been projecting, as I believe they call it, based on her own urgent desire to rip certain people apart. You are also not to worry about your parents. She will handle them."

It was one bright, warm kernel to cling to. Grandmother was on her side. But even Grandmother couldn't make the news less than devastating to Lily's parents. By now her mother knew she was disgraced and would be unemployed once the Bureau got around to the paperwork. Her father, too. Croft would have to fire her. He had no choice.

Suddenly weary beyond words, Lily leaned her head back. She closed her eyes and tried not to think.

Unfortunately, she'd never been good at that. Questions pushed at her until their pressure had her eyes popping open again. "You never answered my first question. Why are you here? For that matter, why are you here with Pete instead of Benedict? Who's taking care of Toby?"

"Toby's fine. Benedict and Arjenie are there. And Pete is well able to see to my safety."

"I'm sure he is, but on those rare times you leave Clanhome, Benedict always goes with you." Pete was good—Lily had seen him in practice bouts—but Benedict wasn't just better. He was the best.

"Oh, Benedict objected at first, but he's too sensible to insist on coming with me, under the circumstances. It would not be wise for me and both of my sons to be out and about for a protracted period."

Because of the mantle. Because if Isen and both his sons were killed, Nokolai's mantle would be lost. "And yet you're here." It was a huge risk, and not just to Isen. To the clan.

"And will soon be at Wythe Clanhome. Wythe doesn't have Benedict, so their security isn't up to our standards, but it would still be extremely difficult for our enemies to penetrate. The danger is much less than you're thinking." He patted her hand again. "You were alarmed for the clan, weren't you? I'm pleased."

She blinked, confused. "You're going to Wythe Clanhome?"

"Of course. That's where Rule and the new wolf are. Rule says that the new wolf—"

"You mean Ruben. Why do you avoid using his name?"

His eyes twinkled with unimpaired good humor. "Do you know, I don't believe anyone had interrupted me for years before you joined the clan? Yes, that's who I mean. A brand-new wolf isn't called by the name he bears in his other form for the first two weeks following the Change. At the new moon, his guide will use that name to recall him to his other form. This new wolf is a Rho. That has never happened, obviously, but we are learning some of the consequences quickly. He can't be controlled by anyone except a mantle-holder, yet he must be controlled until he's able to do so himself. I flew out so I can relieve Rule of that task."

Warmth rushed through her, a dizzy sort of weakness. He'd done it for her. Oh, being Isen, he might have had a dozen other reasons—no, there was no "maybe" to it. He did have other reasons. But in a very large way he'd crossed the continent so she wouldn't be alone in this strange new life she'd been thrust into. Life as not-a-cop.

She touched his hand. Immediately he closed his around hers—a broad hand, warm and brimming with magic. It was nothing like holding Rule's hand, yet it was comforting. Neither of them spoke for several moments. Finally she said, "I really need a shower, don't I?"

He chuckled. "Oh, yes."

TWENTY-SEVEN

LILY got her shower. Then she slept.

She hadn't planned to, but she walked out of the bathroom and the bed was right there and that was it. She figured it was okay to nap because she didn't really have a plan. Not for the rest of the day, the week, her life.

When she woke up, she did. Sort of.

She lay quietly, blinking up at a ceiling grayed out by dusk and listening to rain on the roof. A faint, stretched feeling said that Rule was still far away to the north. The same thoughts she'd gone round and round with in that cell presented themselves to her again . . . only now they lined up better.

Had she been set up? Her gut said yes, and she was going to go with that assumption for now. But that only applied to what, not who or why. "Who" might be Sjorensen, but it was just as possible that Sjorensen had been used. And who better to do that than Special Agent Al Drummond?

She couldn't be sure if she was letting the facts put Drummond at the top of her suspect list, or if she was leading with feelings. Because she wanted it to be him. She remembered the gloat in his eyes, the sheer delight he took in her downfall. But just because the guy hated her didn't mean he'd framed her. Someone could've used his attitude to manipulate him, just as they might have used Sjorensen to tip Lily off. Drummond didn't have magic of his own, and she hadn't felt death magic on him. He could still be part of it. One of *them*.

Or not.

It was the "why," though, that needed more thought. The last time one of Friar's acolytes had tried to get her the plan had been wonderfully simple: kill her in a drive-by. They would have succeeded, too, if LeBron hadn't given his life to save hers.

This time they'd gone for a complicated trick to destroy her as a cop. It didn't jive. It was as if two different minds were coming up with "get Lily" schemes—one convoluted and subtle, the other brutal but straightforward.

Maybe it would help to look at what else Friar & Co. had done recently. They'd started by killing Bixton in a crazily complicated way, presumably so they could frame Ruben. That had to be the subtle mind. Then they'd firebombed Fagin's house and nearly killed him. Straightforward.

Two minds. Well, Friar had two lieutenants, didn't he? If she looked at results in order to determine her enemies' goals, one thing was clear: they wanted Lily out of the Unit, not a cop anymore. Either dead or disgraced worked for that.

So she had to keep being a cop.

Her stomach growled. She hadn't eaten much in lock-up, and she'd slept for . . . ye gods. It was four thirty in the afternoon. She sprang up from the bed, gave her hair a quick brushing, and double-timed it downstairs. The lights were on down there, holding back the early dusk brought on by the rain. Good smells and voices came from the kitchen, which turned out to be full of people sitting at the table . . . Isen, Pete, the Leidolf Rhej, José . . . and Deborah Brooks.

"Ah," Lily said cleverly, stopping in the doorway as five pairs of eyes swung toward her. "Deborah."

Deborah's dimple winked. "You didn't expect to see me."

"No." And she felt obscurely guilty now. "I guess you wanted to find out more about what happened to Ruben."

Deborah nodded, sobering. "Isen and the sera have been telling me about being lupus. About being Rho. What it means, what it will mean. I'm . . . fairly boggled still." She shrugged.

"Also unemployed. Officially I'm on indefinite leave, but from what I'm hearing, I probably won't be able to go back to teaching in Georgetown. Ruben's going to have to stay at Wythe Clanhome."

Lily crossed to the table and sat beside her. "I'm so sorry. Teaching means a lot to you."

"I'll teach again. It's what I do, what I love. But not here, I guess." She sounded sturdy, determined. Her eyes were sad. "And not soon, even though I can't go to Ruben. That's what I meant to do. I came here thinking someone would tell me how to find him, but I hadn't thought it through. If I go to him, I'll lead the—the authorities there."

Isen patted Deborah's hand. "It's very strange to think of Ruben Brooks as apart from the authorities, isn't it? We will work to repair that situation. José," he said, turning his head, "perhaps you'd go ahead and make your corn bread." He nodded at Lily. "I made some of my special chili. You like it, I recall, and it's ready. We weren't sure when you'd awake, though, so the corn bread isn't. If you can wait a small bit longer . . . but perhaps you don't wish to. You missed lunch, and the gods only know what they fed you for breakfast in that place."

Lily agreed that José's jalapeño corn bread was worth waiting another "small bit" for. The Rhej pushed back her chair and stood. "May I?" the woman asked.

"May you—oh. You want to check me out. Sure."

José went to the refrigerator and pulled out the milk. The Rhej moved behind her and rested her hands on Lily's shoulders, humming "Amazing Grace."

It took a while, though as usual Lily didn't feel anything. José had time to mix the corn bread and slide two big pans into the oven before the Rhej spoke. "Your arm is completely healed, aside from a bit of scarring."

Lily nodded. That much she knew.

"The microscopic damage in your brain is healed, too. And the circulation problems that led to it are gone."

Grins sprang out around the table. José spun away from the stove with a huge grin. Even Deborah looked happy. Maybe they'd told her what the mantle had been up to before the Lady got it where she wanted it.

"But this is wonderful!" Isen cried. "Lily, you are no longer angry with our Lady? And not surprised at all to learn about this, I think."

She was a great many things, too many to sort into words. But not surprised. "You'll tell Rule."

"Of course."

The Rhej squeezed her shoulders before releasing her. She came around and sat next to Lily. She had a broad face, the skin a warm, friendly sort of brown, with beautifully arched brows above dark eyes with thick, stubby lashes, and the kind of smile that made you want to smile back. "You want to talk about it, honey? Because I'd surely like to hear."

"About the Lady, you mean?"

"About her. About whatever you'd like to tell me, but I am always most interested in hearing about the Lady."

"She spoke to me this time." Lily paused, surprised that she'd said that. That she wanted to talk about it. "Not in words. I didn't get words like you Rhejes do. Maybe she spoke the other time, too, but the part of me that . . . that can hear her doesn't have words, so the rest of me didn't know about it. But I remember her voice this time. It was a voice," she added as if the Rhej had disputed this. "Not just a feeling or a knowing."

"Her voice is beautiful, isn't it? Like a purring kitten and a thunderstorm all wrapped up together."

Small and vast, cuddly and shockingly powerful. Yes. All of that at once. A pang shot through her and she looked at Deborah. "She asked me to let her put the mantle into Ruben. She let me know what I was supposed to do for that to happen. So I knew what I was agreeing to. Not in words, I didn't know anything in words, but I agreed. The Lady needed my permission to put the mantle into me. She needed my permission to take it out, too. So what's happened to him is partly my fault."

Deborah frowned. After a moment she said, "Maybe he had to agree, too. If you had to give permission, surely he would have, too."

"If he did, there's a good chance he doesn't know it." Lily shook her head. She didn't want to talk about the Lady anymore, but there was one question she couldn't keep back.

"When I said she told me what she'd do, I don't mean she gave details about the project. How could she turn Ruben into a lupus?"

"Ah. We've been discussing that," Isen said, "at some length. I believe she first had to alter the mantle itself. Cullen said it was changing while you hosted it. I think she was—mapping human neurological paths, perhaps. Or other elements that differ from ours. Second . . . but this is your part of the story to tell." He nodded at Deborah.

Deborah leaned forward slightly. "Arjenie Fox found something. I think I told you she'd been looking into Ruben's genealogy for me? Well, after Ruben went through First Change, I guess everyone at Nokolai Clanhome was talking about it. At least Benedict and Arjenie were, and she got the idea to see if any of Ruben's people could have been lupus. It seems lupi keep records. By combining her search with those records, she found . . . you have a term for it." She looked at Isen, tossing the explanation back to him.

"A *pernato*. Yes. One of Ruben's great-grandmothers on his mother's side was the granddaughter of a Wythe Rho. One of his grandfathers on his father's side was descended from a Wythe-Leidolf *pernato*, who was in turn descended from another Wythe Rho. He had the bloodline on both sides. Very thin, but it was present."

Lily gave up trying to track the great-greats. "*Pernato* are the result of recessives on both sides. I get that. But why didn't you know about him?"

"We knew about his grandfather on one side and his grandmother on the other. But beyond the fourth generation, no *pernato* are born, so we don't track our descendents past that point. It's a matter of magic as well as genealogy, you see. The recessive genes may continue to be passed down, but the power is too diluted for a lupus babe to be born. And, indeed, Ruben Brooks was not born lupus. But he possessed the bloodline."

And the Lady, presumably, possessed the power.

Deborah chuckled suddenly. "All that fooling around on the side! Plus there's an elf in the family tree somewhere. Ruben's forebears were frisky folks. I'm looking forward to teasing him about that."

The oven timer dinged. Isen pushed back from the table. "No, no, sit down," he told José, who'd started to rise. "I'll feed my daughter-to-be."

Lily looked at Deborah, curious but cautious. "You seem pretty okay with all this. With Ruben turning into a lupus."

Deborah met her eyes. "He was dying. Now he isn't."

"He . . . dying?" Ruben had said there was damage to his heart. That's why he wasn't going to head the Unit—the regular Unit—anymore. He hadn't said *dying*.

Deborah smiled slightly. "He thinks I don't know. As if he could keep something like that from me by simply not saying it out loud! But yes, he expected to die, and fairly soon, I think. Now he's lupus. Lupi don't get sick, don't have heart trouble. That was the other reason I came here." She nodded at Isen's broad back, bent now to remove the pans of corn bread from the oven. "To find out if that was true. It is." She rested her folded hands on the table. "Am I okay with Ruben becoming lupus? There's a lot about it that scares me, a lot I don't like or don't understand or both. But none of it matters as much as this: Ruben was dying. Now he isn't."

LILY was served homemade chili and corn bread by a barefoot multimillionaire with a dishtowel stuck in the waist of his jeans. Then Isen called all of the guards who were present but not on duty to join them. The kitchen got crowded. Some of them had to eat standing up, but that didn't seem to bother them.

It was early for supper, but the food was ready, and lupi were almost always ready for food. Especially when it was steaming hot corn bread and crazy-good chili made with chunks of meaty chuck instead of ground beef.

Deborah seemed to have forgotten she was shy. Probably being immersed in an ongoing crisis helped, but mostly it was Isen. Lily was willing to bet Deborah had relaxed beneath the weight of that gentle, implacable charm within the first five minutes. He kept her talking throughout dinner.

Yesterday had been a rough day for Deborah. After watching her husband turn into a wolf and try to eat her, Drummond had taken her to Headquarters for questioning. When Deborah was finally allowed to return home, her parents had been lying in wait. They thought she should move in with them, and offered to help find a good divorce lawyer. There'd been a fight. No one was speaking to anyone else.

Lily made another mental note: *call parents as soon as finished eating.* "I hope you're able to patch things up."

"My family fights very politely," Deborah said. "They didn't actually say terrible things about Ruben, but everything they didn't put into words shaped what they did say. I, on the other hand, wasn't feeling polite. I'll be expected to apologize. I don't believe I will."

Lily believed her. Could it be that Deborah's parents had never noticed that beneath their daughter's soft exterior lay solid, stubborn granite? If so, they were in for a rude awakening. "Where do you want to be?" she asked suddenly. "Is your home comforting right now, or too empty, or . . . it may not be safe to stay there."

"I have mentioned that possibility," Isen said blandly. "She didn't care for any of the alternatives I could suggest."

"It's my home," Deborah said. "And yes, it feels empty without Ruben, but I'm not going to stay with my parents."

"Understandable," Lily said, "and not what I had in mind. You might consider that your decision affects the lupi who are guarding you."

"But they were there for Ruben, not . . . oh." Deborah was stubborn, not stupid. Lily watched her chew it over and realize that Ruben's absence didn't mean his enemies would give her a free pass. She was still a tool they could use against him. "I don't see where I can go that would be better."

"I was thinking of Fagin's place."

"I . . . that . . ." Deborah closed her mouth, thought it over. "If the elemental lets me in, you mean?"

"I'm playing a hunch here, but you can communicate with elementals pretty well, from what you said."

"Oh, yes, that part's easy enough. It's worth trying. I wouldn't need guards there, would I? I'd have to ask Fagin first, of course."

Lily had a few things to ask him, too. "I'll go with you, if that's okay."

"Tomorrow," the Rhej said calmly as she pushed back her plate. "You need another eight, ten hours sleep. My, that was good, Isen, José. Thank you."

Lily looked at her, surprised. "I'm healed now, remember? And I just got up from a four-hour nap."

"And I'm guessin' you didn't sleep much last night."

"No, but—"

"You'll see." The Rhej smiled in an annoyingly knowing way. "All that healing took a lot out of you. Stress kept you awake, I guess, at that jail, but your body wants more than the bit of sleep you gave it. You'll crash again soon."

She would not. There was too much to do.

"There's something I'm wondering," Deborah said in her soft voice. "Isen says Ruben won't be trying to fight the Wythe wolves the way he did Scott. They'll smell right to him, like friends."

"They'll smell like they're his," Isen corrected gently. "A wolf doesn't smell clan and think *friend*. He thinks *us*. He feels a deep sense of belonging. This new wolf will feel that belonging, but because he is Rho, instead of *us* he will think *mine*."

Deborah nodded seriously. "And you said Ruben is all wolf right now, so that's how he's thinking. Like a wolf who's a Rho and so he's in charge." Her smile peeped out. "That part's not such a change. Ruben always feels like he's in charge. Not in a smothering way, but like he's a shepherd with a really large flock who is also responsible for the landscape as a whole. Only he feels that even more now, being a Rho?"

Isen nodded. "Not in a smothering way, like you said. He feels responsible for those who are his clan."

"Then why did he submit to Rule? You said earlier that Rule couldn't use his mantle to make Ruben submit any more than Ruben could use his to make Rule submit. So it wasn't the mantle that made Ruben submit. He did it on his own. That's what I don't understand. He's not exactly submissive."

"Ah." Isen nodded. "I can see why that's confusing. Humans do see submission and dominance differently than we do. Perhaps for now you could accept that submitting doesn't make us submissive."

"That's for sure," Lily said. "I've seen Rule submit, and it sure didn't turn him submissive." Isen had given her enough food for two people—or one lupus. She couldn't finish it, but maybe one more bite of corn bread . . . she dabbed a bit of butter on a small chunk. "But there's a whole language of submitting. They do it for lots of reasons other than establishing who's in charge. It's how they acknowledge a fault, settle a dispute, seal a deal between clans—all sorts of things."

A slight frown lingered between Deborah's eyebrows. "But Ruben didn't know any of the—the cultural context about submitting, and he did it anyway. He agreed to let Rule be in charge."

"He didn't know much of anything at the time. That was the problem. But he knew Rule could beat him and he knew Rule would take care of him. That was enough." She popped the bite in her mouth. She'd better stop now or . . . why were all the men in the room beaming at her that way? "What?"

Isen patted her hand. "You've learned a lot since you first came to us. We're pleased. And now, I fear, it's time for me to go. Pete, if you'd bring the car in front?"

Pete left. There was a bit of bustle as the rest of the lupi leaped to their feet and started bussing the dishes and Deborah tried to help. Lily took advantage of the noise to say to Isen, "I'll walk you to the door."

He slid her an opaque smile and told José to put on a little dish-washing music so he could have a private word with Lily. José plugged his phone into a player on the counter and they were all treated to Led Zeppelin.

Lily shook her head at Isen. "That was way less subtle and devious than I expect from you."

"I'm a flexible man. Sometimes the straightforward way works best. You wished to escort me to the door?"

Together they headed for the front of the house. "Are you driving to New York State, then?"

"My route and means are complicated. The Mercedes has GPS, which is potentially trackable. That reminds me. Benedict tells me it's possible to track my location through the GPS on my phone, so I'll keep it turned off. Cullen has made sure Rule's phone is off, also."

She should have thought of that. Why hadn't she thought of that?

Because she was used to being the one using government resources, not the one trying to dodge them. "How will I reach you?"

"Benedict keeps a stock of untraceable, prepaid phones on hand. I brought two with me. I'm told these phones don't roam well away from large cities, but having two networks to choose from may help. These are the numbers." He stopped as they reached the parlor and handed Lily a slip of paper. "I'm glad you wanted a word with me. I wished to speak with you privately, also."

"Oh?"

He smiled. "So wary—and rightfully. I'm offering advice, which is annoying of me, but I hope you'll listen anyway. Has Rule seemed edgy lately? Unusually so?"

"That was a question, not advice."

"And one you don't care to answer, which of course is an answer of sorts. Lily, you know that we are protective of women. You've been in danger often since you and Rule mated. He has dealt with this so beautifully that you may not understand how powerful this instinct is for a lupus with a Chosen. I believe he's been able to handle risk to you for two reasons. First, he knows and accepts that, being who and what you are, you will risk yourself when there is need. His wolf helps him with this," he added. "Wolves don't see their mates as pups to be cosseted and protected, but as partners—in the hunt, in a fight, they act together."

She had to smile. "So it's his wolf side, not the human one, I should thank?"

"Perhaps." He smiled briefly. "But there is another reason. I suspect that on some level, whether he was aware of it or not, Rule has believed you would survive because the Lady would protect you."

"That's . . . not very reasonable."

He sighed. "As a boy, Rule idealized the Lady. It comes of having been mothered by many, but abandoned by the woman who actually bore him. Young boys often feel a fervent love for their mothers. Rule loved the many women at Clanhome who helped raise him, but not that way. His mother-bond was with the Lady . . . or his boyish understanding of her."

"So you're saying he has mother issues."

"That's one way to put it, yes."

And Lily was at risk now because of the Lady. Because of what Rule's mother figure was doing with the mantle. "You haven't gotten to the advice part."

"Rule's wolf still accepts and expects your need to be part of any necessary fights. But Rule the man grew out of that boy who idealized the Lady. He may not be reasonable about your safety. Be patient with him. You can't fix this for him. You can't be less than an equal partner. But you can be patient."

It sounded like fortune cookie advice. That didn't make it bad advice—just annoyingly vague. The rest of what he'd said, though . . . Isen knew people. He knew his son. She nodded slowly. "I'll keep all that in mind."

"Good." He squeezed her shoulder. "Now, are you going to tell me what's hurting you?"

"I'm not harboring any secret troubles. Just the obvious ones."

"No?"

"I am curious about something." It wasn't what she'd meant to ask him about when she finagled this semiprivate moment, but . . . "When lupi hear moonsong, is it the Lady you hear? Her voice?"

He took his time answering. Finally he said, "This question is difficult for me to answer. We don't usually speak of our personal experience of moonsong."

"I've trespassed."

"No." He added a pat of his hand to his reassuring smile. "We don't speak of it because the experience is intensely personal, so I don't know if others would answer as I do. For me, it is not a voice, yet it is the Lady's song. The moon is her instrument, or perhaps she is the moon's instrument."

"You don't hear her in words."

"No. If light were music, it might sound something like moonsong. One thing I know is common to all lupi. We don't hear moonsong with our ears, yet it is very much heard, not sensed in some other way."

Yes. Yes, that's what it was like. Something ripped and words came spilling out. "I never wanted to be Rho. That would've made a mess of my life I don't even want to think about. So I didn't want to keep the mantle. I don't need to turn into a wolf. I'm happy with who I am. Only I guess I'll never hear her voice again, and that . . ." She blinked fast. Dammit. She was not going to cry. "I guess it's pretty wonderful to hear moonsong all the time."

Isen being Isen, he didn't answer her with words. He folded her up in a hug, making it really hard for her to keep back the damn tears, which was stupid. Crying was just stupid. "It's not like I've been longing to be lupus."

"Mmm," he said, and stroked her hair gently.

"It's not like that," she insisted. Her head rested on one broad, burly shoulder. He smelled like laundry soap and warmth. Somehow he just smelled warm. "But I wondered . . . I thought maybe that's what the mantle was doing. Trying to turn me into a lupus. Not succeeding, and maybe damaging me in the attempt, but trying. And part of me . . . part of me thought . . ." A deep sigh shuddered out of her. "But it didn't happen. I don't have the bloodline, do I?" She straightened away from him. "You are not to tell Rule about me getting weepy about this."

"Not if you don't wish me to."

"I don't. And this wasn't at all what I wanted to tell you."

"No?" He waited, benign and patient. Buddha-wolf.

"I'm pretty sure you know about the other Unit. The Shadow Unit."

He nodded.

"Last week Ruben asked me to join. I turned him down. I don't know who to tell that I've changed my mind, but I have. I want in."

Isen smiled slowly. "Ruben is incommunicado at the moment, of course. But he has a second-in-command. I'll make sure Ruben's second is aware of your offer."

TWENTY-EIGHT

~

THE Rhej turned out to be right. Dammit.

After Isen left, Lily headed back to the kitchen, where the Rhej was putting Deborah through Lupi 101. They were talking about what made a clan a clan—the mantles, in other words. "Rule gave me a dirty look when I told Deborah about mantles," Lily said, "but no one has yelled at me about it."

The Rhej gave her a lazy smile. "You're a Chosen. I'm a Rhej. We're Lady-touched, so we've got the authority to reveal the Lady's secret. Most lupi will figure you were just doin' what the Lady wanted."

"The Lady doesn't goose me every time I open my mouth. I've only heard her once."

"Once that you know of," the Rhej said agreeably, and turned back to Deborah.

Deborah didn't need Lily's two cents when she had the Rhej to brief her, so Lily went to the parlor and got it over with. She called her parents.

That was both better and worse than she'd expected. Her father actually overrode her mother, insisting on speaking to her first. He asked her quietly, "In your deepest heart, do you feel you did the right thing?" Lily told him yes. "Then I am proud of you. Do not be a victim or a martyr. Fight, but choose your fights wisely." Her mother claimed the phone while Lily was still tearing up and laid out an ambitious plan of lawsuits—against the Bureau, the arresting officer, the jail where she'd stayed, and possibly the U.S. Senate, though Lily never did figure out why her mother thought the Senate might be particularly culpable for Lily's unjust imprisonment.

So she cried a little, then laughed—her mother did not understand what she was laughing about—and after that it seemed as if she might as well take the rest of her medicine, so she called Grandmother and both her sisters. And then she called Toby. Isen had told him she was out of jail, but it seemed like he ought to hear from her.

Toby wanted to know what jail was like, and did she meet any murderers, and was her arm really all better now? And wasn't that cool about Mr. Brooks becoming lupus? And would she and Dad be able to come home soon?

Her arm was really all better. Jail smelled awful and was the most boring place possible, and the people there were mostly sad people who'd screwed up, not killers, though some of them were mad about being there and thought it was all someone else's fault. And no, she didn't think they'd be able to come home soon.

About the time she got off the phone for the last time, Deborah was ready to leave. Lily tried to persuade her to stay the night, just to be safe, but she refused, though she did agree to meet Lily at Fagin's hospital room the next day.

Deborah left at 7:10 . . . and Lily was exhausted. She got to work anyway. She needed to get her thoughts down on paper. Her time in jail might have been mostly boring, but she had put a few things together. She also needed to line out her investigation . . . the one she'd be conducting with or without a badge. Because dammit, that's what she did.

About an hour and a half in, her brain quit cooperating. She gave up on that and turned on the TV and brooded over the news.

One of Friar's lieutenants was talking to a right-wing pundit. Paul Chittenden was very blond, very well-groomed; he reminded her a bit of Dennis Parrott, though they didn't look alike aside from the gloss. He was assuring the very blond interviewer that the demonstrations Humans First was holding would be peaceful—"While Humans First supports our members' Second Amendment rights, we do not support violence." He talked about how vital these demonstrations were, given how corrupt the government's secretive Unit had proven to be. That was a reference to Ruben's fleeing arrest, of course.

Lily listened long enough to hear her name, then shut it off, stripped, and climbed into bed, so tired she didn't bother with pj's even though there were people in the house.

But for the first time in nearly a year, Rule wasn't beside her, and she couldn't make her mind shut up. It wasn't doing anything useful, just circling around and around various disasters—a couple that were real because they'd actually happened, like getting checked into the holding cell; a couple that hadn't happened yet, but would, like Croft firing her; and fistfuls that were gloom-of-the-night phantasms, all the what-if-if-ifs a hectic brain can conjure. Finally she got up and did some stretches and lunges and such, and that helped enough for her to doze off.

She woke up feeling okay. There was a low-lying dread gnawing at her breastbone, but her brain was clear.

Before she showered, before she got that first cup of coffee, she checked her phone. Rule hadn't called. She'd thought he would once his father arrived and he could switch back to a more verbal form, but he hadn't. Or else Isen wasn't there yet.

That was probably it. Wythe Clanhome was nearly five hundred miles away, and Isen was following some tricky plan to get there without being followed.

The phone chimed when she was still dripping wet from her shower. She wrapped a towel around her and hurried and managed to catch it . . . then wished she hadn't.

It was Croft. He told her she'd been placed on administrative leave pending an investigation; she'd receive the formal notice, which would inform her of her rights and responsibilities, through the mail. She told him she understood and hung up, then stood with the phone in her hand, staring at nothing.

The phone beeped, announcing a text message. She checked, saw that it was from one of the numbers Isen had given her, and read:

This is Rule. I love you. Leaving now. Isen's keeping both non-GPS phones. Mine will be turned off. Love you.

Lily rolled her shoulders and gave a sharp nod. She and Rule were okay. The rest of her world was packed up in the proverbial handbasket and rolling downhill fast, headed for hotter climes, but she and Rule were okay.

When she got downstairs, she found the Rhej waiting by the door with her suitcase. "You're leaving." That sounded especially stupid, so she tried again. "Why are you leaving?"

The woman smiled that molasses smile of hers. "I'm afraid you won't like my reason. I'm off on mysterious Rhej business and can't say a word about it."

Mysterious Rhej business. "You're right. I don't. With everything that's going on right now, if you know something, you really need to share it."

"I can't. I'm hoping you won't hold that against me. I had to empty out my bank account for the plane ticket. Does Rule keep any Leidolf funds on hand you have access to?"

He kept cash in the safe upstairs. Lily had no idea if it was Leidolf money, Nokolai money, or just Rule's money. But she knew the combination, so she went up to get the Rhej some cash. "Is five hundred enough?"

"Oh, yes, I think so. Thank you, Lily."

"You shouldn't be traveling on your own. You should have a guard, I mean."

She shook her head. "Not takin' anyone with me, but Mark's bringing the car around to drive me to the airport."

Lily tried one more time to get some clue what the woman was up to, but all she got in return was a smile and a hug.

Lily's meet with her lawyer was at nine. She got there five minutes early, but was sent straight in anyway. Miriam Stockard turned out to be five foot nothing, with dark gray hair, serious glasses, and a pale yellow suit that had probably cost more than Lily made in a month. More than she used to make in a month, at least. She was all but unemployed now.

The lawyer also turned out to have a trace of a Gift Lily didn't have a name for, save that it was connected to Air. Lily had run across people with that kind of magic before—sort of a nascent telepathy Gift, so faint and unfinished it didn't mess people up. Ms. Stockard couldn't read minds, but Lily would bet she sometimes made good guesses about what a prosecutor or witness was thinking.

Or a client, for that matter. Lily got through the interview okay. Neither of them wanted to be buddies, both wanted to win, and Ms. Stockard was every bit as sharp and icy and focused as her reputation claimed. The arraignment had originally been set for that afternoon, Stockard said, but she'd gotten a postponement. She was in touch with the prosecutor. There was a chance the man would drop the charges. Lily should not get her hopes up, but it was worth a shot. She'd be in touch.

At 9:40 Lily and Ms. Stockard shook hands a second time, and Lily left.

She'd taken Rule's rented Mercedes, not her government-issue Ford. At any moment she expected to have to turn that back in. It felt weird to be sliding behind that wheel, and not her own. She had to pause and take a breath and tell herself to get used to it.

In the pause she noticed something else easing—something that had nothing to do with arraignments or the pending loss of her badge. She checked . . . and yes, Rule was closer. A lot closer, and moving fast. He must have caught a plane.

It helped. It didn't make everything okay, but it helped.

She got to the hospital a good thirty minutes before Deborah was due to meet her. That was intentional. Lily had the idea Deborah knew about the Shadow Unit, but how much did she know? Best to have a brief chat before she got there.

Fagin had a private room. And a police guard. Which was good, but a problem. Lily couldn't badge her way in. Technically she hadn't been fired yet, but she didn't feel right about it. Besides, the officer might have heard about her arrest, and . . . and she was snarling herself up in the unnecessary. She smiled at the officer and raised her voice slightly. "I'm Lily Yu. Can you ask Dr. Fagin if he wants to see me?"

"He's not allowed visitors, ma'am."

She heard muffled voices inside the room. "Are you not allowed to ask him about that?"

"I have to ask you to move on."

The door opened. A lean, dark man with a grave expression and pressed khakis gave the cop a glance, but spoke to Lily. "Dr. Fagin will be out in a minute. I have to help him into the wheelchair."

"Wait a minute," the cop began.

The man looked at him. "Dr. Fagin appreciates your protection, Officer, but he's not a prisoner. He wants to speak to Ms. Yu. If you won't let her in, he'll come out here to do it."

"I've got a list," the officer said stubbornly. "Those on the list are allowed to go in, after showing ID. No one else."

From inside the room Fagin called, "I made the list, you ninnyhammer. Lily's name is on it. Or if it's not, someone removed it without my knowledge or consent, in which case I need to speak to your supervisory officer immediately."

The officer must have been in his thirties, but at that moment he looked like a teen called on the carpet by the principal. "Yes, sir. That would be Lt. Collins, sir. Sixth Precinct."

"Thank you. Now step aside and allow my lovely visitor to refresh my tired old eyes."

Those tired old eyes were twinkling madly when Lily walked into the hospital room. Fagin had enjoyed himself. "You must be feeling better," she said.

"Pain makes me grumpy. Abusing some hapless mote of the bureaucracy is a pleasant distraction. Your arrival will do me even more good. Have a seat, my dear. Ah . . ." He glanced around. There was one chair, which at the moment was next to the window and held a large shopping bag. "Samuel, if you don't mind . . ."

"Of course." He went to fetch the chair.

Fagin did look better. His color was good, his eyes clear. He was sitting up in bed with his legs straight out, his bandaged feet sticking up amid a sea of newspaper pages. He did not wear a hospital gown. Someone must have brought him the blue and purple paisley pajamas.

"Thanks," Lily said when Samuel set the chair next to Fagin's bed. But she didn't sit down right away, and it wasn't Fagin she spoke to first. "It's good to see you, Samuel. I had no idea you were here."

"Rule called while the two of you were trapped by that elemental. He wanted one of us with Dr. Fagin at all times. He asked for me specifically." A smile broke the usual gravity of his face.

Lily's breath hitched. Samuel wasn't LeBron. His smile wasn't quite the same as his father's had been. But there was something about seeing that reflection of the man in his son . . . it eased her. "I'm glad he did."

He shrugged. "He knows I'm still hunting a job and could come right away."

"He knows you can do the job or he wouldn't have asked for you."

"I should hope not," Fagin said, "considering it's my life this dashing young man is protecting. Clearly you two know each other?"

Lily glanced at Samuel and caught him doing the same with her. Yes, they knew each other. Not well, yet it was an intimate connection. She'd heard quite a bit about Samuel before she met him at his father's *firnam*. LeBron had given his life to save Lily's. She smiled and agreed that they did, indeed, know each other. "You're in good hands."

"Glad to hear it. You can't know everyone in both of Rule's clans, so there must be some connection . . ."

"You are incurably nosy, aren't you?" Lily finally sat in the chair Samuel had brought for her. "How are you doing? You don't look doped up."

"Oh, I'm on pain medication still. If I doze off midsentence, that's why. They tell me my lungs are in good shape, which is a blessing. I still cough now and then."

"The expert I talked to thinks it was an SIP. That stands for self-igniting phosphorus. The British stockpiled a lot of them during WWII that they didn't use, but I doubt yours came from one of those stockpiles. Seems like they'd be too old."

His eyebrows climbed. "You've been busy for an incarcerated woman. Have they dropped the charges?"

"No," she said shortly. "I'm out on my own recognizance. Also on administrative leave. I don't think it will take that long for them to do the official firing."

"Lily . . ." Fagin heaved a sigh. "I'm sorry. If there's anything I can do—"

"You can answer some questions about patterning and"—she glanced at Samuel—"about what we discussed at Ruben's party."

Fagin's eyebrows climbed. "Ghosts?"

"We talked about ghosts twice, didn't we? I was thinking of the second conversation."

"How intriguing. Samuel, I believe the things I was wearing when they brought me here must be around somewhere. If you wouldn't mind . . . thank you." Samuel handed him the shopping bag, and he began rooting around in it. "In case you're wondering, Samuel is interested in ghosts, also. Have you seen the news reports?"

Puzzled, she glanced at the TV. A dark-haired woman was talking, but the sound was too low for Lily to catch the words. "About my arrest?"

"No, about the ghosts. There have been several sightings reported in the D.C. area in the last few days. They did a local color piece on it last night."

"I'm told that death magic can throw ghosts."

"So I've heard. Ah, here it is." Fagin pulled his hand out of the sack and held it out. On his palm rested a small crystal. "I don't suppose you have a hammer in your purse?"

"You're more prepared than I am." She took the little crystal. "You carry one of these with you everywhere?"

"That one won't be fully charged," he said apologetically. "I was conducting a small experiment to see how long it took proximity to my Gift to drain the crystal. That's why I had it in my robe pocket—I was keeping it close all the time."

"Better than nothing. I can't set a circle."

"No more can I. We'll have to hope that two sensitives are enough to disrupt the skills of any listeners who might happen to be paying attention."

"I don't know. Friar's shown a keen interest in you. If Rule were here . . ." Though he would be, and soon. The stretched feeling had eased entirely. He was close. "Well, listening isn't seeing, is it? We'll just have to take advantage of Friar's limitations." Lily stood, put the crystal on the linoleum floor, and drew her weapon.

Fagin jerked fully upright. "I don't think that's—"

"I'm not going to shoot it," she said, amused. She knelt, reversed her grip, and smashed the butt on the crystal. It crunched, and she felt the wave of magic roll off it. She stood and holstered her weapon. "That felt a little weaker than at Ruben's. How long do we have?"

"I'm not sure. Maybe thirty minutes. Maybe less."

"We'll keep it as quick as possible, then." Lily pulled her notebook from her purse and handed it and a pen to Fagin. "Write down anything really sensitive. First I'd like to hear about what kind of backup you have for that translation Cullen's so interested in."

Safety-deposit, Fagin wrote. *Thumb drive.* He jotted down the name of a bank, the branch location, and three digits. "I'm afraid I can't recall the entire number, and of course the"—he paused and wrote *key*—"isn't available at the moment."

Because the elemental wouldn't let them in to get it. But if Deborah was able to get in, she could get it for them. "I may have a way to make it available. Where is it?"

Fagin wrote *top desk drawer*. "How?"

"We'll get to that in a minute." The key wasn't enough, not when Fagin couldn't go there himself. Lily took back the notebook and wrote *limited power of attorney*. "If you're willing," she added out loud, "that should do it. I can set it up. Is Cullen okay for the person named?"

"He can't possibly be mobile yet."

"He's not healed, but he is mobile."

Fagin sighed. "How annoying. It will be weeks before I'm on my feet again, and my burns weren't as bad as his. Yes, he'll do. What can you tell me about Ruben?"

"He's with . . ." She hesitated, then finished the sentence by writing *Isen*. She looked at Samuel. "If I tell you not to discuss or reveal anything written or spoken in this room except with your Rho, will you consider that binding?"

He nodded. "Rule said I was to obey you unless there was a conflict with his orders."

"All right. You're not to discuss or reveal what Fagin and I say or write about here except to Rule." She wrote on the notebook: *Ruben is now lupus and the Rho of Wythe clan* and held it up where Fagin and Samuel could see.

"What? But that—that—surely that's impossible!"

"I can't tell you how it happened, but you're aware that lupi have an Old One on their side. She took a hand in things."

"Great heavens above."

"I knew it," Samuel breathed. "I knew the Lady would fix things."

Suddenly curious, she asked Samuel, "Do you think—uh, will they accept him?"

"Of course! I mean, he's got"—he glanced at Fagin—"he's got the authority now."

Authority meaning *mantle*. The thing she'd finally gotten rid of. The thing that would have let them talk freely without worrying about Friar magically eavesdropping.

"But where is he?" Fagin said. "Is he able to . . ." He gestured and she handed him back the notebook. He wrote *Shadow Unit*. "There are lines of communication. It's not good for him to be out of touch."

"The situation's too complicated for me to tell you much when I'd have to write most of it down, but consider him out of touch for the time being. He's got a second, though." She looked hard at him.

Fagin spread his hands. "If you're thinking that's me, I have to disappoint you. I consult. I'm not part of management."

"I figured you'd know who it was."

He shook his head. "I don't. The, ah . . . communications staff will know, and they can authenticate any shift in authority to Ruben's second, but I haven't heard from them."

Lily's lips quirked up. She wondered how Mika would feel about being referred to as part of "the communications staff." "Is that who I need to contact, then? Because I want in, and I need to know what kind of resources I have to draw on. I need to know who I can call on, who—"

"I'm sorry. We don't reveal names, not without authorization. I can't help you."

Lily looked at the door to Fagin's room. With a little leap of her heart and no surprise whatsoever, she watched it open.

"I can," Rule said.

TWENTY-NINE

~~

"I can't believe you thought I'd be mad when I found out you were Ruben's second," Lily said softly.

Rule lowered his head to sniff her hair. He loved her hair, loved the scent and feel and sight of it. She was snuggled into him in the backseat of the Mercedes with Mark at the wheel. He'd been told to take the long way home; they had quite a bit to discuss, and a moving car was extremely hard to target for eavesdropping.

The stereo was turned up high, at Rule's instructions. Beethoven's Fifth was crashing into the crescendo at the start of the fourth movement. With Lily so close, she could speak softly and Mark wouldn't hear unless he made a real effort. He wouldn't.

It wasn't true privacy, but it would do. For now.

There had been a number of things to do and discuss before they left Fagin's room. Lily told him about the limited power of attorney Fagin needed to sign, and why. He told her that Cullen was at the house. Deborah had arrived soon after Rule did, so they'd explained why she was there. It was an excellent solution. Naturally Rule had needed to tell her all he could about Ruben then; while he did, Lily had asked Fagin questions about the grimoire, and about patterning, death magic, and ghosts. As they reached the car, he'd told her he'd talked to Toby and was glad she'd called him earlier. After they got in, he'd mentioned that she didn't seem to be angry.

They hadn't talked at all about Lily going to jail. About the loss of her career.

They would. If she didn't bring it up, he'd see to it. Rule wound a strand of her hair around his finger and spoke close to her ear. "What was I thinking? It's not as if you get upset when I keep things from you."

"First, this is different. I knew you had secrets about the Shadow Unit and why they needed to stay secret. Second . . ." She straightened slightly, but left one hand resting on his chest. "Why do you think I told Isen instead of Mika that I wanted to talk to Ruben's second?"

Both his eyebrows shot up. "You guessed?"

"I wasn't sure, but you were the logical choice. You obviously knew a lot about the Shadow Unit. Then there's the communications staff." She snorted. "That's what Fagin called the dragons. Not many people that dragons will even listen to, much less allow to recruit them."

Bemused, he said, "They are allies of the Shadow Unit, not recruits."

She waved that off. "Plus you've got the whole two-mantled thing going. You can call up Leidolf with a word. It might take a couple words to call up Nokolai, but you're probably already using some of the clan for things I don't know about. You carry your own little cone of silence around as far as Friar's eavesdropping is concerned, and you already know what's going on. Last but not least, Ruben knows you've got what it takes to run a clandestine operation. I figure you were the one Ruben planned to put in charge before he decided he'd better keep the reins himself."

"You're so far ahead of where I thought you were . . ." He stroked her damaged arm with one hand . . . but the damage was gone. His fingers skimmed over intact muscle. Deep inside, he seemed to vibrate, as if . . . he didn't know. He knew what the feeling was, but he didn't like it. "What do you intend to do now that you're a ghost?"

"What I always do. Find the bad guys. Stop them. I've got

a plan—which consists mainly of questions, but with some
assumptions mixed in. I need to know what kind of resources
I'll be able to draw on."

"We can't match what you're used to, but you'll have help.
Some of it will be at the house by the time we arrive."

"Cullen?"

"Yes, though he's not the only one."

"That reminds me. Someone else won't be there. The Rhej
had to leave. I gave her five hundred dollars."

His eyebrow lifted. "Did you?"

"She asked me if you kept any Leidolf funds around, since
she'd blown her bank account on a plane ticket. I didn't know
who that money in the safe was from, but I gave her five hundred of it."

"You did the right thing." He dug a hand into his pocket.
"Did she say where she was going?"

"On mysterious Rhej business. That's what she said. That's
all she'd say."

"I'd give a good deal to know what that business is. Here."
He held out a smooth black pebble. "Your secret decoder
ring."

Puzzled, she took it. "Okay, it's got a tiny tingle of magic,
but it's not a ring and . . . oh." It was glowing.

"If you touch it for five seconds, it glows for two." Hers
had already faded back to dull black. "It won't react to anyone
but you. You use it to identify yourself to other ghosts as an
active agent."

She met his eyes. "You expected me to join your gang of
conspirators all along."

"Not expected. Hoped. I need to give you a quick rundown
of how the Shadow Unit is set up."

She glanced at the back of Mark's head.

"He will be trying not to listen, but if he hears it's all right."
He bent his head anyway to speak closer to her ear. It let him
swim in her scent. "There are three types of ghosts—active
agents, irregulars, and allies—plus an additional resource we
call associates. You can assume that allies and agents know
about Ruben's visions, about the Great Bitch and Friar—
pretty much everything. Agents are able to call on irregulars,

allies, and associates for assistance, depending on the situation and the need."

"Allies like the dragons?"

"Yes. Also brownies, and lupi as a whole are considered allies, though some individual lupi are also agents or irregulars. We're still negotiating with the gnomes, but expect them to ally themselves soon."

She pulled back slightly to look at him. "I can see where gnomes could be useful, but brownies? What can a timid race who never leave their reservations do?"

"Brownies are timid, but intensely curious. And they don't stay on their reservations all the time. They never have."

She blinked. "That's . . . really surprising. I guess it means they're good at sneaking."

"Extremely good."

"How do they report what they see? I'd have noticed if a bunch of brownies were hanging around the house to tell you stuff."

He grinned. "Mostly by cell phone. Modu makes one that's two and three-fourths inches high, less than a third of an inch thick, and weighs about as much as a spool of thread. It's a great favorite with them."

She snorted. "Brownies with cell phones. Okay, what about the irregulars?"

"The majority of ghosts are irregulars, and they vary greatly in duties, capabilities, and knowledge. Most of them are highly trustworthy, but aren't suited for the work of an agent. Some know a great deal about what we're facing. Others don't. They don't get the identifier that you did."

"The secret decoder ring." She rubbed the dull pebble in her hand, frowned, and set it on her thigh. "Fagin said he wasn't an agent."

"He's an irregular, yes." He ran his fingers over her arm again. Her healed arm. "So are Mark and our other guards. Many of the irregulars are what you might call support staff. A few may become active agents, but aren't ready yet. Others have specific, limited duties. A small number are . . . I think of them as sleepers. We may never need to call on them, but if we do, they're in place."

   She chewed that over in silence, then picked up her pebble. After five seconds, it glowed briefly, then winked out. Thoughtfully she slid it in her pocket. "And associates? You called them a resource. They're not part of the ghosts?"

   "Associates provide specific services or information for a fee. Some are decent people. Some are not." He couldn't feel where the bullet had gone in at all, but he could feel a bit of scarring where it had blown out the front of her bicep. Not much. "Associates don't know about the Shadow Unit, and we want to keep it that way. You'll be given access to a database with a list of associates, some background on each of them, and what kinds of skills they offer."

   "It's . . . really weird that you've been setting all this up— you and Ruben and probably others, but you've been part of it. And I didn't know. I'm not angry." A quick glance at him. "It's just weird."

   He slid his hand up her arm to her shoulder. "It's been weird for me, too, Lily." He bent to rub the side of his face along the top of her head. "I'm so sorry I wasn't here. They locked you up and I was far away. I was—"

   She shifted and put her fingers on his lips. "No guilt. None. You did what you had to do, and I did what I had to do. And"— she sucked in a breath—"and I'm not ready to talk about the rest of it. About . . . my job. Not yet. Anyone else asks how I'm doing I'll say okay, and that will be bullshit. It's true, but it'll still be bullshit, and I don't want to give you bullshit. Only I don't . . . I don't have more right now."

   He looked into her eyes for a long moment. He wanted to push, wanted that badly. It couldn't be good for her to keep everything throttled down inside, and he didn't mind angering her. Anger might help her. And yet . . . "I suppose you think that, loving you and trusting you the way I do, I should accept that."

   Her lips moved in a small smile. "Yeah, I do. For now, anyway."

   Slowly he nodded. "For now."

   She sighed and settled against him.

   "You could tell me about the jail."

   "You just agreed—"

"This isn't about spilling your guts. Or about your career. Give me facts, not feelings."

She rolled her eyes. "It was a holding cell. It stank. The food sucked and the company was on a par with the food. You've been in jail. You know what it's like."

"Don't tell me what it's like. Tell me about this particular jail. How many were in there with you?"

"It varied. The lowest number was ten. Made it downright roomy for a while."

He kept asking questions. Solid, factual questions that kept her talking . . . and let him peek between the cracks. She was relaxed now, dealing with facts. He forced himself to stay relaxed, too. He wanted to kill those who'd put her in jail, who'd robbed her of what mattered most—but that was his need. Not hers.

When she paused, he asked, "You were in a county jail? In a holding cell the whole time?"

"Doesn't make sense, does it? Why not a federal facility? Why wasn't I questioned at all? Thinking about it made me paranoid. I kept thinking they'd put me there for a reason, and maybe that was so someone could get to me, so I didn't sleep. Which sounds paranoid, all right, yet I'm still not sure why they didn't try for me. I can't see why 'disgraced and dead' wouldn't work even better for them than just disgraced." She shrugged. "Maybe I'm overestimating them. Maybe they couldn't get someone thrown in lockup with me that fast."

"You weren't where you expected to be. Maybe you weren't where our enemies expected you to be, either."

"If so," she said slowly, "that would mean Mullins isn't one of them. He's the one who took me in for booking. Maybe he took me to the wrong place."

He turned his head so he could smell her hair. "Do you think Drummond is one of them?"

"Could be. Or Sjorensen. She's the one who tipped me about Ruben. Or, hell, maybe it's both of them. Or neither. I don't have enough to make a guess yet." She fell silent, then tipped her head to the side to look at him. "Isen told you what happened, right?"

His brows lifted. "Of course." Isen thought there was a good chance her case would never go to trial—not enough evidence—but in the meantime she would almost certainly lose her job. Her badge. An administrative action didn't require nearly the level of proof that a court did.

"I'm okay, Rule."

She was tough and determined and not about to quit, and he felt her misery as clearly as if he'd turned empath. Maybe he breathed it in, some nuance of her scent he couldn't consciously identify. She hurt, and he couldn't fix it. "You will be." He ducked his head lower, nuzzling her neck, breathing her in.

"You've been all wolfish ever since we got in the car. Petting me. Sniffing me."

"Sorry." He straightened. "I—"

"It's okay." She threaded her fingers in his hair and pulled his head back to her. "You've been scared for me. I guess your wolf wants to check me out."

There was that vibration again.

"But it's just the wolf who's curious. You haven't said anything about me being healed."

"I knew about it, I knew . . ." Not a vibration. A trembling deep inside, as if . . . he had to hold it together. Had to stay calm. Lily needed him to stay calm. "The Rhej. Isen told me she said you're healed. Completely healed."

"It was pretty freaky when it was happening. My head felt weird and I got these tingles. It was like I stood a step back from my body, like it wasn't entirely mine and . . . I didn't know the mantle was putting in a rush job, getting everything fixed before it left. But that's what it did." She paused. "What your Lady did."

His lips lifted in a snarl. "I'll tell you what she did. She used you. She may have fixed you at the last minute, but she used you. I can accept you risking yourself. That's what you do, who you are. I can't accept her risking you that way. Using you."

"I put myself at risk."

"You didn't know what you were agreeing to. You had no idea of the consequences. It's my fault. I should have—"

"Whoa." Now she straightened, pulling away from him enough to frown at him. "Where did that come from?"

"I wanted you to do it. I wanted you to keep Wythe's mantle safe. You knew that, and because I thought it was safe, you did, too. She used me to get you to do what she wanted."

Lily cocked her head, studying him. "You are truly, deeply pissed at your Lady."

Yes. Yes, he was. Too angry to speak, the muscles of his jaws clenched tight on all that anger.

"As I understand it, the deal between your people and the Lady is that she gets to use you. You give her permission for that."

He unlocked his jaws enough to say, "Not against you."

"I gave permission, too."

"You didn't know what you were agreeing to."

"Part of me did. No, wait, listen." She put her hands on each side of his face as if she knew how tight he was there. How much he was holding back, holding in. "The first time, when Brian was dying, I didn't notice anything like that. If the Lady was telling me things about what I'd agreed to, I didn't notice it. But I think she did, because this time . . . in Ruben's kitchen, I knew. I didn't get any of it in words, but I knew exactly what I agreed to when I let that mantle go and flow into Ruben. The part of me she can talk to, it doesn't have words, so I can't hold on to what she says. I just know she cleared it with me first, and I agreed. I think that happened the first time, too, only it was such a different way of—of talking—I forgot it even happened."

He felt like he was swimming in smoke—thick, acrid, and blinding both nose and eyes. He didn't know what to say. What to think.

Lily stroked his face and spoke gently. "So the thing is, if you're mad at the Lady for what she did, you have to be mad at me, too. It turned out okay, but she and I both risked me."

"It didn't turn out okay. You've lost your career."

"I kind of think that's the Great Bitch's fault. And Friar's. And maybe Sjorensen, or Drummond, or even Mullins. Someone set me up, but that someone wasn't your Lady. She took advantage of the situation, I guess, to get me to go to Ruben so she could pass on the mantle. But she didn't set me up."

"You wouldn't have gone there in person if she hadn't tricked you into it. You'd have called, but you wouldn't have been there when Drummond showed up. You wouldn't have been arrested."

"And if Ruben's phone is tapped—and I'm betting it is—calling would have had the same result for me. but Ruben wouldn't have gotten the mantle. He'd probably be in jail now instead of at Wythe Clanhome."

The anger that had ridden him for days was draining out. Or burning down, if not out, leaving everything smoke and fog. He shook his head, but it did nothing to banish the fog. "You're okay with it. You're okay with being manipulated that way."

"I'm okay with it the same way I'm okay with the mate bond. Or your father."

That startled him into silence.

She grinned. "If you could see your face . . . what I mean is, sometimes it drives me crazy, not knowing what the mate bond's going to do, and I hate that, but the bond makes me part of something other than me. There would be an 'us' even without the bond, but it helps, doesn't it? When I was locked up, I knew you were hundreds of miles away, but that was good. It meant you and Ruben had gotten away, and knowing that helped. It helped a lot."

"And my father?" he said dryly.

"He reminds me of the Lady." She paused, her frown saying it was hard to find words. "I heard her. I didn't get words, but I heard her voice, and . . . you know how Isen is. Tricky, sometimes manipulative. He never tells you everything, and you never know what he's going to do. But whatever it is, it will be done with a clean heart. The Lady can be tricky, too, and she sure as hell doesn't tell us much, and I have no idea what she's going to do, and I don't like that. But I think . . . I feel like she's got a clean heart. Like she's clean all the way through."

He put both arms around her and pulled her close and rested his head on top of hers. And sighed. "I think you're right. If I can't stop being angry with her, does that mean my heart isn't clean?"

"It means you're mad. That's all it means."

She was right . . . mostly. There was one other meaning to his anger. One cause that he hadn't wanted to see. Fear was the tinder that anger burned, wasn't it?

He was afraid of the Lady.

It was a thought so foreign he almost couldn't grasp it. How could he fear that which made him who and what he was? Without the Change, the clans, the moon and the magic, he wouldn't be. Someone else might have been born and given the name Rule Turner, but that man would not be him.

Moonsong, mantles, and magic. The half of him that ran on four legs and knew so much of love and blood and loyalty . . . all of that was not just *from* the Lady, but *of* her. How could he fear what was so much a part of him?

The answer floated up as if he'd always known it. For the first time, he'd found something his Lady could ask of him that he was not willing to give. His life, yes. That was hers. But not Lily's.

He knew now that the Lady hadn't asked that of him. Lily was whole and healthy. Perhaps she never would ask it. But he also knew that part of him wasn't the Lady's. Part of him could not be given freely to her, and fear rose from that part like a chilly mist.

He had an image suddenly of his wolf in a deep cavern, advancing cautiously into that cold mist. Sniffing. And snorting, unimpressed. *It's only fear.*

Slowly the knots inside him eased. It was only fear. Nothing strange about fear. For several moments he didn't move as the world returned to him . . . the blare of the stereo, the scent of Lily, of Mark, of the car itself. The warmth along his side and his shoulder from Lily's body. The barely there bump of her heartbeat.

Lily was with him and she was physically healed and whole again. The other problems weren't going away, but in this moment, things were good. She was here, and she was okay. She kept telling him that. Maybe he should believe her. "This was supposed to be my chance to comfort you."

"It's not an either-or deal. Comfort goes both ways."

He found himself smiling. Yes, it did.

THIRTY

～

CULLEN was in the kitchen when they got home—or as close to home as they could manage on this coast. He sat at the kitchen table scowling at a bunch of complicated glowing lines that hung in the air in front of him. On the table in front of him was a battered leather journal—probably the one he'd rescued from Fagin's library.

"The rest of your resources aren't here yet, it seems," Rule said. "Coffee?"

"Sure. I'll start with Cullen." She took out her spiral and sat beside him. "Hey. Have you noticed you aren't alone in the room?"

"It is noisier here than it was a moment ago." He still didn't look at her. He reached up and used two fingers to drag one glowing glyph slightly to the left. "I'm busy."

"Rule says you're one of my resources, so stop doodling and pay attention."

"This is important."

"Whoever firebombed Fagin's library wasn't going after him or his books. They wanted to kill you."

Now she had his attention. Bright blue eyes narrowed at her. "You sound pretty sure of that."

"We've got two minds behind what's happened lately.

One's subtle and devious and likes things convoluted. The other's direct. Guess which one's likely to opt for a bomb?"

"I'll buy that, but why does it tell you what the target was?"

"Fagin's been in D.C. for months. Him and his library. A lot of people knew about that grimoire he's been translating—the Harvard press, for one. Some of his colleagues." She had names. They should probably be checked, just to be sure. But that was a job for someone who could call the local cops and ask for a favor. "The one new element here is you. You show up in D.C. and a day later you nearly get crispy-fried."

He shook his head. "Why would anyone who knows anything about me use fire to take me out?"

"Friar knows you're good with fire. I'm betting he's the convoluted thinker in this deal. I think the direct guy is working with him, not for him. An ally." She glanced at Rule. "Like the dragons are our allies. God knows they don't tell us everything. I doubt Friar tells his allies much."

"I'm not sure Sam would care for the parallel, but you're right." Rule set the filled kettle on the stovetop. "What Friar does tell his hypothetical allies is probably a mix of lies and misdirection with just enough truth to get what he wants from them."

"So let's assume Direct Guy knows Cullen's a sorcerer. He finds out that Cullen's here. He could be having the place watched, or he may have been keeping track of flights to D.C. If he—"

"Wait a minute," Cullen said. "You think one of our villains could get the airlines to watch for flights booked in my name?"

"The Bureau can do that sort of thing, and there's a traitor in the Bureau. So yeah, I do."

Rule moved up behind her and put a hand on her shoulder. "Drummond?"

"He's top of my list, but it could be Mullins. Or Sjorensen, though she's unlikely. At her level, she shouldn't be able to add someone to the watch list." She paused, then got it said. "The one who could do it the easiest is Croft."

Silence.

She kept going. "He knows Cullen's a sorcerer. That's something people might figure out from reading some of my reports, so it's only suggestive, not conclusive. But we need to keep it in mind." She twisted her head to look up at Rule. "I need to know if Croft is part of the Shadow Unit. One of the ghosts."

Rule shook his head. His lips were tight. "Ruben had a feeling Croft shouldn't be told anything. He doesn't know about the ghosts or Ruben's visions. Ruben emphasized that he does not have a hunch that Croft is less than trustworthy, or he'd take steps to remove him. Foreknowledge can alter the way someone responds. Ruben believes that's the case with Croft."

"He believes that, or he had a hunch about it?"

"I've given you his words."

"I don't want it to be Croft. I like him. But we have to keep it in mind."

Rule gave a single nod. The kettle started whistling. He turned to deal with it.

"I wish I knew who was working the bombing." She opened her spiral, frowning at the notes she'd made. "There's a lot of strings to tug on there, but they're the sort that need a lot of manpower. A badge helps, too."

Rule poured the steaming water into the French press. "That I can't provide. Not directly. But I believe one of your resources has arrived."

The doorbell rang.

She shoved her chair back. "How do you do that? We're all the way at the back of the house. You couldn't hear anyone walking up to the door from back here."

"José told me."

"You aren't wearing your earbud."

"He spoke from the backyard."

She shook her head and headed for the door.

The man standing on her front stoop wore a wrinkled shirt, a mud-brown suit, and a bright orange tie. His hairline was receding, his waistline increasing, and she was really glad to see him. Also surprised. "Uh . . . are you my resource?"

"That's not how you do it," Abel Karonski told her disapprovingly. He dug one hand into his pocket and pulled out a small black rock. It glowed for two seconds, then quit.

"Am I supposed to show you mine?" She stood aside so he could come in.

"Nah. Rule told me. Well, technically it was Mika, but the message came from Rule. Took you long enough to make up your mind."

So he'd known Ruben had asked her to join the ghosts. And that she hadn't agreed . . . not until her career was toast. "You found it an easy decision?"

He snorted. "Not easy, maybe, but simple. If the country's survival hangs in the balance, it makes things pretty damn simple."

"I didn't find it either easy or simple."

"I guess you're at that in-between age. Too old to jump off just any old cliff. Not old enough to spot the one cliff in a hundred that's worth the leap."

Jumping off cliffs was not a reassuring metaphor for joining the ghosts. Accurate, maybe, but not reassuring. So why did she feel better? "With your people skills, you should have been a therapist."

"That's me, Mr. Sensitive. Want to tell me all about your feelings?"

"Now there's a cliff you want to steer clear of."

Karonski stopped when they were halfway through the dining room. He sighed. "Lily."

She stopped, too. The parlor, dining room, and kitchen of the row house were shot-gunned, so there were no windows in this dim, interior room. But she could see Karonski's expression well enough. Her stomach went tight. "Yes?"

"I'm here for two reasons. Two units, two different duties. I need to deal with the official duties first. You have to turn in your badge and service weapon, pending the results of the administrative hearing. Croft thought it would be easier this way—me picking them up instead of you coming to HQ to do it."

She swallowed. Swallowed again. Her mouth tasted foul. "My service-issue weapon's back in San Diego. I never carry it. It's too big for my hand. I . . ." Her voice wobbled. She forced it steady. "I can get someone to bring it to the Bureau's office there."

"That should work. Have them do it pretty quick, though."

She nodded jerkily. "My badge. That's in my purse. It's in the kitchen." She turned, moving on automatic. She wouldn't think about this. She'd do it and wouldn't think.

When Karonski's hand fell on her shoulder, she jolted.

His voice was low and rough. "You got Ruben out. Even before you decided to join us, you got Ruben out. You did the right thing, and it cost you a helluva lot."

She swallowed again. Dammit, she was not going to be sick. "I warned him. Rule got him out."

"And I'd sure like to know how he did that."

"I'm not sure I can tell you."

"I can," Rule said from the doorway to the kitchen. He had her purse in one hand. "And will, but it's need-to-know, Abel, and I get to pick who needs to know. Not you." He looked at her. "I can do this. You don't have to."

"No." It was hers to do. Hers to get through. She took the purse from him. Her badge was in a leather folder in the outside pocket. Her fingers were so thick and clumsy it took two tries to pull it out. She held it out to Karonski without speaking.

He sighed heavily. And took it.

Rule moved behind her. She was afraid he'd hug her, try to comfort her. She'd come apart if he did. Maybe he knew that, or maybe he saw her stiff shoulders. He rested one hand there lightly and spoke to Karonski. "Coffee?"

"Sure."

Lily's heart continued to beat too hard as she and the two men went into the kitchen. Something seemed lodged in her throat. But she'd be okay. This would pass and she'd be okay . . . for some value of okay. At some time in the future that she couldn't see at the moment.

Cullen had gone back to messing with his glowing glyphs or runes or whatever they were. The battered journal was open in front of him. Freshly made coffee perfumed the air.

Lily poured herself a cup. Her hands were steady enough for that. Rule handed a mug to Karonski and gestured at the table. They sat. Cullen ignored them.

"So?" Karonski said to Rule. "About that explanation."

"A brief preface for Lily first." Rule looked at her. "The communications staff"—his lips twitched—"sent out word that everyone is to report to me rather than Ruben. I didn't explain. Most will assume it's because he's in hiding. I haven't yet decided who and how much to tell the real reason." He looked at Karonski. "But you need to know, Abel. Ruben is now lupus and the Rho of Wythe clan."

Karonski didn't fall out of his chair. Quite. He wanted explanations. Rule didn't offer them, save to say that Ruben was well, but as a new wolf he wouldn't be able to function as a man for some time—impossible to say how long. There had never been a new wolf who came to First Change as an adult. That might make a difference . . . or it might be years before Ruben could rejoin human society.

Assuming he could rejoin that society outside of prison, that is.

Karonski didn't like it, not one bit. "What the hell were you thinking? If this is supposed to be some kind of improvement, it's a damn sight—"

"It wasn't my idea. Abel, think. Do you honestly believe I have the power to turn someone into one of my people?"

He subsided, still glowering. "Who, then?"

"The Lady." Rule sipped from his mug. "You've been briefed. That's all you're getting. Now it's Lily's turn. Lily, Abel and Cullen will be working under you."

She frowned. "Abel should be in charge. He's got twice the experience."

"Nope." Karonski gave her a steady look. "I have the experience, but not the time. I've got three open official investigations I'm supposed to stay on top of."

And she had nothing but time—interrupted now and then by things like her arraignment. "That makes sense."

Karonski gave her a nod. "Plus you can contact Rule a helluva lot easier than I can, and you can do the mindspeech thing with Mika. I can't."

"Not predictably or consistently," she said, "so don't count on me to—"

Cullen sat bolt upright. "Hot damn. That's it."

"What?" Lily said.

He waved a hand at her. "Not now. I've got the trigger, but I still need to see how the . . ." His voice fell to a low mutter involving phrases like "nine signa" and "west quadrant" and "Mephistophelian dilemma, dammit" as he squinted at his midair squiggles.

She regarded him wryly. "Does Cullen know he's working under me?"

"Technically," Rule said, "yes. You'll have two other resources to draw on. Arjenie will handle research. Ruben set her up with virtually unrestricted access, so that includes pretty much anything in the Bureau's databases. Your other resource comes from one of our allies. The brownies."

"Brownies."

He smiled. "They'll be more helpful than you think. You may recall that I told you Parrott had ties to Humans First. I knew that because the brownies have been watching him. He's met with Paul Chittenden three times in the last two months."

"Chittenden." Friar's East Coast lieutenant. She drummed her fingers on the table. "Parrott's tied in at the top, then, which damn sure changes the picture. You couldn't tell me this before?"

"Unfortunately, no. Brownies are, as you said, timid. Part of their agreement with the Shadow Unit bans us from revealing specific information they've gathered unless that information is obtainable elsewhere. They don't want anyone who hasn't pinkie-sworn to not reveal their secrets to find any link back to them."

Abel grinned. "He means 'pinkie-sworn' literally. That's what they do, all very solemn. I imagine Harry will show up at some point to take your vow."

"Harry. Like my cat?"

"Exactly like your cat." Rule's eyes gleamed with amusement. "He's the leader of the troop who are spying for us. He took that use-name to deal with us in honor of Dirty Harry, whom they consider a great warrior. When that demon showed up here last year—"

"They know about that?"

"Apparently they find you and me too interesting to ignore in spite of the clear drawbacks to being in our company.

They've been keeping an eye on us whenever we come to D.C. When the demon approached last year, Dirty Harry yowled—giving warning—then took off."

"That's their idea of a great warrior?"

"He warned the others and made an excellent escape. Brownies are escape artists. They don't consider courage a virtue. A grim necessity, perhaps. When I first met Harry, he compared courage to taking a laxative. If you must then you must, but you don't want people patting you on the back for it, and you'd be crazy to swallow a whole bottle of cod liver oil if a little sip will do the job."

She had to grin. "So Dirty Harry took the necessary sip, then split, which makes him a hero."

"That's about right, from what I can tell. You'll have to get Harry—the brownie Harry, not the cat—to tell you the story sometime."

Lily had never visited a brownie reservation. There weren't any on the West Coast. "Are they as cute as they look in their pictures?"

Karonski snorted. "They're freaking adorable."

She nodded. She was kind of looking forward to meeting the brownie leader. "Okay. I need to lay out what I need from you two. Cullen, stop playing with your shiny lines and pay attention."

"What?" He scowled. "I need to—"

"At the moment," Rule said, "you need to do what Lily says."

Cullen grimaced, but waved at his air-drawings. They vanished. "I'm listening."

"You said the dagger might be elven made."

"Not the dagger. The spell on it. And I don't know for sure because I need to see the grimoire to confirm, but the spell is a mix of Vodun—that's the part I've been working on in spite of all these interruptions—and what looks almost like Celtic runes. Almost, but not quite. The Vodun segment's the trigger, which makes sense. Vodun specializes in charms and curses that can be used by nulls. Though there's a weird bit to it—but I'll tell you about that in a minute. The thing is, the Celtic-looking runes are not Celtic. I think they're elven, because

Celtic runes were derived in part from elven. But I need the damn grimoire—"

"To confirm your guess. Right. I've got the number for Fagin's safety-deposit box. His thumb drive's there, with a copy of his translation. He's supposed to contact his attorney about getting the thumb drive. Here's the safe deposit number and his lawyer's contact info." She handed him a sheet of paper with the information. "Talk to her."

He grinned. "Guess it was worth listening to you, after all." He pushed his chair back.

"Sit. I'm not finished with you." She looked at the others. "One of the problems with the Bixton case has been the level of magical expertise required to make the dagger. If it's elven work, that solves the problem. Rethna could've made it for Friar long before we came on the scene and spoiled his plans. He could have made other things for Friar, too. Things we haven't run up against yet."

Karonski's eyebrows shot up. "Rethna's the elf lord you two killed last month."

It had been Arjenie's sister who actually killed him, but Lily nodded.

"And you *like* the idea that he might have made all kinds of heavy-duty magical shit for Friar?"

"I like the idea of knowing what we're up against. I like the idea that the guy who enspelled that dagger isn't around to make more. If I'm right, whatever Friar's planning, his best magical tools and assets are limited to stuff he's already got. And I was thinking . . . maybe Rethna made a disguise charm for whoever impersonated Ruben. Elves and illusion go together, right?"

But Cullen was shaking his head. "I can't rule that out a hundred percent, but I really doubt Rethna was good enough at illusion to transfer a solid one to a charm."

"Why not?" she demanded.

"Partly because of how his magic looked—which is a damned unsatisfactory answer, I know." He looked frustrated, as if he didn't like it much, either. "But in addition to that, Rethna's specialty was body magic. Ah . . . something you need to know about elves. The nobility, anyway. They all have a bit of glamour, which is a type of illusion magic. Some of them go on to develop that enough to cast full illusions. And they've all got a bit of body magic, enough to heal themselves and change their own bodies to some extent. All those pretty hair colors? They aren't born with baby blue hair."

"Like that spell that elf lady gave Cynna to turn her permanently blond. That's body magic?"

"That's right. Some elves go on to develop their body magic enough to affect the bodies of others. But body magic and illusion are two very different types of magic. The more you develop one, the harder it is to work the other. It may be different with the High Sidhe," Cullen admitted. "Probably is, but we aren't talking about High Sidhe. We're talking about Rethna. He was aces at body magic, so it's unlikely he could do much with illusion. It would be like a Water Gifted trying to work Fire spells. With a lot of work he might learn a few of the simple ones, but he'd never be that good at them. He'd sure as hell never call Fire." Cullen waved his hand. For a few seconds tiny flames danced there, then puffed out.

Lily nodded. "Then if Rethna was really good at body magic, could he have changed someone to look like Ruben?"

"Probably. I very much doubt he could've made someone smell like Ruben, though."

"The maid didn't say anything about Bixton's visitor smelling like Ruben," she said dryly.

Rule answered instead of Cullen. "Matt did."

She swung to face him, frowning. "I don't know Matt. Who—no, wait, I remember. You were going to send someone to check out the trail I followed into that park across from Bixton's house. That was Matt?"

"He's Cynyr, one of those who've been guarding Ruben. He knows Ruben's scent and he has an unusually good nose, even when two-footed. I heard from him this morning. He found Ruben's scent on that bench in the park."

"But that's crazy."

"Actually," Cullen said, "it's not. Though I just finished putting together . . . can't call it proof, but supportive evidence for my theory. Which I'm warning you is pretty wild, but the trigger on that dagger wasn't just meant to be used by a null. It was made to be used by a magical construct."

She blinked. "And that helps you how?"

"I think Friar used a doppelgänger of Ruben."

A doppelgänger? "Uh . . . isn't that some kind of ghostly double, a harbinger of death? You see your doppelgänger and you die. Something like that."

Cullen rolled his eyes. "I'm talking about real doppelgängers, not fairy tales. Not that real ones are supposed to be real."

"Is there a point you can back up to where you start making sense?"

"Son of a bitch," Karonski breathed. "Son of a bitch. You're talking about a double? An actual, physical double?"

Cullen's eyebrows lifted. "Basically, yes."

Karonski leaned forward. "I need to tell you about one of my open investigations. The one into the attack on Ruben." He patted a closed folder. "It's all in here, but I can sum it up. We know how the potion was administered. According to what Sherry's group found, it was added to a pot of coffee. The problem is, Ruben says Ida brewed that pot. Ida says she didn't. She washed out the pot like usual, then went back to her desk and didn't go back in Ruben's office until he had the heart attack. Whoever made the pot, it was brewed between five and five fifteen. Ruben had the heart attack at five forty. Three people had access to the pot between five and five forty—Ruben, Ida, and the director."

Lily jerked back. "Ida? No. That's not . . ." Ida Rheinhart had been Ruben's secretary forever. Sure, she was kind of scary, but scary like Lily's third-grade teacher. Lily, like the rest of her class, had been convinced Mrs. Brown was an alien. She had to be, since she was either telepathic or really did have eyes in the back of her head. Unlike some of the kids, however, Lily hadn't thought Mrs. Brown was a kid-eating alien. No one had gone missing, after all.

Ida didn't eat children, either. Or FBI agents who failed to file a report properly, however much it might seem that way at times. And if you pulled out her fingernails one at a time, she'd give you the Gorgon gaze, but she would not betray Ruben or the Bureau. "But it can't be the director, either. Can it?"

"None of the above, if Seabourne here's right." Karonski's eyes gleamed. "We've been looking for some kind of compulsion charm, which is several shades of unlikely, especially since Ida claims she doesn't have any blank places in her memory. But compulsion is all we could make fit—until now."

"Oh, yeah." Cullen was almost purring. "I don't feel quite so crazy now. I don't suppose you found any puddles or wet places near Ruben's office?"

Karonski frowned. "Nothing like that in the reports. I didn't arrive on-scene until long after puddles would have dried up."

"A wet spot." Lily frowned. "Water, or something else? The carpet was damp near Bixton's body."

"Hot damn." Cullen's eyes glowed almost as brightly as his wiggly lines had—and a lot more blue. "Hot damn, it fits. It all fits."

"Explain," Rule said.

"Okay." He brooded a moment, probably translating his jargon into something resembling English. "A doppelgänger is supposed to be a temporary magical construct that exactly duplicates a living person. Or a cat or a canary, for that matter, but most people are not interested in going to that much trouble to get a spare Tweety Bird. Problem is, doppelgängers are like the lead-into-gold bit early alchemists wore themselves out on. Or like cold fusion is for physicists these days. It seems like it ought to work, but no one can get it to. Every century or two there'll be a flurry of rumors that someone's cracked the problem, but those stories are like Elvis sightings—the true believers get excited, and everyone else rolls their eyes.

"So 'doppelgänger' crossed my mind when I heard about Ruben's apparent double, but only in the way 'alien abduction' might pop into your head if you hear about mysterious lights in the sky on the same night someone disappeared on a lonely road. It fits the plot, but the plot's screwy. Then I saw the runes on that dagger, and it didn't seem quite so ridiculous."

Lily drummed her fingers. "Are doppelgängers an elf thing?"

"Maybe. I should probably tell you about the guy who wrote the grimoire. Eberhardus Czypsser chased doppelgängers back in his day—it's one reason he was discredited for a century or two and most copies of his book disappeared. But never mind that for now. He claimed to have successfully made a doppelgänger of a bumblebee."

Rule's eyebrows lifted. "A bumblebee?"

"You start small, especially if a spell takes an ungodly amount of power and you aren't willing to use death magic."

"Death magic."

"Yeah, which is another way doppelgänger fits. If you could make one at all, it would take mega-oomphs of power. Magic had thinned out by Czypsser's time, so he made something small. A bumblebee. Or so he claimed, but he refused to demonstrate or prove his claim in any way, saying he didn't give a damn if anyone believed him. And sure enough, people mostly didn't.

"But there're two reasons he might not have been just passing gas. Number one is that in his youth he was apprenticed to an honest-to-God adept. His master was said to have spent time in one of the sidhe realms and returned knowing a lot about sidhe spellcasting—including their runes. Czypsser's grimoire has a list of runes passed to him by his master. It may or may not have details about his purported creation of a bumblebee doppelgänger, but there will be something about it, even if he didn't put it all down."

"What's reason number two?" Lily asked.

"Ah." Cullen leaned back in his chair, smiling like the proverbial cat with feathers stuck to his mouth. "Reason number two, children, is the type of magic I think it would take to create a doppelgänger. You'd need someone who was naturally Gifted in some form of body magic and had spent a few centuries getting better. An elf lord, in fact. Someone like our dear departed friend, Rethna."

"That's it. It fits. Why didn't you say something earlier?" she demanded. "We spent hours at Fagin's place and you didn't say one word about this."

"I didn't tell you the aliens ate my homework, either. You don't get how outlandish this would sound to anyone who knows anything."

Rule chuckled. "He didn't say anything because he hadn't put it all together until just now."

"I just figured out the Vodun trigger," Cullen said, "in spite of constant interruptions."

Rule grinned at his friend. "You also just realized—because Lily said it—that Rethna could have made the necessary charm or whatever it is before he was killed."

Cullen scowled. "An amulet. It's probably an amulet."

"Whatever you say. You were thinking we had a second elf hanging out with Friar, weren't you?"

"Sure, it sounds obvious now, but I had to swallow two impossible ideas to get there. Number one being that dopplegängers are even possible. Number two was that Rethna was not just good enough to make a dopplegänger, but so ungodly good he could make a dopplegänger amulet that others could invoke a month after he died. One that outlasted the limit on charms. You don't have any idea how crazy that sounds. He'd have to have been a goddamned adept."

Lily tilted her head. "Isn't that exactly what he was? You've got that gem he wore. The bullet-stopping one. You called it an artifact. It takes an adept to make an artifact, so—"

"So we don't know that Rethna made it himself." Cullen grimaced and ran a hand over his head, making his hair stand up. "But yeah, okay, maybe he did. Only it gives me retroactive creeps, thinking we went up against an adept. We shouldn't have won. He was away from his realm, his land, so he didn't have the power to draw on that he would have back home, but still." He shook his head. "We shouldn't have won."

"We wouldn't have, if it hadn't been for Dya. So is the dagger an artifact? It lasted more than one moon cycle, but the spell on it isn't hidden. You said you couldn't see the spells on artifacts."

Cullen grimaced. "That's another thing that kept me from fingering Rethna at first. All the artifacts I've seen have the spellwork hidden, but I was extrapolating from too small a sample. Maybe Rethna didn't know how to do the hiding trick.

Maybe he just didn't bother, since almost no one here can see magic."

"I imagine it's a lot of work to—hey!" Movement glimpsed out of the corner of her eye had Lily spinning around.

He stood in the doorway to the dining room grinning at her. He was brown all over—shaggy brown hair, skin midway between caramel and chocolate, brown cargo pants with oversize pockets, brown sweater, brown loafers. And green eyes. Grass green, leaf green eyes with crow's feet tucked in the corners. Eyes round and large like a cat's set low in his face, giving him the look of an oddly aged child. He had a little dab of a nose and a wide, merry smile. He was about eighteen inches tall.

He was freaking adorable. Lily smiled back. She couldn't help it. "Harry, I presume?"

Rule's eyebrows shot up. Karonksi looked baffled. Cullen rolled his eyes. "Oh, great. The runt's here."

THIRTY-ONE

◆━━◆

THE pinkie-swearing took less than five minutes and was, indeed, a solemn business. Cullen left the room right after that, saying he wanted to call Fagin's lawyer then talk dirty to Cynna . . . "and you know how that makes Lily blush."

Though Harry was the only brownie Lily met, the rest of his troop was nearby—out in the backyard, having fun hiding from the guards. Whatever magic brownies used to hide in plain sight didn't work on Lily or Cullen, who was shielded against mind-magic. It worked great on everyone else. Very good spies, indeed.

"*Dul-dul* works on scent," Harry said when Lily asked why the lupi couldn't find him or his troop. He was perched on a small stack of books set on one of the chairs so he could join them at the table. "Not hearing or touch, though. Just sight and scent."

"Why scent but not hearing?"

He rolled his big green eyes. He had long lashes and cute little eyebrows that made perpetually surprised arches. "Because we *need* it to work on scent, of course. We can learn how to move silently, but we can't learn how to not smell, can we?"

That wasn't exactly an answer. "How did you get in? Everything's locked."

That just made him giggle.

Before asking him about his ability to hide, Lily had asked several questions about Parrott's meetings with Chittenden. It turned out that brownies loved watches and clocks and had a keen sense of time on the hours, minutes, and seconds level. They had very little grasp of calendars. Harry knew Chittenden's last visit to Parrott had taken place the day Sadie's cousin Hermie let the pigeons out of that coop over by the park with the cannons—and hadn't that been fun? He didn't have any idea what day that was. After some nose-wrinkled thought, he decided it might have been ten days ago. Or maybe five. Or fifteen?

Fortunately, Rule knew what day Harry had reported the meeting to Ruben: a week ago yesterday.

However lacking they might be with calendars, they were aces at details. The kind of details that interested them, at least. Lily learned a great deal about the flora and fauna in Parrott's yard and a fair amount about his neighbors. The couple on the west side had three kids, two dogs, and a nanny—who was playing hide the pickle with the husband and oyster diver with the wife.

It was a rambling report, but there were some good nuggets in it. "I'm wondering if you could follow someone for me." She glanced at Rule. "That homeless woman you talked to. If we knew where she sleeps, we'd have an idea where to ask questions, see if anyone else has seen anything. I'm thinking we could show pictures of Parrott, Mullins, Drummond, and Chittenden."

They arranged for Harry to meet them at the Twelfth Street Kitchen at three. "How do you get around the city?" Lily asked.

"Cars, mostly. Motorcycles are more fun, but it's hard to keep from touching the driver." Harry hopped down—straight down to the floor, which seemed like a long drop for someone only eighteen inches high. But Lily knew Harry could jump a lot farther than that without harm. Like everyone else in the country, she'd watched videos of brownie acrobatics on brownies.com. The *Wall Street Journal* said the brownies made a tidy amount of money selling ad rights on their site.

"They perch on the bumpers, I'm told," Rule said, rising. "Harry, you'll take my good wishes to the others?"

"Sure." Guileless green eyes beamed up at Rule.

"And this goes along with those wishes." He knelt and held out a small plastic Baggie filled with Hershey's Kisses.

Harry nodded happily as he accepted the Baggie. In the old days, brownies were happy with a saucer of milk. That was before they discovered chocolate.

Rule went to the back door. "And Harry?"

"Yes?"

"Give Lily back her ring."

Lily's gaze jumped to her left hand . . . which was bare. "How the hell—"

Harry chortled and slapped his thigh. "You're getting better, big wolf!" He reached into one of his many pockets and took out her ring. "Here you go!"

Rule accepted it. "This ring is off-limits for the game."

"Sure." Harry nodded, his eyes twinkling. "Whatever you say."

Karonski spoke. "Harry, what would you do if someone played the game with your grandmother's *ti-tutwelli?*"

Harry giggled. "No one would do that!"

"Pretend someone did."

The brownie wrinkled up his cute little face and thought about it. "I guess I'd pull their guts out through their nose."

Karonski nodded as if that's what he'd expected. "The way you feel about your ancestors' *ti-tutwella?* That's how humans are about their wedding rings. Now, Lily's ring is an engagement ring, not a wedding ring. An engagement ring is not quite as important as a wedding ring. What would you say, Lily—maybe seventy percent as important? Eighty?"

Harry squeaked like a mouse. Amber skin paled to an ashy shade. His gaze darted between Lily and Rule. "I didn't know that. I really, truly didn't know that. Are we okay?"

"The ring," Rule said, "is off-limits."

"It is! It is one hundred percent points off-limits!"

"Then we're fine. See you at three." Rule opened the door. The little brownie bounded out as if a werewolf was after him, the Baggie of Hershey's Kisses slung over his shoulder.

Lily watched, bemused. "What in the world was that about?"

Rule shut the door and came to her. "You don't seem upset." He handed her the ring.

"Baffled, more like." She slid the ring back where it belonged. "But he's so cute it's creepy. At least now I know what's behind all that cute—larceny." She frowned and took the ring off, then slid it back on. "How in the world did he get it off my finger without me noticing?"

"That I can't tell you. Harry would be deeply wounded if you called him a thief, though. Taking your ring was part of the game. Brownies play it constantly. I don't know all the rules, but I think anything that's in plain sight is fair game. If they snitch something and leave without you noticing, you have to pay a forfeit to get it back. The forfeits can be quite imaginative."

"And if you catch them, they just give it back. They don't have to pay a forfeit?"

"There are points involved," Karonski said. "But don't ever ask them how the points are figured. The scoring seems to change on a whim."

"Huh." Lily frowned at her ring. Harry should not have been able to remove it without her feeling it move. He couldn't have used magic on her, so how . . .

Cullen breezed back into the kitchen "The runt's gone? Good."

"Why do you dislike Harry?" Lily asked.

"Because he's a sneaky little bugger."

Rule said dryly, "Several years ago, before Cullen got those shields, a brownie snitched an old document he'd recently acquired. He wanted it back badly enough to pay the forfeit—which meant running around the block three times. Backward."

"The little bastards ran alongside me and laughed the whole time. I couldn't see them, but I damn sure heard them." Cullen sat at the table. "Sneaky little buggers, every one. Now, I've got to meet Fagin's lawyer at the bank in an hour, so we have to be quick. And don't give me a hard time about rushing off," he told Lily. "If we're really lucky, that grimoire will give me something solid about dopplegängers. What I've got is rumor and conjecture and not worth much. Oh, and you may be getting a call from a priest."

"A priest."

He nodded. "The one who married me and Cynna. Father Michaels. Cynna's going to call him. It's possible the Church knows something about dopplegängers."

"You discussed this with Cynna over the phone? I don't like to be paranoid, but your phone could be tapped."

Rule spoke. "Cullen has a new spell that's supposed to block anyone trying to listen in technologically. I have no idea how it works, but it's tricky and requires physical components. Which I imagine is the real reason he made his calls in his room."

"Okay." She looked at Cullen. "And you think the Church knows something about dopplegängers."

"Something, yes." He shrugged. "The pope declared them anathema back in the sixteenth century and trained a special group of priests to banish them. That's one reason the rumors about them never quite died out—the Church took them seriously."

"The sixteenth century was a long time ago. Surely this Father Michaels won't know how to banish dopplegängers."

"No, but he's got a mentor who's pretty far up the ladder in the Jesuits. Those people know how to hang on to information—and secrets. If anyone has anything solid about dopplegängers, it'll be them. The real question is whether Father Michaels can pry anything loose from his buddy."

"I'm going to have to go pretty soon, too," Karonski said. "But I've got a question for Seabourne first."

"Shoot."

"If it was a dopplegänger that put the potion in Ruben's coffee, does that mean we don't have a traitor in the Bureau?"

Lily's heart jumped. She hadn't thought of that.

"Afraid not," Cullen said, "if what little I think I know about dopplegängers turns out to be true. Dopplegängers are physical doubles, but they don't get the mind and memories of the original. They have to be piloted or controlled, and the pilot has to be fairly close to the dopplegänger. I don't know how close, but Ruben's office is in a subbasement. Underground, in other words. Earth blocks mind-magic, so the pilot pretty much had to be on the same level as the doppelgänger to direct it."

Lily drummed her fingers on the table. "So making doppelgängers takes lots of power, which our perps are supplying with death magic. They're made mostly of water, and they don't have minds of their own—"

"Hold off on the assuming. They don't have the original's mind and memories. Whether or not they can think, if they're aware at all, I have no idea. A couple more things that all the accounts agree on. They're temporary constructs. I don't know how temporary, but it's probably related to power. The more power poured into them, the longer they'd last."

That made sense. "And this amulet we're assuming Rethna made. The thing that makes doppelgängers. It wouldn't be a one-shot deal, would it? They can make more doppelgängers. But would they be more Idas and Rubens? Can they change the setting on the amulet to make doppelgängers of other people? Or do they have more than one amulet, with each one set to a specific doppelgänger?"

Cullen frowned. "Hmm. I think the amulet could be reset each time it's used. No, I think it would have to be. I suspect the amulet does the heavy lifting—the parts of the spell no one here would be able to handle. Whoever uses it supplies part of the spell, though—probably through a fairly simple ritual—as well as the blood or tissue from whoever they're copying. The user would need to be Gifted and have some knowledge of spellwork. Not a lot, maybe, but some. I'm sure about the tissue and blood part," he added. "That's definitely part of the spell or ritual. The rest is guesswork."

Rule asked, "Would they need to do the ritual with the artifact at the same time they killed to create the death magic they need? Does it all happen in one location, all at the same time?"

"The artifact would've been the focus of the death magic ritual, the place their leader directed the power. The ritual invoking the amulet could be done at any time after it was charged. If Rethna was an adept, we have to assume he could make an amulet that stored power well. The one real limit is on how long the dopplegängers last. No, there are two limits. First, our bad guy had to be in Headquarters, probably on Ruben's floor, when he invoked it. Second, there's timing. Unless you've got a constant power source—like ritually killing people every hour or something—any dopplegängers you make are going to be short-lived. Or so I think. I don't—"

His phone chimed. He took it out, glanced at it. "José says the rental car I sent for is out front. I'd better go. I have to drive the rental company guy back to their lot, wherever that is, before I head to the bank. You got so surly when I used yours last time," he said, rising and slipping his phone back in his pocket. "I thought I'd better get my own wheels—on your dime, of course."

"Of course. You're here on clan business."

Cullen grinned. "Who says I can't be considerate? I was frugal, too, and passed on the Ferrari."

"You'll take a guard with you."

Cullen stopped. "You've got to be kidding."

"Our enemies want you dead. You're still injured. You do a good job of hiding it, but you are. You'll take a guard with you."

Rule was using his mantle voice. Lily couldn't feel it the way Cullen undoubtedly did. Cullen managed to argue anyway. "You don't have enough guards here as it is."

"More are on the way. Leidolf, since they're close. I called Alex this morning." Rule had his phone out. He tapped the screen a few times. "José has assigned Steve to you. He'll meet you out front."

Cullen rolled his eyes. "All right, but I drive. Oh. I almost forgot. I don't know that it will help, but there's one other thing you might need to know. The tissue or blood used to make a dopplegänger has to come from a living person. Or bumblebee, as the case may be."

"I don't see how that's significant," Rule said.

Cullen shrugged. "I don't, either, but—"

"I do." Lily's hands were cold. Her stomach was knotted. "I think I do." She looked at Rule. "You remember I couldn't figure out why I was put in that particular jail. Why was it suddenly best to get me locked up instead of killing me? It's almost always easier to kill someone than to frame them. I couldn't figure it out."

Rule didn't say anything. He didn't have to. The tightness in his face said he was following her very well.

"That jail has a policy," she went on. "Everyone—even those just in holding—are tested for HIV. They took blood from me."

THIRTY-TWO

~≥

TWENTY minutes later, Cullen was gone, eager to get his hands on Fagin's translation of the grimoire. Karonski was gone, too, after calling the jail to ask about Lily's blood sample. Surprise! No one could find it. He'd headed out to lean on them, see if he could find out who might have swiped it.

Lily had asked Karonski a couple questions before he left. He didn't remember what Drummond's alibi was for the day of Ruben's heart attack—they'd checked literally hundreds of alibis. He'd get that information to her, he said. Lily told him to hold off—she might have a faster way of getting it.

Lily made a couple phone calls then. So did Rule. First he ordered lunch, then he called Arjenie back in California. He told her to set up access for Lily to the database, then handed her his phone. Lily told Arjenie what she needed her to find out.

So after those twenty minutes passed, they were alone in the house—no Rhej, Isen, Cullen, Deborah, or Karonski. No one but the two of them.

Made it easier to fight.

"That makes no sense!" Lily took three quick paces away, turned, and glared at him. "I said I'd take a guard with me."

"I go with you. That's not negotiable." Rule's face was

closed up as tight as a vault. "You seem to be forgetting that I am in charge."

"I don't believe you just said that." She took a deep breath and let it out slowly, trying to bank her temper. "At the moment, our enemies want me alive. What good would my doppelgänger do them if I was dead? Whatever my double is supposed to do, people would know it wasn't me."

"Killers have been known to dispose of bodies."

It was hard to argue when he was right. She did her best. "Rule, we'll get twice as much done if we split up."

"If you're worried about efficiency, consider the fact that if your temper leads you to take off without me, I'd have to follow you. Taking two cars would certainly be inefficient." The last was delivered with icy sarcasm.

"Look. I get that you've been worried about me, but—"

"Do you?" In two quick paces he was in front of her, his eyes blazing. He seized her arms. "Do you really have any idea? Because *worried* is a thin and puny word that would snap like a twig beneath the weight of my feelings."

Last month, Lily had discovered just how terrifying it could be to know, deep in her soul, that she could not keep those she loved safe. That death could strike at any moment, no matter how clever or strong or quick she might be. It had been a hard lesson . . . and she wasn't a control freak of a Rho.

She reached up and put both hands on Rule's face. "Anyone can die," she said softly. "In fact, with a very few weird exceptions, everyone does die. On any given day, there's a chance you won't make it, or I won't, or my mother, or Cullen . . . the thing is, there's every chance we will. We have to put our weight behind the second deal, not the first."

For a long moment he didn't speak. Then he took one of her hands, folded the fingers gently into her palm, and held it to his lips. He kissed her knuckles one at a time, all five, including the one at the base of her thumb. "You are very wise." His mouth crooked up. "And I am still going with you."

THEY went to Sjorensen's apartment together.

Karonski said that Anna Sjorensen had been put on administrative leave, just like Lily. He didn't know how they'd learned it was Sjorensen who'd tipped Lily off about Ruben's arrest—shoot, maybe she'd confessed—but she was in trouble, too. That pushed her to the bottom of Lily's list of suspects, but she still wanted to talk to the woman. It would be good to know just how Sjorensen had learned about the impending arrest. "We still don't know what they're planning," Rule said.

Rule and Lily were in the backseat of the Mercedes with Scott at the wheel and Mark riding shotgun. José had decided that Scott could drive just fine with a broken arm, leaving the rest of them free to repel invaders or catch bullets in their teeth or whatever.

Rule had already finished the two huge roast beef sandwiches he'd ordered for himself. Lily was still eating hers— grilled cheese made with havarti and cheddar on rye. The deli had great cheddar and didn't stint on the pickles.

Lily swallowed and slugged down some Diet Coke before answering. "We know they want to duplicate me. We know they can duplicate Ruben and Ida. We know they're thinking big, since the end result if they win is lots of dead lupi and the country in chaos—martial law, riots, the president and vice president dead, the government splintered."

Rule went along with her by adding to her list. "We know they didn't plan on Ruben turning lupus. We know they're using death magic, which means there are bodies somewhere." He glanced at her. "We know someone in the Bureau's involved."

"Yeah." She brooded on that a moment. "We're pretty sure Parrott is, too. He'd be a suspect even if we didn't know he's tied in with Chittenden. First, he's Gifted, and he hides it. Parrott could've been lying about Bixton knowing about his terrible taint. Or Bixton might have known, then found out Parrott hasn't been staying on the wagon, magically speaking." She flipped her hand. "Two birds, one stone. Take out Bixton and frame Ruben."

"Or Bixton could have learned something about Friar or Chittenden that made him dangerous to the movement."

"True. I wish I knew if Chittenden was Gifted. I'm betting yes, but we don't know. It would help if we knew where he was."

"Unfortunately, my people lost track of him last week."

Her eyebrows shot up. "Which people—ghosts or lupi?"

He smiled grimly. "Lupi, in this case, though they're acting in accordance with Ruben's plans. We've been keeping an eye on both Chittenden and Jones. Chittenden managed to slip away."

"Huh." There'd been a lot going on she hadn't known about, hadn't there? She glanced at what was left of her lunch. "Anyone want the other half of my sandwich? I can't eat the whole thing."

"I'll take it," Mark said.

She passed it to him and took another sip of soda. Living with lupi meant never having to worry about wasted food or leftovers. She looked at Rule. "Anything else I should know?"

"Perhaps." He considered a moment, then said, "The president knows about Ruben's visions."

She choked on a swallow of Diet Coke. "The what? She what?"

"You knew she and Ruben have had a close working relationship."

Yes, but . . . "How much does she know?"

"Nothing about the Shadow Unit specifically, but about the Great Enemy, Friar's transformation . . . she has the basics. The White House has been quietly observing heightened security this past month."

"And no one's noticed? There hasn't been anything about heightened security in the news."

"She cancelled her visit to Mexico last week."

"Because of the vote coming up on—oh. You mean that wasn't the real reason." Lily chewed that over. "Congress doesn't know any of this, do they?"

"No. I'm not sure she's told any of her cabinet. What could she say? That her pet psychic has had bad dreams?"

"They'd freak. At least half of them would think she'd lost it. Someone would leak it to the press, and before you know it the whole country would be debating whether the president was non compos or if everyone should be buying guns and stocking their bomb shelters."

"And possibly getting rid of the Gifted in their midst."

Thereby doing part of the enemies' work for them. "I guess Ruben didn't have one of his hunches to *not* inform the president."

"He felt sure that was the right thing to do."

"Shit. I just thought of something. We don't know if Ruben's still a precog, do we? I mean, normally lupi don't have Gifts. Cullen does, but he's the exception. I should've touched Ruben before the two of you took off."

"You'd have lost a hand," Rule said dryly, "so I'm glad you didn't try. I suspect Ruben's still a precog, but you're right, we don't know for sure. And I hadn't thought of that until you mentioned it."

He didn't look happy to have thought of it now. "I guess we'll find out. Do you—" Her phone cheeped like a baby bird. She grimaced. When she first heard the ring tone she thought it was cute, but it was already driving her crazy. She took it out and checked the number. It was the Etorri Rhej. Lily had left a message for her while they waited on lunch. "This is Lily."

"Hi, Lily. I was so sorry to hear about your recent trouble."

"Geez, that was on the news up in Canada?" She couldn't believe her arrest had made even the national news, much less gone international.

A moment of silence. "No, I heard about it from others in the clan. Is your arm improving?"

Oh. Right. She was talking about the shooting. It made Lily want to laugh or groan. That news was a whole month old, and plenty of new troubles had replaced it. "It's healed really well. There's more to the story, but I'm pressed for time. Can I owe you the details for now?"

"Sure. Your message said something about a ghost that's been bothering you."

Like all the Rhejes, the Etorri Rhej was Gifted. She was a medium—a powerful one—plus she knew a lot about ghosts and death and all that, and was able to put it in language that mostly made sense. "Not bothering me exactly, but I have some questions. Killing people to make death magic tends to

throw ghosts, right?" It had to do with what the Rhej called
transitioning and the power involved in that process. Lily
didn't really want to hear the explanation again, so she hurried
on. "That may be where my ghost came from, plus there've
been other ghosts seen in the city recently. And I know someone's been making death magic."

"Ugh. Nasty stuff."

"It is. There may be a lot of it involved, too, so—"

"How much?"

"Ah—I don't know how to quantify it."

"I see your point. I asked because . . . well, mediumship
runs in my family, and has for a very long time. Mothers and
grandmothers have passed down the Gift, the lore, and the stories for many generations. When you talked about a lot of
death magic, I thought of one of the oldest stories. This would
have been pre-Purge, probably by several hundred years."

"That's a long time for a story to keep its shape."

"It is, but bear with me. The story tells of how an evil magician put a small village to death ritually to fuel a Great Spell."

"How many in the village?"

"Fifty-five, I think. I can call my grandmother to make sure
of the number."

Which could have changed a hundred times over the years.
"No, that's okay. I was just wanting a ballpark on how many
deaths we're talking about."

"Anyway, the evil magician ended up being killed by a
rival magician—the Bán Mac. There are a lot of stories about
him. You can find some in most folklore compilations. Apparently he rode all over Ireland on his 'horse of flame' seducing
matrons, rescuing maidens, defeating evil magicians, and
drinking enough ale to kill most men. Also tricking the little
people and getting tricked," she added, "because this was Ireland, after all. Most of the tales focus on Bán Mac, but the
story passed down in my family tells about what happened
after the battle. The area near the sacrificial site was plagued
by instabilities."

"What kind of instabilities?"

"Oh, the usual—water turning to blood, animals born mal-
formed, cows going dry. And of course a lot of ghosts. But

there were also reports of 'divvil beasts' and frequent earth tremors, and something about 'time gang awry.' I can't say how accurate any of this is," she said apologetically, "but there's probably some truth in it. The solution is the point of the tale, to those in my family. The neighboring villages brought in a priest to lay the ghosts. He did that, but he also 'poured Spirit onto the land to knit up its break,' and the odd occurrences stopped."

"Hmm."

The other woman laughed. "You sure can pack a lot of skepticism into a single sound. I think you need to talk to a priest." She laughed again. "I didn't mean it to come out that way. What I mean is that the Church may know more about these odd occurrences at sites of death magic than I do. But even aside from that, you need to let the Church know. The Catholic Church is very good at laying certain kinds of ghosts. The souls of those killed may need the power of the Church to replace what was stolen in order to complete their transitions."

That made two people who wanted Lily to talk to a priest. "A priest Cynna knows is supposed to call me about some stuff related to the case. I'll ask him about it."

"Good."

"The other thing I wanted to ask was if there's any way I could talk to that ghost if he shows up again."

"I can't help you with that. If you were a medium, I could offer suggestions, but mediums and non-mediums experience ghosts so differently that my training doesn't really apply to you."

"Is there any way you could come to D.C.?"

A moment's silence, then: "I'm afraid not. I have a prior obligation I have to honor."

It was the brief pause that made Lily suspicious. "Some kind of mysterious Rhej business?"

Another pause, then a chuckle. "You could say that."

"It's what the Leidolf Rhej said when she hit me up for five hundred dollars before heading for the airport."

That seemed to make the Etorri Rhej's day. She laughed and repeated it, then said goodbye in high good humor.

"I'm begining to think," Rule said as the car slowed, "I

should call my father and see if the Nokolai Rhej has also departed for an undisclosed location."

"Surely not." The Nokolai Rhej was blind. She couldn't jet off on mysterious Rhej business . . . could she? "Maybe you should. Not that it will do any good, since we still won't know what they're up to. I'm starting to have some sympathy for Cullen's attitude about Rhejes."

"They do know how to be silent."

The car had stopped for a light. So had a couple dozen other cars. As backed up as they were, it would take a couple of light changes to get through the intersection. They were only a couple blocks from Sjorensen's place. Lily tapped her foot, considering getting out and walking the last bit.

"Assholes," Scott muttered.

"What?" Rule said.

"Sorry. I shouldn't have said anything. The bumper sticker on that gray SUV bugs me."

Lily couldn't see it until their own lane of cars crept forward—then there it was. A shiny gray Nissan SUV with three kids in the back—two boys and a cute little girl in pigtails—and two bumper stickers on its rear window. One read "Humans First." The other said, "Honk If You Hate Weers."

Lily couldn't believe it. "Jesus. Honk for hate. They think they're being cute." One of the boys threw something at the other. The mother turned around and said something to them. She looked like a nice woman, not yelling or anything, just wearing her Mother Face.

"They're probably here for the Humans First demonstration," Rule said. "The big rally is tomorrow."

She'd lost track. With everything that had happened, she'd pretty much forgotten about the demonstrations Humans First had planned. "Rule. Tomorrow. Are you thinking what I am?"

"I don't think it's coincidence, no."

Their eyes met. He looked as grim as she felt. If whatever Friar was cooking up was scheduled to coincide with the demonstration tomorrow, they didn't have much time. And they still had no idea what Friar was planning.

Anna Sjorensen was staying in an ESH studio suite, with

ESH meaning extended stay housing, and "studio suite" meaning it was basically a hotel room with a kitchenette. It was the sort of place the government parked clerks, agents, and other human miscellany when it wanted them in D.C. temporarily. Sjorensen was still technically part of the Nashville office, temporarily assigned to D.C. for training, so she qualified for ESH.

Unless Croft had gone ahead and pulled her into the Unit. Lily would ask about that.

These ESH units weren't bad; the location was decent, if noisy, being on a busy street. No parking, though. Scott dropped her, Rule, and Mark off in front. He'd have to circle the block until they came out again.

On the sidewalk, the two men flanked her. Lily sighed and decided not to make an issue out of it. At least Rule was on her right. He knew better than to get in the way of her gun hand. "We aren't all going to fit going through the door this way."

Rule slanted her a smile. "Mark will go in first."

"Good grief."

"It's standard practice," Mark assured her. "The Rho never goes through a door first."

"I'm not a Rho. I'm the one who makes sure the area's safe for the other people."

"Not this time," Rule said.

"I'd like to argue, but that's Arjenie's ring tone." She took out her phone as they reached the revolving doors that led to the lobby. With a sigh, she waited beside Rule while Mark went first. "Hey, Arjenie. Does this means you've got something for me?"

"I'm not interrupting, then? Good. I e-mailed you the files. You didn't ask me to call, so I wasn't sure if I should, but I had a hunch you'd want to hear about this."

Lily had asked Arjenie for the complete personnel files on Sjorensen, Mullins, and Drummond. She was absolutely not entitled to see those. Even if she'd still been Unit, she would've needed Ruben's written authorization to see the complete files. But Arjenie had the highest clearance possible now, Rule had said. She could access anything.

Mark had reached the lobby without being shot. He nod-

ded, and Lily and Rule took the wild risk of entering the revolving door themselves. "This is a good time, actually," Lily
said as they emerged in the small, empty lobby. "You found
something interesting?"

"Nothing much on Sjorensen. She was a good student and
did well at Quantico. Not much on Mullins, either, except that
he's a recovering alcoholic—that's how they say it, you know,
even if they've been sober a long time, and he has. Twelve
years. But that's not why I called."

Lily smiled. Arjenie had trouble summarizing. "You found
something on Drummond?"

"I think so. Maybe. His wife died last year. They'd been
married twenty-two years. No children."

They headed for the elevators. "This is important?"

"It's how she died. She was killed by a woman named Martha Billings whom Drummond had arrested years ago. Billings was Fire-Gifted and mob-connected, and had a bad habit
of burning things down for money."

"Ah." Some Gifted had killed his wife. "What happened?"

"Billings got out of prison, partied for about a week, then
went and burned down Drummond's house. He wasn't home,
but his wife was, and she died of smoke inhalation. They know
it was Billings even though no one saw it because she confessed. She was mad that it hadn't killed Drummond, so she
sent him a video where she raved about how she'd killed his
wife and she'd be coming after him next. Can you imagine
that? She confessed in a video."

"Criminals are often not all that bright." The elevator doors
opened and the three of them got in.

"She might have confessed, but she didn't hang around to
be found. Drummond went nuts. He tore up his office and did
some raving of his own. Then he vanished. Just poofed, abandoned his cases, went missing. He's gone for two weeks, and
in that two weeks, Billings turns up dead."

"That is definitely worth a phone call," Lily said. "I take it
there was nothing linking him to Billings's death?"

"No, it was ruled an accident. The car she was driving burst
into flames. There were witnesses, and no one saw anything
except that it was suddenly engulfed in flame. No sign of ac-

celerants, shots fired, nothing. The investigating officers decided she'd suddenly lost control of her Gift. She had a rep for doing drugs, and drugs do mess up your control," Arjenie added, "so that wasn't implausible. This happened four days before Drummond turns up. He'd been drinking the whole time, he said, and he doesn't remember everything real well, but he had credit card receipts to show that he'd stayed at an inn down in Tennessee, a long ways from Boston. Boston's where Billings died. It wasn't a real alibi, but Billings's death wasn't ruled a homicide, so it didn't matter."

They'd reached the seventh floor. The doors opened. Mark went first again, with Lily and Rule right behind him. No one in the hall. "That was not all in Drummond's personnel file."

"No, but there was enough in it that I knew you'd want the rest of the story, so I went digging."

"I'm glad you did. Thanks, Arjenie. Feel free to bother me anytime you get a hunch like that. Did you find anything about Drummond's alibi for five to six on the day of Ruben's heart attack?"

"He had his teeth cleaned at three thirty, and the dentist says he probably left about four thirty. The agent's notes suggest he could have gotten to Headquarters by five if the traffic wasn't bad, but in the end he was eliminated based on scan and visual records and the testimony of the guards on duty at the entrances that day. They know Drummond by sight," she added. "He's been at Headquarters for years."

"Hmm. Well, send me the dentist's contact info and address, okay? Thanks." Arjenie told her to take care of herself and Lily disconnected. She looked at Rule. "You heard all that?"

He nodded. "You said Drummond had an attitude about magic. Now we know why."

"It's not proof, but it's suggestive. If he decided once to take justice into his own hands, he could decide to do it again. Maybe wiping out one Gifted wasn't enough. Maybe he wants to get rid of all of us."

They'd reached a door with 715 over the spyhole. Lily knocked.

No answer. She waited a moment and knocked again. She'd been reluctant to call ahead. Too easy for Sjorensen to turn her down. "Damn. Guess we'll have to try back later."

"Lily. Step aside a moment, please."

Something in Rule's voice kept her from asking why. She moved away from the door. He moved up—and put his face next to the crack where the door met the frame. Slowly he crouched, sniffing all along that crack. He straightened and turned. "I smell blood."

She dug in her purse with one hand. Pulled out her weapon with the other. And elbowed him aside.

To her surprise, he let her. "Anna!" she called loudly, banging on the door with the hand that held her weapon. "Anna, are you okay?"

No answer. She wasn't expecting one. The hand groping madly in her purse connected with what she wanted. She pulled out a single latex glove, handed her weapon to Rule, and tugged the glove on. "Anna!" she called again, even louder. "I have reason to suspect you're injured. If you don't respond, I will force entry."

Weapon ready in her right hand, she reached for the door-knob with her gloved left hand. The door had a key card lock like a hotel and the light was red, so she was startled when the knob turned. She swung the door open—and quickly, before the two lupi could shove her aside, she stepped in.

A short entry hall, angling almost immediately to the left. Blank wall dead ahead. Drops of dried blood on the pale beige carpet. And a very stubborn, very fast man dodging around her to run inside.

"Stay back," she ordered Mark without knowing if he'd obey, and she followed as quickly as her merely human self could, weapon out.

On the left, a kitchenette. Directly ahead a single room—bed to one side, couch, desk, and tiny two-person table on the other. Big windows with the drapes closed. And a nice, reddish-brown stain on the carpet directly in front of her.

No body. No signs of a fight, aside from the blood.

Rule was moving quickly through the small space, pausing here and there to listen and sniff. Making sure they were alone, she supposed. Mark—wonder of wonders—had stayed out, guarding the door. Lily crouched and studied the bloodstain.

It wasn't fresh, but the center looked to still be damp. There was some spatter. She tilted her head. She was no expert, but that didn't look like spray from a bullet. "You smell gunpowder?" she called. Rule had vanished into the tiny bathroom.

"No."

The wound hadn't spurted. There was just that bit of spatter. Head wound, maybe? It looked like the victim had been struck, staggered a step or two, then fallen to the floor. The biggest spot would be where she'd lain, unmoving, her blood soaking into the carpet.

Lily turned her head. Brown spots led away, as if the wound had still been dripping when the victim was carried out. Or walked out on her own? "Can you tell for sure if that's Sjorensen's blood?"

He came out of the small bathroom. "Probably. I'll need to get close."

"Just don't touch it."

He came and knelt near to the stain, bent, and sniffed. Held still a moment, his mouth slightly open. "This is Anna's blood."

"There's a trail leading to the door. Drops of blood. I don't know if it's enough to suggest she was still alive then, her heart still pumping, but maybe. Maybe she was. What I'd like to know is if she walked out or was carried. Can you tell by sniffing?"

"Not in this form. Probably not as a wolf, either. There are other smells here." He sniffed the carpet again, this time a couple feet away from the bloodstain, then shifted position and did it again. "Mostly it's Anna, but two of the not-Anna scents are recent. I don't see how I could tell if they carried her out, though. They walked in, walked around, and walked out, but I can't say if they were carrying her."

"Okay." She took out her phone. "You want to have not been here?"

His eyebrows snapped down. "What?"

"I'm calling Croft. Maybe I should call the locals, but Croft can get everything rolling quickly, and speed is important. She might still be alive. But that means we'll be stuck here awhile. It might be that you and Scott dropped me and Mark off. You never came in. You're on your way to the Twelfth Street Kitchen right now."

"We're not separating. If you're here, so am I."

She gave up and called it in.

THIRTY-THREE

~

RULE did not hit or harm any cops in the next few hours. Not Special Agent Ron Fielding of the FBI. Not Sergeant Willy Spaulding of the Washington Police Department, either, and that took more willpower. As Lily said at one point, Spaulding might not be an asshole, but he did a damn fine impression of one.

Lily had wanted Rule to leave, to stay free to continue their own investigation. It made sense. Rule hadn't even considered doing so. He'd abandoned her once to get Ruben away, and she'd been arrested, locked up. It didn't matter that his leaving hadn't caused her arrest, and his presence couldn't have averted it. He couldn't abandon her again.

They did end up separated for a while. Two sets of law enforcement wanted to question them, and the federal contingent, at least, was smart enough to separate them for that. The FBI claimed a meeting room on the second floor to coordinate their investigation; Rule was questioned there while Lily was questioned elsewhere. The two of them were then stashed in the manager's office next door to the meeting room.

The separation was probably good policy, but it came too late. They'd discussed the situation by the time Agent Fielding arrived. Lily didn't want to call her lawyer; she wanted Anna found, and intended to cooperate as fully as possible. She warned Rule then that she'd be a suspect. Croft had told her not to reveal anything about the Bixton investigation, but Lily's arrest was not a secret. It was quickly obvious that Fielding knew about it and what role Anna's actions had played.

Fielding didn't know Lily, and it was his job to speculate. Maybe Lily had suspected Anna of setting her up and had gone to confront her; the argument escalated, and Anna ended up dead. Lily then got rid of the body—probably with Rule's help, since Anna Sjorensen outweighed Lily. Lily was alibied for almost the entire day by Mark, Scott, Cullen, and some of the others, but Fielding assumed that Rule's people would lie if he told them to. As, of course, they would.

But Fielding was both professional and reasonable, and it was a stretch to suspect that Lily had not only killed Anna and enlisted Rule to get rid of the body, but had gone on to stage an elaborate discovery of the scene a few hours later. What was the point? Lily might be a suspect, but mostly because she couldn't be crossed off the list altogether. After a couple hours he was ready to let them go.

Detective Spaulding was neither reasonable nor professional. Mostly he was pissed. The feds should've called him right away, not waited forty damn minutes. The feds were holding out on him. The feds thought they could come in and take over when this was by damn his city, his case, and he wasn't going to put up with it. Add Lily's recent arrest to that mountain of attitude, and he was convinced that either Lily had killed Anna or Rule had done it for her. He didn't seem to need a reason—and, since the feds were indeed holding out on him, he didn't have one. Lily was a fed and Rule was a werewolf. That was enough for him.

Unfortunately for the detective, he lacked a body. It was hard to build a case without one.

The afternoon wasn't entirely wasted. Rule had his phone and could tend to some business while he waited. Plus humans constantly forgot that lupi had good ears, and the little office where Rule spent most of that time abutted on the meeting room. Rule heard a great deal about what went on with the federal part of the investigation.

Not only had they not found a body—they hadn't found anything. The knock-on-doors didn't turn up anyone who'd seen or heard anything suspicious. There were no fingerprints on the doorknob, and several surfaces inside the apartment had been wiped, too.

He reported all that to Lily as they finally headed back to the house. "Anna's attackers were lucky," he finished. "They seem to have carried her out of there without attracting any notice."

"There has to be someone around to notice. We were alone in the lobby, remember? And the elevator, and the hall. No one's home during the day at an ESH building. It's temporary housing, no families or retirees, and everyone's at work. The best you could hope for is a delivery at the right time."

"I suppose most people in the Bureau would be aware of that."

She nodded. Her expression was abstracted.

He reached for her hand. "What?" he said softly.

"I didn't say anything to Croft. Nothing about dopplegängers or what's really going on. What we think is going on," she corrected herself. "I left him in the dark about almost everything."

"Because there's a chance Croft is involved." Rule didn't believe it . . . but that could be because he didn't want to.

"I hate this. I hate it. I think Drummond's the bad guy, but maybe I think that because I want it to be him. Because I so much don't want Croft to be one of them."

He squeezed her hand. "Even if Drummond's involved, he might not be the only one."

She swallowed. Nodded.

He shifted the subject. "I keep wondering why they went after Anna. What did she know or guess that made her a threat?"

"They didn't just want her. They wanted something at her place, too."

"Why do you say that?"

"Why else were so many surfaces wiped clean? They were

looking for something. Plus there's the amount of blood in the carpet. It wasn't a spurting type of injury. To get the carpet soaked that way, they must have left her lying there awhile. There are other possible reasons for that," she added. "Maybe they didn't go there expecting to have a body to remove and needed some time to arrange things. But the likeliest reason is that they left her there while they searched for something."

For a moment he could see it—Anna's crumpled body bleeding into the carpet while her attackers went through her things. Anger rose. "She was alive still," he said, his voice rough. "When they searched, she must have still been alive to have bled so much."

"Yeah, I think so, too." She was silent a moment. "I even wondered for a bit if maybe it wasn't Sjorensen who called me. What if it was her doppelgänger, and they had to get rid of Sjorensen so no one guessed? But the blood spot was still damp in the middle. She was attacked in the last twelve hours or so. If they'd made a doppelgänger, wouldn't they want to get rid of the original sooner than that?"

Rule frowned. "Maybe not. If Anna didn't call you, she'd deny having done so. But they would expect that, wouldn't they? Both sets of 'them'—the authorities and our enemies. Our enemies might have used a doppelgänger to call you, but not seen the need to remove Anna until something else happened."

"Whoever called used Sjorensen's phone. But maybe . . ." Her fingers started tapping on her thigh. "Maybe they snitched it from her, then planted it on her again. Maybe that's what tipped her that something was wrong, and she started digging. Maybe she learned something, or they were afraid she did." She sighed. "That's a whole slew of maybes, and they don't get us any closer to finding her."

Rule didn't respond. Lily knew as well as he did that it was unlikely they'd find Anna. Her body, perhaps, if they were lucky. And patterners tended to tip luck their way.

Scott turned onto their street. It occurred to Rule he hadn't prepared Lily for what awaited them at the house. "I sent for more Leidolf."

"You mentioned that."

"I'm afraid it will mean decreased privacy for you. Some of them will be sleeping in the basement. It's uncomfortable in its current state, but at least there's a sink and toilet. They'll have to shower in the first-floor bathroom, however, as will those bunking in the garage."

Her head swung toward him. "You're putting them in the garage and in the basement?"

"Most of them. The shift leaders and José will sleep in the front bedroom. José texted me that the bunk beds have been delivered. Did I tell you that I named Scott José's second?"

"No." There seemed to be a lot he hadn't told her. Had he arranged all of this while they were at the ESH building? "Ah—congratulations, Scott."

He nodded, facing straight ahead. "Thanks."

"José will need a second, given the number of guards now in his charge. We discussed this and agreed on Scott. It helps that he's Leidolf, but the promotion is based on ability and temperament, not clan."

"How many guards are you talking about?"

"Twenty in addition to those already here."

"You've got to be kidding."

"Ruben isn't the only one who can have a hunch."

THEIR little parlor was wall-to-wall lupi. They didn't really fit. Lily stood beside Rule facing the sea of lupi and wondered why she was there. Sure, she had to meet them, but she didn't think she could memorize everyone's names this fast.

Rule had told them all to sit and was giving them a truncated version of what they were up against—not everything, but he told them about doppelgängers, and that they were to watch for the scent of death magic, which should distinguish the fake from the real. José and Scott were at the back of the room, the only ones standing other than Lily and Rule.

"As for your immediate duties," Rule finished, "José has already sorted you according to his needs and your strengths. Those of you—"

"No, he hasn't."

The blunt-featured man who'd contradicted Rule sat at the

front of the mob. His name was Mike. Lily remembered that because he looked a bit like a pale-skinned Mike Tyson—well over six feet of muscle and mad.

Rule's attention lasered in on the man. "What did you say?"

"José hasn't sorted us according to our strengths. I'm the best fighter here. Ask anyone. Plus I've planned and led raids. I've got nothing against Scott, but I've got twice his experience. I should be in charge, not some Nokolai wetback who—"

He didn't get the chance to finish. In a split second Rule had him by his shirt, jerked him to his feet—and threw him. All two hundred and fifty pounds or so of him. He sailed over two men who managed to duck and crashed into the wall—then fell onto an end table that broke beneath him, sending a lamp and a couple of ugly knickknacks crashing.

Rule stalked up to the man, weaving around the seated lupi. Mike started to get up. Rule put his foot on the man's back and shoved him down again, leaving his foot in place. Had there been any sound in the room at all, Lily wouldn't have been able to hear him, his voice was so soft. "You are mine. José is mine. *I* say you obey José. If he wants you to wash the floor with your tongue, you will start licking."

"Y-yes." The man couldn't offer his belly. He was lying on it, and Rule's foot kept him pinned. But he managed to tilt his head so part of his throat showed. "Yes."

No one moved. No one spoke. Lily wasn't sure the roomful of lupi were breathing. She might not be able to feel it when Rule pulled mantle, but she could hear it in his voice—and see the results. He'd all but flattened them with it.

She shook her head. "I've always hated that table, but that's the second wall you've damaged this week. You're really hard on walls lately."

For reasons known only to the testosterone crowd, that brought a bright grin to Rule's face. He looked about eighteen. "I have been, haven't I?" He stepped away from the man on the floor, speaking to Lily as if they were alone in the room. "My apologies for the mess, *nadia*. Mike will clean it up. The rest of you . . ." He glanced around. "Those who will bunk in the garage can—"

The doorbell rang. José spoke from the back of the room.

As usual, he wore an earbud. "It's Seabourne with another man—pale skin, brown hair, looks about forty. He's wearing a clerical collar."

The priest. Cynna's priest, who was supposed to call, dammit, not drop by. Lily sighed. "Maybe Mike could hurry."

LILY remembered Father Michaels from the wedding. Not everyone would have taken a ghostly poltergeist and an angry dragon in stride the way the priest had, so she was inclined to like him. He looked the way she thought a priest should look, too—not the bluff Irish version, but the scholarly sort. Abraham Michaels was slim and pale, with a long neck and elegant hands. He wore gold-rimmed glasses, dark slacks, and a tweed jacket. And the collar, of course.

"We were about to order supper," Rule said as he led the way to the kitchen, as bland as if they hadn't all walked past a scary man crawling around on the floor picking up broken bits. Most of the rest of the lupi had vanished before Lily reached the front door—either out back or down to the basement—but the just-promoted Scott was still with them. "You'll join us, I hope. Do you enjoy Mexican food, or would you prefer Chinese?"

"Nothing for me, thank you."

"Mexican," Cullen said promptly.

"So noted. Lily?"

"No preference."

"Scott, you'll take care of ordering, please. Three pans of the enchiladas from Café Lopez."

Scott nodded, pulled out his phone, and left the room, heading for the front of the house. Three pans wouldn't begin to feed thirty lupi plus Lily, Rule, Cullen, and Father Michaels—who'd be offered dinner again when it arrived, Lily was sure, if he was still here. The guards must have already eaten. Not surprising. It was pushing eight o'clock.

Rule gestured at the table. "Please have a seat, Father, and tell me what I can get you to drink. We have a decent selection of wines—the Cabernet is my personal favorite, but if you prefer white you might try the Riesling. Lily favors it. Or I could put on coffee. We have various sodas, too, of course."

"Nothing, thank you. I'm sorry for barging in on you," the priest said, seating himself at the table, "but I need to ask you some questions. The situation could be both urgent and dangerous. Extremely dangerous."

"Yes, I believe it is." Rule opened the wine cooler.

Lily went to get glasses. "Riesling for me. I don't care if it goes with the enchiladas. Cullen?"

"Cabernet." Cullen pulled out a chair and sat beside the priest. "Father Michaels called me instead of Lily after talking to his Jesuit buddy. He has questions and I didn't know how much to tell him, so I brought him to you."

Rule had retrieved two bottles and was opening one. "I wonder why you called Cullen instead of Lily?"

"I was alarmed, and . . . well, Cullen is not one of my parishioners, but I officiated at his marriage. I feel some responsibility toward him. When I learned there was a chance someone was creating dopplegängers—"

"He wanted to make sure it wasn't me," Cullen said dryly.

"Not because I had the slightest suspicion Cullen would use death magic," Father Michaels said firmly. "He has a highly developed curiosity that might lead him to experiment unwisely, but he wouldn't power his experiments in such a foul way. I didn't know how certain it was that death magic was involved."

"That part's solid," Lily said. "I'm a touch sensitive, and I felt death magic on, uh, something related to an investigation. Something we believe was handled by a dopplegänger."

"Did you see it?" he asked urgently. "This dopplegänger. Did you see it, and are you certain it dispersed?"

Cullen's eyebrows shot up. "They don't last, Father."

"Humor me."

Cullen shrugged. "Okay, sure. Then no to the first—none of us have seen a dopplegänger—and yes to the second. They left wet spots behind."

"They?" His eyebrows shot up. He shook his head. "I don't quite see how wet spots—"

"About half of their mass comes from water. When they dissolve, some of that water remains. Wet spots."

"I see." He sat back, breathing out audibly in relief. "Yes, that should indicate they're gone."

Rule had wrestled both corks free and was letting his bottle breathe. Lily poured herself a glass of the Riesling and brought it to the table. "Are you sure you don't want some wine, Father?"

He looked from Lily to Rule to Cullen, a frown pulling at his brows. "You don't seem to grasp the seriousness of the situation."

"We grasp it just fine," she said, sitting across from him. "We've had a little more time than you to adjust, and . . . forgive me for the assumption, but we're maybe more accustomed to dealing with this kind of sh—stuff than you are. I've got some questions for you."

"As I have for you. How certain are you about these dopplegängers, if you didn't see them? How many dopplegängers are you talking about?"

"Two. There may have been a third, but that's iffy. As for how sure we are . . ." She glanced at Cullen. "What would you say—about ninety-five percent sure?"

"Something in that neighborhood."

"This is not good." The priest sighed unhappily. "Not good at all. That means we're talking about multiple deaths. Multiple souls who haven't been able to complete their passage."

"How many?" Lily asked. "A medium I know told me that large amounts of death magic can cause what she called instabilities. Do you know anything about that?"

"I'm afraid not. Father Moretti may. I have to call him. I'll ask."

"Father Moretti is your friend in the Jesuits?"

"No. No, I'm telling this all out of order. I . . . thank you." Rule had ignored the priest's refusal and set a glass of wine at his elbow. He sat beside Lily as Father Michaels continued. "I have to ask you to promise you won't reveal what I'm about to tell you."

Lily exchanged a glance with Rule. She let him say it. "We can't promise that."

"This is information the Church has kept secret for centuries. I must have your word."

Rule shook his head. "My people take vows seriously. If I promised that, I wouldn't be able to speak of it even if it were necessary to save lives. I . . ." His brows drew together. He blinked, then nodded. "What if we promised not to speak of it—except to those who already know, of course—unless we are in truly urgent and dire circumstances?"

The priest looked troubled, but after a moment he nodded slowly. "Yes, I think I can accept that. Very well. About all I knew of dopplegängers when Cynna called me was that they probably fell within the responsibility of a certain group of Jesuits. I called a friend of mine in that order. Alejandro intended to do some research, then call me back. Instead I heard from Father Moretti. Ah . . . he's a senior advisor to the Superior General of the Order. Extremely senior. Alejandro's inquiries sent up a red flag, it seems."

Absently he sipped his wine—paused, and seemed to notice the glass he held. "This is quite good."

"Thank you," Rule said.

"As I was saying, Father Moretti is in charge of a particular group of Jesuits. You might call them watchdogs. Some of what they watch for is unlikely to ever occur, but inquiries such as Alejandro's draw their attention."

"So dopplegängers have been created before?" Lily said. "Copies of humans, that is, not bumblebees."

"Cullen mentioned the bumblebee." Father Michaels glanced at Cullen, a small smile briefly lightening his expression. "The Church has encouraged the idea that dopplegängers are a pipe dream, but yes, they are possible. Until shortly before the Purge, they were not considered a grave threat to anything but the souls of their makers. They lacked sufficient duration to be a real problem. But in the seventeenth century, someone discovered how to make a new type of dopplegänger that lasted much longer. Some accounts claim . . . but I'm getting ahead of myself. This new type of dopplegänger was created using death magic, just as you believe yours are. The Church called them *nex in vita.*"

"Death-in-life," Rule murmured.

Father Michael's eyebrows lifted in surprise. "Yes, exactly. They were different from previous dopplegängers in significant ways. For one thing, they were unsouled."

Lily frowned. "Like demons?"

Cullen snorted. "They're constructs, Father. Of course they lack souls. So does my computer."

The priest shook his head. "Involving death magic in their creation changes things. I don't know enough about it to explain. I can only repeat what Father Moretti told me. These dopplegängers lacked souls, but unlike your computer, they were capable of volition. If their *presul* was killed—ah, that means the director or controller of the dopplegänger. If the person directing the dopplegänger was killed, the creature didn't disperse, as happened with the older dopplegängers. Instead it went on a killing spree. There are accounts of *nex in vita* lasting up to a week—and one account of one lasting an entire month, dispersing only when it had killed everyone and everything in the village."

"A *month*?" Cullen was incredulous.

"I don't know if the story is accurate," Father Michaels said apologetically, "and I'm afraid the medieval Church took steps to alter the historical record, so you'll be unable to verify it on your own. But Father Moretti takes that account very seriously."

"I'm not buying it." Cullen looked more grim than dismissive, however. "It would take massive amounts of death magic to fuel a dopplegänger for a month. Even if a practitioner was able to channel that much power—and that's a big if—we're talking at least a hundred people killed in a short time in a controlled ritual. I don't see how anyone could do that—or how the Church could keep it quiet if someone did."

"But it wasn't done in ritual. Not once the dopplegänger had been created, that is. Father Moretti believes that the *nex in vita* can feed upon death directly, without ritual, to avoid dissolution. If a dopplegänger's creator doesn't dispel it—or if he is killed and no one controls it—then as long as it can keep killing, it won't cease."

"Until someone kills it," Rule said.

Father Michaels shook his head. "They exist in a sort of

half-life. Death-in-life, as it were. Because they aren't fully alive, they can't be killed."

Lily's eyebrows shot up. "At all?"

"Perhaps with modern weapons . . . but according to the historical record, they cease when they run out of power, but they can't be killed."

After a moment Rule said, "Are you sure of this, Father?"

"Father Moretti is, and I believe him."

"Then how do we stop a doppelgänger? The Church must have found a way to do so."

"I don't know." Lines grooved his face as if he'd aged a decade since he arrived. "The method the Church used back then isn't one we'd want to repeat. I don't want to see a second Purge."

THIRTY-FOUR

LILY rubbed her face and thought wistfully about coffee. "For a while there, I thought you were going to tie him up."

It was after ten. She, Rule, and Cullen were seated around the table once more. Father Michaels had just headed upstairs to the bedroom Cullen wasn't using. Rule had been utterly insistent that the priest was in danger and should stay with them. At first Father Michaels had refused, but he had agreed to call Father Moretti from their house. That way they could answer questions—some of them, at least—and between Rule's presence and Cullen's debugging spell, they could be sure no one listened in on the call.

Father Moretti had spoken with Cullen and Rule, but hadn't asked to talk to Lily. *Quel surprise*—there was sexism in the biggest, oldest boys' club in the world. He'd then spoken privately with Father Michaels for nearly an hour.

The upshot of all that talking was that Father Michaels would stay with them, after all—and the Jesuits were sending specially trained priests to D.C. Lily hoped they were trained in something other than killing all the Gifted they could find. The first Purge hadn't worked out well.

Not that Cullen had any doubts how to handle it. Mage fire, he'd pointed out, had destroyed an ancient staff created by an Old One. It could burn up some dead elf's trinket, too.

Cullen had been known to be overconfident, but Lily was betting with him this time. At least on that score. On another subject, he was becoming a real pain.

"I'm not buying it," Cullen said for the fifth time. "The Purge did not take place because some renegade German spellcasters managed to cobble together an evil, death-eating dopplegänger that the Church didn't know how to deal with. I don't care how good the Church was at hushing things up back then. There would have been rumors, speculation—something about it would have reached the magical community."

"History is written by the winners," Rule said. "The magical community lost that round in a big way. And Father Michaels didn't claim that the Purge was caused only by the advent of these *nex in vita*. They might have been the deciding factor for the Pope, but God knows secular authorities were behind it, too."

The priest believes what he said, a crisp mental voice announced.

Lily jolted. "Mika? You've been listening?"

Did you think my only function was to act as your personal e-mail service?

Rule raised his eyebrows at Lily. "I thought you knew. Mika chimed in with a suggestion about the wording when Father Michaels asked us for that promise."

She grimaced. "He must have just spoken to you."

Sam says that Arcan in Rome says that some priests there believe as this one does. Mostly the ones in the red robes.

"The cardinals?" The ones high enough up in the hierarchy that they were privy to most of the secrets.

In English they are so called. Were they named after the birds, or were the birds named for them?

"The birds were named for the red-robed priests," Cullen said, still peevish. "People thought one gaudy creature resembled the other."

English is a flexible language. Often confusing, but flexibility can be an advantage. Cullen Seabourne would do well to remember this.

Rule gave Cullen an amused glance. "That's telling you."

"Never mind about the Purge," Lily said. "If the rest of

what Father Michaels told us is true, our enemies have the ability to make doppelgängers that can last a hell of a lot longer than the two we know about did. Doppelgängers that want to kill so they can eat death magic and stay . . . I guess *alive* isn't the right word. So they can continue. And they can't be killed."

A puff of feeling arrived, almost like a contemptuous mental snort. *The priest is not right about everything. In the past it has taken an Old One to create any form of the undying. I do not believe abysmally ignorant spellcasters of a backwater realm succeeded in doing so.*

"That's telling all of us," Lily said dryly. "I'm not about to get a big head now. But these doppelgängers may be hard to kill."

Possibly. If so, Sam suggests you obtain possession of the focus.

"You've told all this to Sam and the other dragons?"

Of course. We have informed most of the Shadow Unit, also.

"By focus," Cullen said, "are you talking about the artifact used to make the doppelgängers?"

Yes. You will need to destroy it. Ah. Sam has reminded me of something.

"Is Sam listening to us now?" Rule asked.

Sam is monitoring several situations. Be quiet while I speak with Lily Yu. Lily Yu, you will be unable to absorb power from the doppelgängers or the amulet. Sam believes it is best you are aware of this so you can plan your tactics properly.

"I wouldn't want to try. It's death magic, isn't it? Ugh."

Your understanding is as dangerously inadequate as Sam suspected. Absorbing death magic would turn you into a creature we would have to hunt down and kill. Sam believes that under sufficient stress—to save Rule Turner, perhaps, or the lives of young children—you would violate this ban. To ensure you do not, during our recent session I created a barrier.

"You did *what*?"

Do not be alarmed. I am young for such advanced and delicate work, but I did an excellent job. I am unusually skilled at perceiving and manipulating the . . . bah. Your language lacks a word for this. I refer to the interface between power and physicality. I cannot manipulate your Gift directly without destroying you, but I was able to place a barrier in this interface. You are still able to use your Gift in the way normal for you, but you will not be able to pull power from others.

Lily was on her feet. "This was Sam's idea?" she demanded. "Sam wanted you to do this? Without asking me—you deceived me, tricked me—"

It is unlikely you would give permission without a great many explanations we were and remain unable to offer. I tell you now so you can plan accordingly. Oh, and I will need to remove it later, or your Gift will burn itself out attempting to override the barrier. Now I must go. I have a great deal of distance to cover by dawn.

"What? What do you mean, you're going?"

Neither I nor any of the dragons in North America will be available to pass on messages for two or three days.

"Mika!" Rule was on his feet, too. And furious. "You're leaving at a critical time, and without notice or explanation! Is this the way allies support each other?"

The mental voice was fainter. *I regret the lack of notice. I have trouble differentiating threads in . . . from the not-now. I had intended to give you more . . . as well, perhaps. You would have . . . quite annoying. I am nearly out of range, so . . .*

And that was it. Mika was gone.

"Son of a *bitch*." Rule spat out the last word.

"Has everyone been messing with my head?" Lily was so angry she was shaking. "The Lady, the dragons—is there a sign on my head that says 'please tamper with my brain?' "

Cullen leaned back in his chair, frowning. "Once the two of you are done cursing the damned know-all, see-all, tell-nothing dragons, we might try to figure out why they're taking off so suddenly. It isn't for one of their sing-alongs. They wouldn't have kept that a secret until the last moment."

Lily drew a shaky breath. She was okay. At least she thought she was. How could she tell anymore? "What's to figure? We don't have anything to go on."

"We know Mika's traveling a long way, but expects to get there by dawn."

"Do you know how fast a dragon can fly? I sure don't."

"There were fighter jets pacing the dragons when we returned from Dis."

She remembered. In retrospect, it didn't make sense. How could wings carry dragons anywhere near as fast as a jet? Even if those jets were intentionally going well below their top speed . . . she turned to Rule.

Who had an odd look on his face. "This is farfetched, but . . ." He looked at Lily. "Mysterious Rhej business?"

She blinked. "It has to be coincidence. Doesn't it? The Rhejes don't take orders from the dragons. Or vice versa. I doubt they're in contact at all."

"No," Cullen said slowly. "But what if the dragons are in contact with the Lady?"

THE land was rock and dirt without a shred of green, lit by the eerie fluorescence of a sky lacking sun, moon, or stars. Lily crouched behind a rocky outcropping, firing an M-16 at the nightmare swooping down upon her from that empty sky. The horrific blasts from her weapon had her head pounding as if something was trying to get in, but the creature kept coming—

Cheep, cheep, cheep.

Her eyes popped open. It was dark—dark as in nighttime. Normal night. She was not in Dis . . . stupid damn nightmare. Blindly she groped for her phone on the bedside table, sitting up. Rule was gone. Maybe it wasn't the middle of the night, after all. Her hand connected with the phone and she thumbed it on. "Lily Yu here."

"Lily, I'm so sorry if I woke you."

It was Deborah Brooks. Lily glanced at the clock. 6:35. It wasn't night anymore, though it was still dark; sunrise was thirty or forty minutes away. Rule must have messed with the alarm again, dammit. He did that when he thought she needed sleep. "Not a problem," she said. "Something's wrong, or you wouldn't have called."

"It's the elemental. It's leaving."

"Everyone's leaving." No, wait, Deborah didn't know about the exodus of dragons and Rhejes, and this couldn't be connected. Could it? Lily reached for the lamp and switched it on, hoping light would get her brain working. "What do you mean?"

"It's difficult to put what it tells me into words, but it's being called—or maybe offered something. I think someone has promised it something. Or perhaps it wants to see the others. There are other earth elementals there. I'm not sure how many, but it wants to go where they are. I think I should go with it."

"Wait. Go with it? Where and why?"

"The National Mall. I'm almost sure it's going to the National Mall. That's where those Humans First people are. That can't be good, can it? So I need to go with the elemental. I thought you and Rule should know. I wasn't sure who else to tell."

"You did right." She threw back the covers and headed for the chest of drawers. "Stay where you are. We'll be—"

"I'm sorry, but I can't do that. I need to go now, Lily. It likes me and is happy for me to go with it, but it won't wait for me. You won't be able to call me because it doesn't like cell signals. It says they itch. I have to go now." The line went dead.

Lily didn't waste time cursing. She called Rule loudly as she grabbed underwear from the drawer. She never slept naked when there were people in the house, but last night they'd made love so late and she'd fallen asleep without dragging on a T-shirt or anything else and . . .

The door slammed open. "What is it?"

"Deborah Brooks called. Fagin's elemental is headed for the National Mall. At least that's where she thinks it's going, and she's going with it." How? Deborah couldn't ride on the thing. Follow it in her car? On foot? Lily had her panties on and was fastening a bra. "I tried to get her to stay put, but she wouldn't. She said there are other earth elementals there now. And someone's offering them something."

"Cullen," Rule called as he moved to the closet. "To me. José! Send someone for the van, double-time. I want ten guards downstairs and ready to leave immediately. The rest here and on high alert." He pulled something dark from the closet and tossed it at Lily.

She caught it. A T-shirt. Good. She pulled it on and went to get her weapon. A pair of jeans sailed her way, but landed on the floor.

Cullen burst in. He was wearing even less than her—as in nothing.

Lily grabbed the jeans as Rule continued briskly, "Earth elementals are headed for the National Mall—we think. So is Deborah Brooks, who called Lily with the information. Can you stop or interfere with a summoning?"

"Depends on what they're doing, how far along it is, and how close I can get." He scrubbed at his face with both hands, clearly trying to wake up. "Why would Humans Firsters summon elementals?"

"Bet it will look like me or Ruben is doing the summoning," Lily said, fastening her slacks, then reaching for her shoulder harness. "They plan to use the elementals to inflict damage—the Washington Monument, maybe? The Smithsonian?—and blame us. The Gifted in general, but specifically the Unit. They want the Unit completely discredited."

"It won't be you doing the summoning," Rule said. "Ruben. He's in hiding so he won't be alibied, and too many people know that sensitives can't work magic."

"Shit." Cullen said. "Yeah. I'll get dressed." He dashed out.

"Dammit," Rule said. "Where's my phone?"

"Here." Lily plucked it from the dresser and handed it to him. "Do we have a plan?"

"We're winging it."

"One good thing. They can't know we've been tipped. They don't know about Deborah, so . . ." Her phone beeped. A text. She grabbed it. Maybe Deborah had something to add to their too-short conversation.

It wasn't from Deborah. It was from Doug Mullins:

Found Anna. Still alive. Others too. Need backup at 1225 N Hammond in D.C. Approach from FRONT. Bad guys behind me on Webster.

THIRTY-FIVE

～

HE woke nameless and naked and clogged with dreams. The images choked him. He whined, but the sound frightened him. It was wrong. He was wrong. Shaped wrong. Bare and furless and—

"Shh." A comforting smell, a heartbeat and presence he knew, drew near. The leader. He was in his tall-shape, the furless one where his forelegs could grasp and hold things. At first that had been terrible, seeing the leader's proper form vanish, replaced by the alien shape, but the leader kept doing it.

After a while he'd understood that the leader wanted him to acknowledge him no matter what. To know that this one was leader no matter how he was formed. Once he understood that, it made little difference which shape the leader took.

"You slipped into your other form while you slept," the leader murmured. "That's unexpected for both of us, but you're okay. You're all right."

Dimly he struggled after the words, the sense of them. Oh—he *remembered* words. Language. He hadn't known he'd forgotten until this moment, when he remembered. He needed words now. "Dreams . . ." he whispered.

"You dreamed?" The leader laid a hand on his shoulder.

"We . . . go. We go." He tried to sit up, but he'd forgotten how this form worked and thrashed awkwardly before managing it. "Stop them. Must stop them." He panted as if he'd been chasing for hours instead of sleeping. Then more words tumbled out, surprising him because he didn't know what they meant. "Albany. D.C. Albuquerque. S-San Diego."

The leader thought for a long moment. He smelled calm, and that helped. But he had to understand. Had to help. They must *go*.

"Well, you're breaking enough rules all on your own," the leader said at last. "Why shouldn't I break one, too? Ruben," he said firmly.

Something yanked at him. Something inside that twisted his thoughts, opening . . . opening . . .

"Ruben. It is time to remember. You are Ruben Brooks."

THIRTY-SIX

"**I**T'S a trap."

"Maybe." Lily gnawed on her lip. Was it really from Mullins? She had—maybe—been tricked by someone using Sjorensen's phone. She texted back:

Why do you have to beat women off with stick?

He replied:

Massive charm and intellect and my goddamn sense of humor. Hurry.

"It's Mullins." She texted her reply—*On my way. 20m.*—then looked at Rule. "I have to go. If it's a trap, I'll just have to be smarter than they are. If it's not . . . he says she's alive."

Rule was rigid. "All right. I go with you." He started to turn. "José—"

She grabbed his arm. "No. Rule, you can't go with me everywhere. You can't. I need to do this. You need to lead your people. You've got a mix of Leidolf and Nokolai and they aren't all—"

"They'll do as they're bloody well told!"

"José isn't you! He doesn't know enough to lead them into who-the-hell-knows-what with dopplegängers and elementals!"

"I'm not going to leave you."

His phone sounded. It was "Dueling Banjos," Isen's ring tone.

He released her and spun around, grabbing the phone like he wanted to choke it. "Yes." His expression darkened, but he said nothing for several moments. Then: "You're sure? . . . I see. I . . ." His jaw clenched. "Give me a moment."

He paced away, the phone gripped at his side. Turned and looked at Lily. "Ruben woke as a man. He had dreams—visions—and they seem to have propelled him back to his original form. He is not yet in full possession of language, but from what Isen pieced together, events will take place very soon in Albany, Albuquerque, San Diego . . . and here. At the National Mall. He's already spoken to Benedict and Manuel. Benedict will take a troop of Nokolai into the city. Manuel agreed that Albuquerque was Ybirra's to handle. Ruben . . . with Isen's help, Ruben will lead Wythe to deal with events in Albany." Bleakly he finished, "My Rho orders me to go immediately to the National Mall."

Softly she said, "Then you have to go."

He closed his eyes. Shuddered. "Yes."

She went to him and put her arms around him. "I'll live if you will."

"You can't promise that."

"Tough. I am anyway."

1225 N. Hammond was a box. It had once had pretensions toward being a house, but the shape was all that was left; the roof lacked much in the way of shingles and the windows were gaping holes. The front door tilted drunkenly, a single hinge being insufficient to hold it upright.

It didn't stand out all that much in this neighborhood. The Mercedes did, but that couldn't be helped. "Okay," Lily told Mike. "Chris and Scott should be in place by now. Let's go."

If Mullins did need backup, he'd be getting it. Lily hadn't waited for Rule to tell her to take guards with her. She'd asked for Scott and three men of his choosing, one of whom was really good at sneaking. The sneak he picked was Shannon, a skinny young guy they'd dropped off a couple blocks up. The other two were a Nokolai she knew and liked named Chris . . . and Mike of the bad attitude and broken table.

She thought she knew what Scott was doing. Rule had taken Mike down hard and publically. This was his chance to redeem himself. But Mike must also be nearly as good as he thought he was, or Scott wouldn't have taken the chance.

At least she hoped so.

The abandoned house didn't offer much in the way of cover, so Lily hoped Scott and Chris were good at sneaking, too. She wanted them as close as possible. They couldn't use phones to stay in touch; even texts were out, since the lit screen would give away their positions. But Scott had said five minutes, and she trusted him.

Unlike most lupi, Scott was good with a gun, plus he'd learned the basic hand signals Nokolai used. Chris, being Nokolai, knew them all, including ASL, which was more than Lily did. But she knew enough to direct them silently, if necessary . . . and if they could keep a visual on her.

That was why Mike walked beside her down the dirty sidewalk instead of one of the others. He didn't know the hand signals. He didn't have a gun, either, but he made a fine display of strength—which wasn't his main purpose, but it didn't hurt.

Lily had her weapon out, though she kept it at her side. Even if someone in the houses they passed could see what she held, she didn't think they'd call the cops. "You have any problems taking orders from a woman, Mike? You could take me in a fight. Maybe you think you should be in charge here."

"You're a Chosen. My Rho's Chosen."

"Which means you think I'm cool as cream cheese, but doesn't answer the question."

He was silent a moment. "Rule said we are to obey you as long as your orders do not contradict his. He also said you are a warrior. LeBron said that, too. I don't know Rule well enough to know what he means by that word, but I knew LeBron. I can take orders from a warrior."

Startled, she glanced up at him. Way up. "You knew LeBron?"

"We trained together. Fought together. He was a good man."

"He was." And she wished fiercely and futilely he was walking beside her now . . . but in a way, he was. In a way he was still watching out for her. It was his word that inclined Mike to trust her to lead.

Across the street a dog barked over and over—the endless repetitive barking of a bored and lonely animal. The wind was up, blowing Lily's hair in her face. Should've grabbed an elastic to hold it back. It wasn't doing much to dispel the cloud cover, though; Lily could see a glow behind those clouds where the full moon rode low in the west, but it was dark down here.

Mike could probably see pretty well. Lots better than she could, anyway. "You ever worked with a human?"

"Not this kind of work."

"Compared to you, I'm scent-blind. I don't hear half what you do, and to me it's still too dark to see much. Don't assume I see, smell, or hear what you do."

"Maybe you don't see the guy leaning against the wall of the house next to our target, then. He's in the shadow."

"Ah—no. Wait. Now I do." He'd moved toward the front of the house. The houses were spaced closely, with only a narrow strip between; that strip was completely black to Lily's eyes.

"Can't see his face well, but what I see matches the description you gave me of Mullins."

The man beckoned urgently at them. Lily broke into a quick jog. "If he draws, take him down."

A whisper reached her as she drew near. "Jesus. Who's the mountain?"

Lily stopped a couple paces away. It was Mullins, all right. She kept her voice low. "You said you wanted backup. He's mine. This is 1223 Hammond, not 1225."

"So sue me. I lied. I picked you to call because they wanted to take you out, so you're probably not one of them, but I don't know for sure."

"Who's they?"

"I wish to hell I knew. The house behind us"—he gave a quick jerk of his head to indicate the rear of the house—"I think that's where they've been conducting their rites. That death magic shit. They've got Sjorensen and fourteen others stashed there, drugged and unconscious. There's four thugs watching the place—three in the house, one out back."

"How do you know all this?"

"How do you think? I got a tip, checked it out. We've got to move fast. Come on." He turned, easing back into the deep shadow between the houses.

Lily didn't really trust him. She followed anyway. It was so dark she trailed a hand along the side of the house to keep her bearings. A couple steps in, it occurred to her she was being stupid. One of them was able to see a lot better than the others. "Mike. Take point."

She couldn't see Mullins, but the sound of his footsteps stopped. She felt more than heard Mike move past—and keep going.

Maybe Mike had heard something. It wasn't smell that tipped him off, not with the wind at their backs. Maybe he just decided to show initiative. He rushed to the back of the house, where he turned and leaped at someone or something out of sight.

"Shit," Mullins whispered.

Lily took two quick steps forward and jammed her gun into Mullins's back. "Keep moving."

He sighed heavily, but obeyed. They rounded the corner, Mullins first. Lily's heart pounded madly.

Mike had a man on the ground, pinned with an armlock. Lily couldn't see the man's face, but something about the build was familiar.

A low voice grated, "Get this son of a bitch off me."

Drummond. It was Al Drummond.

"Look," Mullins whispered, "I didn't tell you about Drummond because you wouldn't have come. But he's the one who tipped me."

She grimaced. "He's with them. The death magic, the attack on Ruben—he's part of all that."

"Yeah." The single syllable ached with sadness. "I know."

EN route, Rule tried and failed to reach Deborah. He called his father and told him about the elementals—maybe D.C.

wasn't the only city where they'd been summoned. He called the guards who'd been stationed at Ruben's house, and—because Lily had insisted—he called Abel Karonski. And he called Harry.

Parking was always a problem near the Mall, and it was impossible today. They ended up leaving the van in an illegal spot four blocks from Pennsylvania and running the rest of the way—across Constitution Avenue, which took some expert dodging, and between the Natural History Museum and the American History Museum. When they reached Madison Drive, they stopped.

Madison had been closed to traffic for the occasion. Just past it lay a stretch of grass, then the broad pedestrian path that outlined the central area; imitation gas streetlights provided plenty of light for lupus eyes.

The dawn prayer service that would kick off the daylong rally would start in forty minutes or so, and the Humans Firsters were gathering. At the east end of the Mall, a tall stage had been erected. Unlike most, it was closed on the front and sides, giving it a very finished appearance. The stage was backed by the Capitol Building—which was partly obscured by an enormous Jumbotron screen so distant ralliers wouldn't miss a single twitch of their leaders' faces.

It all looked very peaceful at the moment . . . and crowded. Rule didn't know how to estimate crowd size the way Lily could have, if she'd been here. If only—

Enough. She was doing what she had to do. So was he. She'd promised to live. And by all that was holy, he would hold her to that promise.

So he'd take his best guess. The crowd was certainly not the quarter of a million that Humans First claimed had signed up for their rally, but it was large. Perhaps ten thousand people had gotten up well before dawn to get a good spot, eager to show their hatred for lupi.

"What do you see?" he asked Cullen softly.

"Too damn many people," he muttered, giving the area a slow scan. "I can't see through them, you know. Wait. Down by the Washington Monument. That's an earth elemental. Not a big one, nowhere near the size of Fagin's, but . . . shit.

There's another one under the Smithsonian. It's deep, but I can see a glow."

"Can you tell who's summoning them?"

Cullen crouched and put one hand on the ground. "I suck at Earth magic, but here goes." His lips moved, but all Rule caught was a cadenced sort of murmur. An incantation, he supposed. Cullen straightened. "No clue who's doing it, but I think it's a call, not a summons. That's good news."

"The difference being—?"

"A call is just that—'hey there, how ya doing, want to come have some blood?' A summons is a compulsion and takes beaucoup power, especially with earth elementals. I'd rather not go up against anyone who could summon multiple earth elementals, then keep them from trying to kill each other. Highly territorial, earth elementals. Or, hell, anyone who could summon a single elemental the size of the one Deborah's hanging out with. If . . ." His voice trailed off. He squinted, then started walking toward the stage at the far end of the Mall.

Rule kept pace. "Manny, Tom—your job is to keep Cullen alive. Stay with us. The rest of you, fan out, centered on me. Fifteen-foot perimeter." He lowered his voice. "What is it?"

"I just caught a glimpse. Something leaked, but only for a second. Maybe someone broke the circle, then closed it up again. But I could swear someone's working a spell under that damn stage."

" . . . **EXCEPT** for the death magic," Mullins finished. "Al didn't know about that, didn't believe you when you said it. But he's been a cop too long. He got itchy, checked something out. Found that setup on Webster. You were right. They've been collecting homeless people, killing them to make death magic. Al couldn't stomach what they were doing, what they planned to do, so he called me. Two of us couldn't do it alone, though. We'd just get killed, then they'd go ahead and kill everyone. So I called you."

They'd moved inside—all of them, or almost. Maybe 1223 Hammond wasn't as completely derelict as 1225, but it was equally abandoned. Lily had summoned Scott and Chris, and the five of them sat or squatted on a kitchen floor every bit as dirty as the ground outside. In here, though, they didn't have to worry as much about being heard.

Lily looked at Drummond—who was technically under arrest. Mullins had informed him of that before calling Lily. Mike had disarmed him and sat next to him now, ready to stop him if he tried anything. He hadn't said a word since his demand to "get this son of a bitch off me."

He didn't look like a man undergoing a crisis of conscience. More like a balked fanatic. "You're okay with violating your oath," she said. "Okay with killing Ruben Brooks—"

"He's not dead."

"Not your fault he lived, though, is it? You didn't object to your buddies killing a senator, either—one who was as anti-magic as you are. Did he find out too much about Dennis Parrott, or was he just a convenient way to frame Ruben? I'm not even going to ask you what part you had in bombing Fagin's library and nearly killing him and Cullen. You probably don't think they're real people, seeing as how one's lupus and the other's Gifted. You're cool with massacring lupi and Gifted, but I'm supposed to believe you draw the line at killing homeless people."

"I don't give a damn what you believe."

"Al," Mullins muttered, "you're not helping."

Drummond shot him a look Lily couldn't read. "Look," he said impatiently, "she's not going to buy it if I play the repentant sinner. She and all her magical crowd are an imminent and ongoing danger to the people of this country. That's fact, and if you can't see it now, you will. But yeah, I do draw the line at killing innocent people. Especially killing them in such a foul way. It . . ." His lips tightened to a thin line. After a moment he went on, eyes blazing. "And if you don't quit talking this all out and give me back my weapon so we can do something about it, they'll all die."

"Who's in this with you?"

He shook his head, a small, bitter smile on his thin lips.

"You want my help, you're going to have to—" Her phone vibrated. She pulled it out of her pocket, saw who the text was from, and smiled tightly. At last. She read it, sent a quick reply—*I'm clear to talk—you? Call if u can*—and gave Scott a nod so he'd know she'd heard from Shannon. Then she spoke to Mullins. "Some of your story's been confirmed. There were four thugs at the Webster house—three inside, one out back. The place reeks of blood and death magic. But those four have just been joined by two more in a catering truck."

"Fuck!" That was Drummond. "If we'd acted right away—"

"We'd have been shot by the two who showed up late for the party." Her phone vibrated again. This time it was a call, not a text. Shannon again. "Go ahead." She listened, asked a couple questions, and told him to stand by for instructions. "They've begun loading their victims into the truck. Not bodies—victims. Out cold, but still alive." She looked at Drummond. "They're taking them somewhere else to be sacrificed, aren't they?"

He was silent.

"To your friends at the Humans First Rally." When he still didn't speak she leaned forward. "Goddammit. Don't you get it? Your buddies are perfectly willing to sacrifice their own people along with the ones you consider innocent. What do you think they're going to do with the death magic they conjure by killing twenty-two people? I know about the doppelgängers. They must plan to make a lot of them, not just duplicate me and Ruben. Or maybe they're planning to feed the earth elementals they've called. Those elementals can do a lot of damage if they're fed well."

"They wouldn't—" He shut himself up quickly.

"They killed a United States senator who was *on their side*. Hell yes, they would. They'd do anything. There are children at that damn rally. Are you going to let kids be killed to protect your righteous cause?"

"I'm not the one who insists on talking and talking and talking. You going to shut up and do something? Or are you planning to sit this out while they carry off and kill twenty-two people—including someone who's supposed to be a friend of yours?"

"You're right. I'm not going to let them do that."

His mouth twisted. "There's six of them now. Armed. You'd better give me back my weapon."

"You want in? I don't need you. There's me and Mullins and four lupi. Hell, the lupi probably don't need me and Mullins, but we'll tag along. What about you? If you want in, you're going to have to prove to me that you mean it."

Scott's head swiveled toward her. He opened his mouth—and shut it again without telling her not to be an idiot.

Good man. "Who are you working with?" she repeated. "And what are they planning?"

"Al," Mullins said slowly, "you're so far wrong, and you can't see it, and it breaks my heart. But if you've ever trusted me—not just to take your back, hell, you know I'll do that—but really trusted me, listen to me now. These people you're in with, they're bad. They're going to kill people. Not just collateral damage in this unholy war you think you're fighting—they'll out-and-out murder people because they don't give a shit. If it's easier to kill, if they think it works, they'll do it. You think you're doing this because of Pat, to keep others from dying like she did. But it's revenge you're really after, and you're taking it on people who never hurt you or her. If she could see you now, see what you've done, she'd be sick. You know she would."

Drummond's gaze switched from Mullins to Lily and back again. His face didn't give away a thing, no sign at all that he'd caved. But he started talking.

THIRTY-SEVEN

～

IN the flat, grassy plains of northeastern Colorado, the sky was barely tinged with pink in the east. Three modest late-model cars pulled off onto the shoulder of State Highway 14 between Raymer and Stoneham, about twenty-five miles south of the Nebraska border.

Headlights shut off. Doors opened. Seven women stepped out into the darkness. Seven small globes of light sprang into being, holding back some of that dark.

The women looked nothing alike; in age they ranged from early thirties to over eighty, and they were as varied in build, hair, and coloring as they were in age. They weren't quite as dissimilar in dress. All wore jackets, and three had hats. October mornings are chilly in the Colorado plains. Six of the seven wore jeans. One wore a beautifully embroidered dashiki and an elaborately wound headscarf with her jeans. The seventh wore a battered leather aviator's jacket over an eye-searing muumuu with enormous fuchsia flowers on a green and turquoise background.

They gathered and talked for a few minutes, sounding variously calm, keyed up, worried, or pragmatic. The one in the dashiki didn't speak. Now and then a fifty-ish woman with a dramatic silver streak in her black hair would take the silent

woman's hand, smiling and nodding at her, then would relate
something to the others as if the silent woman had spoken.

The one in the muumuu was the oldest and heaviest of
them. She seemed to be in charge. Her eyes were as milky
white as her hair. "Enough chitchat. They'll be here when they
get here," she told the others. "We'd best be where we need to
be when they arrive. Come on."

"You know where to head, then?" asked a tall, husky
woman with milk-chocolate skin and a thick southern drawl.
"I can't see a thing."

The oldest of them chuckled. "Dark, light, it's all the same
to me. The feel of the place is clear enough—thick metal
doors over a big hollow tube going straight down. Susan, you
might take my arm. I won't be paying attention to what's up
close, so I could trip over a twig and embarrass myself."

A mild-looking woman in her early thirties took the old
woman's arm, and all seven set off into the grass, the little
lights bobbing along with them . . . headed directly for the underground missile silo.

"Oh," said the one in the muumuu. "Here's Sam now."

THIRTY-EIGHT

~~~

PAUL Chittenden was Friar's East Coast lieutenant, but he wouldn't be taking the stage at the rally. He kept a low profile. Humans First's official organizer for the D.C. rally was Kim Evans, a tall, nervous powerhouse of a woman who liked cameras just fine and had a problem distinguishing between fact and fiction.

Rule had met her recently at a D.C. party, the sort of event he used to attend more often. The sort of event Lily hated, which was why he accepted far fewer invitations than he used to. But he'd heard Kim Evans would be at this one, and he'd been determined to meet her and size her up.

It had been worth the effort. In five minutes' conversation, Evans lied three times—twice about things she'd said that were on record, available to see and hear at various news sites. The third lie was her insistence that Rule himself had just said something he hadn't. She'd lied passionately and sincerely, and when called on it, brushed it off with "don't be ridiculous."

Evans's fierce insistence that the truth was whatever she said it was created its own odd sort of charisma. Heaven knew the press found her fascinating. There were television cameras set up on stage—those operated by the Jumbotron people, yes, but also from various news outlets.

Rule stood beside Cullen at the north side of the crowd, where it thinned slightly, way back from the stage. They'd been unable to get closer without forcing a path. Rule had been ready to do just that when Abel found them. Abel had decided to pay a visit to the people hosting the event. He could badge his way in, he said.

The crowds had swallowed them up ten minutes ago. Rule was getting increasingly nervous. Abel hadn't called. The brownies were either late or they couldn't get through the mob, and the show was starting. A swell of music announced Kim Evans as she mounted the steps. Evans had a racehorse's elegance—thin and quick and nervous. She was immaculately turned out in a bright pink suit and three-inch heels; she'd worn her blond hair loose, and the wind whipped it around her narrow face. The crowd went crazy cheering.

Rule's phone sounded. It was Lily. His heart pounded in a mix of relief and anxiety—relief because he'd hear her voice. Anxiety because she wasn't *here*. "Yes?" he said, then, blocking his other ear: "Say again. There's too many people screaming and clapping. I couldn't hear."

Even with his hearing, even with his other ear stopped up, he missed a few words when she repeated her message: ". . . going to be kinda busy here, but you need to know. Pass the word. They . . . making lupus dopplegängers. Wolf form. A whole lot of them. Must have used Brian's tissue. Turning them loose on . . . here and . . . buquerque and . . . iego and New York."

THE plan was simple enough. Let the bad guys get all their unconscious victims loaded up—then stop them, take their wheels, and show up in their place at the rally.

Having all the bad guys outside was obviously best. Having all the victims in one place and secured inside the truck made it harder for the bad guys to use them as hostages. The tricky part was that she was trusting Drummond. Sort of.

Lily was going with her gut—and maybe with Mullins's gut, too. Drummond's sense of right and wrong might be twisted as hell, but it was strong. Strong enough for him to sacrifice his career and his bloody stupid war against the Gifted to keep a bunch of homeless people from being sacrificed. In his screwed-up head, everything he'd done was supposed to protect people. Lily and Ruben, the lupi, the Gifted in general—they weren't really people to him. But he couldn't let "innocents"— people without Gifts or the knack of turning furry—be killed.

She wouldn't turn her back on him, but she'd use him. He had an advantage she couldn't overlook. He'd supplied the thugs in the first place.

Or rather, he'd arranged things. Dennis Parrott hadn't known how to go about hiring muscle who wouldn't object to wet work. Drummond might claim he didn't know about the death magic, but he'd known his compadres were planning murder. Like most cops, he knew people on the other side of the law. He'd set up a meet between Parrott and Randy "Big Thumbs" Ballister. "Big Thumbs" got his name from saying he'd "squish that prick like a bug," accompanied by a motion with his thumb. Word was, he did a lot of squishing.

Most of the operation would be carried out by the lupi. If everything went right, Lily wouldn't even be needed. That grated on her. She didn't like sending others into danger while she stood around giving orders, but she wasn't going to risk lives just to soothe her ego. Lupi could do things she couldn't.

So Lily squatted across the street from the Webster house, tucked behind a hugely overgrown juniper. The world was growing lighter, though still wrapped in shades of gray; she could see clearly enough. The catering truck was parked in the cracked driveway, its open rear facing the house. Its driver had just climbed back behind the wheel and rolled the windows down so he could enjoy a smoke.

He was a bit of a wild card; surrounded by metal, he'd be hard to take, and there was no cover to reach him unseen. They were hoping Big Thumbs's men were scared enough of him to obey, no matter what. If not . . . that's why Lily had picked this spot. It was the only place with cover that gave a good view of the man.

Two men emerged from the front door, a long, blanket-wrapped bundle carried between them. Another man—Big Thumbs himself—stood by, watching.

If the count was right, that was the next-to-last hostage. And here came two more men with another bundle. Where the hell was . . .

She sighed with relief as a white Ford that any self-respecting criminal would make for a cop car pulled up, blocking the catering truck. Drummond climbed out, slammed his door.

The first two men hastily heaved their bundle into the truck and hurried to back up their boss. They didn't bother with subtle. Both drew their weapons.

Lily could hear Big Thumbs clearly. "What the hell you doing here?"

"Parrott thinks I'm his goddamn messenger boy, that's what. He says he left something behind last time. Fancy card case, metal—might make it through the fire when you torch the place, and it's got his initials on it, so he wants you to find it."

"Why the hell didn't he call me?"

"He doesn't have a throwaway with him, asshole. He's not making calls to you on his regular phone."

Big Thumbs thought that over, then grunted. "I hate working with damn amateurs. He pays good, but he's a pain in the ass. Where is his goddamned card case supposed to be?"

"Wherever he's been holding those ceremonies. He said you'd know what he meant."

"Okay, but if we run late, he'd better not bitch about it." Big Thumbs nodded at the last two men, who'd deposited their burden in the back of the truck and slammed the doors. "Look for the man's fancy card case. Should be out back."

There was a brand-new, eight-foot wooden fence closing off the backyard. It stood out like a sore thumb in this neighborhood. According to Shannon, the backyard was where the worst stink of death magic came from.

That's also where Scott and Chris were waiting. Those two men wouldn't be coming back.

Big Thumbs waited impatiently for a full forty-five seconds. "Hell with this shit. No point in the delivery running late. You two, get aboard." He looked at Drummond. "Move your damn car."

Why did the bad guys never read the script? Time for Plan B: shock and awe. Lily pulled a small metal whistle from her pocket.

"What's taking them so long?" Drummond said with equal impatience. "I don't need to be seen standing around shooting the shit with you. I'm going to look for that damn case myself." He started for the house.

Shit. Drummond had gone off-script, too.

Big Thumbs grabbed his arm. "Did you hear what I said? Move your damn car."

Lily put the whistle to her mouth and blew once, twice, three times. And heard nothing, because it was a dog whistle.

Drummond jerked his arm away—or tried to. Big Thumbs was a big man, and he had a tight grip. "Listen, you jerkwad, you'd better—"

Two enormous wolves streaked around from each side of the house, running flat out.

One of the men shrieked like a girl and fired wildly. The other stared in frozen horror for a second—which is way too long when lupi are moving at top speed.

The next bit, at least, went smooth as silk.

The wolves took down the two gunmen like clockwork— two great leaps, two downed men with snarling wolves pinning them. Mullins fired from a window inside the house—an attention-getting shot, aimed high. "Freeze, assholes! This is the FBI!" And Drummond—who was supposed to have moved away from Big Thumbs so he couldn't be taken hostage—seized the man's arm, twisted, and landed him on the ground. He drew his gun and stuck it in the man's face. "Tell the driver to climb out. Do it now. I'm in a real bad mood."

Lily drew a shaky breath. Adrenaline had her on hyperdrive. She eased out from behind her juniper.

The driver shot Drummond. He fell on top of Big Thumbs.

Lily stopped, braced her right hand with her left in the approved stance, took a full second to aim, and fired twice.

The driver jolted as the bullet smashed into his face. Lily felt that moment viscerally—no emotion, just the fact of it, her bullet smashing into his brain and ending him.

The door of the house shot open and Mullins raced out, with Chris and Scott right behind him.

Big Thumbs shoved Drummond's body away and snatched the .357 that had fallen from Drummond's hand when he was shot. Lily didn't have a clear shot, dammit—one of the wolves partly blocked her, but she saw Big Thumbs take aim at Mullins. She started running, knowing she'd be too late.

Drummond shoved himself up with one arm and rolled back on top of Big Thumbs.

The gun went off.

Scott got there first. Before Lily finished running across the street, he'd kicked Big Thumbs in the head—he wouldn't be moving again soon and maybe not ever—and gently rolled Drummond onto his back. Blood drenched Drummond's white shirt and trickled from his mouth. His eyes were open and staring. "No heartbeat," Scott said tersely.

"The driver," Lily flung at Chris as she skidded to a stop. "Check him. If he's dead or incapacitated, get that truck open and start getting those people out of there. Shannon! Mark! Change back and get those two goons restrained, then help Chris."

"Al." Mullins went to his knees beside his friend. "Al, oh, shit. Al."

Something white and filmy began condensing over Drummond's body.

ON a grassy plain of northeastern Colorado, six women stood in a circle near a fence enclosing a place bare of grass, where a set of steel doors were set into the ground. They chanted in a language so old no record remained of it. The seventh woman—the dark-skinned one in the beautiful dashiki—sat apart, eyes closed, quietly doing nothing at all that anyone could see . . . but whatever eyes the U.S. government kept on this site normally, today they wouldn't work.

Overhead, four dragons flew . . . and joined their voices with the women's.

Slowly, almost silently, the steel doors began to move.

* * *

RULE had not been able to come up with any clever plans for dealing with "a whole lot" of lupi dopplegängers, other than what he'd already put in place. He'd warned Isen, Benedict, and Manuel, who didn't have any suggestions, either—but at least they, too, were in their appointed places. Waiting, as he was.

Rule's primary target was the amulet or artifact or whatever was used to create and control the dopplegängers. Preventing general carnage was a major secondary goal, but they *had* to find and obtain the artifact, then destroy it. Which was why he had two men whose sole job was protecting Cullen . . . the only person on the planet known to be able to call and control mage fire.

The control part was important. Rumors in the magical community said Mrs. O'Leary's cow was innocent—the Great Chicago Fire had been cause by a Fire Gifted who managed the calling part, but flunked on control.

Rule had opted to split his men. Fourteen were with him and Cullen. Nine were with José about halfway down the length of the crowd at its fringes, ready to move where they were needed. And one was on the roof of the Smithsonian Castle, keeping an eye on the whole spread of people.

Rule and his squad had made themselves unpopular by shoving their way close to the stage. The men were bunched up tightly around him and Cullen, both because of the press of people and because their bodies should keep others from seeing his too-familiar face. That was also why they hadn't pushed to the very front, where crowd control barriers and three men in security guard uniforms kept everyone back from the stage. He didn't want Parrott to see him.

Interesting that the event's organizers didn't want anyone within fifteen feet of the stage . . . that tall, enclosed stage with room beneath it for an entire coven.

Lily was on her way here. He'd spoken to her, knew her plans, could feel her moving closer. It was nothing short of delusional to feel such relief that she would be with him soon. How could he keep her safe in the midst of the kind of chaos likely to ensue? Especially when she'd be doing her damned-est to be right in the middle of that chaos. But the closer she got, the more he settled. Steadied.

Sometimes he didn't make sense at all.

He hadn't heard from Abel and couldn't reach him by phone. Maybe Abel had found out what was under that stage. Maybe that hadn't worked out well.

Rule's phone was in his pocket, but he was wearing a head-set that should stay on through even vigorous activity. He spoke into it now. "Does she have any control over the ele-mental at all?"

"Not much, she says, though it promises it will protect her. Uh . . . she says it's pretty excited."

An enormous, excited earth elemental was not good news. But at least Deborah's guards had found her and were jogging along beside her now at the far west end of the Mall as she and the elemental headed this way. Deborah's phone wasn't working, which was why Rule was talking to Matt instead of Deborah.

She was on a bicycle. A bloody bicycle in D.C. traffic! She'd found it in the shed behind Fagin's house and had ridden over eight miles to get here. She couldn't track the elemental in a car, she'd told Matt, so wasn't it lucky Fagin had an old bike?

Rule was certain Ruben wouldn't consider that good luck, any more than he did. "Keep me posted if anything changes," he told Matt and reached up to disconnect. He glanced at his watch. Ten more minutes. Maybe less.

The minister of a Maryland megachurch finally reached the "amen" in a lengthy but surprisingly inoffensive opening prayer. Rule had no problem with people asking to be pro-tected from the forces of darkness—he only hoped some Power was listening and would give him a hand with the pro-tecting. The minister went back to his chair on the right side of the stage. Four people—two men and two women—sat in those chairs, waiting their turn.

Kim Evans was one of them. She returned to the podium, where she proceeded to whip up the crowd about the great evil in their midst, focusing on their recent martyr: Senator Bob Bixton.

"—and a man who was supposed to protect us all, a man sworn to the service of this country—a *Gifted* man who ran the very Unit designed to deal with magical crimes in this country—walked into Senator Bixton's home and stabbed him. Why? Do we even have to ask?"

She paused dramatically while the crowd screamed their responses—*no, killer, traitor*—then continued. "Here to talk to you today about the danger posed by those corrupted by magic—a danger we all know is increasing and has penetrated every level of our society and even our government—is the senator's longtime friend and chief of staff, Dennis Parrott!" She stepped to one side and began clapping.

The crowd screamed and clapped. Parrott hadn't been among those waiting on the stage. He walked up the steps at the side.

"Son of a bitch," Cullen said, his voice raised to be heard over the din created by thousands of enthusiastic Humans Firsters. "That's Parrott?"

"Yes."

"He's got a charisma Gift. A real powerhouse of a Gift, augmented by a nasty smear of death magic. And . . ." He stopped, squinting. The Jumbotron screen was no help with what Cullen needed to see.

A charisma Gift explained how the aliens had gotten people like "poor Meggie" to go with them. When a strong charisma Gifted turned his attention on you, you trusted. You wanted to please. Poor Meggie, indeed. Maybe it explained what had happened to Abel as well. Parrott could have distracted him long enough for one of the others to knock him out . . . or worse.

"Parrott might be wearing it," Cullen said suddenly. "The artifact, I mean. I can't tell from here, but there's something interacting with his power."

"Drummond told Lily that Parrott isn't the one who makes the dopplegängers. Would their creator hand over control of the artifact to someone else?"

"Well, Drummond's a lying, murdering sod, but who knows? He could have been telling the truth about this. But Parrott's got something. I can't tell what. I think it's on a ring, though. There's a bit of an extra glow on his right hand . . ." He scowled. "I need to get closer."

Rule didn't respond. There was one way to get closer, but they would use that only if they had to. If, say, a few slavering, oversize wolves suddenly appeared on the stage.

Parrott advanced across the stage, pausing once to wave and nod as if recognizing someone particular in the audience. He reached the podium and held up his hands, urging everyone to be quiet. The cameras zoomed in, and the Jumbotron screen filled with the man's smooth-shaven face looking grave and sincere.

Rule's phone vibrated. He pulled it out, touched the screen . . . "Harry. I'd about given up on you."

"We're here, Rule! We're here! Traffic sucked, but we made it. I never saw so many people in one place before. Humans are crazy, aren't they?"

"I often think so. Where are you, specifically?"

"I'm up by the stage, like you said. Oh, you mean my troop. Don't worry," he said proudly. "I've got them stationed like you told me."

"That's great, Harry. I also told you I needed someone who was very, very good at the game."

"That would be me! I am the best. I am the juggernaut of the game! What do you need?"

"You see the man on stage now? He has a ring on his right hand . . ." Rule went on to tell Harry what he needed him to do. Parrott was talking. Rule wasn't really listening . . . until the man spoke Lily's name.

THIRTY-NINE

❦

THE catering truck had been stripped of everything usually found in such a vehicle to make room to stack twenty-two unconscious people in back. Those people were, Lily hoped, being revived or at least tended back on Webster Street. Shannon had first aid training; she'd left him at the house to help, and Mullins had planned to call it in as soon as they left.

Mike was the driver of the truck now. No lupus would have been fooled by the substitution; the front seat must reek of blood to them. But he'd tossed a jacket over the back of the seat, covering the worst of it, and humans are visual creatures. So far no one had noticed anything out of the ordinary— including the cop who'd stopped them when they needed to enter the closed-off street.

Chris was up front, too. Lily and Scott crouched on bare metal in the back of the truck, their weapons out, and listened.

So did Al Drummond. He didn't look much like himself, being all white and filmy . . . except for that glowing gold ring on his left hand.

He gave her a tight smile. He had his weapon out, too, as if he planned to charge out of the truck with the rest of them, but since it was as insubstantial as the rest of him, she didn't think he'd be much backup.

He hadn't spoken to her. It was clear he knew she could see him, though, and that the others couldn't. It was clear he meant to stick with her.

Why and how had his ghost started appearing days before he died? Was that one of those "instabilities" the Etorri Rhej had mentioned, some sort of astral time warp?

Did Drummond even know he was dead?

Lily had been told by someone who ought to know that ghosts weren't souls, but the shadows cast by souls. She'd wondered at the time what the hell that meant. She still did. And she really, really wished this one would go into the light or something and quit following her.

"What the hell you mean, the cargo don't go here?" Mike demanded. "I was told to bring it to the stage. This is the stage."

A muffled voice told Mike he had to take the truck to Fourteenth Street—"at the back of the gathering, by the Washington Monument. You've heard of it? Big pointy thing sticking way up in the air?"

"Shit. I gotta call Big Thumbs."

"You've got to move this thing, and quick!"

"I do what Big Thumbs says, asshole, not you."

Lily nodded at Scott, then at the doors at the rear of the truck. He moved into position.

So did Drummond.

RULE ended the conversation with Harry quickly—and his phone immediately vibrated again. He answered.

It was Mark from on top of the Smithsonian. "Silver catering truck just pulled in behind the stage."

He'd known she was here. He felt her. "Good."

"And there's some kind of upset at the back of the crowd near the Washington Monument—people moving away from one spot. Not running, just avoiding that spot for some reason."

"Keep an eye on it. You see Deborah?"

"She and her guards are just the other side of the Monument. She seems to be resting."

The elemental could be doing something that made people uneasy . . . but Matt would call if that were so. Assuming Deborah could tell, that is. "Okay. Notify José. Out." Rule disconnected. "The catering truck's here. They're behind the stage."

Parrott had kept his speech brief and was introducing someone. "Give her a warm welcome, because she's seen the light and is here to tell the truth about what happened when Ruben Brooks fled justice. Ladies and gentlemen, Lily Yu!"

And Lily walked up the steps. Only it wasn't Lily.

It looked precisely like her. It moved like her. It wore black slacks and a red jacket identical to one that hung in Lily's closet . . . that thing was wearing her face, her form, stolen from her while she was locked up. The mate sense told Rule where Lily was—behind the stage, not on it. And moving. Lily was in motion, which meant she'd made her move—yes, look at Parrott turning to look behind the stage.

Crisp now and certain, Rule spoke. "That's not Lily. It's a doppelgänger. Lily's making her move, though, so we need to as well. As planned—positions!"

Rule had kept the Nokolai guards with him. He'd expected trouble to come from the stage, and his Nokolai knew many useful tricks. Like this one, which was part of one of the training dances.

Six men dropped to their hands and knees, shoulder-to-shoulder in the short grass. Three men leaped onto their backs and linked arms to steady themselves.

Cullen grabbed Rule's arm as he started to move. "There's something weird about the Lily-double."

Rule shook him off. "It's not Lily. Of course it's weird." And along with Andy and Sean, he quickly scaled the lupi pyramid to crouch atop Jacob's shoulders, with Andy and Sean doing the same on either side of him. Jacob's hands gripped his ankles.

When he leaped, Jacob shoved. And Rule sailed toward the stage.

The human record for the standing long jump was a little over eleven feet. Rule wasn't human, and Jacob's push gave him extra momentum. He still wouldn't make it to the stage in a single leap, but he passed over the heads of those at the very front to land lightly in the clear strip between the crowd and the stage. Andy and Sean landed on either side of him.

Their order had been settled ahead of time. Rule wanted to go first, but he was a Rho. He couldn't risk himself unnecessarily. So when Sean bent, cupping his hands, it was Andy who accepted that stirrup. Sean heaved. Andy sailed onto the stage.

Rule was right behind him. He grabbed the edge of the stage with his hands and heaved himself up.

The not-Lily thing stood halfway between the podium and the stairs, unmoving. Parrott was nowhere in sight. Kim Evans had surged to her feet and started forward, telling them to get off, get off—

Not-Lily's face lit in a sudden grin. It sprinted fast—faster than anything human could move—to Kim Evans, stopping behind her, drawing something from its pocket. As Rule raced toward them, it grabbed the woman's hair, tipped her head back. And slit her throat.

Blood geysered out, some of it splattering Rule as he reached them. He seized not-Lily's arm, using his momentum and a twist of his hip in a simple throw.

It spun with the throw, twisting so fast it landed with its feet under it, that huge grin still on its face, a bloody knife gripped in its left hand. "Oooh, yes, let's play! Catch me if you can!" With impossible speed it darted toward the three people who'd risen from their chairs on the stage.

But while it had paused briefly to taunt, Andy and Sean hadn't. They shot past Rule. Andy got to it a couple feet ahead of Sean. It swung one fist almost casually—and Andy went sailing off the stage. Sean closed with it, grappling for the knife. Rule ran to help him.

And from the strip of ground next to the stage Cullen yelled, "It's possessed! That's how they work it—they summon demons to possess the dopplegängers!"

Shit. Rule kept running.

A wolf landed on his back.

LILY heard Cullen shouting about demons possessing the dopplegängers as she raced after Dennis Parrott. Parrott had heard the commotion when she and the others burst out of the truck. It hadn't taken him more than a second to decide to clear out. He was running flat out, headed for a long black limo.

Scott shot past her as if she'd been on a leisurely jog. Just as Parrott reached the limo, Scott tackled him.

Lily slowed and looked around to see where she was needed. She'd sent Mike and Chris to check under the stage. Mike had thrown a couple security types aside and was vanishing through the door now.

Chris, dammit, was right beside her.

"Those sons of bitches are fast," a gravelly voice said.

She glanced quickly to her left—not at Chris. At Drummond. Or some variation on Drummond. "You can talk!"

"Huh. I guess I can. This is confusing as . . ." His voice faded out, though his mouth kept moving. He scowled and stopped trying.

"Lily?" Chris said.

"It's that ghost. Never mind. Why aren't you backing up Mike?"

"Uh—"

"I'm with Scott. I'm protected. Go!"

He sped off.

Scott had Parrott on the ground. He wasn't moving. "He unconscious?" she asked.

A rising swell of screams drowned him out, but he nodded. Then paused with his head up as if he were sniffing the air. "Smells weird."

Demon-possessed dopplegängers might. "You find any jewelry?"

Scott shook his head. "Just a watch. Could a watch be the magical whatsit you're looking for?"

Someone giggled. "No, silly. I've got it."

Lily looked down. "Harry?"

The little brownie was jigging from foot to foot excitedly. His high-pitched voice cut through the crowd noise better than Scott's deeper tones had. "I got the ring like Rule said, but I can't give it to him because he's fighting with a wolf. And I can't give it to Cullen because he's fighting with some other wolves on the other side of the stage."

Fear jumped into her throat and clogged it. She swallowed. "You could give it to me."

His face scrunched up like a wizened apple. "He didn't say to give it to you."

"It's okay, though. I'm wearing the engagement ring, re-member?"

His face cleared. "Yeah, you are! Here." He tossed some-thing up at her.

She caught the ring—heavy worked gold holding a dark red cabochon gem—then nearly dropped it. Death magic coated the thing with such thick foulness she could hardly stand to touch it. Quickly she stuffed it in her pocket. "We've got to get this to Cullen." Who was fighting "some other wolves."

Over the stage, or around it? Around was the long way, but whatever was happening on that stage was keeping Rule too busy to come check on her. Anything able to do that would keep her from getting the ring to Cullen. She set off at a run with Scott beside her.

And no ghosts. Thank God. Drummond must have gone on or whatever ghosts did.

People were fleeing. That was her first second's impression as she rounded the end of the stage—people shoving and streaming away from the carnage and the wolves.

Some hadn't made it. She glimpsed bodies, gore—other wolves chasing the wolves that chased the people trying des-perately to get away. A pair of men faced one of the wolves. And in the trampled grass near the stage, a furious man with a movie star's face flung a thin ribbon of fire.

Black fire. Mage fire.

It struck a wolf as the creature leaped for the stage. And burned—black flame rippling out to eat fur, skin, and muscle so fast it seemed instantaneous. The burning body fell to the ground, limbs twitching.

Another wolf leaped at the beautiful man's back.

"Cullen!" she screamed.

He spun. The wolf slammed into him and they fell to the ground. The two men who'd been trying to keep it from Cul-len leaped onto the wolf and pulled it off. One had its head, the other hugged the body tight. The one holding the head pulled it back, snapping the neck. They dropped the body.

Only it got up again. The head hung down, twisted at an insane angle. Even as Lily watched, still running, the head twitched—and started to resume its usual position. Slowly, but the damn thing was healing as she watched.

Cullen had rolled away. He sprang to his feet, threw out a hand, and sent another ribbon of black flame from his finger-tips. The demon thing burned.

"I've got the ring," Lily said as she came to a stop. "Parrott's ring. It's lousy with death magic. I hope you've got some juice left."

"I've got juice. Put it—" His head swiveled to look up at the stage.

An Asian woman with long, straight hair leaped off it—right onto Cullen. She wore a red jacket, black slacks, and a face Lily looked at in the mirror every day. She was giggling like a teenage girl at a slumber party and she moved every bit as fast as Cullen ever had—grabbing the arm he tried to hit her with as she hauled back with a fist and punched him in the side of the head.

His head snapped back on his neck. She pulled her arm back to do it again—

And Rule leaped down from the stage, grabbing the demon-Lily's arm as he landed, spinning her around. She grinned and swatted him playfully.

He staggered back, going to one knee.

Cullen shoved to his feet again, shook his head, and circled around the two of them to get to Lily. "Put it down! Put it on the ground!"

She bent and did that, then got out of his way. He skidded to a stop, flung out his hand, and showered the damned ring in mage fire. An awful lot of mage fire.

Lily scrambled back. As she did, black smoke erupted from the small inferno—smoke that smelled like a week-old floater. Lily choked on a whiff and coughed.

The smoke cleared as quickly as it had appeared. Cullen was on his knees—and swaying. And the demon-Lily was gone. One second she'd been dodging Rule's kick. The next she simply . . . wasn't.

And a buff and gray wolf charged Rule.

Lily glanced frantically around. None of the wolves had vanished. Just the demon version of her.

"Rule," she called, "I think Cullen's out of it as far as mage fire goes!"

"Yeah," Cullen muttered, looking dazed as he swayed in place on his knees. He lifted one hand to his head. "Seeing double and mage fire—not a good mix."

Scott tackled the wolf just as it reached Rule. The two of them tumbled to the ground, ending with the wolf on top and Scott holding the beast's head, trying to keep its open jaws from his face—and losing.

Until Rule kicked it in the head—a solid roundhouse kick that should have killed it outright. It shook its head as if briefly dazed and lunged for Scott's throat again.

Rule's second kick was to the beast's body, sending it tumbling.

A white form drifted in front of Lily—Drummond was back. "Come on!" he rasped. "I found him. The bastard with the kill-switch, the master control—whatever the hell you call it. He's at the other end of this mess."

"Who is he? What does he look like?"

"Tall, blond, prissy mouth . . ." Drummond's mouth kept moving, but without sound.

"You faded out again!" Behind him she saw Scott and Rule weaving and dodging, keeping the demon wolf busy but unable to stop it.

Drummond's scowl deepened as if he was concentrating. He spoke slowly. "Four rings. One here, one at each rally. The master controls them all. Powers them. You have to . . ." His voice faded out again.

Should she trust him? He'd claimed not to know about death magic, but all of a sudden he knew about the rings and the master control—or whatever the hell it was. Did she have any damn reason to believe him? Drummond had died to save Mullins. That didn't mean he wasn't rooting for the demons at this party.

But if she didn't go and he was telling the truth . . . what else was she going to *do*? If they didn't destroy the amulet, they couldn't stop the demon-possessed dopplegängers. Who wouldn't die without a dose of mage fire, which Cullen couldn't provide until he stopped seeing double.

"Rule!" she called "I think Chittenden's here"—the description could fit Friar's lieutenant—"and has the amulet! I'm going after him!"

He flung his head up. *"No!"* And the demon wolf charged him. He threw himself aside, rolled, and sprang to his feet.

Lily holstered her gun, which was no damn use whatsoever against creatures who considered a broken neck an inconvenience. And turned away from the man she loved while he battled for his life. Turned and ran.

Within seconds, Scott caught up with her. He didn't say a word.

Rule must have sent him. Her eyes burned.

The field was clearing out faster than she would have thought possible, but it was far from empty. There were living people still fleeing. And there were bodies. A woman huddled next to one of those bodies, a man whose face and chest were so saturated with blood it was hard to see the ruin of his throat. It was horrible to do nothing. Horrible to keep running, but Lily did, chasing a white shape as vaguely formed as when she'd first seen it at the shooting range. A shape that was always a few yards ahead of her.

She ran. And ran. Scott kept pace beside her. They passed three clusters of fighting—lupi in both their forms, but mostly wolves, keeping demon wolves busy so they wouldn't kill the humans who'd assembled here to root for an end to lupi.

As they drew near the Washington Monument, her ghostly guide suddenly veered to the left, toward a huddled mob of twenty or thirty people being circled by a pair of wolves. She followed, focusing on her breathing, on the even rise and fall of her legs, so she wouldn't arrive too winded to do anything. And wondering what the hell she was supposed to do to save those people.

Wait a minute. She recognized one of the wolves. It was José. And he and the large gray wolf weren't circling the people—they were patrolling, keeping one of the demon wolves away.

Stupid—she hadn't noticed till just now, but the demon wolves were all alike. Of course they were. They'd all been made from blood or tissue from Brian's wolf-form, so they were identical.

The ground shook.

Lily staggered, her stride broken. Someone screamed. The ground gave a second, harder shimmy, and she had to stop. Scott took her arm, steadying her.

A huge something rose from the ground. It was brownish gray and long, really long, and seemed to grow itself out of the earth, absorbing grass and dirt and rocks into itself as it *became*. No eyes, no legs, not much of anything but body . . . a segmented body three or four feet thick. Like an earthworm.

This time when the earth shook, Lily fell to her knees. So did Scott. And it kept on shaking.

Another form emerged, this one breaking and absorbing bits of Madison Street as it reared itself out of the earth . . . out and up, one end questing in the air as if seeking a scent. This one was even bigger, and it pulled itself together faster than the first one had.

It was not as big as the third one.

From the stage at the east end of the Mall to a spot just short of the steps to the Washington Monument, the earth bulged. It swelled up like the wall had at Fagin's, shaping itself into segment after segment of stony worm eight feet thick . . . ten feet thick . . . twelve. Bodies rolled off as it formed itself. And, horribly, some bodies remained, incorporated into its mass along with sticks and stones, purses and grass.

The earth groaned as the creature began undulating. Moving slowly toward the first elemental.

A white but detailed Drummond darted in front of her, his mouth moving. Clearly impatient, he tried to grab Lily's arm. His hand went right through her. She didn't feel a thing. No cold chills. Nothing.

He grimaced and beckoned fiercely.

For one more second she stared at the enormous monster of

earth and stone advancing slowly toward its smaller cousin. She couldn't do anything about elementals. Nothing. Maybe Cullen could—if he was still alive. If he healed from the concussion fast enough.

She spun and followed Drummond.

José and the other wolf who'd been harrying the demon wolf had chased it well away from the knot of people. They didn't seem to realize yet it was time to get away. Maybe they didn't know where to go. Someone shoved to the edge of the mob. A woman. A woman in dirty jeans and a red shirt, with a face that would make any man hunt for a cloak to throw over puddles. "Lily!" Deborah cried. "It won't listen to me! It's angry—terribly angry—that it was called and wasn't fed, and it's angry that those others invaded its territory!"

A man slipped up behind Deborah. He wore a good-quality suit, no tie, and was tall and thin, with short honey-blond hair. And—like Drummond had said—a prissy mouth. "That's the way it goes sometimes," Paul Chittenden said as he slid his arm around Deborah's neck and squeezed. "Lily Yu, isn't it? Stop right there. I can break her neck in a second."

Lily slowed, not quite stopping, holding her hands out to demonstrate her lack of a weapon. "Scott," she whispered. "Can you—?"

"We're too far," he whispered back. "If he knows what he's doing, he could kill her before I get there."

Chittenden applied more pressure. Deborah's face turned bloodless. "I said stop."

Lily did. So did Scott.

The people closest to Deborah and Chittenden had pulled back a few paces. "Hey," said a beefy man with a crew cut. "What do you think you're doing?"

"Stopping evil from spreading," Chittenden said, smiling. "Do you believe in the Second Amendment, sir?"

"Yes, but—"

"So do I." He drew a gun from inside his jacket and shot the man.

No one screamed this time. Maybe they'd overloaded on the horrors of the day. No one moved or spoke.

"Now," Chittenden said, turning that prissy smile on Lily,

the gun held casually in the hand that wasn't choking Deborah, "we'll have a chance to get acquainted while my pets are doing their work. So . . . do you come here often? What's your sign? If you were stranded on a desert island—"

The woman who jumped Chittenden must have been at least sixty, and probably weighed a hundred pounds soaking wet. She belted him in the head with a purse the size of a small suitcase. He staggered, his gun-hand swinging around, his smile gone—and his attention diverted.

Scott shot forward like a bullet from a gun.

Chittenden backhanded the woman, who collapsed. And, from ten feet away, Scott leaped.

Quickly Chittenden brought his gun up. At point-blank range, he fired.

Scott smashed into Deborah, knocking both her and Chittenden to the ground.

Lily had shoved into a run the same moment as Scott. She was slower, but she got there. She got there seconds after Chittenden shoved Deborah and Scott off of him, just as he started to scramble to his feet. She got there with her weapon in hand, and she jammed it into his ear while he was still couched on one knee.

"Give me a reason," she gritted. "Give me one tiny little reason. I'd love to blow your brains out."

He froze.

Deborah lay on the ground, breathing hard, but stirring. Scott didn't move.

"Hell with it," Lily said, and reversed her weapon and struck him in the temple, hard, with the butt of her gun.

He collapsed.

She followed him down and hit him again, just to be sure. Then checked his eyelids. Oh, yeah, he was out. "Deborah, you okay?"

"Yes, I . . ." She wheezed. "Hurts, but I'm okay."

"Check on Scott." Lily grabbed Chittenden's right hand. No ring. She reached for the other one.

"Oh, no." Deborah sat up and felt Scott's neck. "He's . . . there's a pulse."

Relief barely had time to register. Drummond swept into

Lily's field of view. He patted his upper chest urgently, scowling.

She scowled back. Then she got it. A necklace. Chittenden wore the thing around his neck. She reached inside Chittenden's shirt. A moment's groping and she touched it—and recoiled.

The ring had been foul. This was . . . putrescence. Needles and slime and decay, glass shards, blood gone rotten. Touching it was like being kicked in the chest. For a second she forgot to breathe.

How many? How many people had he killed to load this thing with so much death magic?

Grimly she forced herself to retrieve it, but this time she felt for the chain first. A couple of hard yanks broke the clasp and she pulled it free.

It was an amulet, as Cullen had predicted, the stone a match for the one in the ring—a dark, dull red that didn't look like any gemstone Lily knew. The stone was oval in shape and about two inches long, set in some plain metal. Not gold, and it lacked the sheen of silver.

She sat back on her heels. Now what?

Now she took it to Cullen and hoped like hell he'd healed his concussion enough to attempt mage fire. She shoved to her feet and looked down what used to be a grassy field . . .

The stage was gone. Weirdly, the Jumbotron screen still reared up, but it loomed over a rubble of broken boards. In front of that rubble, dozens of wolves fought.

All of them, she realized as she looked around, a sudden, sick lurch of her heart making her squeeze her hands into fists. All of the demon wolves had congregated in that one spot. Where Rule was.

The elementals were battling.

The giant one had wrapped most of its length around the smallest one like an enormous boa constrictor. Neither made any sound, not a vocalization, anyway, but there was a dull grating of stone against stone. And while the giant one squeezed the smallest, the third elemental took the giant's tail—or its far end, anyway—in its jaws and chomped.

Stone crunched.

"Oh, dear," Deborah whispered.

Earth elementals move slowly. That's what Lily had been told. And the giant one had seemed to be especially slow. Managing that much bulk wouldn't be easy, especially if you didn't practice having a physical form very often. But it turned out that elementals could move fast—when they really, really wanted to.

The coils wrapped around the smallest one loosened and the head—if that was a head—whipped around and around, unwrapping itself enough to lunge at the third elemental like a striking snake. Its jaws opened. And kept opening.

Yeah, that was definitely the head. Eyeless and blind, and not that much like an earthworm after all. Not when most of that head became a gaping, tooth-lined maw. Rows of teeth, like a shark's—not huge teeth, not for the size of that mouth, but there were a lot of them. It caught the other elemental's head in its jaws . . . and crunched.

The captive elemental shook. Its body began to crack, like rock struck by a hammer. Cracks, fissures, opened up in it—then all at once it exploded into dust, dust that hung in the air in a huge, dirty cloud.

Twenty or thirty tiny figures dressed all in brown raced out of the dusty cloud, little legs pumping. Brownies could move amazingly fast. "Lily, Lily!" yelled the one in the lead. "Rule's hurt! Cullen's hurt! Everyone's in trouble! Do you have the nasty thing?"

"I—yes!" she called back. "But—"

"You have to break it!" Harry screamed. "Make it not-be! You have to do it now!"

"I can't—it takes mage fire to—"

"No!" He was still yelling at the top of his little lungs even as he came to a stop in front of her. "Give it to *it!* Hurry!"

Do what?

"To the Great It!" He pointed at the enormous elemental, which seemed to be considering renewing its attack on the other one. But that one was beginning to subside. To sink back into the earth. Slowly, but it was on its way out of here.

"Are you nuts? You want me to feed an enraged giant elemental a colossal amount of death magic?"

He rolled his eyes. "Stupid! Earth doesn't cleanse as quick as fire, but it cleanses. Hurry!"

Deborah spoke in her husky, damaged voice. "It's too angry. I can *feel* how it rages . . . it will kill anything, anyone, that comes near."

Lily had promised Rule she wouldn't die. But if the only way to save Rule was to break a promise—

"Never mind. You're too big and slow, anyway."

"I—hey!" she cried.

The chain she'd been gripping dangled loose. The amulet wasn't on it anymore.

And a whole troop of brownies were running away—and they were amazingly fast. Running straight toward a giant, enraged earth elemental.

"Lily?" Deborah said. "Who were we just talking to?"

Lily turned her head, incredulous. "You didn't see them?"

"See who? I heard someone, but I didn't see a thing."

"Brownies," Lily said numbly as she turned back to watch the timid little brownies charge a creature as long as a football field. "A whole troop of brownies."

They pelted straight for it. It noticed them—apparently it didn't need eyes all that much—and swung its head around, opening those jaws once more, lowering its head to the ground. They split into two streams, one group veering to each side of that enormous head—and scrambled up onto it.

The head reared up. And up. They clung to it—its surface wasn't smooth, after all, being full of stones and sticks and the occasional body part—and they were little and light. They clambered around on its head, then formed a chain, a brownie ladder. The ones at the top of the beast's head somehow anchored themselves so others could dangle, hands gripping hands or feet, some upside down, some rightside up, all assembling themselves so quickly it was like magic.

Maybe it *was* magic—of a different sort. One that called for skill, not power.

One brownie climbed down that living ladder . . . which dangled right over the great elemental's mouth.

That mouth opened wide and wider, a horrible, gaping maw. The elemental flung its head once as if it was nodding emphatically—and the chain of brownies swept out, then in. Right into its mouth. Which closed—but brownies spurted out even as it did. With delicious, desperate speed they shot out, slipped out like watermelon seeds, and scampered down stony, segmented sides. Down and down and . . .

The elemental stopped moving.

"Oh," Deborah murmured. "Ohh . . . that tasted nasty, but it feels so full now. Content."

Escape artists, Lily thought. That's what Rule had called them. Brownies valued nothing so much as a great escape— and oh, what an escape that had been!

Slowly the elemental began to subside. The stony mass lost its shape gradually, even gracefully, clods of dirt, rocks, and sticks breaking loose to fall to the ground as it sank itself back into the earth.

It was gone.

Lily looked toward the east end of what used to be the National Mall. There were a few patches of grass left, but no people. They'd fled or been killed.

Except at the far end. Where the fighting had stopped.

She shivered. He was alive, she *knew* he was alive, but how badly hurt? How many others were dead? She glanced at Deborah, at Scott so still on the ground. "Take care of him," she pleaded. And set off at a run yet again.

FORTY

～

RULE lay flat on the ground, his eyes closed. He felt her coming. At last. At last.

Cullen was loosening the tourniquet he'd tied high on Rule's left leg. "Bleeding's stopped," he announced with satisfaction. "Or almost. It's a godawful mess, but you aren't bleeding anymore."

Good. He'd lost so much blood he couldn't sit up. Best if he held on to what was left.

"I wish I knew what was happening inside . . . but if the artery's stopped bleeding, you'll be healing up whatever was causing the internal bleeding pretty quick now, if you haven't already."

"Don't . . . mention the . . . internal bleeding to her." Gods, but talking hurt.

Cullen snorted. "She'll cripple me good if I lie. But if it doesn't come up . . ."

Rule nodded slightly. That was good enough.

I'll live if you will, she'd said. He'd done his best, but for a while it had seemed he'd default on his end of the bargain.

She was nearly here . . .

And then she was. "Rule." She took his hand. Warmth and ease spread through him in a sigh of contentment. "You're a mess." Her laugh was shaky. "A really bloody mess. Can you see at all?"

"One eye is just swollen shut. The other . . ." He stopped to gather enough energy to finish. "That one will have to regrow."

"I guess you didn't see the brownies, then."

Brownies? Not since Harry's troop stood on the edges of the crowd, letting themselves be seen for once, yelling at everyone to "run this way!" Brownies were good at giving warnings, after all. And they'd helped, directing people where to go . . .

"They're heroes. The most incredible heroes. I'll tell you about it in a minute." The sound of Lily's voice suggested she'd turned her head. "His leg?"

Cullen answered. "Broken. The femoral artery got ripped open, but the bleeding's stopped."

He heard her swallow.

Cullen's voice went soft, as it so rarely did. "He'll be okay, Lily. Not able to do much, not for a while, even with his super-duper speedy healing. But he'll be okay."

That was good to know.

The sirens he'd been hearing were close now. Good. They'd need a lot of ambulances. So many injured . . .

"And the others?" Lily asked, her voice low and raw. "I see some of them, but . . . Karonski. Did anyone ever find him?"

"He's alive. Got knocked out, but Mike found him and brought him out."

"And Chris?"

Silence.

So many dead . . .

"They converged on us," Cullen said after a moment. "About the time that giant elemental Fagin had been keeping as a pet rose up, all of the demon wolves came after Rule. The rest of us were just obstacles. There'd be more dead if they'd cared about killing us, but they didn't. Everyone's hurt, but not as many lupi died as might have. All they wanted was to get to Rule."

"I thought—they seemed to be after you, Cullen. First one wolf, then the demon Lily, then another wolf."

"Oh." Rule could hear the shrug in his friend's voice. "A

demon will usually go after a sorcerer if it can. They never know what one of us might be capable of, so they like to take us out quick."

Funny that Cullen was just *now* mentioning this.

"Something changed," Cullen went on. "They seemed to be acting on their own at first. When they came for Rule, they weren't. They were under someone's control."

"Chittenden," Lily said. "He sent them. He must . . . I think at first he stuck to the original plan, turning the demon-ridden doppelgängers loose. The more people they killed, the better. Lupi would be blamed. It sounds like he changed his tactics when he realized he wouldn't be getting an on-site delivery of victims to feed to the elementals. I don't know what he'd planned to do with the elementals, or how he planned to sacrifice twenty-two people right out in public. Maybe he thought everyone who saw him slitting throats would end up dead, so it didn't matter."

"Yeah, that fits," Cullen said. "By then he'd seen Rule, though, so he sent the doppelgängers after him. It must have seemed like too good an opportunity to pass up. Is Chittenden dead?"

"I knocked him out. I wanted to . . . but I didn't. He'll live to stand trial."

"That's something, I guess." Cullen was silent a moment. "You want to tell me what happened with that enormous elemental? I saw the brownies scaling it like it was a climbing wall, but I don't know what they did."

She told them. Rule felt a smile stretch across his face. It hurt, but so did everything else.

Someone—Mike, it sounded like—called Cullen to come help with setting a bone. Cullen told Lily to "call me if he starts bleeding again, but he won't"—and moved away.

The wail of one of the sirens peaked, then shut off. Some kind of help was here. Rule needed to speak before they lost this brief privacy. "Lily."

She bent closer. Close enough that he could breathe her in, the sweet, comforting scent of her . . . and her tears. She'd worked so hard to keep those tears from her voice, but she'd been crying from the moment she settled down beside him. He must look bloody awful. "You did the right thing. If you'd obeyed . . ." Obedience was not something his *nadia* was inclined toward, no, and he was so glad and grateful for that. "If you'd heeded me when I tried to forbid you, we'd all be dead."

"I did what I had to do, but I was just guessing. It was all such a guess."

"A guess backed by great courage." He made the effort and raised one hand to touch her hair. He didn't touch her face, though he wanted to. But she didn't want him to know about the tears, so he avoided discovering them. "I knew you had to go, to do what you could. I just couldn't . . . you're braver than I."

His beautiful, brave *nadia* snorted. "Yeah, right. Why did you send Scott with me instead of coming yourself?"

"I couldn't." That moment rose up and choked him again— Lily racing off into God knew what, her very motion a lure to whatever wolfish instincts lived in the demon-ridden doubles of his people. "Scott isn't fully healed yet. He couldn't fight properly. Too many would have died if I left. I had to stay."

"I know," she said softly, and miraculously found the one spot on his face that didn't hurt, and stroked it. "I know. Which means you did what you had to do, just like me, doesn't it?"

TWO hundred fifty-nine people died at the four Humans First rallies—one hundred and twelve of them in D.C. alone. That had been by far the largest rally, so there had been a great many targets. Plus it was the only rally where elementals had been summoned, and estimates put the number of demon wolves there at more than twice those at the other rallies. The second highest number of fatalities occurred in Albuquerque, mostly because Manuel and his clansmen had had the farthest to travel, and had arrived late.

Of those two hundred fifty-nine people killed, thirty-seven were lupi . . . which didn't sound too disproportionate until you looked at all the numbers. Which Arjenie did, because her mind worked that way. She sent Rule an e-mail with those numbers, which he read while being given the last of the four pints of blood he'd needed.

He immediately called several of his media contacts and arranged to speak to reporters from his wheelchair as he was being released from the hospital. One of his eyes was covered by a gauze pad. The swelling had gone down around the other one, just as he'd said it would.

At that press conference, he told reporters and their cameras that there had been an estimated thirty-five thousand humans altogether who'd attended the four rallies. Seven-tenths of one percent of those people were killed. There had been one hundred sixty-four lupi who raced to save the humans at those rallies.

One-fifth of them were killed. Nearly a third of them died in D.C.

Rule's press appearance garnered attention for several hours, until an announcement that night by the Secretary of Defense eclipsed everything else for a while.

A nuclear warhead had been accidentally deployed that morning due to a mysterious series of glitches that no one was able to explain. The missile had apparently been on course for the West Coast when—with even greater mystery—it had vanished from sight and radar. No trace of the missile or the warhead was ever found.

WITH everything that happened that day, it wasn't surprising that no one noticed that four of the U.S. cities with dragons were temporarily without dragons. Since they were gone a single day, people might not have noticed even without the dramatic events.

It was the next day when six women boarded planes at the Denver airport at various times, headed back to their various homes.

The seventh woman didn't need to catch a plane. She'd left as soon as her work was done. An enormous black dragon had flown her home already, his talons wrapped carefully around the empty body, her bright muumuu flapping merrily in the wind of their passage.

Dragons cannot open gates on their own. They can manipulate them, power them, even close them, but they can't open them. For reasons they do not explain, song magic alone isn't enough. The Rhejes could open a gate; that knowledge was held in the memories. They couldn't shift one in front of an ICBM boosting at thousands of miles an hour, so they needed the dragons as much as the dragons needed them.

It takes a godawful amount of power to open a gate. The dragons supplied much of that, but the Rhejes had had to channel it. An eighty-one-year-old heart, however valiant, can only take so much strain, and the two healers present couldn't stop chanting to help. She'd held on, though—held on until the gate opened and the missle shot into a realm that had held no life for over three thousand years.

Nokolai clan had a new Rhej.

TWO days later, Lily was called to Croft's office to "discuss the results of the administrative hearing." The sound of his voice told her it was good news, so she was hopeful, really hopeful, that she was going to get to keep her job. Maybe there'd be a black mark on her record, but she could live with that.

"They want to *what*?" she said, dumbfounded.

"It's a great honor. The Presidential Citizens Medal is the second-highest civilian award in the country. The president will, of course, present it herself."

It made her furious. "I'm no hero. I showed up. That's about it. Oh, and I did manage to give Chittenden a skull fracture, which makes me personally very happy. But if the president wants to hand out medals, I can name a dozen who deserve it more. Harry and his troop. Chris, Mike, Scott, Rule, Isen—" She had to stop, her breath hitching. Not everyone she spoke of was still around to receive a stupid medal. "That old woman with her handbag—now, there's a hero! It's not right to single me out this way. It's not right."

"Sometimes showing up is what it takes. Showing up over and over and over in spite of how hard it gets."

She shook her head, out of words.

"Besides, I disagree about you not doing much. There are

twenty-two other people alive today who'd disagree, too. And
if you hadn't acted on that tip . . ." Croft paused a moment,
clearly uncomfortable. He knew who had tipped Lily about
Chittenden's possession of the amulet, though it wasn't in her
official report. He always avoided mentioning it, clearly uncomfortable with the idea of ghostly tips. "If you hadn't acted,
the brownies couldn't have done what they did."

"So give the brownies a medal."

"The president wanted to. Their spokesperson said they re-
spectfully declined to receive any sort of award, and besides,
they never leave their reservation, so what were we talking
about?"

That startled a laugh out of her. "I'm told they don't like to
have a fuss made about bravery."

He smiled. "Apparently not." The smile faded. "As for pub-
licially honoring the heroism and sacrifice of the lupi . . . I
hope that happens eventually, but right now the country is too
divided. There's a great uneasiness, even among some who
agree that they were heroes—a feeling that if the country
didn't harbor lupi in the first place, none of this would have
happened. And, of course, there's that vocal minority that believes the government is engaged in a massive cover-up and
the lupi really were behind it all, not Paul Chittenden."

Lily grimaced. The Humans First movement hadn't died. It
was diminished, but not dead.

"Lily." Croft leaned forward earnestly. "People need heroes. Let them have one."

"Yeah, don't be a dick," Al Drummond said. He was sitting
in the other visitor chair, looking his usual pallid self. "Take
the damn medal."

She wanted to tell him it was physically impossible for her
to be a dick. She wanted to tell him to *go away*—which he had
so far refused to do. Not that he was around every minute, but
every so often, he popped up, usually with unwanted advice.

But people look at you funny if you start talking to your
invisible friends, so she didn't. And in the end, Lily agreed to
accept the medal. It would be months, maybe a year, before
they did the big presentation ceremony. Who knows? She

might still end up dismissed and disgraced and not have to go through with it.

THREE days after that, on the night before Lily and Rule were scheduled to fly home—at last—they were in their bedroom at the Georgetown house, getting ready.

Rule sat on the bed as he slipped on his shirt. He could stand without using the crutches; it had taken some insistence on his part, but they'd casted the leg as soon as the outer wound closed, and having it casted helped. But standing hurt more than he liked to admit, so he stayed seated as much as possible.

The femur had barely begun healing; his eye hadn't started. He kept a square of gauze taped over it, knowing it was an ugly sight. His healing had prioritized the internal injuries. That was normal. But it was taking forever for him to *feel* normal.

So many dead. Too many, and the war had only begun.

"Am I the only one who thinks it's just weird to be going to a dinner party?" Lily asked as she turned away from the closet, a necklace in one hand. "Or for Deborah and Ruben to be giving one, for that matter."

"Deborah wants to feel normal. And it's just us and Isen, not really a party."

"Fasten this for me?" Lily said, and held out a necklace. The one he'd given her . . . gods, was it only two weeks ago? "No, don't stand up." She huffed out an impatient breath and dropped to her knees in front of him. "Here." She pulled her hair aside. "I'm hoping Fagin's right about those white stones."

He took his time fastening the necklace, enjoying the slight, involuntary shiver his touch gave her. He'd been too damaged for them to make love, but his guts were healed now, so tonight, that would change. He promised himself that. "What about the stones? They're agates, by the way."

"That's what he said. He also said that white agates are supposed to offer protection against malign or confused spirits."

That made him grin. "You're hoping to keep Drummond from dropping in while we eat our steaks?" Lily said the ghost wasn't around constantly. Just now and then—usually with some sort of unwanted advice.

"Damn right. If it works, I'll wear this all the time." She stood. "I'll get your shoes. No, stay there," she told him firmly. "Why was it okay for you to help me constantly when my arm was messed up, but you don't want to let me help you?"

That was apparently a rhetorical question, for she went back to the closet without waiting for an answer. Rule finished buttoning his shirt and waited obediently.

Coming to First Change as an adult had made a big difference in Ruben's adjustment. He'd returned to Washington yesterday in his two-legged form—but only temporarily, and not alone. In addition to Isen, he'd brought five Wythe guards. Isen had judged that Ruben's control was good enough for him to make an appearance around the two-legged crowd, as long as he was with Ruben. Ruben still had trouble with speech sometimes when the wolf was too much present, but he could hold it together pretty well.

They'd decided to keep Ruben's transformation as much of a secret as possible. The president knew. Croft knew. But even the head of the Bureau was unaware that his briefly disgraced, newly reinstated head of Unit 12 was the werewolf who'd helped lead the fight against the demon dopplegängers in Albany.

The charges against Ruben had been dropped. He would remain in command of Unit 12 . . . but Croft didn't get to give up his desk job. Ruben wasn't close to being ready to resume hands-on control of the Unit. He and Deborah and Isen would be leaving for Wythe Clanhome tomorrow.

The story was that they were going to a secret location where the privacy-obsessed healer who'd helped Ruben right after his heart attack could continue treatment. That treatment would be seen to have worked in another few weeks when the Brookses returned home. Their swimming pool would have been filled in by then and construction finished on the two-story "guesthouse" they were going to add . . . which would in fact be a barracks for Wythe guards.

The Brookses would be spending a great deal of time in upper New York State, of course. But Ruben should be able to resume control of Unit 12.

Lily returned from the closet carrying Rule's favorite loafers in one hand . . . and a small box wrapped in shiny white paper in the other.

"What's that? My birthday's not for another four days." And he would spend it with Lily and Toby. His heart lifted slightly. This was the first time he'd have his son with him on his birthday—and Lily to share that with.

"Three days," she corrected him. "You mean you forgot? It's our eleven month, one week, and, uh . . . three days anniversary."

He smiled. "Eleven months, two weeks, and five days."

"Don't be difficult." She sat on the bed beside him. "The point is, this is not an early birthday present. You know I don't believe in those. It's just a thing." She handed him the box.

There was a big silver bow on top, dwarfing the little box, which was very lightweight. He pulled off the bow and ripped the paper.

She'd given him an eye patch. A black silk eye patch.

"So you can look piratical instead of like a patient," Lily said. "It sucks being a patient, but a pirate—well. That's dashing."

"I'm not vain." But he handed her the patch so he could yank off the gauze pad, suddenly eager to be rid of it.

"Yes, you are." The eye patch was attached to a strip of silk, elasticized in the back. She tugged it on. "Good. It fits."

It did. His fingers told him that the patch covered his eye from brow to cheekbone. "Am I dashing now?"

"Absolutely." She leaned in and kissed him lightly. "A man in a cast and bandages looks injured. A man in a cast and an eye patch looks dangerous. So I've been thinking."

"It's a habit of yours, I've noticed." He slipped on his shoes. "Pass me the crutches, will you? I want to see how this looks."

She handed them to him. "About the wedding."

He stopped. "Yes?"

"We still haven't settled who's going to perform the ceremony. Maybe we should talk about that."

The last time Rule brought that up, she'd all but run in the other direction. Lily had an issue with religion in general. What was she . . . oh. He smiled.

She was making things normal for him, or trying to. What had he told her two weeks ago? She'd asked how he could spend time planning a wedding and picking out a necklace for her, and the answer had been so clear to him then.

How else could he live?

Nothing seemed as clear to him now . . . except for Lily. Who had picked out a present for him, and suddenly wanted to talk about wedding plans. He levered himself to his feet with the crutches, bent, and kissed her. "Perhaps Sam would conduct the ceremony for us."

She stared at him. "Sam? But he isn't—that is—I don't think that's legal."

"Or we could ask Father Michaels. He did a nice job with Cullen and Cynna's wedding." He swung himself over to the full-length mirror and smiled. The patch did look rather good.

"But we aren't Catholic. And he lives here, and we're getting married in San Diego."

"That could be a problem, I suppose. I have another idea. I think Carl was a minister at one point. It was under a different name, but that shouldn't matter." He got himself turned around. "Would you like to be married by Carl?"

"Your father's cook."

"Yes, and I've been wanting to talk about the doves."

"Doves." Her eyes widened in horror. "My mother wanted doves."

"Perhaps she had a point. Wouldn't it look splendid, releasing a few dozen white doves all at once to carry our message of hope and love up to—"

"You are so full of shit." But she started laughing. "Doves, sure. Our guests would love some flying hors d'œuvres. Maybe we should have some cute little bunnies for them to chase after the ceremony instead of cake, sending our message of fuzzy, yummy love to flesh eaters everywhere."

He had to kiss her again—which took some arranging, dammit, with the crutches, since he wanted to do more than peck her on the cheek. But he managed, and after a long, delicious moment, raised his head. "Lily, I love you."

"Yeah," she said, smiling. "I know."

Keep reading for a preview of
the next lupi novel by Eileen Wilks

MORTAL TIES

Available fall 2012 from Berkley Sensation!

SHE hadn't brought flowers. It would be tacky to bring flowers to the grave of the woman you killed, especially when you
didn't regret it. When you knew that, given the same circumstances, you'd do it again.

And yet here she was. And there were flowers on the grave
she'd come to visit. Not an expensive bouquet—more like the
kind you pick up at the grocery store, with dyed carnations
and baby's breath. They were in a cheap, narrow glass vase
that still held about an inch of water.

Lily Yu crouched down, frowned at the flowers, and
brushed the dirt off the small plaque set into the ground that
the vase rested on: Helen Anne Whitestone.

Lily had learned the woman's last name a week after killing her. She hadn't known much about Helen at the time, save
for the things that mattered then. Helen had been a telepath,
and she'd been nuts. She'd tortured and she'd killed; she'd
done her damnedest to open a hellgate, and she'd intended to
feed Rule to the Old One she served. She'd also been doing
her damnedest to kill Lily just before Lily put a stop to that
and all her other plans.

No regrets, no. And since Helen hadn't had a spouse, lover,

or any living family, Lily didn't even carry the burden of bringing grief to those who had once loved the woman.

And yet here she was. And someone had brought Helen flowers not too long ago.

Maybe she should have visited Helen before this.

Lily had found out where Helen Ann Whitestone was buried months ago, even though she couldn't have said at the time why it mattered. Mount Hope had been San Diego's municipal cemetery for about a hundred and fifty years. Raymond Chandler was buried here. So was Alta Hulett, America's first female attorney, and the guy who established Balboa Park and the city's library system. So were the few who, every year, were buried at the county's expense.

Helen had died a virgin and intestate, but the taxpayers hadn't had to pick up the tab for planting her. Turned out she'd socked away over a quarter million. Telepaths had an inside track on scamming people, didn't they? If they could shut out the voices in their heads enough to function, that is—which Helen had been able to do, thanks to the Old One she served. That's how she'd met her protégé, Patrick Harlowe . . . who'd also died badly, but not at Lily's hands. Cullen Seabourne had done the honors.

But Lily had killed again. Helen was her first, but she'd added to the tally this past year. That was apt to happen in a war, though, wasn't it?

"Goddamn morbid sort of thing to do, isn't it?" said a gravelly voice. "Hanging out at the grave of someone you killed."

Lily jolted, then twisted to scowl at the intruder. "Oh, hell. I thought you were gone."

"Guess you were wrong." The man leaning against a nearby palm tree wore a dark suit with a wrinkled white shirt and a plain tie. He was on the skinny side of lean, with a broad, flat forehead and dark thinning hair combed straight back, and he was pale. Pale as in white. Also slightly see-through.

Al Drummond. Formerly an FBI special agent. Currently Lily's own personal haunt, though she'd thought—hoped— he'd gone on into the light or something, since she hadn't seen him in over a month.

Death didn't seem to be any more fair than life. Why had

she gotten stuck with Drummond's ghost? She hadn't killed him. "How do you know whose grave I'm visiting?" Lily demanded.

He snorted. "I can read."

"And you know who Helen was."

"Did you think I didn't do any digging before I set out to get you?"

Drummond might have gone spectacularly wrong, but he'd been a good agent before that—competent, thorough, and bright. Of course he knew who Helen was, knew that Lily had killed her. God only knew how much else he'd dug up about her.

Lily stood and started for her car.

Drummond followed, damn him. "Not going to ask me where I've been?"

She reached the path and kept walking.

"Most people are curious about the afterlife."

"I wouldn't believe anything you told me anyway, so why ask?"

He scowled. "I was straight with you. Once we made a deal, I told it straight."

True. And he'd risked his life to rescue twenty-two homeless people, then given it to save a friend. But first he'd betrayed the Bureau, tried to kill Lily's boss, conspired in the murder of a U.S. senator, and gotten Lily thrown in jail. "The only thing I want to know is why you're here. Why are you pestering me?"

"Damned if I know, except . . . I've got this idea you're going to need me. I don't know when or how, but you will. It's . . ." He shrugged stiffly. "I guess I'm paying a debt."

"The debt's forgiven. Go away."

"We don't always get what we want, do we?"

EILEEN WILKS

USA Today **Bestselling Author of**
Mortal Danger* and *Blood Lines

NIGHT SEASON

Pregnancy has turned FBI Agent Cynna Weaver's whole life upside down. Lupus sorcerer Cullen Sea-bourne is thrilled to be the father, but what does Cynna know about kids? Her mother was a drunk. Her father abandoned them. Or so she's always be-lieved.

As Cynna is trying to wrap her head around this prob-lem, a new one pops up, in the form of a delegation from another realm. They want to take Cynna and Cullen back with them—to meet her long-lost father and find a mysterious medallion. But when these two born cynics land in a world where magic is common-place and night never ends, their only way home lies in tracking down the missing medallion—one also sought by powerful beings who will do anything to claim it…

penguin.com